W9-BUE-564

THE
WORLD
AT THE
END
OF
TIME

THE
WORLD
AT THE
END
OF
TIME

FREDERIK
POHL

 A DEL REY BOOK

BALLANTINE BOOKS · NEW YORK

A Del Rey Book
Published by Ballantine Books

Library of Congress Cataloging-in-Publication Data
Pohl, Frederik.
  The world at the end of time.

  "A Del Rey book."
  I. Title.
PS3566.036W67   1990   813'.54   89-18462
ISBN 0-345-33976-2

Design by Holly Johnson

Manufactured in the United States of America

First Edition: June 1990

10 9 8 7 6 5 4 3 2 1

THE
WORLD
AT THE
END
OF
TIME

CHAPTER 1

Although Wan-To wasn't at all human, he (or one might prefer to refer to him as "it," but "he" was not an inappropriate pronoun) would have put that statement in a very different way. Wan-To would have said he was *at least* human. He certainly had all the human characteristics that he would have considered worth having—if he had known that such a thing as the human race existed, which he did not. He was strong. He was intelligent. He had an inquiring mind—which meant he had a scientific one—which meant that, technologically, Wan-To was a very slick article indeed.

He had, too, that quintessentially human trait that you never seem to find in things like tarantulas or termites. He had a hell of a great sense of humor. His idea of what was funny was not subtle. Basically, it was the pie-in-the-face or the pull-the-chair-out-from-under-you kind of thing. But that's just as true of a lot of human beings.

He was also an extraordinarily (and very humanly) competitive individual. Wan-To definitely wanted to be the best of his kind. He wanted that *at least*. Sometimes, when things got dicey with his only "friends," he wanted to be the only one.

Of course, the ways in which Wan-To was all these things was not exactly a human way, but that would not have troubled Wan-To. He would have been sure his way was better.

The place where Wan-To lived—which was not exactly a

3

"place," since Wan-To was a dispersed sort of being—was the interior of a medium-sized G-3 star not readily visible from the surface
of the Earth. He hadn't always lived there. He certainly hadn't been
"born" there, or in any place near it, but that is a whole other story
and even Wan-To didn't know all of it. Wan-To could move easily
enough when he wanted to. In fact, he had packed up and moved
about as often as any American city apartment dweller, from one
star to another—and once, long ago, he had moved a lot farther than
that. But, like a New Yorker blessed with a rent-controlled apartment, he did his best to stay put. Moving was a great annoyance to
him. It was also a little dangerous, since going out there into interstellar space, away from the friendly multimillion-degree heat and
pressure of his star, frightened him. At such times he was naked and
exposed, like a molting crab hiding while it grew a new shell. Leaving his star left him vulnerable to the attentions of predators—who
were no less frightening because they were, in some degree, himself.

Of course, Wan-To enjoyed his star. He knew it as intimately
as a man knows his bedroom. He could easily have moved about it
in the dark, if there had ever been any dark. Human astrophysicists
would have envied him that first-hand knowledge. For a human
astronomer to make a model of what the inside of a star was like
was an exercise in observation, deduction, and just plain guessing.
Humans could never see inside a star. The longer the humans
worked at it, the better their guesses on the subject got—but Wan-
To didn't have to guess. He *knew*.

That isn't all an Earth person might have envied Wan-To for.
Really, he had a pretty joyous life—at least, when he wasn't terrified.
For Wan-To, living in a star was *fun*. In any star he happened to
occupy he could always find a satisfying variety of environments.
He could even find a wide choice of "climates," and he had all sorts
of vastly differing particles to amuse himself with, though some
elements were a lot scarcer than others. For instance, if you took a
random sample of a million atoms out of Wan-To's star, mixed well
from all of its parts, only one of those atoms would be the element
argon. Two or three atoms each would be aluminum, calcium, so-
dium, and nickel; sixteen would be sulfur; thirty or forty each would
be silicon, magnesium, neon, and iron. You'd probably find eighty
or ninety atoms of nitrogen, 400-plus of carbon, nearly 700 of oxy-

gen. (If you took a larger sample—if you counted every atom in the star—of course you'd find a lot of other elements. In fact, you'd find *all* the other elements, from beryllium to the transuranics. Inevitably some freak of fusion would manufacture at least a few of every atom that could possibly be made, somewhere inside Wan-To's star. But all the elements named—*every* element that ever existed, save two—would still amount to fewer than 2,000 atoms in your sample of a million.)

The rest of your million-atom sample would be just those two heavy hitters, though not at all in equal proportions. You would find some 63,000 atoms of helium; and then the rest, 935,000 atoms out of the million, would be hydrogen. So you might think of Wan-To's star as being a very dry Martini indeed. Hydrogen was the gin, helium the dash of vermouth, and all the rest were just contaminants leached off the olive, the stirring rod, and the glass it came in.

There were plenty of all these things in Wan-To's dense central core to play with, and anyway, if he tired of them he didn't have to stay in the core. He had the whole star to play in, and it was a million miles across, with a hundred different regimes. He could "wander" at will from "room" to "room" of his "home"—spending some time in the outer shells, even the photosphere; venturing (with care, because they were so thrillingly diffuse) into the corona and the nearer parts of the solar wind; riding up and down in the upwellings of hot gases that made sunspots and speculae.

That part of Wan-To's star was the convection zone, and in some ways it was the best of all. The convection zone was the layer of the star where simple mechanical transport took over from radiation in the escape of energy from the star's core. For the first four-fifths of its escape from core to surface, a photon of energy traveled purely radiatively. Not exactly in a straight line, of course; it bounced from particle to particle, like a ball in a pinball machine. But a fifth of the way down from the surface the pressure was lessened enough so that the gases could move about a bit—which is to say, convectively, and so it was called the convection zone. There the heat from the core made its way the rest of the distance to the surface by being transported in cells of hot gas, like the outwelling of warmth from a hot-air heating system. Some of the gas rose to the surface and again began radiating, ejecting its heat away into space. Some, cooling, fell back. In the convection zone Wan-To could cavort freely, letting himself be carried along by the convection cells when he chose, twisting their paths into amusing tangles when that seemed more interesting. Oh, there were a million places to play inside a star!

For that matter, there was no reason for him to be bored with the core. There was plenty of variety even there. If he decided the center was a little too warm (it ran about fifteen million degrees), there were cooler spots farther up. He enjoyed the physical sensations the star's interior offered. The varying rotation rates (its poles slower than the equator, its core faster than any part of the surface) and the twisting magnetic field lines that looped below the surface and, here and there rising above it, produced sunspots—they were to Wan-To as a Jacuzzi is to a Hollywood film writer.

So for Wan-To his star was a house with many mansions. It should be stated, though, that Wan-To didn't exactly *move* when he "went" from place to place. In a sense, he was always in all the places at once. It was more a matter of paying attention to one place rather than another, like a TV addict with a wall of sets, each tuned to a different channel, now looking at this one, now at another.

Even a medium-sized G-3 star is a vast place, and so the pieces of Wan-To were separated by thousands of miles. What held him together was the network of neutrinos that served him for neurons. Only neutrinos could do that for him, for nothing else could move freely about in the choked, squeezed interior of the star, but that was all right. The neutrinos worked just fine.

What Wan-To was composed of was that strange state of being called plasma. Plasma isn't matter, isn't energy, is some of both; it is the fourth phase of matter (after solid, liquid, and gas) or the second phase of energy, whichever you prefer to call it. In Wan-To's view, it was simply the stuff that intelligent beings were made of. (He had never heard of "human beings," and wouldn't have cared about them if he had.) Sometimes, some of Wan-To's colleagues (or children, or brothers—they were a little bit of all three) did suspect that a *kind* of intelligence might have developed from other things, like solid matter. Sometimes Wan-To thought that himself, but any such thing could not be very important, he was pretty sure, because no "matter" entity could ever amount to much on a cosmic scale. No, the logical home for a truly sentient being, like himself, had to be in the great compact core of plasma at the heart of a star.

It was a great pity, in Wan-To's view, that there were so many stars.

Although only a tiny fraction of them had managed to become "alive"—and then only because he or one of the others had made them so—sometimes he would have preferred to be the only one there was.

It wasn't that Wan-To didn't enjoy company. He did, very much, but he didn't like paying the price for it. He could see, now, that he had made some serious mistakes in indulging his desire for companionship. It had been a dumb idea to create siblings. For that matter, it had been a dumb idea the first time it had been done, long ago and very far away, and what made Wan-To sure of that was that in that particular case he had been one of the ones that had been created.

Still, Wan-To could understand how his unfortunate progenitor had felt, because no one liked being entirely *alone*. Creating companions hadn't worked out well this time. The ones he had already made weren't much company anymore, because few of them dared communicate with any of the others in the present uneasy situation. But it was still an attractive idea. It was just that next time he would have to do it in a different way. It would be quite all right, he thought, to have more of his kind around—provided the others were just a little less strong, smart, and competitive than himself.

When they weren't, they were dangerous.

Stars generally live a very long time. So would Wan-To; in fact, he could easily outlive most stars by quite a lot. He intended to see that he did; in fact, he meant to make his life last about as close to forever as possible.

The difficulty with that plan was that it wasn't entirely up to Wan-To. The companions he had created had their own views on the subject. Indeed, at least one of them was doing his best to murder Wan-To at that very moment.

CHAPTER 2

One of those "human beings" Wan-To had never heard of was a boy named Viktor Sorricaine. Of course, Viktor had never heard of Wan-To, either; their paths had never crossed in Wan-To's long life and Viktor's so far fairly short one.

On Viktor's twelfth birthday (or, you could say, his one hundred and fifteenth), he woke up, sweating and itchy, to stare into someone's eyes. "Mom?" he asked fuzzily. "Mom, are we there yet?"

It wasn't his mother looking down at him. It was an old woman he had never seen before. She didn't hold herself like an old woman, bent-backed and tottering. She stood straight and her eyes were clear, and she looked at Viktor in a way that made him uneasy—sad and amused, tolerant and angry, all at once. He thought she looked as though she knew everything there was to know about Viktor Sorricaine, and forgave him for it. She was definitely old, though. Her hair was thinning, and her face was terribly lined. "You don't remember me, do you, Viktor?" she asked, and sighed to show that she forgave him for that, too. "I'm not surprised. I'm Wanda. Your mother will be here in a moment, so don't worry. We've just had a little problem."

"What kind of problem?" Viktor asked, rubbing his stinging eyes, too polite to ask her what it was she thought he should have remembered.

"Your dad will take care of it," the woman said. Viktor couldn't press her, because she had already turned away to call for someone to help her get Viktor out of the shallow saucer kind of thing he was lying in.

Viktor was beginning to wake up. Certain things were clear to him at once. He knew that he was still on the interstellar ship *New Mayflower*, from the fact that he weighed so little. That meant that, no, they hadn't arrived yet. He knew what the pan he was lying in was, because he had expected all along that sooner or later he would find himself in one like it. It was the warming pan where frozen passengers were thawed back to life when the journey was through. But since it seemed the journey wasn't through, what could be the reason for waking him now?

He allowed himself to be helped up and was badly surprised to find that the help was needed; his young limbs were shaky. He let himself be tugged, like a skiff towed by a motorboat—only the old woman who said her name was Wanda was the motorboat—to a shower cubicle. There the woman gently stripped off his thin freezer robe to bathe him. It was a rougher bath than he was used to. There were many decades of dried perspiration and dead skin for the warm jets to flush away, but that was what they were for. They did their job, and the hissing, gulping suction pumps sucked the wastewater away.

By the time he came out he knew exactly where he was. He was in the ship's sick bay.

Viktor knew all about the sick bay. He had seen it from time to time, had in fact spent several boring hours there before it was time for his family to be frozen, when the last of his baby molars had had to be helped out so his adult ones would come in straight. The old woman patted him dry. He let her. He was more interested in what was going on in the warming pan he had awakened in. Two little kids, no more than four or five years old, were in it now, huddled in each other's arms under the bath of directed infrared and microwave as they warmed. The pan around them was filled with the thick, milky liquid that kept them oxygenated through perfusion until their lungs began to work, and their limbs were already beginning to move with tiny random twitches. He even recognized the kids: Billy and Freddy Stockbridge, the sons of his dad's navigation partner—two nasty little bits of business if he'd ever seen any.

By the time he was dressed in tunic and shorts and had drunk two enormous glasses of something sweet and hot, his mother came hurrying in from the next chamber, white robe fluttering behind her. "Are you all right?" she asked anxiously, reaching out for him.

He allowed her to give him a quick kiss, then fended her off with dignity. "I'm fine," he said. "Why aren't we there?"

"I'm afraid there was a little complication, Vik," she told him, her voice uneasy. "There's something wrong with the flight plan, so they've got your father up to straighten it out. It'll be all right."

"Sure it will," he said, surprised. There wasn't really any doubt in his mind about that; after all, the man who was in charge of straightening such things out was his father.

"Marie-Claude's up, too," she said fretfully, touching his forehead as she used to do when she thought he might have a fever. "Between the two of them they'll have it all cleared up, but I've got to go help out. Are you sure you'll be—"

"I'm *sure*," he said, exasperated and a little embarrassed at being treated like a child.

The old woman interrupted. "Vik needs to eat and get himself oriented, Mrs. Sorricaine-Memel," she said. "I'll see that he's all right; you go ahead."

Amelia Sorricaine-Memel looked at her curiously, as though trying to place her, but only said, "I'll be back again as soon as I can."

When she was gone, the old woman took Viktor's hand. "You're supposed to go in the treadmill for a few minutes," she told him. "Then the doctors will check you over. Do you want to do that now?"

"Why not?" he asked, shrugging. "But I'm hungry."

"Of course you're hungry," she said, laughing a little. "You always were. You stole my chocolates when I was on the teaching machines, and your mother took away your candy for a week."

Viktor frowned at the woman. It was true that he had stolen chocolates and been punished for it, but the child he had stolen them from had been Wanda Sharanchenko, the tiny blond daughter of one of the engineering officers, two years younger than himself. "But—" he began.

The woman nodded. "But that was a long time ago, wasn't it? More than a hundred years, while you were a corpsicle. But it's me, all right, Viktor; I'm Wanda."

The ship *New Mayflower* wasn't "there." It wasn't even close to the "there" they were aiming for. According to the original flight plan there was to be more than twenty-eight years of deceleration time left before they would be at the planet they were meant to colonize.

But, unbelievably, it seemed that the original flight plan was wrong.

Wanda tried to explain it to Viktor as she led him to the huge rotating barrel that was the ship's treadmill, spun at nine revolutions a minute to simulate enough of normal Earth gravity to prevent calcium migration and muscle loss.

The treadmill was familiar enough to Viktor. He'd spent plenty of hours in it in the two years before he went into the freezer; it was where he played games with the other children in their compulsory daily exercise routine. He trotted around the barrel like a veteran, working out a century's worth of kinks in his young muscles, achieving a sweat and a decently high pulse without trouble. Wanda was hanging at the hub of the wheel, talking to him as he ran.

When he asked her what had happened, she called, "Flare star."

"A what star?" he panted.

"A flare star. Or maybe a nova, I don't know—they say there are some funny things about it. Anyway, something blew up. It's really bright, Vik. Wait till you see it. And it's only about thirty degrees off our course, so—"

She didn't have to explain. Viktor had heard enough from his father to see the problem. The unanticipated flare would be pouring out wholly unexpected floods of photons, and, as the light sail had already been deployed to help in *Mayflower*'s long, slow deceleration, the flare would be shoving them off course and their speed would be decreasing too rapidly. New course settings had to be calculated, and so, of course, all the navigators had been recalled from freezing, nearly three decades ahead of schedule, to assist in the work.

Even for Viktor, who had spend most of the unfrozen part of his conscious life as the son of one of the ship's navigators, that was not easy to understand completely. What made it worse was the person who was telling it all to him. He could not reconcile the hundred-year-old Wanda Sharanchenko (no—even that was wrong—her name turned out to be Wanda Mei now) who was telling him all this with his quite fresh memory of the tiny little girl who had cried and tried to bite him after he ate her chocolates. Panting, he called up to her perch on the hub, "But why didn't you get frozen, like everybody else?"

She paused, peering at him while she thought her answer out. "I suppose," she said finally, "it was fear."

"Fear of *freezing*?" Viktor demanded, incredulous. How silly could you be? What was there to fear in being gently frozen and then reawakened when the time came? It wasn't any different from going to sleep and waking up in the morning, really. Was it?

But, Wanda told him, it was. "Not everyone survives freezing. About one person out of a hundred and eighty can't be thawed. Something goes wrong, in the freezing, or the suspension, or the thawing, and they die, you know."

Viktor hadn't known that. He swallowed. "But that's not bad odds," he protested, for his own sake mostly.

"It's bad odds if you're the one that dies," she said decisively. "My parents thought so. And that's not counting the ones that get freezer-damaged. They can come out blind, or paralyzed. Who wants that?"

"Have you ever seen somebody blind from the freezer?" he challenged.

"Keep running," she ordered. "No, but I never saw a dead one, either. I still know they're there! Anyway, my parents volunteered to stay on as part of the caretaker crew, and I stayed with them . . . all these years. Now come off the wheel, Viktor, you're ready for your physical."

Which he passed, of course, with flying colors. But what he was to do after that was much less clear. If the ship had been where it should have been when they woke Viktor up there would have been no problem. Even a little kid had things to do to get ready for landing.

But they weren't there yet, and Wanda was no help. "Just stay out of the way," she advised, and hurried off to some kind of work of her own.

The fact that Viktor had been revived early from the freezer didn't mean that anyone wanted him up and about. The grown-ups he encountered made that clear. It would have been better all around if he had stayed cold and senseless, like the eleven hundred other passengers in the freezatoria. But that wasn't Viktor's fault. It was his parents who had opted for storage as a family unit, Mommy and Daddy and young Viktor all in the same capsule in the cryonic chambers, and once the process of resuscitating his father had well started the other two had already been much more than halfway back to life.

They couldn't, after all, break the sleepers apart with a fork, like a block of frozen spinach. They had to thaw a bit before they could be separated, and then—well, there was always that one-in-a-hundred-and-eighty chance Wanda had mentioned.

The room Viktor was supposed to share with his parents was no bigger than his own personal bedroom had been in California, back down on the surface of Earth, before they left to join the interstellar colony ship. It was pretty cramped.

That was not the fault of the ship's designers. They had allowed ample living space for the handful of men and women who were to take their turns on unfrozen watch as the other eleven hundred aboard slumbered at the temperature of liquid nitrogen. But they had only planned for thirty-five or forty watchkeepers to be awake at any one time. Now, with thirty others roused unexpectedly to deal with the problem of the flare star, living space was in short supply. Not quite as short as it had been in the first moments after launching, of course, when Viktor's family had taken the first watch until the ship was well clear of the solar system. And by no means as short as it would be when the ship arrived at its destination and all the corpsicles were defrosted to get ready for landing. Then it would be ten in a room instead of three, and in around-the-clock sleeping shifts, too.

Still, living space was pretty cramped. Worse, Viktor was bored. When his parents were out working, or at least awake, he could watch old films from Earth. He could even see whole recorded baseball games, taped by broadcast from Earth as they were played, though of course there was not much suspense in watching them. The results had been history for decades. Come to that, if he got desperate enough he could even dial up the teaching machines and please his parents with a few hours' study of algebra or antimatter engine maintenance or the history of the Holy Roman Empire.

None of that was enough to keep a young boy busy. Viktor didn't want to watch baseball. He wanted to play it. But there were never eighteen people to make up two sides, even if any of the grown-ups had been willing. He was lonesome. Grown-ups were about all he had for company, because all the other kids on *May-flower* were still corpsicles. Not counting the Stockbridge infants. They certainly couldn't be counted as friends, and none of the adults on the ship had much time for them, either. The adults were all busy, not to say obsessed, with the unexpected, and definitely unusual, flare star. The general idea, as much as any of the adults thought about it at all, was that the teaching machines would keep the children busy most of the time, and Viktor could look after the two little ones the rest of it.

Viktor was having none of that.

He hung around the working rooms of the ship as much as he could, watching his father and Marie-Claude Stockbridge and the others peck away at their computers, listening to snippets of conversation.

"It looks like an extra eight months travel time—that's not too bad."

"There's plenty of fuel reserve." That was his father. "I've calculated a first-approximation vector, but what about the light sail? Pull it in? Leave it out?"

"Leave it out. Just cut engine deceleration thrust. Then—" That time it was Marie-Claude Stockbridge speaking, and she looked up at the screen that showed the heavens before them. The bright blue-white flare star dominated everything, dimming that fainter, yellower one that was their destination. "Then when we get there, I wonder what we'll find. That star's putting out a lot of radiation."

What she said was what was on everybody's mind. The place they were going, the probes had said, was a livable planet—in fact, the name they had given it was "Newmanhome"—but heavy radiation could change the parameters of what was "livable." Of course, the first ship, six years ahead of them in flight, would find all that out before them—but if things were bad, what could they do about it? There was no way to return. "Newmanhome's got Van Allens and a pretty deep atmosphere, Marie," Vik's father told her. "It'll be all right. I hope."

And then there was silence for a moment until one of the others turned back to his computer and tapped a few keys. "Right now it adds up to a little under seven light-years to go," he announced. "First thrust approximation, a six-percent reduction ought to do it, adjusting it back as the flare dies away. That's the hard part, though. Anybody know how to calculate the decay rate?"

"For a regular flare star? Maybe," Viktor's father said irritably. "For this thing, how can we? It's not really flaring. It's more like it just blew up."

"But you say it isn't a nova," the man said, and then he glanced up and caught sight of Viktor. "Looks like your son's come to help us, Pal," he said to Viktor's father. It was an amiable enough remark, but it carried a message, too, and Viktor turned and got out of the room before the message had to be made explicit.

For lack of anything better to do, he turned to the teaching machine to explain some of what was going on. For instance, he knew that a light-year was a very long distance indeed. But exactly how long?

The teaching machine tried to help. It told Viktor that a light-year was the distance traveled in one year by a beam of light, speeding along at its unalterable pace of 186,000 miles per second, but it wasn't easy for Viktor to visualize even a "mile." The machine tried to be helpful. Some 734 of those "miles," it explained, lay between New York and Chicago, back on Earth. Six thousand of them took you from any point on the Earth's equator to one of its poles. But that meant little to Viktor, who had been only six years old when he and his parents launched to join the ship's crew assembling in space. He thought he remembered Los Angeles, because of the amusement parks and the seals, but he also remembered the snow-man his father had made for him in the courtyard of their home—and there couldn't have been any snowmen in Los Angeles. (His mother had explained to him that had been in Warsaw, where Vik-tor had been born, but to Viktor "Warsaw" was only a name.)

The closest the teaching machine came to defining a mile for Viktor was to point out that it was a little more than twenty-five times around the revolving exercise treadmill where every wakeful person had to exercise his muscles and preserve the calcium in his bones.

So that was a mile. But the datum wasn't all that much help. Multiplying twenty-five laps around the revolving drum by 186,000 by the number of seconds in a year was simply beyond Viktor's capabilities. Not to do the arithmetic—the teaching machine wrote the answer out for him—but to grasp the *meaning* of the simple sum $25 \times 186,000 \times 60 \times 60 \times 24 \times 365.25 = 146,742,840,000,000$.

Call it a hundred and fifty trillion laps around the revolving drum . . .

What was the use of calling it anything, though, when nobody could really grasp the meaning of a "trillion"?

And that was just one light-year. Then, of course, you had to multiply even that huge number by another 6.8 to find out how far you still had to go before landing . . . or by 19.7 to find out how far you were from home.

The thing about young Viktor Sorricaine was that he hated to give up. On anything. He wasn't a very impressive kid physically—tall for his age, but gangling and pretty clumsy. Viktor had nearly abandoned the hope of becoming an All-Star center-fielder, but that wasn't because he despaired of ever getting his co-ordination on track. It was only because he was pretty sure that no one in the place where he was going to spend the rest of his life was going to have time to organize any professional baseball teams.

Viktor was determined, but he wasn't crazy—although his par-

ents might have thought he was, if he had told them of his other
long-range ambition.

But that other ambition he didn't tell. Not to anybody.

He didn't let himself be thwarted by the teaching machine. He
dismissed it and tried another tack. He turned to the outside viewers
to see for himself just how distant Earth's old Sun looked. It took
some doing, but then he found it—barely—an object pitifully tiny
and faint among ten thousand other stars.

Then he heard the noise of scuffling and childish voices piping
in rage. Of course he knew who it had to be. He groaned and went
to the door. "Quiet down, you kids!" he ordered.

The Stockbridge boys didn't quiet down. They didn't even acknowledge hearing him. They were concentrating on trying to maim
each other. Billy had hit Freddy, because Freddy had pushed Billy,
and now the two of them were slapping and kicking at each other
as they rolled slowly about the floor in the microgravity.

Viktor didn't at all mind their punching each other. What he
objected to was that they were doing it in front of his family's door,
where he might be blamed for any wounds they might wind up
with. Not to mention the amount of noise they made and the language they used! Viktor was certain he had not known so many bad
words when he was their age. When he got them pulled apart, he
heard Billy pant ferociously at his sobbing brother, "I'll kill you,
you whoreson!"

That did it for Viktor. He hadn't been going to tell on them,
but that was too much. He would not allow even her own child to
say such a think about beautiful, desirable, undoubtedly chaste
Marie-Claude Stockbridge—since, improbable as any happy out-
come of his ambition must seem even to Viktor, Marie-Claude
Stockbridge was the other ambition he had no intention of giving
up on. "All right, you two," he growled. "We're going to see your
parents about this!"

But by the time he got them back to the Stockbridge family
quarters on the far rim of the ship Viktor had a change of heart.
Werner Stockbridge, their father, was webbed into his bed, sound
asleep. He looked too frayed and worried as he snored there to be
wakened for a punishment session, and their mother wasn't there
at all. The phone told Viktor that Marie-Claude Stockbridge was on

duty in the Operations complex at the heart of the ship, along with
his own parents. He didn't want to disturb her there. He looked
gloomily at the little culprits, sighed, and said, "All right, you two.
How about a nice quiet game of dominoes in the rec room?"

An hour later Mrs. Stockbridge came looking for them,
full of praise for Viktor. "You're a lot of help," she told him. "I
don't know what I'd do without you, Viktor. Look, as soon as I
get the kids in for a nap I'm going to get something to eat and then
bed. Will you keep me company?"

Viktor knew perfectly well that that invitation was for the meal
and certainly not for the bed. All the same he felt a sudden electrical
heat at the bottom of his belly and only managed to growl, "Okay."

In the refectory Marie-Claude Stockbridge had the tact to let
Viktor carry her tray to the table. He was extremely careful about
it. In the gentle gravity of the ship's fractional-G acceleration slip-
pery foods could slide right off the plate if you moved too fast in
the wrong direction, but he delivered the trays to the table magnets
in perfect order. Then he set himself the task of making grown-up
dinner-table conversation. "Vegetable protein again," he announced, stirring the thick stew. "I can't wait to get there and get
a decent meal."

"Well, don't get your hopes too high. The meals might not be
too good right away," Mrs. Stockbridge said politely. There were
plenty of food animals in the livestock section of the freezers, but
of course they would have to be allowed to breed and multiply
before many of them could be turned into steaks or pork chops or
fried drumsticks. "Although the first-ship colonists ought to have
some stocks built up by the time we're there." She looked absently
past Viktor, catching a glimpse of herself in the wall mirror—half
the walls on the ship were mirrored to make the rooms seem more
spacious. She touched her hair and said remorsefully, "I'm a mess."

"You look all right," Viktor growled, frowning down at the
rest of his stew.

But that wasn't the whole truth. Marie-Claude looked a lot better than "all right" to his lascivious pubescent eyes. She was taller
than his father, and more curved than his mother. Her hair was

tangled, and her fingernails were still cracked from the freezer, and there was a faint, sweet smell of healthy female perspiration about her . . . and all of that was inexpressibly alluring to twelve-year-old Viktor Sorricaine.

Although Viktor wished no harm at all to Werner Stockbridge, one of his best daydreams (and sometimes night dreams) involved Marie-Claude's husband somehow losing the power of reproduction. He had learned that such things sometimes happened to men. He viewed it as a potential opportunity for himself. After all, everyone knew that when the ship landed it would be everyone's duty to have children. *Lots* of children—the planet had to be populated, didn't it? Lacking the ability to participate in the process himself, Werner Stockbridge would surely accept the necessity of his wife becoming pregnant now and then—and who better to do the job for him than their good family friend, young (but by then, with any luck, not too young to do the job) Viktor Sorricaine?

Some of the details of Viktor's fantasy were pretty hazy. That was all right. The important parts of the fantasy came later on. After all, Mr. Stockbridge was much older than his wife—thirty-eight to her twenty-five—and males were at their sexual peak in their teens. (Viktor knew a lot about the subject of reproductive biology. The teaching machines had not always been a disappointment.) After that age male vigor slowly declined, while the sexuality of women grew from year to year. Viktor took comfort in the fact that the thirteen-year difference between Marie-Claude's age and her husband's was exactly the same as between hers and Viktor's own, though of course in the opposite direction. So (Viktor calculated, as he gallantly escorted Marie-Claude back to the room where her husband and sons slept) in a few years, say seven or so, he would be nineteen and she would be no more than thirty-two; very likely, he speculated, the very peak years for both of them, while old Werner Stockbridge would be well into his forties and definitely well on the downhill path at least, if not actually out of it . . .

He turned and glanced up at her. "What?"

Marie-Claude was smiling at him. "We're here, Viktor. And, oh, Viktor, I know what a nuisance those two little monsters can be. Thank you!" And she reached down and kissed his cheek before she disappeared into the family cubicle.

So, of course, then there was no help for it. From then on Viktor doggedly baby-sat the two Stockbridge brats, however hateful they got. Which could be pretty hateful. When they awoke from their nap he organized a game of gravity-tag in the treadmill, hoping to tire them out. When they still wouldn't tire he took them on a tour of the ship. By the time it was their bedtime he realized it was also his own; he had never before understood how wearying taking care of small children could be for an adult, or anyway a near-adult, like himself.

When he woke up it was because his parents were calling him. "I thought we'd all have breakfast together for a change," his mother said, smiling at him. "Things are almost getting back to normal."

Breakfast was no different from any other meal except that they had porridge instead of stew, but what was different was the atmosphere. His father was relaxed for the first time since their defrosting. "The flare star's dying out," he told his son. "We're watching it pretty closely—there are some funny things about it."

Viktor always had permission to ask for explanations. "Funny how, Dad?" he asked, settling down for one of those wonderful father-and-son talks he remembered from the old days. His father was one of those priceless few who didn't think little children should ever be told "You'll understand when you're older." Pal Sorricaine always explained things to his son. (So did Amelia Sorricaine-Memel, but other things, and not as interesting to Viktor.) Some of the things Pal had explained as he tucked his son in, instead of telling silly children's stories about the three bears, were the Big Bang, the CNO hydrogen-to-helium cycle that made stars burn, the aging of galaxies, the immensity of the expanding universe. Of course, Amelia had interesting technical things to talk about, too, but her specialty was physics and mechanics. Things like entropy and the Carnot efficiency of heat engines weren't nearly as wondrous to a child as the stories of the stars they were wandering among.

This time Viktor was disappointed. All his father said was, "It just doesn't match any of the known profiles of flare stars. It might be a nova, but it's a funny one. It's got two big jets. Matter of fact, I've sent a report to the International Astronomical Society about it—who knows, they may even name it after me as a new class of objects!"

"They ought to," Viktor said decisively, pleased because his father looked pleased too—almost as pleased as he was puzzled. But his father shook his head.

"It'll be twenty years before they hear it and another twenty before they acknowledge, remember?" he said. "Anyway, it looks as though we can handle the navigation."

"Maybe," Viktor's mother said.

"Well, yes, maybe," his father conceded. "There's always a maybe." He pushed aside his empty porridge bowl and took a deep swallow of the one cup of coffee he was allowed each day. Fifth Officer Pal Sorricaine was a plump, smooth-faced, blue-eyed man with a cheery disposition. He smiled often. He was smiling now, though with a little quizzical twist of the lip to acknowledge the "maybe." He had close-cropped pale hair, and he ran his hand over it as he gazed benignly at his son. "Marie-Claude says you've been a sweetheart about her kids," he said.

Viktor shrugged, scowling into his bowl.

"Got a case on her, have you?" his father asked, grinning. "I can't say I blame you."

"Pal!" his wife warned.

Sorricaine relented. "I was only teasing you a little, Vik," he apologized. "Don't be touchy, okay? Anyway, I think we can go back in the deep freeze in a day or two, after all. So if there's anything you specially want to do on the ship this time . . ."

Viktor made a face. "What is there to do?"

"Not much," Pal Sorricaine agreed. "Still—have you taken a good look at the ship? It's changed a lot since we took off, you know. And you'll never see it this way again."

Later on, being a surly "sweetheart" once more for Marie-Claude Stockbridge, Viktor was minding the kids in a rough-house game of catch. After a wildly thrown ball had bounced around a corner of the passage and hit one of the maintenance crew in the face, Viktor remembered what his father had said. "Enough ball playing," he announced. "I want to show you something."

"What?" Freddy demanded, wresting the ball away from his brother.

"You'll see. Come on."

Viktor's parents were both at work, so he had the little room uncontested. For a wonder, the Stockbridge brothers were reasonably quiet as Viktor turned on the screen and found the menu for exterior real-time observation.

It took him a little experimentation before he was able to lock onto the view he wanted, but then he had it.

New Mayflower was a ramshackle contraption. You could have held it together with string—it would never experience any strong forces to tear it apart—and the designers pretty nearly did. The bits and pieces of it were random, irregular objects, but the screen clearly showed the vast bulk of the light sail, half deployed.

Even the little kids knew about the light sail. To travel from star to star took vast amounts of energy. The antimatter mass thrusters were not enough. Light sails had helped lift *Mayflower* out of the gravity well of the Sun's attraction, using the Sun's own endless flood of photons to help thrust it away. The same light sail was now already half deployed to use the light of the new star to help slow the ship down. There it was, fanning out from the ship like a huge frail ruff of silver—but only halfway deployed. "Look at it," he commanded.

"It's crooked," Freddy announced.

"*You're* crooked," Billy told him. "Give me my ball!"

"Yes, give him the damn ball," Viktor gritted.

"It isn't his."

"It is so!"

"No, it's mine, because you lost it and I found it. Finders keepers!"

"Well, I don't have it anyway," Freddy lied, concealing the ball as he ducked behind Viktor. "It's home."

"It *isn't* home! I see it—"

"Will you two shut up about the stinking ball?" Viktor roared. "Here, let me show you where we're going."

"I don't want to see where we're going," Billy whined, but Viktor was already adjusting the image. Now it was direct line of

sight—toward the "stern" of the ship, naturally, because *Mayflower*
had long since been turned around so the main engines could thrust
in the direction that would slow it down. It wasn't a very good
picture. Around the edges the stars were bright, ten thousand of
them or more, hues from firebox red to sapphire and white, and
the ghostly pale haze of the Milky Way washing out one corner
of the screen. But the center of the picture wasn't very clear. The
optical overload sensors dimmed the flare star enough to let the
others show, but the haze of ions streaming from the drive jets
fuzzed everything. Including the star they were heading for. "That's
it," Viktor said. "Right under that bright one."

"I can't see it," Billy whines. "I want a Coca-Cola."

"A what?"

"A Coca-Cola. It's a drink. I saw it on television. I want one."

"Well, I don't have one," Viktor said, "and if I did your mother
probably wouldn't want you to—oh, my God."

The boys stopped whining and looked up anxiously at him.
"What is it?" Freddy demanded, apprehensive.

"Nothing," he said, staring at the view he had just succeeded in
tuning in on the screen. "No, it's nothing. It's just that I, well, I
kind of forgot. I forgot that half the ship would be gone by now,"
Viktor said.

When *New Mayflower* left Low Earth Orbit to begin
its long journey to a new home, it was six years behind *New Ark*.
And even before it pulled out of Low Earth Orbit the skeleton of
New Argosy was beginning to take shape behind it. The three interstellar ships, combined, had a single assignment: to populate a world,
and thus to establish a bridgehead for the human race in its long-
term destiny of seeding the entire galaxy with people.

That was a pretty fantastic idea, even for bumptious humans.
But the project wasn't purely a fantasy. It could be done. The whole
human total on all three ships came to under four thousand people.
But human beings are really good at procreating. In two or three
centuries, if they put their minds to it, the population of the new
planet could be bigger than that of bulging old Earth itself.

Practicality wasn't the question.

The question (and some asked it) was: *Why?* Why travel a hundred years and more to people another planet with human beings, when the Solar System already had enough of them for any reasonable need?

Really, there was only one answer to the question of why anyone would want to colonize the new world, and that answer was: Because it was there. Newmanhome wasn't only there, it had *life*; the long-ago probe, no bigger than a washing machine, had established that definitely as it sped through the new solar system. The proof was that the presence of reactive gases in the planet's atmosphere showed that it was a reduced-entropy world. The reactive gases in its air hadn't reacted with each other. Something was keeping them from doing so, and thus attaining chemical equilibrium. And the only thing that could do that was the only known anti-entropic force in the universe:

Life.

Oh, not *human* life. Not even anything technological—the probe had detected no signs of radio, industry, cities—nothing like that. But there was an atmosphere with oxygen and water vapor, and so human people (they were *nearly* sure) would be able to live there.

So *New Ark* was designed and (oh, after a *terrible* amount of argument and delay; Viktor hadn't even been born then, but his father had told him about it) even funded and built. And even before it was finished *New Mayflower* had been begun.

Each ship was purpose-designed, and the purposes were slightly different—*Ark* had to be self-sufficient, *Mayflower* would have the advantage of *Ark*'s colonists already there. Also, by the time they began assembling *Mayflower* the state of the art had leaped a generation ahead, so the two ships didn't look much alike. *Ark* was only a squat cylinder. *Mayflower*, with many added refinements, was longer and narrower. It started out 450 feet long and 90 feet in diameter at its widest point—it was more lozenge-shape than cylindrical—and once in orbit around the new planet its duties would have just begun. It would stay in orbit around Newmanhome indefinitely, to microwave power down to the colonies. (And, of course, *Argosy*, a generation more advanced still, would actually *land* on the planet!—but that was many years in the future, because the funding battles had begun all over again. The building of *Argosy* was still going on, but at a snail's pace.)

The ships all had one thing in common, though. To travel through interstellar space, each of them had to eat part of itself.

So the new shape of his ship was startling to Viktor. His eyes refused to recognize it. *Mayflower* was far shorter and stubbier than when last he had seen it, ten decades earlier. The long mass thruster, shaped like a skinny tulip, stuck straight out from the back of the ship where once it had been almost completely within the fabric of the ship itself.

To power its flight to the new star, *Mayflower* had fed more than half of itself into the plasma reactors already.

The string ball of fuel—twisted cables, thick as girders, of antimatter iron—had unraveled and reacted with the normal steel structure that had once enclosed it. The normal iron and the antimatter iron destroyed each other to produce the vast flood of charged particles that drove the ship.

Of course, not all the real iron in the ship was annihilated in the suicide pact with the anti-iron. Even interstellar travel didn't need *that* much energy. Most of the normal iron simply flashed into plasma and streamed out the thrust nozzles as reaction mass. There was no mystical reason why the normal matter had to be iron, either—iron didn't need anti-iron for the two to annihilate each other; it was just what was easiest to spare.

It was a very efficient reaction. Much better than that pathetic "atomic power" the old people used to use.

It is always true that $e = mc^2$, all right, but it is not easy to get all of the *e* out of the *m*. The sort of nuclear power plant that human beings built in the late twentieth century had a lot of mass left over when its reactions were complete. Ninety-nine point nine percent of the fuel mass remained mass and stubbornly refused to turn into energy at all.

But when antimatter reacts with an equal amount of normal matter no mass whatever is left. It isn't only a tenth of a percent of the mass that becomes driving force when you react normal matter with its antiparticles. It is all of it.

––––––––––––

By the fourth day after Viktor's unplanned defrosting, the crew of *Mayflower* had gotten over their first heart-stopping fear. The flare star showed signs of dimming. The situation didn't seem critical, exactly. Puzzling, yes: Why had a very ordinary little K-5 star suddenly blossomed into flame? But it didn't seem to be life-threatening.

As panic subsided to surprised resentment aboard the *New Mayflower*, and then as the resentment changed to the work of coping with the consequences, Viktor Sorricaine's days became routine. Everybody's did. Fifth (Navigator) Officer Pal Sorricaine stopped being a navigator so he could become an astrophysicist, since one of his CalTech degrees had been on the dynamics of stellar cores. That was what was needed. The problem wasn't just how to rig the light sails and decide how much thrust to order from the deceleration engines, it was to predict how long the flare would last—and precisely what its curve toward extinction would be.

For that even Viktor's father's skills weren't quite enough, so they defrosted *Mayflower*'s best astrophysical brain. And so Frances Mtiga (three months, or you could say ninety-odd years, pregnant) woke up, blinking, to find a dandy dissertation problem facing her.

When she was thawed and bathed and fed and dressed Pal Sorricaine sat her before a screen and punched up the relevant menu for her. "This is what we've got on the flare star, Frances," he said. "I've filed it under NEWFLARE, and here are all the relevant studies I've been able to find—they're under FLARECITES—and this is the preliminary report that I sent back to Earth. That file's marked TENTATIVE. Maybe I should have called it GUESSWORK. It doesn't matter much anyway, Fanny. By the time any of this gets to Earth and back we'll be getting ready to land on the new planet."

"Or we won't," Frances Mtiga said dourly, rubbing her belly for reassurance as she studied the citation file.

"Or we won't," Pal Sorricaine agreed, grinning. "But there isn't any real reason to doubt that we will, Fanny. It looks like it's an interesting problem in astrophysics, that's all. Not any real threat to the mission. Anyway, we just won't go back into the freezer until we've got the whole thing studied out and under control."

Mtiga sighed, scratching her belly again. It was barely beginning to round out. "We'll give it as long as it takes," she said fretfully. "But tell me, Pal, don't you think my husband's going to have a surprise when he wakes up and finds he has a ten-year-old kid?"

Indeed it began to look that way. The astrophysical information stored in *New Mayflower*'s databank was comprehensive, but there wasn't much that was useful on flaring K-5 stars, because K-5 stars of that spectral type had never previously been observed to flare that way.

Viktor happily shared his father's puzzlement, all the more happily because no one expected him to solve the conundrum of the flare. His father was less lucky. He laid out the latest stretch of film to show his son, scowling at it. Although Viktor knew that it was supposed to be a spectrum, because his father had told him so, the film wasn't in color. It wasn't a rainbow. "It's a spectrogram, Vik," his father explained. "It shows the frequencies of the light from a star, or anything else. The diffraction grating bends the light, but the different frequencies bend to different amounts. The shorter the wavelength, the more it bends, so the red end doesn't get bent very much and the violet bends way over to here. Well, actually," he corrected himself, "this end is really the far ultraviolet, and down here is infrared. We can't see them with our eyes, but the film, can ... Only it's not a very good spectrogram," he finished, scowling again. "That grating's been out there for a hundred years, and all that time it's been bombarded with gases and fine particles of interstellar dust. The lines are blurred, do you see?"

"I guess so," Viktor said, peering uncertainly at the ribbon of grayed lines. "Can you fix it?"

"I can put a new one in," his father said, and displayed the thing he meant. It was a curved bit of metal, as long as Viktor's forearm, the shape of a watermelon rind when the flesh has been eaten away. His father handled it with care, showing Viktor the infinite narrow lines that had been ruled onto its concave face.

Well, that part was pretty exciting—it meant somone would have to suit up and crawl out onto the skin of *New Mayflower* to pull the fuzzed grating out and put the new one in—anyway, it would have been exciting, if Viktor had seen it. To his annoyance it all happened while he was asleep. By the time he knew it was

over his father was pondering over a newer, sharper, but still baf-
fling spectrogram.

"Christ," he grumbled, "*look* at the thing. It looks like that
star's spilling its guts two ways at once. Only Doppler interferome-
try doesn't show any increase in diameter, so it's not a nova-type
explosion. So what is it?"

No one expected Viktor to answer that question. They did expect it of his father and of Frances Mtiga, but the astrophysicists
didn't know the answer either. Every day they checked twenty-four
hours of observations, which the computer matched against the latest revised models Sorricaine and Mtiga had prepared to draw its
best-fit curves. And every day the fit wasn't really good enough.

"But it's going to be all right, Pal," Viktor's mother told her
husband. The three of them, for once, were having dinner together
in the big refectory. "I mean, isn't it? There's plenty of fuel. You
can just shove the ship around on the drive and forget about the
sails, can't you?"

"Sure we could," Pal Sorricaine said absently. "Oh, we'll get
there all right, I guess."

"Then—"

"But it's not very goddamn *elegant*!" he barked.

Viktor understood what his father meant. The wondrous thing
about astrophysics was that the more you learned, the better everything fit together. Things didn't get more complicated, they got
more breathtakingly clear. In Pal's view (as in the view of all scientists) oddball events spoiled the symmetry of the laws that ruled
the universe. They were a *disgrace* that could only be repaired by
figuring out how, after all, they did fit. "Anyway," Pal Sorricaine
said after a moment, "there's a price tag on this thing. That fuel's
not just supposed to get us there. It's going to power industry and
stuff. The more we use, the more we're stealing from our future."
And that was true enough, because when *Mayflower* was just a hulk
in orbit the colony would need the microwaves it would be beaming
down to the surface. "But mostly it's not elegant," he said again
dismally. "We're supposed to know all about these things. And we
don't!"

They defrosted a mathematician named Jahanjur Singh to help them out, but Viktor could tell from the way his father kept staring into space that it wasn't helping enough. Still, Viktor found with pleasure that his parents had time to relax with their son. Amelia kept as busy as Pal—her own specialty of thermodynamic engineering wasn't very relevant, but at least she could run a computer for the astrophysical team—but still there were times when they all played tag together in the centrifuge; they watched tapes of Earthly TV together; they even cooked fudge together, one night, and Viktor's mother didn't stop him however much he ate.

Viktor was no fool. He could tell that there was something on his parents' minds that went beyond the astrophysical problem and the navigation of the ship, but he expected they would tell him about it when they were ready. Meanwhile he had the ship to explore. With so few humans awake, he had a lot of freedom to do it in. Even Captain Bu tolerated his exploration.

Before he was frozen Viktor had been pretty much afraid of Captain Bu Wengzha. It took him a while after defrosting to get over the feeling, too, because Captain Bu wasn't happy about the jawbone course corrections he had to make when he was thawed out himself. *New Mayflower* was, after all, *his ship*.

Captain Bu was the oldest man aboard *Mayflower*—well, to be accurate, he wasn't anymore; he'd spent more than eighty years frozen, daring the odds to be thawed out for a while every decade to make sure the ship was shipshape in all its myriad parts. People like Wanda Mei had had their biological clocks running much longer than he. Bu was still biologically fifty-two, with a wide, strong-toothed mouth in a wide, plump face the color of the beach sand at Malibu. He had no hair on his head at all, but he had carefully cultivated a wispy beard. Most of the time he didn't smile. He didn't smile when things were going smoothly, because that was simply the way they were supposed to go, and he certainly didn't smile when Fifth Officer Sorricaine came apologetically to the bridge to tell him that that day's sail-setting order, still in the process of being carried out, had to be revised because the flare's light pressure hadn't fallen off quite the way the model predicted.

Peering over the captain's shoulder in one of those discussions, trying to be invisible so as not to be sent off the bridge, Viktor

looked wonderingly at the sail. It spread out in an untidy sprawl at
the bow of the ship—which was now, of course, its stern—like a
drop cloth for untidy house painters. Only it was not meant to
catch spilled paint, but photons. The sail was almost more nuisance
than it was worth, except that, of course, everything on *New Mayflower* was designed to serve at least two purposes and some of the
sail's later purposes made it, in sum, very worthwhile. The trouble
with it now was that at stellar distances there weren't very many
photons for it to catch.

The film of the sail was tough, tricky stuff. It was "one-way"
plastic, and it weighed very little. But to keep it spread at all, with
the dynamic force of the ship's engines tearing at it, it needed a lot
of structural support; nearly a quarter of its mass went into the
struts and cables that spread it at the right orientation (complex to
figure, because the thrust on the sail varied with the square of the
cosine of the angle it made with the source, doubly complex because
there were many sources), and the motors that changed the orientation as needed. Even so, the sail's contribution to *Mayflower*'s
acceleration and deceleration could be measured only in tiny fractions of one millimeter per second squared.

But those tiny delta-Vs all added up, when you had to bring a
vast ship from near relativistic velocities to relative rest in just the
place you wanted to insert it into orbit. So the varying flux from
the flare star mattered a lot to Captain Bu, and to everyone on
the ship.

Captain Bu wasn't always fierce. He turned out to have a weak-
ness for kids—at least, as long as there weren't very *many* of them
to get in the way. He not only didn't chase Viktor from the bridge,
he actually encouraged him to visit there. He even tolerated the
Stockbridge boys there—for brief periods, until they began acting
up, and always with Viktor clearly understanding that his life was
held hostage if the kids got in trouble.

Captain Bu even joined Viktor and the two boys in the gravity
drum, laughing and shouting, his wispy beard flying about—and
then afterward, when they were all cleaned up and hungry, he shared
almond-flavored bean-curd sweets with them out of his private stock.
Viktor didn't like the bean curd much, but he did like the captain.
Captain Bu was a lot better than the teaching machines (though not

really, Viktor was loyal enough to believe, as good as his own father) at explaining things.

When the bean curd was finished and the boys made less sticky,
he showed Viktor and the Stockbridge kids just where everything
was. "This is my ship," he said, putting a spoon on the table before
him, "and Freddy's plate there is the star we're heading for, six
point eight light-years away. It has an astronomical name, but we
just call it Sun. Like the one we left." He made a fist and held it in
the air over the table. "And my hand is the flare star, about five
light-years from us, about four point six from the destination, and
here"—another spoon—"is the *Ark*, maybe a tenth of a light-year
from landing. They've already felt the radiation. It comes at a bad
time for them, velocities are getting critical, but it won't bother
them much, I think. They're a lot farther from the flare than from
the new Sun."

"Where's home?" Freddy Stockbridge piped.

"Shut up," Viktor said, but Captain Bu shook his head forgiv-
ingly.

He bared those big white teeth at the boy. "*That* is home, boy,"
he said, tapping Freddy's plate. "The place we're going to. I know
when you said that you meant Earth, though—well, that's back
somewhere by the door."

And as Freddy turned to look at the door he saw his mother
standing there, hesitant to invade the captain's quarters until Bu
nodded to her to come in.

"Captain," Marie-Claude Stockbridge said, nodding. She looked
very beautiful—as always, Viktor told himself yearningly. "Viktor
dear, how are you? Are my little wretches giving you any trouble
today, Captain?"

"Not a bit, Dr. Stockbridge," Captain Bu told her stiffly. Now
in the presence of an adult the smile was gone. "I do have to go
back to the bridge, though," he mentioned, and nodded them out
of his room. Marie-Claude looked wryly back at the closed door.

"Doesn't he like you?" one of her sons asked.

"Captain Fu Manchu doesn't let himself like grown-ups. He
puts up with a lot from you two, though," Marie-Claude told her
sons, and then had to explain who Fu Manchu was.

"He was showing us where all the stars and ships and things

were," Freddy volunteered. "Viktor said he was going to tell us why messages take so long, but he didn't."

"Oh," Marie-Claude said, "that's easy enough. See, the star flared about five years ago, and the light reached the ship just a week or so ago, that's when they started reviving us. And then—"

"Excuse me," Viktor interrupted. "I have to go home now."

Of course, he didn't, really. His reasons were quite different. He just didn't want Marie-Claude explaining things to him as though he were a *child*.

Not even the hope of an ultimate fleshly reward—well, another kiss, anyway—could make Viktor Sorricaine tend to the Stockbridge boys in all of his free time. True, his main hope was so faint and improbable that he hardly dared admit even to himself, but that wasn't what made him hide from them. The boys caused that all by themselves. They were simply unbearable. Viktor was amazed at the troubles they could get into, and even more amazed at the energy stored up in those small bodies to do it with. No twelve-year-old has ever remembered what he himself was like at five.

So, with the boys at least temporarily in the custody of their mother, Viktor arranged to keep it that way by getting out of sight. After a little thought he headed for the most remote habitable part of the ship, the freezatorium.

"Habitable" was almost too strong a word. The narrow aisles between the frost-clouded crystal coffins were freezing cold. The crystal was a good thermal insulator, but the liquid-gas cold inside each casket had had a hundred years to chill through it. Each casket was rimed with hoarfrost. The air was deliberately kept dryer than comfort would suggest in that section of the ship—Viktor could feel his throat getting raw as he breathed it—but even those faint residual traces of water vapor had condensed out on the crystal.

Although Viktor had had the forethought to borrow a long-sleeved sweater of his mother's, it wasn't enough. He had no clothes warm enough for that place. As he tiptoed along the corridors he was shivering violently.

He rubbed some of the frost off one of the caskets with the

sleeve of the sweater. Inside was a woman alone, dark-skinned, her
eyes closed but her mouth open, looking as though she were trying
to scream. The card in the holder at the corner of the casket said
Accardo, Elisavetta (Agronomist–plant breeder), but Viktor had never
seen that woman before, or heard that name. Likely enough she was
one of the ones already in the freezer by the time his parents joined
the ship.

And he wasn't much interested in thinking about her, either.
The cold was getting *serious*. It would be better even to face the
Stockbridge boys again than to stay here, he thought.

As he turned to hurry back through the double thermal doors,
he heard his name called. "Viktor! What are you doing here, dressed
like that? Are you crazy?"

It was Wanda Mei, furred and gauntleted, her old eyes peering
out at him over a thick scarf that wound over her head and across
the lower part of her face. Viktor greeted her uneasily. He didn't
particularly want to see Wanda Mei; he had been making a point of
avoiding her, because it gave him an uneasy feeling in his stomach
to know that this decrepit human wreck had once been his bouncy
playmate. "Well," she said, "as long as you're here you can give me
a hand. We'll have to put some more clothes on you, though." And
she tugged him down to a bend in the corridor where it widened
out to a little workshop. From a locker she pulled out a furred
jacket like her own and furred overshoes and a soft, warmly lined
helmet that came down over his ears, and then she set him to work.

Her job had been tugging some of the huge crystal caskets out
of their wall racks, setting them in place at the workshop. Empty,
they weren't heavy, but Viktor's help was welcome. "Why are we
doing this?" he asked.

"For the people that are going into the freezer again, of course,"
she said crossly. "What, are you too weak to help me? I was doing
it myself until you came along, an old woman like me." And indeed
the work was mostly just awkward. "That one," she said, pointing
to one already stacked, "that one was yours, Viktor. For you and
your family. How did you like it, all those years you slept there?"

He swallowed, looking at it without joy. "Are we going to be
frozen again?"

"Not right away, no, not you; that's why yours is on the bottom. But before long, I think. This one here, this is for the Stock-bridges; they go back in about three days, I think."

"In three *days?*"

She sighed. "It is my hearing that should be weakening, not yours. Can't you understand me? The emergency is over, they say, so the extra people can be corpsicles again." She looked at him, then softened. "Ah, are you worrying?"

"You told me to worry!"

She smiled, then apologized. "If I am frightened, that is my business. I didn't mean to scare you. You've already been frozen once, and survived. Was it so bad?"

"I don't remember," Viktor said truthfully. All he remembered was being given a tiny shot that caused him to fall asleep, with the freezer technicians hovering reassuringly around him; and then waking up again. Whatever had happened in between had happened without his consciousness present to observe.

He worked silently with ancient Wanda Mei for a while, doing as he was told but thinking about Marie-Claude going back into the freezer. A thought had occurred to him. He would, he calculated, be sure to gain at least a few days on her by staying unfrozen longer than she. If only there were some way of prolonging that time— If he could stay thawed and living on the ship until it landed— Why, then he would be almost her own age, even old enough to be taken seriously by her!

That thought, however, still left the problem of her husband unsolved. "Hell," he said, softly but aloud, and Wanda looked at him.

"You're tired," she said, which wasn't true, "and you're cold—" which certainly was. "Well, we've done enough; thank you for your help, Viktor." And then, back in the warm part of the ship, she thought for a moment and then said: "Do you like books, Viktor? I have some in my room."

"There are plenty of books in the library," he pointed out.

"These are *my* books. Kid's books," she amplified. "From when I was your age. I've just kept them. You can borrow them if you want."

"Maybe some time," Viktor said vaguely.

She looked cross. "Why not this time? Come on, you haven't seen my room."

Indeed he hadn't. Actually, he didn't much want to now. There wasn't any real reason for that, only the kind of queasy, uneasy feeling that Wanda gave him. It wasn't just that she was old. He'd seen plenty of old people—well, not usually as old as Wanda, of course; but for a twelve-year-old anyone past thirty is pretty much in the same general age cohort anyway. Wanda was different. She was both old and his own age, and seeing her reminded Viktor, in terms he could not ignore, that one day he, too, would have wrinkles and age spots on the backs of his hands and graying hair. She was his future displayed for him, and unwelcome. It shattered his child's confidence that he would remain a child.

He entered Wanda's room diffidently. It smelled terrible. He saw that it wasn't in any way like the one Viktor shared with his parents. It had started out identical, of course—every room on the ship was basically the same standard cubicle, since each one would become a separate landing pod when the colonists arrived at their destination—but over a hundred years she had decorated it and painted it and added bits of furnishings and knickknacks that were her own . . . and it had one bit of furnishing that Viktor had not at all expected and saw with astonished delight.

Wanda Mei had a cat!

The cat's name was Robert, a whole tom who was, Wanda said, nearly twenty years old. "He won't last any longer than I will," she said, sighing as she sat down. The cat stalked toward her, then soared into her lap, but she gave him a quick stroke and handed him generously to Viktor. "You hold him while I find the books," she ordered. Viktor was glad to oblige. The old cat turned around twice in his lap and then allowed his back to be stroked, nuzzling his whiskery cheek contentedly into Viktor's belly.

Viktor was almost sorry when Wanda produced the books. But they were grand. She had *Tom Sawyer* and *Two Little Savages* and *Mistress Masham's Repose* and a dozen others—worn, dog-eared, the bindings sometimes cracked, but still entirely readable.

Only the catbox smell of the room began to get to him. He stood.

"I have to go now," he announced. She looked surprised but didn't object. "Thank you for the books," he remembered to say, politely. She nodded.

And then, as he reached the door, he asked the question that had been on his mind all along. "Wanda? Why did you do it?"

"Why did I do what?" she demanded crossly.

"Why did you let yourself get old?"

She glared at him. "What impudence, Viktor! And what a question! Everyone gets old, that is what human beings do. You will get old, too!"

"But I'm not old now," he pointed out reasonably.

"You are not even grown-up enough to be courteous!" Then she said, softening, "Well, I told you. I was afraid. I didn't want to die . . . only," she sighed, "it appears that I am going to die before very long anyway. I did want to see the new planet, Viktor. All the planets. Nebo and the one we're going to live on, Enki. What they call Newmanhome. And Ishtar and Nergal—"

"And Marduk and Ninih," he finished for her. Everyone knew the names of the planets in the system they would live in. "Yes. But why don't you—"

"Why don't I get frozen now, after all?" she demanded bitterly. "Because now it's too late, Viktor. What would they do with an old useless woman when we land? What would my husband do?"

Viktor stared at her. He hadn't known she had ever had a husband.

"Oh," she said, nodding. "Yes, I was married once. For seven years, while Thurhan was thawed out for his turn at engineering duty. Why do you think my name is Mei now? But we didn't have any children, and he went back into the freezer, when his tour was over, and when he wakes up again what would he want with a wife older than his grandmother? And besides—"

She hesitated, looking at him sadly. "And besides," she finished, "I'm still afraid."

He spent the rest of the day alone, reading. When he got to the refectory for the evening meal almost everyone was there, looking excited. The rumor was now fact. The emergency crews weren't needed anymore, and they were being sent back to cryonic storage.

Most people looked pleased at the word that the emergency was over, but Viktor's mother wasn't looking pleased, and his father looked abashed. All the feelings of the last days came back to Viktor. Something had been kept from him. "What's the matter?" he demanded, alarmed.

"I had to make a decision," Pal Sorricaine said reluctantly. "See, I'm going to stay awake for a while, Viktor. Not long—well, maybe not long; it's too soon to tell. But they need an astronomer-navigator to keep an eye on the flare star, and I guess I'm it."

Viktor pondered, blinking. "You mean my mother and I are going to be frozen, but you're not?"

"It'll be all right, Vik," his mother put in. "For us, anyway. For your father, well—well, perhaps it will only be for a few months. Or a couple of years at the outside—don't you think, Pal?" she appealed, turning to his father.

"I'll do it as soon as I can," he promised. "After all, the flight's got sixteen years to go—I don't want to wind up that much older than you!"

Across the room, Werner Stockbridge was whispering in his wife's ear when he caught sight of Viktor. He detached himself and burrowed through the crowded hall, aiming a friendly slap, or pat, at his son, Billy, on the way. He lowered his head to Viktor's level and said confidentially, "You're just the man I'm looking for, Viktor. Do me a favor?"

"Sure, Mr. Stockbridge," Viktor said at once, though his tone was doubtful.

"Take the kids off our hands for a while, will you? I mean, we're going back in the deep freeze in a little while and—and Marie-Claude and I need a little private time first, if you know what I mean."

Viktor flushed and looked away, because he did know. "Okay, Vik?" Stockbridge persisted. Viktor nodded without looking up. "Give us an hour then, all right? Two would be better—say, two hours, and I'll owe you a favor."

Viktor checked ship's time on the wall clock: 1926 hours. Without very good feelings about it, partly because of the thought of two hours with the Stockbridge kids, mostly because of the thought of what the elder Stockbridges would be doing with those two hours, he led the boys to his own family's room and turned on the teaching machine. "I'm going to show you where we're going," he promised.

Freddy looked startled. "Heaven? You mean because we're going to die? Mrs. Mei said—"

"You're not going to *die*, and it doesn't matter what Mrs. Mei said," Viktor told them sourly. "I mean I'm going to show you the planets. Look," he said as the blue-white one flashed on the screen. "That's where we're going to live."

"I know," Billy said, bored. "It's called Newmanhome, but its real name is Enki. It's just like the Earth."

"It isn't *just* like the Earth. The days are a little bit shorter, and the year is a *lot* shorter."

"Dummy," Billy said scornfully. "How can a year be shorter than a year?"

"It is, though. There are twice as many years there." He tried to explain, and when he had, more or less, succeeded, they were first appalled, then delighted.

"Twice as many birthdays!" Billy caroled.

"Twice as many *Christmases*!" his brother shouted. "Show us some more planets!"

But really they weren't much interested in baked little Nebo, so close to its sun, or the far-out Marduk and Ninih. And when Viktor showed them the glowing coal of Nergal, squat and cherry red, and told them it was a brown dwarf, they rebelled. "It isn't brown," Billy pointed out. "It's red."

"It's *called* a brown dwarf. That's its *name*, because it's almost a star, but not quite. You see," he lectured, having listened to his father's explanations a few nights earlier, "a *star* has nuclear energy, like a bomb."

"What's a bomb?" Billy asked.

"Like our ship's drive, I mean. A *planet* is just like rock and things. But in between a star and a planet there are these other things. They don't have nuclear energy. They're only hot because they're so big that they're all squeezed together."

"It's dumb to call them brown when they're red," Freddy said, siding with his brother. "Viktor, have you got a crush on our mother?"

Viktor stopped short, suddenly flushed and angry. "Have I *what*?" he demanded.

"Have you got a crush on her?" Freddy insisted. "Mrs. Mei says boys get crushes on older women and you follow Mom around all the time."

"Now you're being really stupid, if you want to know what's *stupid*," Viktor said furiously, gritting his teeth. "Don't ever say anything like that again."

"We won't if you'll play treadmill tag with us," Billy promised, grinning in triumph. "And you have to be It!"

Dinner the next night was a sort of ceremonial affair, a good-bye party for the ones who were going back into the deep freeze. Captain Bu gave a short speech and the chef, Sam Broad— he was really a food chemist, but he was the best cook on the ship, too—had made four big cakes with icing that said *Till We Meet Again*. Pal Sorricaine was especially attentive to his wife and son that night. He kept one hand in hers all through the meal, so that they both had to eat one-handed, and he told Viktor all sorts of stories about astrophysics. When he got to the point of how the Big Bang had created only hydrogen and helium, so that all the rest of the elements had to be cooked in the cores of stars that then exploded and scattered them around to form new stars and planets the Stockbridge boys crept near to listen. And when he pointed out the logical deduction from that—"So you see, most of your body—all the oxygen and carbon and nitrogen and calcium and everything— all of it was once inside a star"—they said respectively, "Oh, wow!" and "Yuk! But that isn't in the Bible, is it?"

Viktor grinned at them. "The Bible's one thing," he told them, in full lecturing swing. "Science is another. Even scientists think about Heaven and Hell, though. Did you ever hear of a man named Arthur Eddington? Well, he was the first one to figure out what the temperature inside the core of a star had to be in order to cook all those heavier elements out of hydrogen. Only when he published his figures some other scientists told him he was wrong, because it wasn't hot enough to do the job. So Eddington told them to go look for a hotter place."

He looked at the uncomprehending faces expectantly. "It was a kind of way of telling them to go to Hell," he explained.

"Oh," Billy said, deciding to laugh.

"Dr. Sorricaine?" Freddy said. "Hell's hot like Wanda says, isn't it? So if we get frozen that can't be Hell, can it?"

By the time Pal Sorricaine, startled, had reassured the boy, their parents came to take them away, and Viktor and his parents went to their own cabin. As his father tucked him in Viktor asked, "Dad? Are you really going to do it?"

His father nodded.

"For just a little while?" Viktor persisted.

His father paused before answering. "I can't say that for sure," he said at last, reluctantly. "It depends. Viktor, this is kind of important to me. Any scientist wants to be the one that makes a big contribution. This is my chance. That flare star—well, there's nothing like it in the literature. Oh, they'll see it on Earth—but from long, long away, and we're right here. I want to be the one—well, one of the ones; Fanny Mtiga's involved, too—that they name it after. The 'Sorricaine-Mtiga objects.' How does that sound?"

"It sounds okay," Viktor told him. He wasn't content or happy about it, but he heard the tone in his father's voice. "Are you going to tell me a story tonight?"

"Sure am. I know," his father said. "Do you want me to tell you about some of the famous people before me? What they did? What they're remembered for?"

And when Viktor nodded, Pal Sorricaine began to talk about the men and women whose shoulders everyone stood on. About Henrietta Leavitt, the nineteenth-century Boston spinster who spent seventeen years studying Cepheid variables and found the first good way of measuring the size of the universe; of Harlow Shapley, who used her work to make the first nearly recognizable model of our own Galaxy; of Edwin Hubble, champion prizefighter turned astronomer, who found a way to employ supergiant stars in the way that Henrietta Leavitt had used Cepheids, thus extending the scale; of Vesto Slipher, who first linked red shifts with velocity and then with distance; of a dozen other forgotten names.

Then his father got to names Viktor had heard of. Albert Einstein? Oh, of course! Everybody knew about Albert Einstein. He was the—wait a minute—wasn't it relativity he discovered? And something about e equals m c squared? Right, Pal Sorricaine told him, hiding a smile, and that was the key to understanding why stars are hot—and to making atomic bombs and power plants, yes, and ultimately to designing the kind of matter-antimatter drive that was shoving New Mayflower on its way. And why the speed of light is always thirty million centimeters a second, no matter how fast the star—or spaceship—that emitted the light was going. New Mayflower might have been going a million centimeters a second, but that didn't mean that the light, or the radio waves, that went ahead of it to carry its picture and messages were traveling at 31 million cps; no, it was always the same. c never changed, and there was nothing anyone could do that would ever change that.

About then Viktor's mother came in with a glass of milk and a pill. "Why do I have to take a pill?" he asked.

"Just take it," she said quietly, affectionately. It occurred to Viktor that it might have something to do with getting ready to be frozen again, so he did as told and kissed her back when she bent to his face.

Then his father went on to the English Quaker, Arthur Eddington, the man who had figured out the connection between physics—stuff that people studied in laboratories on Earth—and the stars, the things that interested astronomers. You might even say, Pal Sorricaine told his son, that Eddington invented the science of astrophysics. Then there were Ernst Mach and Bishop Berkeley, and the geometers Gauss and Bolyai and Riemann and Lobachevski, and Georges Lemaître, the Belgian priest; and Baade, Hoyle, Gamow, Bethe, Dicke, Wilson, Penzias, Hawking . . .

Long before he finished his recital Viktor was asleep.

He slept very soundly. He almost woke, half woke, to find he was being carried somewhere; and almost realized where he was being carried. But the pill had done its work, and he never opened his eyes . . . for sixteen more years.

When Viktor Sorricaine woke up again he was still twelve (or, you might say, very nearly a hundred and fifty), and the first feeling that flooded through him as he gazed up at the face of his father was joy, purest joy, for he had beaten the odds one more time.

The second feeling was not as good. The Pal Sorricaine who beamed down on him was graying and much thinner than the one who had stood by as he went to sleep. "You didn't get frozen at all," Viktor said to his father, accusingly, and his father looked surprised.

"Well, no, Viktor," he said. "I couldn't. We had to watch that star, and—well, anyway, we're all together again, aren't we? And we're there! We're landing! The first parties have already dropped down to the surface, and we'll be going as soon as our chutes are ready!"

"I see," Viktor said, not actually seeing. And then he remembered something. "I have to give Wanda's books back."

His father looked startled, then saddened. Before he even spoke Viktor understood that Wanda wasn't going to want them back, because she wasn't alive anymore. A chill ran through him, but he didn't really have time to think about it. The ship was incredibly noisy now. Not just the chattering of two or three hundred people, the ones already revived, the ones working to revive more, and the ones checking them over and getting them ready for the drop, but loud sounds of crashing and crunching and battering of metal to metal. The interior of the ship was being gutted, as it had been designed to be; the interior cubicles were being wrenched loose from their neighbors, since each one would be a capsule in which eight or ten human beings, or several tons of parts, machines, supplies, or other cargo would drop to the surface of the new planet. Viktor caught a glimpse of a surveillance camera, keeping an eye on crews outside the ship. He could see that the immense stretches of the light sail were deployed in a different way now. It was not one single vast expanse of film anymore, it was a dozen smaller segments, long narrow strips like the sails of a windmill, stiffened by the dynamics of rotation around the main body of the ship. That, he knew, was for greater efficiency in the orbit-insertion maneuver; but that phase was over. Now the sails were being furled and stowed, to shape into the four hundred parachutes that would slow the fall of the para-drop capsules that would carry everything useful on New Mayflower to the ground.

When he caught a glimpse of Marie-Claude Stockbridge he saw that she was weeping. Even weeping she looked desirable, but he could not bear the thought of her being in sorrow. "What is it?" Viktor asked his mother.

"Oh, it's Werner," his mother told him sadly. "Poor Marie-Claude! Werner didn't come out of the freezer. He's dead."

CHAPTER 3

Pal Sorricaine was not the only observer who had been thinking hard about that anomalously flaring K-5 star. So had Wan-To, with a good deal more urgency.

The mere fact that one of his misbehaving relatives had blown up a star didn't bother Wan-To very much. There were plenty of stars to spare. The universe was littered with the things. If the idiots exploded a million of them it would make very little difference to Wan-To—there would still be hundreds of billions left in just this one little galaxy—provided, of course, that the star he lived in wasn't one of them. (Still it would be a pity to wreck them all and have to move on to another galaxy, so soon after having had to get out of the last.)

It was the motives behind it that made this unnatural flaring of stars so distasteful to Wan-To. It was an unsettling development, and one for which, justice would have forced him to admit, he had mostly himself to blame.

He excused himself, though. He couldn't help the fact that he had been lonely.

The game Wan-To's "family" was playing with him had its counterpart on Earth. Artillery officers called it "probing fire," meaning that you pulled the lanyard and wondered if you'd hit anything. The fact that they hadn't, this time, didn't mean anything very reassuring. If they kept it up, in the long run they were sure to score a bull's-eye . . . and when Wan-To thought about anything, it was always the long run he thought about.

Wan-To *liked* his star. It was big, but not too big, and it was comfortable. Its diameter was just under a million miles, its surface temperature was between six and seven thousand Kelvin—it varied a little, because Wan-To's star was just a touch variable. Well, that was what you got when you chose a medium-sized star. But you also got a lot of energy to play with, and, anyway, he had made sure that it was prudently below the "Chandrasekhar limit" beyond which the damned thing might go supernova. Its actual mass was about 2.4 times 10^{27} tons. Getting a little bit smaller all the time, of course. It was, like any star of its class, turning more than four million tons of hydrogen mass into energy every second, but that wasn't worrisome. Wan-To knew well that it had some twenty-four sextillion of those 4,000,000-ton masses to spend. So it had a good long life expectancy to begin with. It should still have at least a few billion years to go before it began to swell unpleasantly toward the red-giant stage.

Of course, it had used up quite a lot of that life expectancy already. It had not been new when Wan-To moved into it. Wan-To knew that. Like any suburban householder aware of doors that were beginning to stick as his house settled and damp spots where the roof was almost beginning to leak, Wan-To understood that some day or other he would want to move into something newer and less likely to give trouble . . . but not for a while yet.

For now he was perfectly happy in his snug little house. He wanted to stay there—if he could.

Thinking along these lines, Wan-To restlessly extended himself into the convection zone of his star. It was like a worried human getting up and pacing about his room. It also cheered him up, because that was one of his best places for play. There was pure pleasure in twisting the convective cells so that rising and falling ones hit each other head-on. Besides being fun in itself, like playing with Silly Putty or stroking a textured worry stick, he knew that it made pretty patterns on the surface of his star. He could stop heat transport in an area a thousand miles across that way, and so that part of the star's surface would be what human astronomers called a "sunspot." In that place a little patch of the star would cool a little. Not much. Only by a couple of thousand Kelvin, say, but enough so that to humans those areas looked dark by comparison. They weren't really dark, of course. They were infinitely brighter than any human illumination, but everything around them was very much brighter even than that.

Abruptly Wan-To halted his play as a fresh fright struck him.

The sunspots! If he played about in the convection zone, the sunspots he made would be *visible*! The patterns would not be the same as natural ones, and anyone looking at his star could see that someone was doing that to its surface!

Hurriedly, worriedly, Wan-To released his magnetic grasp on the pockets of hot gas. Delicately, fearfully, he extricated himself from the convection zone entirely. He could only hope that none of his competitors had happened to have a close-in optical surveillance of his star just then, and enough intelligence to figure out what he had revealed.

Then, when (a few dozen years later) enough time had passed for even a fairly distant colleague to have seen it and reacted to it if he were going to—and nothing dire had happened—Wan-To began to relax.

It was true that he couldn't play in the convection zone anymore. That was a pity. It had been fun. But, on the other hand, a very satisfying thought had occurred to him:

Perhaps some of his competitors still did.

Wan-To then set certain observational procedures into operation, with particular emphasis on the optical frequency human beings called the color blue. While he was waiting for results, he paused to think seriously for a bit.

It had been a long time since Wan-To had seen his "parent"— the one who, like Wan-To, had created some copies of himself for company and, like Wan-To, then regretted it very much. Wan-To couldn't even see the galaxy where he had been born anymore. It was on the far side of the core of the galaxy humans lived in, the one they called the Milky Way, and observation through the masses of gas clouds and dust and stars and other highly obscurant things was almost as difficult for Wan-To as it was for human beings. Earthly astronomers knew it was there, though. They had observed it, though sparsely, by radio, and deduced it, though uncertainly, by its effects on the motions of the bodies near it; they called it "Maffei 2." Wan-To didn't much want to see it. He had a pretty good idea of what it would look like if he did, for when he left it it was getting too hot to live in (in the vernacular, not the cosmological, sense), because the squabbling among his various relations had erupted into veritable cascades of stars wrenched open, spilling their guts into space.

He saw with regret that the same thing was beginning to happen here.

The fact that he didn't want to see Maffei 2 didn't mean he was incurious about the rest of the universe. Indeed, he was intensely curious; in fact, he had plans for a lot of it. He wanted to know what was happening, and he wanted to make sure that things happened his way.

For the two tasks of satisfying his curiosity and making things happen, Wan-To had four major tools at his disposal. In increasing order of importance, they were matter, photons, tachyons, and packets of twinned particles that performed according to what human beings had called "the Einstein-Rosen-Podolsky Separability Phenomenon."

The twinned Einstein-Rosen-Podolsky packets—call them "ERPS" for short—were the best. For one thing, they were the fastest. As humans had discovered, under certain conditions pairs of particles, however far apart in space, are somehow so sensitive to each other that an action performed on one of the particles, anywhere, will instantaneously be reflected in its twin, anywhere else. *Instantaneously.* That generally universal speed limit, the velocity of light, just doesn't come into it when you're talking about ERP pairs. It doesn't apply. Knowing these facts, it was easy enough for Wan-To and his colleagues to devise complex particle pairs and gave them what amounted to instant sending and receiving stations. One of Wan-To's sets was kept at home with him, the other was deployed anywhere in the universe he chose to plant it.

Wan-To had planted plenty of them. He liked them very much,

not least because there was no "directionality" about them. There was no way of telling, from one of his distant ERP packets, where its twin was—and therefore, where *he* was. Since Wan-To definitely didn't want just anyone to know where he was, he used the twinned ERP packets for talking to his worrying colleagues. They were his equivalent of an unlisted telephone number.

His other tools were also good, in different ways.

Tachyons, for instance, were almost as fast, and in some ways better. You could carry a lot more information a lot easier on tachyons—particles whose existence had been surmised, but not detected, on Earth. More than information could be carried. You could, for instance, hit someone pretty hard with a tachyon blast, if you wanted to do him harm. (From time to time Wan-To did want to do someone harm, if only to keep that one from doing the same to him.) A tachyon was a quite legitimate particle, even within the ancient confines of relativity theory. It obeyed the law of the limitation of the speed of light. The only thing that distinguished tachyons from less exotic particles was that for tachyons the velocity of light was the lower speed limit, not the upper. They could never go as *slowly* as *c*. Speed wasn't much of a problem when you used tachyons. Indeed, since the lowest-energy tachyons were the fastest ones, for any *normal* purpose—say, at distances of up to a few hundred light-years—they were almost as speedy as the ERP pairs.

The objection to using tachyons wasn't technical, it was tactical. Tachyons were noisy. They moved *through* space (instead of simply ignoring space, as the twinned pairs did), and so a person at the receiving end could rather easily figure out the direction they had come from.

Wan-To definitely did not want that done.

Then, of course, for lesser tasks he had the whole spectrum of photons at his disposal, too—radio, heat, visible light, gamma rays, X rays, even gravitons. All of these were useful, for different things, but they were all so terribly *slow*. None of them could move faster than that old 186,000 miles a second.

Still, they could be very handy when used in the right way, especially the range of particles that mediated the force of gravitation. With them, it wasn't hard for Wan-To (or his brethren) to zap a star. Even human beings could have done it, if they had had access to the necessary gravitons, graviphotons, and graviscalars, and in all those supplies Wan-To was immensely rich. If you flooded a target star with the right particles you could pull it right out of shape. All that held any star together was gravitational force. When stretched on the particle rack, the core bubbled and fountained like a geyser, and no structure inside it could survive.

Wan-To could imagine that happening to his own comfortable home very easily, and the thought gave him the creeps.

Finally, Wan-To could use that slow, gross, clumsy stuff—matter.

It was easy enough for Wan-To to make things out of ordinary matter, but he mistrusted the stuff. It was completely foreign to his everyday life. He used it only when there was no alternative. And yet, when he thought over his options, it began to look as though this were one of the times when no good alternative could be found.

Although his mind—you wouldn't really want to say his "brain," because there wasn't much of Wan-To *but* brain—although his mind, that is to say, was very widely dispersed about the fabric of the star he lived in, the messenger neutrinos flashed their signals about as fast as any animal dendrites in a human skull. It didn't take him long to decide that, this time, the employment of a certain amount of matter was his best strategy.

What helped him to that decision quickly was a sudden urgent signal—his "senses" perceived it as something between the ringing of a loud alarm bell and the sting of a wasp—from one of his ERP pairs.

The signal told him that another nearby star had just gone flaring to its death.

That meant that his siblings were still shooting at him with their probing fire. Sooner or later those random shots would find him . . . and so it was time for Wan-To to act. It was war!

It is civilians who get the worst part of wars. Wan-To can't be blamed for what happened to the innocent bystanders in this one, though, since he had no idea there were any.

CHAPTER 4

The innocent bystander named Pal Sorricaine was now (biologically) in his sixties. That was a lot, compared to his wife's biological thirty-eight, but he still had youth enough to do his duty by the colony. Accordingly, when Viktor was (again biologically, anyway) fourteen, his mother provided him with a sibling.

Viktor had some trouble welcoming the thing. It was female. It was also tiny and noisy at all hours of the day and night; and, in Viktor's view, it was very ugly.

For reasons Viktor could not understand, the wretched look of the thing didn't seem to worry his mother. It didn't put his father off it, either. They held it and fondled it and fed it, just as though it were beautiful. They didn't even appear to mind the bad smells it made when it fouled itself, as it did often.

Its name was Edwina. "Don't call her an 'it', either," Viktor's mother commanded. "Call her by her name."

"I don't like her name. Why couldn't you call her Marie or something?"

"Because we picked Edwina. Why are you so crazy about the name Marie?"

"I'm not *crazy* about it. I just *like* it."

Amelia Sorricaine-Memel gave her son a thoughtful look but decided not to press the matter. "Marie's a pretty name," she conceded, "but it isn't hers."

"Ed-*wee*-na," Viktor sneered.

His mother grinned at him. She rumpled his hair fondly and offered a compromise. "You can call her Weeny if you want to, because she is kind of weeny. Now let me show you how to change her diaper."

Viktor gazed at his mother with teenage horror and despair. "Oh, *God*," he moaned. "As if I didn't have enough to do already!"

In fact he had plenty to do. Everybody did. Building a new colony wasn't just a challenge. It was *work*, and every colonist had to face the facts of frontier life.

The first fact of Viktor's new life had been the dwelling he and his parents were given to live in. It was a long, long way from the beach house in Malibu. It was bigger than the cubicle on *Mayflower*, but that was all you could say for it. It wasn't even a cubicle. It was a tent. More accurately it was three tents run together, each made out of several plies of the light-sail/parachute material, and all they had to furnish it with was a couple of beds—pallets, really; they had no springs—and some metal cupboards brought down from *Mayflower*. (Even those they would have to give up, they were warned, as soon as wood equivalents could be carpentered from the native vegetation. Until the new mines and smelters were fully operational, metal was precious.)

The second fact was time, also in short supply. In fact, there wasn't any of it. Every one of the skimpy daylight hours was filled— if not with work (farmhand, construction helper, general laborer; the kids who landed from *Mayflower* were at once put to work at whatever they could do), then with school. School wasn't any fun, either. Viktor was shoved into a class with thirty-two other kids of about his age, but they weren't a congenial lot. Half of them were from the first ship, seasoned and superior in the ways of the new planet, and very aware of their superiority, and the other half were greenhorns like himself. The two kinds didn't get along.

That situation the teacher would not tolerate. He was a tall, one-armed man named Martin Feldhouse, chronically short of breath. Short of patience, too. "There won't be any fighting in this school," he decreed, coughing. "You have to live together for the rest of your lives, so start out doing it. Line up in size places for your buddies."

The students stood up and reluctantly milled into order. Viktor wasn't sure how to take Martin Feldhouse; he had never seen a human being who was missing an arm before. The thing about Feldhouse was that he had gotten himself crushed under a truck of gravel out at the pit. Back on Earth, or even on the ship, he would have been patched up in no time. Not here. In this primitive place, at that early time, he had been too far from the medical facilities for immediate attention, and so when he got to the clinic the arm was too far gone to be saved, though the injuries to his chest and internal organs had been repaired. More or less repaired. Except for the persistent cough, anyway. When all his disabilities were added up the total pointed to the only job he was still fit for, so now he was a schoolteacher.

"Now count off," Feldhouse decreed. "When I point to you, say where you come from—Ship, or Home. You first!" And he pointed to the tallest boy, who promptly announced that he was Home, and so was the girl next behind him, but the one after that was from *Mayflower* and so she was paired with the first boy.

When they got down to Viktor his "buddy" was a girl named Theresa McGann. They looked at each other with speculative hostility, but took their seats together as instructed, while Feldhouse looked on the four unpaired planet-born children. "You four belong to me," he declared. "The rest of you are going to work together. You from the Ship, you teach your buddies as much as you can remember from what you got out of the teaching machines. You from Home, you teach geography and what the farms are like and everything else about what it's like here—what is it, what's your name?"

"I'm Viktor Sorricaine," Viktor announced, putting his hand down. "Why do you call this place 'Home'?"

"Because that's what it is," the teacher explained. "That's the first thing you all have to learn. This planet's name is Enki, according to the astronomers, but its right name is Newmanhome. We call it Home for short. From now on you only have one home, and this is it."

It had taken eight months for the last of the corpsicles in *New Mayflower* to be thawed, oriented, and paradropped to New-manhome's surface. Most of that time was spent tearing the crew and cargo sections of the ship apart to make them into the modules that would carry everybody and everything down, and assembling the light-sail/parachutes and streamers that would keep the landing from being a catastrophe. The colonists already there welcomed the new arrivals, to be sure. They welcomed the cargoes each brought down even more. For that matter, the empty modules themselves were fallen upon with joy; each one, when emptied, contributed nearly half a ton of precious steel.

In all this work everybody had to lend a hand, kids included. Kids also had to go to Mr. Feldhouse's school (if they were twelve to fourteen biological Earth years; there were other schools for younger and older ones). For three hours a day they used the teaching machines and drilled each other in grammar and trigonometry and Earth history and music and drawing, under Feldhouse's short-tempered and sketchy supervision. The good part of the school was that Viktor had other children of his own age for company, even if one of them was the bratty Reesa McGann the teacher had forced on him the first day. The bad part was that almost all of the kids were strangers. And a lot of them—the children from the first ship, that was—were really stuck up.

Because he and Reesa were "buddies" they shared a seat in the crowded school hut, and she was the one who had the privilege of pointing out to him how little he knew about how to live on New-manhome. Every time he complained about shared books or heavy labor, she was sure to tell him how very much worse it had been six years before, when *they* landed. Their *Ark* hadn't been designed for disassembly, like the *Mayflower*. All the first colonists could do was strip it of its cargo and most of its moveables. Then, reluctantly, they abandoned it. It was still up there in orbit, drive almost dead except for the trickle of power that fed its freezer units, otherwise just a hulk. With all its precious steel.

"If you'd been a little smarter," Viktor told the girl in a superior tone as he was trying to make a fire in the fireplace outside their tent, "you'd at least have fixed the drive so it could beam power down, like our ship."

"If we were smarter," she answered, "we'd have come in the second ship like you, so somebody else would have done all the hard work for us before we got here." And then she added, "Pull out all that wood and start over. You've got the heavy chunks on the bottom and all the kindling on top. Don't you know *anything*?" And then she pushed him out of the way and did it herself. The girl was so *physical*.

If Viktor had really looked at Theresa McGann he would have discovered that she wasn't such a bad girl after all. True, she kept reminding him of his immense areas of ignorance (but he was grimly repairing them as fast as he could). True, she had scabby knees. True, she was several centimeters taller than he, but that was only because fourteen-year-old girls are generally taller than fourteen-year-old boys. He didn't look at her that way, though. It wasn't that he wasn't interested in the opposite sex, even such a touchy-squeezy physical specimen of it as Reesa McGann. He was often *obsessed* with the opposite sex, like any healthy, horny male teenager, but the focus of his interest hadn't changed. It remained the beautiful (and now widowed) Marie-Claude Stockbridge.

Marie-Claude remained widowed, too. Suffering, Viktor observed that she often "saw" other men, but he took some comfort in noting that she seemed to have no intention of marrying one of them.

Apart from his schoolwork Viktor's contribution to the community was officially defined as "scutwork"—meaning the kinds of low-skilled jobs other people didn't have time for. When he possibly could, he tried to get into a work party with Marie-Claude, but most of the time he possibly couldn't. There was too much work, of too many kinds. Up on the rapidly emptying *Mayflower* the cleanup crews were emptying the cargo holds and launching the contents to the surface. The most precious and fragile of the new supplies came down in one or another of the three-winged, rocket-driven landing craft *Mayflower* had carried in its hold, but there wasn't enough fuel made yet to use them for more than one trip each. Sturdier shipments, including passengers, came down in the big pods.

There were all kinds of things in those pods—tractors, stills, hand tools, lathes, stores, drilling equipment, rifles, flashlights, cooking utensils, plates, surgical instruments, coils of copper wire, coils of fencing, coils of light-conducting tube, coils of flexible pipe; then there were cows, sheep, pigs, chickens, dogs, cats, carp, tilapia, trout, bees, dung beetles, earthworms, kelp, algae, catfish—each fresh out of the freezer, wrapped in protective foam or immobilized in a plastic bag. The living things didn't all come down at first; many of them (and many, many tubes of ova and sperm and seeds and spores) stayed frozen on the ship against a future need.

The pods kept coming. Almost every time *Mayflower* came around in orbit in the right position—only about one orbit in twenty was right, because of the planet's rotation—the orbital crews launched clusters of twelve or fourteen separate loads, linked until the retrofire rockets slowed them, then shaking apart, popping their light-sail/parachutes, coming down in fleets of bright gold film canopies, with the gray metal pods hanging underneath. Those were smart parachutes. Each one had sensors that kept it posted on where it was drifting and shroud controls that could maneuver it toward its planned drop point—fairly well, anyway—at least, well enough, provided the linked pods had been ejected at just the right moment and the retrofire burn had been precise.

But even with everything going right, the chutes could land anywhere within a ten-kilometer radius of the drop point, inshore of the colony on the shore of what they were calling Great Ocean.

It would have been nice if the drop point could have been right on the little town itself. But that would have meant that half the pods would surely have fallen into Great Ocean, and that meant a whole different order of difficulty in getting them back. It was easier to send people like Viktor out to drag them back on tractor-drawn sledges. So that was what he did—half a dozen times a week.

The most urgent cargoes to reclaim were the living ones. They had to be put in pens, tanks, barns, or breeding ponds at once (sometimes when their new homes were still being built for them by other sweating, hurrying laborers). Then the next priority was the machines that were needed ASAP, so the colony could live and grow—the plows, the tractors, the helicopters, the outboard motors for the colony's growing little fleet, and the spare parts to keep them all going. Fortunately fuel was not a problem after the first few weeks. The fuel wasn't liquid gases of the kind the rockets used— that would have to wait a while yet—nor was it diesel fuel or gasoline. There was oil on Newmanhome, everyone knew that, but there hadn't been time to drill much of it out. So, instead, the first-ship people had filled huge ponds with Newmanhome flora of all kinds, chopped up and drenched, making a kind of sour beer mash that they distilled into vats of alcohol fuel. That drove the tractors that brought in the goods, and Viktor helped. Almost every waking hour of the day when he wasn't in school, and every day of every week.

It was, at least, certainly good exercise.

As though Viktor didn't have anything else to do, he was assigned care of the baby when his parents were at work. He even had to bring the brat to school with him sometimes. Luckily, the thing slept a lot, in a basket behind his desk, but when it woke and began to cry he had to take it outside to shut it up. Sometimes it only needed to be fed, but when it—no, *she*—when *she* had wet herself, or worse, he had to face the disgusting job of changing the damned thing.

The only saving graces were that he wasn't the only kid with a baby sister or brother, and he didn't always have to do it alone. Theresa McGann took her buddying seriously. "You don't know diddly-shit about babies," she told him, watching critically as he tried to stretch one leghole of the rubber pants to fit around Edwina's waist.

"I suppose you do," he snarled.

"Ought to. I've had the practice." And she proved it by shoving him out of the way and taking over.

Reesa not only did not seem to mind changing little Edwina's filthy messes, it appeared she could even put up with the Stockbridge boys. In her free time she showed them things to do in the little town. When they were standing by, thumbs in their mouths, watching the older kids square dancing in an exercise period, she was the one who invited them in and taught them some steps. (She even taught Viktor a few.) She even once, when everyone was miraculously free at the same time, took Viktor and the boys to picnic in the hills north of the settlement.

Viktor had reservations about all that. Her taking care of Billy and Freddy deprived him of one more chance to keep a high profile in the eyes of Marie-Claude, but then he didn't really have the time to do much of that, anyway. And the picnic was fun. Reesa's very best quality, in Viktor's opinion, was that like himself she was planning to be a space pilot. Or if there weren't any openings along that line, as there was every reason to think there would not, at least an air pilot. There was plenty of flying to be done in the air of Newmanhome—whole continents to explore, and shoals of islands; the orbiting *Mayflower* kept sending down photographs taken along its orbit, but there was more to see than an orbiting hulk could cover. And then, someday . . .

"Someday," Reesa said, gazing up at the emerging stars, and she didn't have to say someday *what*. They both knew.

The sun had set. The campfire had been stomped out, and the Stockbridge boys sent grumbling off to haul water to pour on the coals. Overhead were the stars and planets of the Newmanhome sky.

"Someday," Viktor agreed confidently, "I'll be up there again. *We* will," he amended, to avoid a fight. Then he craned his neck toward where the boys had disappeared into the scrubby Newmanhome woods and lost a little of his confidence. Viktor had never lived on the edge of the unknown before.

He saw that Reesa was grinning at him and reddened; one of the things that he hated about Reesa was that she always seemed to know what he was thinking. "The kids are okay," she reassured him, with another of those friendly pats. "There's nothing out there to hurt them. They can't even get lost, because they can see the town lights."

He didn't dignify the remark with an answer. He said firmly, "After *Argosy* gets here there'll be spaceships again. Have to be. We're not going to be stuck on one lousy little planet all our lives."

"And we'll be just about the right age," Reesa agreed. "Where do you want to go? First, I mean?"

Then, of course, there was an argument. Neither of them wanted to bother with Ishtar: it was big—Jupiter-sized—but that meant no one was ever going to land on it, because it didn't have any more of a surface to land on than Jupiter did. It didn't even have Jupiter's interesting retinue of moons, because gravitational interaction with giant Nergal seemed to have stolen them all away. Nergal was Viktor's choice. "All those moons!" he said. "Some of them have to be decent, and anyway it's a brown dwarf—nobody's ever got near a brown dwarf before!"

"That's what Tiss Khadek says," Reesa said.

"Well, she's right."

"She's *always* right," Reesa told him, "or anyway says she is. She thinks she owns this place."

Viktor snickered. The Iraqi astronomer from *Ark*, Ibtissam Khadek, was the granddaughter of the man who had run the first robot probe and named the planets after his "ancestral" Babylonian gods, as was his privilege. "The fact that you don't like her doesn't mean she's wrong," he told Reesa. "Where would you go?"

"I want to go to Nebo," Reesa declared.

"Nebo!"

"Captain Rodericks thinks so, too. He says we ought to establish an outpost somewhere, and that's the best place."

Viktor said pityingly, "There are *moons* bigger than Nebo!"

But she was insistent. Nebo was the nearest planet to their new sun, the size of Mars but hotter than Mercury. "It's got an atmosphere, Vik. Why does it have an atmosphere?"

"Who cares?" Viktor asked.

"I care. I want to know *why* . . ." And the argument continued until the Stockbridge boys were back and they were nearly home. It was a fun argument. It made it seem as though they really were going to have the chance to get back into space, though both knew that the day when that would be possible would not come until they were a great deal older.

Funnily, one of the worst spats between Viktor and Reesa McGann came over the question of getting old—or, anyway, over just how old they were.

It started when they were sprawled on the spiky Newmanhome grass in the schoolyard, panting, just after finishing the morning's calisthenics. What they all usually wore when they exercised was the plain white jockey shorts that were standard issue for all colonists as underwear; what was annoying Viktor that particular day was that Reesa had done ten more pushups than he had, and so he looked at what she was wearing and sneered, "Why are you wearing a top?"

She looked at him with understanding contempt. "I'm a girl," she informed him.

She wasn't the only female teenager to wear a shirt, but there weren't many others. "You've got nothing to hide," he pointed out.

She said, adult to child, "That's not why I wear the top. I wear the top to show what I *will* have. Anyway," she added, "I'm older than you are."

It began with that. The argument went on for days. They had both been six when her ship, the *New Ark*, moved out of orbit. When Viktor's *Mayflower* landed, they were both twelve—so Viktor insisted, because they had each spent the same length of time frozen, just about, and the same under of Earth years growing.

But, Reesa said with that superior old-timer sneer that made Viktor's blood boil, he hadn't calculated right. *Mayflower* was a tad faster than *Ark*, being a generation later, so she had spent less time in the freezer and more growing up.

"You've got that backwards!" Viktor howled in triumph. "You spent *more* time frozen!"

She scowled, flushed, and quickly backtracked. "But that's not the important point," she insisted. She had spent six more Earth years than he had on Newmanhome. That made her older, because Newmanhome had twice as many years, just about, as Earth in any given period of time.

Viktor strongly protested her arithmetic.

It was true, of course, that the Earth calendar didn't match up well against the realities of Newmanhome. Newmanhome's day, sunrise to sunrise, was about twenty-two and a half Earth hours; and it swung around its sun so fast that it only had about a hundred and ninety-eight of those days in each year. So a Newmanhome "year" was not much more than half an Earth (or "real") year.

The discrepancy played hell with birthdays. That wasn't much of a practical problem, but it made a major annoyance when you got into arguments like the one with Reesa McGann. Viktor's birthdays were terminally confused, anyway. Everybody's were, for how could you allow for a couple of stretches of freeze time? Of course, you could count back to time of birth. At any time the teaching machines could easily tell you the exact Earth day, year, and minute it was right then in Laguna Beach, California, U.S.A., Earth (or, in Viktor's case, should they reckon from Warsaw, nearly a dozen time zones away?). But Reesa flatly refused to consider Earth standards applicable.

Viktor pondered over the question at school. It wasn't just birthdays. Even worse was the question of holidays. Where in the Newmanhome calendar did you put Christmas, Ramadan, or Rosh Hashanah? But as it was birthdays that established the pecking order between him and Reesa, Viktor took time to do a lot of arithmetic on the teaching machine, and then he presented his teacher with a plan to recalculate everybody's age in Home years.

Mr. Feldhouse squashed it firmly. "You haven't allowed for relativistic effects," he pointed out. "A lot of the transit time for both ships was at forty percent of the speed of light or better; you have to figure that in."

So grimly Viktor put in some more of his precious few hours of spare time with the teaching machines . . . which Mr. Feldhouse approved, grinning, because it was wonderful math practice for the whole class.

Slowly, painfully slowly, the reinforced colony digested its new additions and began to incorporate the cargoes *Mayflower* had brought into their lives. Steel from the ship wouldn't last them forever. Ore bodies existed, taconite mostly, but the surface outbreaks were limited and there wasn't the manpower to dig deep mines.

That was where Marie-Claude Stockbridge's machines came in, and that was when Viktor got closer to his life's ambition—though, of course, Reesa spoiled it for him.

She came to Viktor's tent early one morning and leaned in.

"Get up," she ordered. "If we get there first we can help Stockbridge with her Von Neumanns."

Viktor pulled the sheet indignantly up to his chin and glared at her fuzzily. "Do what?" he asked.

"Help Marie-Claude Stockbridge," she repeated impatiently. "They've given her the okay to send the machines out, and she's going to need help—us, if you get off your dead ass and get there before everybody else does."

That woke him up. "Get out of here so I can get dressed," he ordered, suffused with joy, and pulled on his shorts and shoes in no time at all. He knew about the Von Neumanns, of course. Everybody did. They were going to be very important to the colony, but they'd had to take their turn, like every other very important project, until the utterly urgent ones of survival had been taken care of.

On the way to the machine shed Reesa explained. "Jake Lundy told me about it. He's kind of got eyes for me, you know; he's helping Stockbridge prepare the machines, and I think he liked the idea of having me around for a few days. So right away I thought of you."

"Thanks," Viktor said happily. He didn't much care for Jake Lundy—five years older than Reesa or himself, a tall, muscular man who was already known to have fathered at least one child for the colony, though he showed no signs of wanting to marry. But Viktor could put up with Lundy—could even put up with Reesa—if it also meant being near Marie-Claude.

Then he stopped because what she was babbling on about had just reached him. He glared at her. "What did you say?"

"I said I think Stockbridge is kind of hot for Jake, too, you know? I mean, he's a gorgeous hunk of man." Then she paused to peer at him. "What's the matter with you?"

"Nothing's the matter with me!" he snapped.

She walked around him, looking at him curiously from every side as he stood, mute and belligerent. "Oh, I get it," she said wisely. "You've got a crush on Marie-Claude."

"Shut your mouth," he said, trembling.

She did her best to be patient with him. "But, Vik, that's just normal, you know? You shouldn't get pissed because she's making it with a guy. She's a woman, isn't she?" She stepped back a pace before the look he gave her. "Hey, don't get mad at me! I didn't do anything!"

"Just shut up," he blazed.

She looked at him thoughtfully, then led the way toward the machine sheds. But she couldn't keep quiet indefinitely, and just before they got there she cleared her throat. "Viktor? Don't get sore if I ask you something. When you were all on the ship, did you ever see Marie-Claude and her husband make love?"

"Don't be *disgusting!*"

"Oh, Viktor," she sighed. "*Doing* it isn't disgusting. Watching somebody is, maybe, so the reason I asked—"

"I said *shut up.*"

And for a wonder she did, because his tone was really dangerous. But his internal pain didn't heal.

Marie-Claude Stockbridge had in her charge a dozen prototypes of Von Neumann finder-homer machines, great, simple-minded automata that weren't in any real way alive, but shared with living things the ability to forage in their environment, to ingest the kind of chemicals that they were made up of, and to replicate themselves, as people do when they have babies, by making copies of themselves to grow up and do the same thing all over again, generation after generation. And each had a "homing circuit," like that of the freshwater salmon or the migratory birds, which would bring it back to the place it started from (or its ancestors had) when it was of a certain size, there to be dismantled and forged into whatever metal parts the colony needed.

They were ugly things, but they sure beat the hell out of digging holes in the ground.

The Von Neumann machines came in several varieties. There were digging kinds, that looked like iron bedbugs; there were swimming kinds, to exploit the thermal springs they hoped to find at the bottom of Great Ocean, that looked like chromium-plated versions of the sort of shell people picked up on Earthly beaches. They weren't purely mechanical. The iron-miner, for instance, had a complex "digestive" system like the second stomach of a ruminant, where genetically tailored iron-concentrating bacteria helped extract the metal from the rock after the jaws of the Von Neumann miner had pulverized it.

What Reesa and Viktor and a couple of other drudges did was only to fetch and carry, to hoist the Von Neumanns in slings while Marie-Claude and Jake Lundy pried off their inspection hatches and checked their circuits, and to test the seals and make sure the mechanical parts were freed from their shipping constraints. It was hard, hot work. Viktor was stiffly ill at ease at first, eyes always on Marie-Claude and Jake Lundy to see if there was any visible affection going on between them; but in the pursuit of her specialty Marie-Claude was all business. And best of all, she was there. She was where he was hardly an arm's length away, for hours at a time; and if she thought of him as a child she treated him as a colleague. Even Jake Lundy wasn't so bad. His muscles were a big help when the massive machines needed hoisting or turning, but Viktor was getting pretty strong, too, and he was the one Lundy yelled for when something hard had to be done.

They worked from sunup to school, two or three hours every morning. Reesa was always the first one to tell Viktor it was time to leave, because Viktor had no incentive to leave Marie-Claude's company for the schoolmaster's—except one day. On that day Reesa disappeared into the backhouse for several minutes when work was through, and when she appeared she grabbed his arm, looking oddly triumphant. "Look at this, doofus," she ordered, flushed and excited.

"We're going to be late for class," he complained. He wasn't much annoyed. He was only irritated by the fact that she was *touching* him again—he tolerated with difficulty the fact that she was a touching, hugging kind of person, always wanting physical contact—until he saw what she was displaying for him. Then he recoiled from the scrap of stained white fabric in disgust. "Ugh! Gross!" he cried. "It's your dirty *underwear!*"

Her face was rosy with pride. "Look at what it's dirty with! That's *blood!*" she crowed. "That means I'm a grown-up *woman* now, Viktor Sorricaine, and you're still just a dumb little kid."

He looked around apprehensively, to see if anyone was observing this, but the others were still hard at work. He understood what she was showing him. What he didn't understand was *why*. Of course he knew what menstruation was, because the teaching machines had been quite specific about all the physiological details of sex. But, as far as the female reproductive systems were concerned, the overriding impression Viktor had come away with was that it was *messy*. Viktor wasn't a male chauvinist pig. At least, he didn't think he was. He didn't consider himself superior to females simply because of gender. What he thought about sexual dimorphism was mostly charitable compassion for the nasty predicaments females found themselves in every month, and the even worse ones that confronted them in childbearing.

It had never occurred to him that any female would *boast* about it.

"That means I could have a *baby*!" Reesa chortled.

"Not without some guy to help you," Viktor pointed out defensively.

"Oh," Reesa said, starry-eyed, "there isn't going to be any problem with *that*."

And the colony grew.

Even while Marie-Claude was turning loose the first few of her Von Neumanns, her fingers crossed in the hope that they wouldn't break down, that they would work the way they were supposed to, that they would find their way back as they should—even then the construction workers were finishing the great steel skeleton of the vast rectenna that, very soon, would deliver the first *Mayflower*-generated microwave power to the colony. A model steel plant was half done, ready for the first of Marie-Claude's Von Neumanns to come back with raw metal. And wells were being sunk into the hot water that underlay the hills behind the town they were beginning to call Homeport. When those geothermal wells were beginning to produce electricity there would be plenty to spare, enough to run the immense freezers whose foundations were being dug, to store all the samples still on *Mayflower* and *Ark*.

That wasn't all. Real homes were being built, with a lottery every week to see which half-dozen lucky families would get to move out of their tents into something with walls. The beamed broadcasts from Earth still came in, all the hours of every day, along with the regular reports from *New Argosy*, now more than halfway to Newmanhome; but people watched them now only for entertainment, not with the hopeless yearning of the first years.

It was a time for—well, not for rejoicing, exactly, because there were still endless years of hard work ahead. But at least it was a time when the three thousand and more (every day more) human beings could look back on how much had been accomplished, and look around at the farms and the docks and the sprawling town with satisfaction that the planet was being tamed to their needs.

Of course, they hadn't yet seen any new strange objects in the sky.

Fifth (Navigator) Officer Pal Sorricaine had no ship to be an officer of anymore, and nowhere to navigate anyway.

It meant a considerable comedown for him. He was still a kind of astronomer, of course. But the flare star was only a memory, which meant there was nothing much to do about that still-troubling puzzle, and anyway there wasn't much he could have done about solving it. There weren't any decent-sized telescopes on the surface of Newmanhome. *Mayflower*'s sensors were still operating, but they weren't telling anybody anything they didn't already know, except for some peculiar readings from the innermost planet, Nebo. There was a little group of interested people who got together to talk about it from time to time, Sorricaine and Frances Mtiga and the Iraqi woman, Tiss Khadek. They spent hours trying to find in the datastores some suggestion of why the hot little planet had an atmosphere, and what the gamma radiation that seemed to come from parts of its surface might mean, but there was nothing in previous astronomical history to help. It didn't seem very urgent, even to them. No one thought the readings were important enough to spend scarce man-hours on, not while the rectenna was still unfinished and the new food warehouses were still almost empty.

So Pal Sorricaine did odd jobs.

It was the kind of work the kids did when not in school. Unskilled work. Hard labor, sometimes, and in inconvenient places. He was away from the community two or three days at a time,

with a team of other men similarly among the technologically unemployed. They spent their time collecting the low-priority cargo
pods that had fallen at the inconveniently far perimeter of the drop
zone, or even outside it. They sledged them into the city; not only
hard work, but not even very interesting.

Pal Sorricaine didn't seem to mind. He took on the job of car-
tography when he was out in the wildwoods, searching for lost
pods, and his maps became the best the community had. When he
was home he was cheerful. He took his turn at minding Baby
Weeny. He was loving to his wife and affectionate to Viktor. It was
puzzling to Viktor that his mother seemed to worry about her husband. But when he asked her about it she simply laughed and said,
"It's a kind of a problem for your dad, Viktor. He was one of the
most important men on the ship. Now he's sort of—well—general
labor, you know? When things get more settled and he can do real
astronomy again . . ."

She let it trail off there. Viktor didn't bother to ask her when
she thought things would be that settled. Of course, she didn't know
any more than he did. Maybe the only right answer would have
been "never." But that night, when his father returned with the
tractor team, four great pods of steel bumping and scraping behind
them, he seemed content enough. Pal was in a good mood, anxious
to hear about what had been going on in the town while he was
away, and bursting with a couple of pieces of gossip he had brought
back from long night talks with the other men. "Do you know
what Marie-Claude's been doing?" he asked his wife, chuckling.
"She's pregnant, that's what!"

Viktor dropped the spoon he was trying to feed his baby sister
with. "But—her husband's *dead*!" he cried, appalled at the news.

"Did I say anything about a husband?" Pal Sorricaine asked
good-naturedly. "I just said she's going to have a baby. I didn't say
she was getting married. I guess she likes the idea of being a merry
widow."

"*Pal,*" Viktor's mother said warningly, looking at her son.
"Don't make it sound awful, Pal. Marie-Claude's a good person,
and besides we need more babies."

Pal grinned at her. "So it's all okay with you? You wouldn't
mind if I, uh, volunteered to help out along those lines next time?"

"Pal," she said again, but the tone was different; she was almost laughing. "What's the matter, aren't I keeping you happy?"

His father grinned and began to mix a cocktail. Halfway through, he paused and looked thoughtfully at his son. Then he glanced at his wife and added more of the gin—it was real gin, almost the last they had—to the mix. "You're old enough to try one now, Vik," he said kindly.

In pain and misery, Viktor took the plastic tumbler and gulped a mouthful. The juniper stung the inside of his nasal passages; the alcohol scorched the inside of his mouth. He swallowed and coughed at the same time.

"Viktor!" his mother cried in alarm. *"Pal!"*

But Pal was already beside his son, arm around his shoulder. "It's better if you just sip it a little at a time," he said, laughing.

Viktor was having none of that. He wrenched free and, as soon as he could postpone a cough long enough to swallow, downed the rest of the drink. Fortunately, there wasn't much of it; his father had measured out only a junior-sized amount for his son's first of-ficial cocktail.

Viktor wasn't short of willpower. He used it all. He managed to strangle the coughing fit, though his voice was hoarse while he was reassuring his mother that, really, he was absolutely all right. His throat burned. His eyes were watering. His nose still stung. But there was a warmth, too, that started in his chest and spread through his whole body.

It almost seemed to numb his stark interior pain. It was, really, not a bad sensation at all. Was that why people like his parents drank this stuff?

Now that his mother had realized her son wasn't dying she was sipping her own drink, but not in any relaxed or jovial manner. Her gaze stayed on Viktor. Pal Sorricaine tried to jolly her out of it, without much success. Viktor ignored them both. He sat hunched over the empty tumbler, staring into it as he turned it in his hands, as he had seen an actor in a transmitted Earth film do when he, like Viktor, discovered the woman he loved had been bedding another man.

Viktor was crushed.

For Marie-Claude to make love with her husband had been bad

enough. This was incomparably worse. There was a sudden knot of physical pain in Viktor's stomach, like a stab wound. Even the warm, ginny glow didn't stop the pain.

His mother turned from studying her son to face her husband. "Pal," she said seriously, "we've got to talk to Viktor."

Viktor felt the tips of his ears burning with resentment. He refused to look up. He heard his father sigh. "All right," Pal Sorricaine conceded. "I guess it's about time. Viktor? Vik, listen to me. Are you—" He fumbled for the right words. "Uh, all right?"

Viktor raised his head to give his father the cold stare of a stranger. "Sure I am. Why wouldn't I be?"

"I mean about, you know, Mrs. Stockbridge," his father persisted. He looked more embarrassed than Viktor had ever seen him, but determinedly sympathetic. "Son, I didn't mean to say anything that would get you upset. Do you understand that? Listen, it's only natural for a b—for a young man to be attracted to an older woman, especially when the woman is as sexy and—" He caught his wife's look just in time. "When she's as nice a person, I mean, as Marie-Claude. There's nothing wrong about that. I remember, when I was sixteen, there was a dancer in the ballet school at the Warsaw Opera, about twenty, so thin and graceful—"

He stopped, on the verge of another unexpected precipice. He carefully avoided looking at his wife. She regarded him thoughtfully but didn't speak.

"You don't know what you're talking about," his son said severely.

Viktor had never spoken to his father that way before. He stood up, testing for dizziness, and headed with precise, careful steps for the door. He left Pal Sorricaine biting his lip behind him. His son's glare had looked pretty nearly like hatred, and Pal Sorricaine had never expected that sort of emotion from the son he had always loved and cherished, and thought loved him back.

Outside Viktor paused, leaning against the door.

Because they had been one of the lucky families in the lottery they had two rooms now, two cubicles together, in the long row that lined the muddy street, joined like ancient American tourist cabins. Behind him, through the thin film windows—last and long-est use for the remaining scraps of light-sail/parachutes—he could hear his parents muttering to each other.

But, queerly, there were people muttering to each other in the street, too. They were standing in clumps, faces uplifted to the sum-mery Newmanhome sky. Viktor instinctively glanced up himself. In the starlight he could make out that there were patches of warm-weather convection clouds obscuring much of the moonless heav-ens, but there were hundreds of stars shining through the gaps, too.

Well, there always were clouds and stars, weren't there? Why were these people staring so? True, one star, all by itself, seemed quite bright, almost as bright (Viktor dimly remembered) as the planet Venus from Earth, brighter than any Newmanhome star had ever seemed . . .

With a shock he saw that the star was getting brighter.

How strange! And it kept on getting brighter still, almost Moon bright, bright enough to throw a shadow; and Viktor realized that it had been that incredibly bright all along. What had deceived him was that he had seen it only through a clump of cloud at first. When the last fringe of cloud had rolled away it was a blue-white beacon in the sky, brighter, Viktor was sure, than any possible star should be—

And he went running back into the house, stumbling but now suddenly cold sober, to shout to his parents that another nearby star had gone flare.

After that, there was no objection to Pal Sorricaine becoming a full-time astronomer again. Pressed though the colony was for able-bodied workers, everyone agreed that this second Sorricaine-Mtiga object definitely needed to be studied. Pal was re-leased from his scavenging duties, Frances Mtiga from her school, Jahanjur Singh from his work as an accountant for the stores comp-troller, and Ibtissam Khadek from the guidance systems for the rec-tenna.

The difficulty came when the four of them asked, no, *demanded*, that the colony instruct the orbiting crews to put aside other work in order to make the observations only they could make, with the ship's sensors that were the only eyes the colony had for investigating what was going on in space.

It took a full-scale colony meeting to decide—more than three thousand people crowding around the open-air platform where the speakers urged their cases.

When Pal Sorricaine heard that the decision would go to a meeting he swore and poured himself a drink. That meant it would go by majority vote, and Pal Sorricaine, like a lot of *Mayflower* people, thought the majority was unfair. The second shipload had begun by outumbering the first, 1,115 to 854—but then the first colonists had had six Earth years to make more babies, so the combination of the colonists from *New Ark* and their Home-born offspring now totaled 1,918, while *Mayflower*'s total had only reached a little over 1,300. Of course the newborns weren't old enough to vote, but who was, exactly? At what age did the franchise begin? And by what sort of calculation?

Sorricaine went to the meeting grimly determined to battle out the voting age question. But this time the line wasn't drawn between the two ships' people. The question split both fractions almost down the middle. There was one side—headed by Pal Sorricaine and his little group, along with Captain Rodericks from the first ship and Marie-Claude Stockbridge—who insisted that the star had to be studied with all the resources possible. There was another side that included Reesa McGann's parents, but also Sam and Sally Broad from *Mayflower* and a lot of others from both ships, who were even more emphatic that the orbiting crews had all they could handle to finish converting the drive engines to MHD microwave generation, and didn't the others understand the colony *needed* that power?

They all settled in for a long town-meeting argument. Even allowing only three minutes to each speaker meant long hours of debate. Worse, they were unproductive hours. Men and women debating policy were not planting crops or putting up houses or exploring the planet.

It took them an hour just to decide, by raucous voice vote, how many could be allowed to speak. The decision was a hundred—three hundred minutes—five hours of talk; and, even though some of the lottery winners immediately turned their times over to allies more articulate and convincing than themselves, a lot of those three-minute talks amounted only to saying, over and over, "The safety of the colony is threatened!"

What they couldn't agree on was which threat—whether the threat from the sky was more dangerous than the threat of postponing the arrival of beamed power from the ship.

It ended badly for Pal Sorricaine. He and his colleagues got their observing time, but with a bad condition. The allotment of ship time was to become effective only after the ten Newmanhome days of additional work it would take for the microwave installation to be completed.

By then the flare was still bright, but not as bright; the vital first spectra had been missed. Sorricaine, Mtiga, and the others did what they could with the data that began to flood down on them, but they learned nothing they hadn't known before. The star had somehow pulled itself apart, and no one could guess why.

The star continued to dominate the night sky for more than a hundred Newmanhome days. Then Pal Sorricaine filed his last report to the distant Earthly astronomers, gave up his privileges, and went resentfully back to laboring, mourning the lost chance.

At least he wasn't reclaiming lost pods any more. The last of them had been found and brought in; someone else had done that for him. He found other jobs. He drove a tractor on the farms; he sailed to an island a hundred miles south of the colony, to seed it with earthworms and Earthly clover to prepare it, one day, for crops; he shifted goods in the storehouses with a forklift . . . and that was the job that did him in, for one day he stacked the sacks of seed potatoes too high, and the lift overturned.

There was not enough of Pal Sorricaine's right leg left to save when they got him to the hospital.

It was a torment to him that, in the next year, there were two new flare stars, two months apart. "I think we didn't pick a good part of the galaxy to colonize," he told his son, wincing as he tried to find a comfortable position for the stump of his right leg. "Pieces of it keep blowing up." And then he asked his teenage son, please, to save his liquor allotment for him—to help, he said, with the unremitting pain.

CHAPTER 5

Wan-To's interest in the Sorricaine-Mtiga objects (which, of course, he never called by that name) was becoming pretty nearly frantic. He saw a lot more of them than Pal Sorricaine did, because he saw them a lot faster. He didn't have to wait for creeping visible light to bring him the information. His Einstein-Rosen-Podolsky pairs relayed the images instantly. The things were popping up all over.

However, he was beginning to have hope. The results from his blue-light studies were beginning to come in.

Blue light was particularly good for looking for starspots. Although the spots seemed relatively dark, they were quite bright enough to be seen by Wan-To's great and sensitive "eyes"— particularly if you looked in the blue. Because the spots were cooler than the areas around them, their gases were ionized in a somewhat different way; and it was the spectral lines of the singly ionized calcium atoms—the ones that had lost just one electron— that stood out in blue.

When Wan-To found blue-light images that were not natural he knew just what to do. He summoned up the necessary graviphotons and graviscalars and hurled them in a carefully designed pattern at that star.

That would have been quite a wonder to human physicists, if

they could have known what Wan-To was doing. It would have been a marvel for them if they could even have detected any of those particles, though they had sought them as long, and as unsuccessfully, as any medieval knight had sought the Holy Grail.

It was in the early twentieth century that Theodor Kaluza and Oskar Klein formulated the human race's first decent model of how gravity worked. It wasn't a wholly successful model. There was still a lot to learn. But it managed to relate electromagnetism and gravity as manifestations of a higher-dimension space-time in ways that seemed to fit together pretty well—in ways, in fact, that Wan-To had understood for many billion years. His own understanding of gravitation was more or less a Kaluza-Klein model, though with considerable important amendments. He understood that the three basic mediating particles of the gravitational interaction between masses were what human scientists of the Kaluza-Klein faith would call the vector bosons—the graviton, the graviphoton, and the graviscalar. His command of them was perfect. With the resources of his star to draw on, he could generate any or all of those particles at will. He often did—in copious amounts. He found them all very useful.

He didn't bother much with the simple graviton. That was the uncomplicated spin-2 particle that seemed to pull masses together at even infinite distances—the only one that Isaac Newton, for instance, would have understood. Of course, the graviton was highly important in holding stars together and keeping galaxies rotating around their common center, but you couldn't *do* much with it. The others were rarer, and more fun, especially when you wanted to attack a colleague's star. A dose of graviphotons, the spin-1 repellers, would churn up the star's insides in a hurry; no organized system of Wan-To's kind could survive inside a star that was tearing itself apart that way. Alternatively, or better still in addition, he could pull at the star from outside with one of the other particles. The more useful of those was the spin-0 graviscalar, which pulled matter and energy toward it just as the humble graviton did, but only over finite distances. The graviscalar was a very *local* kind of particle.

The great virtue of the graviscalar, in other words, was that it couldn't be detected by Wan-To's enemies unless they were right on the spot—and then they wouldn't be in any position to do anything about it.

When Wan-To saw his target star erupt—very satisfyingly—he began to relax.

Nothing could have survived in that utter holocaust, of course. Wan-To was pleased. He wondered which of his competitors he had killed.

It would, he thought, surely have been one of the dumber ones. The others—the ones he had first made, the ones who were almost as smart as Wan-To himself—would, like Wan-To, have figured out that they shouldn't give their locations away by playing in the convection zones. But at least one was gone—one possible threat, but also, of course, one possible promise of companionship.

Philosophically, Wan-To turned his mind to his next step.

There was no help for it. It would be matter. He was going to have to work with nasty *matter*.

Wan-To had made copies of himself before. That was why he was having his current problems, in fact—if he hadn't wanted company he would have been alone and, therefore, safe. There was no particular problem in preparing a pattern of himself for occupying another star. He knew exactly how to organize inanimate plasma into a living, reasoning being like himself, because he had himself always at hand as a model.

Working with cold, dead, tangible *matter*—that was another problem entirely. He had done that, too—well, there wasn't much Wan-To *hadn't* tried, in the ten or so billion years he had been alive. Once he had made a nonplasmoid copy of himself to live in a cold, diffuse cloud of interstellar gas, once even out of solid matter, on an asteroidal body orbiting the star he had occupied at the time. Both were disgusting failures. The gas-cloud doppel was terminally *slow*—it simply had too little energy to work with to be any kind of real company. The one made of matter was just matter, and thus repellent to Wan-To; he had obliterated it after a mere century or two.

But at least he knew how to do the job.

The distance of the star system he was working on didn't present any problem. He had long ago planted an Einstein-Rosen-Podolsky set in each of the places where he now wanted them to be. (Wan-To always planned ahead.) The problem was that matter was no fun to manipulate. In Wan-To's opinion it was slow, it was unfamiliar, and it was pretty nasty stuff all around. What made the work even harder was that he wasn't there, so he had to perform all the complicated operations involved through the limited signals that could be carried through an ERP pair. In human terms, it was like a paraplegic trying to play a Space Invaders video game with the kind of controller that responded to puffs of his breath, or like a cardiac surgeon trying to snip and stitch and ream a dammed-up ventricle into shape with a flexible probe that snaked up through the blood vessels from the femoral artery in the patient's crotch.

The limitations of the Einstein-Rosen-Podolsky pair made it all harder, of course. The ERP effect was a probabilistic, quantumlike event.

That meant that there was no guarantee that the message received at one end would be identical to the one that had been transmitted at the other. In fact, it almost certainly wouldn't be.

Naturally Wan-To and his brethren knew how to deal with that problem. Parity checks and redundancy: If the parity check showed nothing wrong, then the message was *possibly* intact. Then it was compared with the same message transmitted three times. Majority ruled.

All that meant in the long run was that it took longer than it should to carry on a conversation—not because of travel time, but because of processing.

But Wan-To didn't have an alternative.

He didn't want to construct another plasma intelligence. That could well attract attention. Matter would not; beings like Wan-To didn't pay much attention to matter, and there was little chance that any of his feuding relatives would see what was going on on this little satellite of the stellar system he had chosen. He had plans for that system and its neighbors. To make the plans work, he needed some very potent particle-generators.

It would have been possible to create the particle-generators directly, but Wan-To was cleverer than that. What he was constructing wasn't the generators, it was a sort of little Wan-To, a matter analogue of himself, which when completed would do the job of constructing the generators and running them as long as necessary, in just the ways that Wan-To desired.

That little matter Wan-To wasn't anything like an exact copy of himself, of course, and it certainly didn't have all of his powers. What Wan-To was building was only a kind of servomechanism. It had exactly as much intelligence as it needed to do what Wan-To wanted it to do, and no more. It would do what Wan-To himself would have done—up to the limits of its powers, anyway. But by human standards those powers were vast.

Working with solid-phase matter was even a kind of intellectual challenge. So he was pleasantly occupied at his task, like a human terrorist whistling as he puts together his time bomb, and happily contemplating the success of his plans, when a signal reached him.

It was wholly unexpected, and it came through one of his ERP complexes. It wasn't an alarm, this time. He experienced it as a sound—in fact, as the sound of a name—*Haigh-tik*.

That was Wan-To's "eldest son"—which was to say, the copy of himself he had made first and most completely. As a natural consequence, that was the relative who gave Wan-To the most concern; if any of the eight intelligences he had produced was capable of doing their creator in, Haigh-tik was the one.

So Wan-To paused in the labor of creating his matter analogue and thought for a moment. He knew Haigh-tik very well. He didn't want to talk to him at that moment. It was tempting to start a conversation, in the hope that Haigh-tik would inadvertently say something that would give away his location. The trouble with having a little chat was that Haigh-tik was as likely as Wan-To himself to learn something. But there was a better possibility, Wan-To reflected. He knew quite a lot about Haigh-tik's habits—including what sort of star he preferred to inhabit.

So Wan-To took time to study some of the fairly nearby stars.

Of course, he had done that before—many times, over all the billions of years he had existed, because looking at the outside universe was one of his principal recreations. He saw them quite clearly.

In fact, he saw *everything* quite clearly for, though Wan-To's eyes were no more than patches of sensitive gas, they worked extremely well. What they looked at, they *saw*. They could trap a single photon, and remember it, and add it to the next photon that came in from that source. And it didn't matter how long the next photon took to arrive.

A human astronomer on, say, Mount Palomar would have been wild with jealousy. A Palomar astronomer might take an interest in a particular star, or a particular remote galaxy, and turn his 200-inch mirror on it for a whole night's observation. If the night sky were really cloudless—and if the cars and filling stations down the hill and the streetlights of San Diego didn't pollute the seeing with too much extraneous light—he might get twelve whole hours on a single charge-coupled plate. He wouldn't do that very often, of course, because there were too many other astronomers clamoring for time to gaze at their own precious objects.

Twelve hours!

But Wan-To's eyes could soak up photons from the faintest object for a thousand *years*. And if a thousand years wasn't long enough, why, then those eyes would stay unwinking on that single object for a million.

Nor were they limited to the so-called visible frequencies. All the frequencies were visible to Wan-To. He could "hear" a lot at radio frequencies, particularly when studying the great gas clouds, some of them a thousand light-years across, up to hundreds of thousands of solar masses. In the clouds, atomic hydrogen shouts at 1.4 gigahertz; molecular hydrogen is mute. But there are other compounds in the molecular clouds that speak right up: Carbon monoxide is noisy; so is formaldehyde; so is ammonia. He could easily pick out, in the clouds, the things that dirtied them with single molecules and clumps of silicates (rock) and carbon (graphite, charcoal, diamonds) all frozen over with water ice. If radio and optical studies weren't good enough, he had high-energy X rays and gammas that went right through dust.

He saw *everything*.

On Earth, the early stargazers named the bright points of light they saw overhead at night. The Arabs of the Dark Ages did it best. They had dry air and thus clear night skies, and no power plants or oil refineries to dirty the air, or illuminated highways or shopping malls to fill it with unwanted glow. Before Galileo invented the telescope they could see as many as three thousand stars, and they gave most of them names.

Wan-To could see many more stars than that. One way or another, he could see just about every star in his own galaxy (which at that time was also Earth's)—roughly two hundred and thirty-eight billion of them, depending on which giants had just gone supernova and collapsed into black holes and which new ones were just beginning to shine. He didn't bother to give them names. Type, distance, and direction were good enough for him—but he *knew* them all, and most of those in the Magellanic Clouds and quite a few in M-31 in Andromeda as well. And he also "knew" just about all the external galaxies this side of the optical limit, too, right down to the "blue fuzzies." He was himself a catalogue far better than Harvard or Draper or the Palomar Sky Survey.

So to survey just the nearest stars didn't take Wan-To long at all. After all, there were only about twenty thousand of them.

The important thing was that he had a piece of useful information about Haigh-tik. Haigh-tik was known to prefer young stars, probably of the kind Earthly astronomers called T-Tauri objects. Therefore Wan-To sought ordinary-looking stars with a strong lithium emission at 660.7 nanometers.

He found three that were close enough to be possible residences for his undutiful son.

Giving his equivalent of a humorous shrug, Wan-To zapped them all. In one sense, he thought, that was a waste of two stars, at least. Still, there were plenty of stars, and anyway, in just a little while—no more than a million years or so—they would have settled down from being wrung out and so be habitable again if wanted.

After he had sent the instructions on their way he went back to his other project, feeling more cheerful. A dozen other stars had flared up and died while he was working. If Haigh-tik had been the one directing that probing fire, maybe he was now out of the game.

But whoever it was, Wan-To did not want him to know he had missed.

CHAPTER 6

On Viktor Sorricaine's forty-first birthday— Well, it probably wasn't *exactly* his birthday, although it was the 38th of Spring, and Viktor, carefully calculating back in Newmanhome years, had long before chosen that date as a base point for his age— Anyway, when he reached that birthday he was the equivalent of twenty, in Earth years. A man grown. Old enough to vote. On Newmanhome he was also definitely a man grown and old enough for any adult activity at all. He had fathered two small babies to prove it.

He didn't have a wife to go along with the two children, but that wasn't anything special on Newmanhome. Almost everybody past puberty was producing kids for the colony, whether they were married or not. Even his own father had helped the baby boom along again. By the time little Edwina Sorricaine was fourteen (Newmanhome years; Earth equivalent, about seven) she had two younger brothers and was beginning to learn how to change a diaper on her own. The human population of Newmanhome stood at more than six thousand. Two thirds of them were younger than Viktor, which was probably why Viktor had seniority enough to have risen to be the pilot of an ocean-going cargo ship. Where he really wanted to be was in space, of course, but there weren't any of those jobs open. Nor was he quite senior enough to be an airman. But ship's pilot was still pretty good.

He was certainly grown up enough to be married, if he had been inclined that way. His mother frequently reminded him of that fact. "Reesa's a nice girl," she would say, sometime during the days he spent at home, between his voyages to the farms on South Continent or the new tree plantations on the islands in Archipelago West. Or in her letters she would tell him how young Billy Stockbridge—now, would you believe it, twenty-six (Newmanhome) years old and pretty nearly grown up himself—had begun playing his guitar to accompany Reesa McGann's flute in duets and, although there was that great difference in their ages, people didn't take those things as seriously in the new world, and wasn't it about time that he, Viktor, *made up his mind?*

He had made it up, long ago.

Viktor had never stopped dreaming of Marie-Claude Stockbridge. In spite of the fact that she laughed at him when, once, he tried to kiss her. In spite of the fact that he was despondently aware that she had become pregnant four times in thirteen Newmanhome years, by three different men. In spite of the fact that, although all that was bad enough, she had just made it worse still by marrying the father of her latest two.

The name of the cur she married was Alex Petkin. It infuriated Viktor that Petkin was at least eight Newmanhome years younger than his bride—or, as Viktor saw it, not all that much older than himself, for God's sake, and if Marie-Claude had wanted to rob the cradle why the hell couldn't she have robbed *his?*

In Viktor's view, his own two children were beside the point. He was only doing what everybody else was. On Newmanhome, kids were supposed to experiment before they settled down. Naturally, such kids' experiments frequently produced more kids.

Getting laid now and then was one thing. Getting married was another matter entirely. To marry, in Viktor's lexicon, necessarily meant to *love*. He did not feel he had been in love with either of the mothers of his children. Certainly he was quite fond of Alice Begstine, the mother of his four-year-old. Alice was a ship's navigator who was also frequently not only his bedmate but his shipmate on the long voyages across the Great Ocean. Undoubtedly, he was very used to Reesa McGann, who had borne him his newest one, still an infant. But he had never associated either Alice or Reesa with the word "love."

That word was reserved for Marie-Claude—ah—Petkin. In spite of the fact that she had gone and married a stripling still in his fifties, who was quite unlikely to become enfeebled with age in time to do Viktor Sorricaine any good.

Since Viktor was not an idiot, he no longer really expected that was ever going to happen. His own father, crippled as he was, much older than the cur, Petkin, was a permanent testimonial to middle-aged male vigor. At least, the toddler Jonas and little Tomas, sucking his knuckles in his crib, surely were.

None of that mattered to Viktor. Marie-Claude was still the woman Viktor made love to, tenderly and copiously, in every night's drowsy imagining just before he drifted off to sleep in his bed—no matter whom he happened to be sharing the bed with.

Crossing Great Ocean took four or five weeks each way, depending on the winds, plus a week or two loading and unloading at each end. It came to more than a quarter of a Newmanhome year for each round trip. Things happened fast on Newmanhome, and every time Viktor came back to the growing city they called Homeport everything was changed.

As Viktor's ship sailed into Homeport on the morning of that 38th of Spring the broad bay glistened in the sunlight. Fleecy clouds drifted overhead. The breeze was warm, and Viktor saw lots of progress in the colony. The new grain elevator for the docks had been completed since he had sailed away, and up on the hill the two microwave rectennae loomed behind the new geothermal power plant, the second antenna already half covered with its wire net. That was good; the colony was getting plenty of electrical power at last.

It was Alice Begstine's turn to supervise the unloading of the ship. So as soon as they were docked Viktor leaped off, waved farewell to Alice and headed toward the new houses on the edge of town. He was looking forward to spending his birthday with his youngest child, Yan—and maybe with Reesa, the little boy's mother, if she seemed to be in a friendly mood.

She wasn't home. Freddy Stockbridge was sitting in her front room, reading his prayer book, while Reesa's two children napped.

Viktor looked at him with suspicion, but all he said was, "Hello, Freddy." Viktor wasn't sure how to take Freddy Stockbridge, who had decided, of all things, that what he wanted to be was a priest. "What are you doing here?"

The question was really "Why aren't you working?" and Freddy answered it that way. "They made today a secular holiday," he said, sounding aggrieved. "They call it First Power Day. They're having some kind of an anniversary celebration up at the power plant."

"Another damn holiday," Viktor said, trying to make friendly conversation. Landing Day, *Mayflower* Day—every major event in the colony's history had to be commemorated, it seemed, though Viktor rather liked the thought of his own birthday being a planet-wide day off.

"Another darned *secular* holiday," Freddy corrected him. "It isn't really fair, you know. Would you believe they won't let us have Good Friday off? Or even All Saints' Day, although they close the schools the day before for Dress-Up Night?"

"I'll sign your petition," Viktor promised, lying. "Is Reesa up there?"

Freddy shrugged, already back in his prayer book. "I guess so," he said, not looking up.

"Thank you very much," Viktor said, snapping the words off because Freddy was irritating him. Viktor thought of looking in on his parents, who at least would remember that it was his birthday, but he was curious about what Reesa was doing, and why she had left his child to a baby-sitter—Freddy Stockbridge, at that!

The only way to settle that was to ask her, so, still irritated, he trudged up the hill.

There was a crowd there, all right, five or six hundred people at least. Captain Bu Wengzha was up on a flag-bedecked platform, making a speech, though most of the people were picnicking on the grass and hardly listening to the captain at all. What the speech seemed to be about was electrical power, and Reesa was nowhere in sight.

". . . this wonderful geothermal power plant," Captain Bu was saying, "has delivered energy for us for one year now without interruption and, God willing, will go on doing it for a thousand years to come. That is God's gift to us, my friends, limitless energy from the geothermal heat under our feet. Let us praise His name! And let us thank, too, the skills and painstaking labor of our comrades who have given so unstintingly of themselves to create this wholly automatic technological marvel, which supplements the flood of energy being beamed down to us by that sturdy ship, New Mayflower . . ."

Viktor listened for only a second—not very interested, though a little surprised to hear the old ship's captain sounding so godly—then turned off his ears. He spotted a young woman holding a baby, listening patiently to the captain. He nudged her. "Valerie? Have you seen Reesa?"

The young woman glanced at him. "Oh, hi, Vik. No, not lately. Is she helping them get ready for the dancing over there?"

She was looking toward a group setting up a plank dance floor on the grass. Viktor nodded thanks. "I'll go look."

Captain Bu's amplified voice followed him as he stepped among the picnickers to the dance committee. ". . . and by this time next year, they promise, all of our cryonic facilities will be complete on this very spot, along with liquid-gas generators to refuel our shuttles so that our heroic friends in orbit above us can have the regular relief they rightfully . . ."

She wasn't hammering down the flat boards for the dancing, either. Viktor buttonholed the nearest worker he recognized. "Wen, have you seen Reesa?"

The young man blinked at him. "Oh, she's not here," he assured Viktor. "I think she's up at the observatory."

"The observatory," Viktor said, not meaning to sound disparaging. He had always thought of the "observatory" as a rather pointless hobby of his father's. "What does she think she can see in broad daylight?"

"No, they're not looking through the telescope. It's the space course. You know, the astrophysics course they're having for space pilots—it was on the bulletin boards weeks ago."

"For space pilots?" Viktor was suddenly alert. "I wasn't here weeks ago!"

"Oh, have you been away?" Wen asked. "I thought you'd know. After all, it's your father that's giving it."

A course for *space* pilots! And given by his own father! Viktor was more irritated than ever as he climbed swiftly toward the little plastic dome on the peak of the hill. If there was any hope of anybody getting into space again, why hadn't he been *told*?

Viktor knew, of course, that his father still had a few people interested in astronomy hanging around him. Not very many. There wasn't any reason for anyone to be very interested, for the most exciting things in the Newmanhome sky, the flare stars, had stopped coming. There had been eight of them over a dozen Newmanhome years, then the flares had stopped.

That had left Pal Sorricaine high and dry, because the whole team of investigators into the "Sorricaine-Mtiga objects" had been disbanded. There was no longer anything for them to do. Jahanjur Singh had been coopted by the power teams to help design transmission facilities to the new colonies on Christmas Island and the South Continent, and Fanny Mtiga had emigrated to South, with her family, to start a new career in farming. "Don't go!" Pal had pleaded. "You're wasting your skills! Stay here, help me."

"Help you do what, Pal?" she asked, patiently enough. "If there's another flare I'll see it on South, won't I? And I'll get the same reading from the *Mayflower* instruments. And anyway, they've all been about the same—"

"We owe it to our profession! Back on Earth—"

"Pal," she said gently, "back on Earth they're seeing it all for themselves now, aren't they? Some of those flares were closer to them than to us, and they've got a lot better instruments."

"But we were the first to report!"

She shook her head. "If they elect us to the Royal Society we'll hear. Meanwhile what the colony really needs is food. Give me a call if anything comes up—to the South Continent."

So she had gone; and Pal Sorricaine had stayed and driven the half-dozen people who constituted his group of disciples to help him with such projects as cataloguing the nearby stars so they could have better names than they had ever been given on Earth.

Then Pal had an inspiration. He wheeled the council into letting them divert a little effort into casting some low-expansion glass blanks, then set his acolytes to grinding a mirror. It took forever to

finish, but when it was done and silvered and mounted in a tube
Pal Sorricaine and his class had a real telescope, right there on
the surface, with which to look at their new neighbors in space: the
six other planets, their dozens of moons, and the largest of the
asteroids.

Of course, it was all pretty pointless in any *serious* astronomical
sense. Any real astronomy would be done by the optics on the
orbiting hulks, which still worked perfectly. The few crew members
still up there, desultorily running the microwave generators and
going slowly ape from loneliness, didn't bother to tend the sensors,
but they didn't need tending. Even back on Earth, astronomers in
Herstmonceux, England, had routinely operated instruments in the
Canary Islands or Hawaii by remote radio control; telescopes didn't
need a human hand on the controls. But Pal was determined to
force his students to *look* at the skies. Though the 30-centimeter was
far from perfectly curved, and the sky over the hill it was mounted
on was frequently obscured by clouds, at least his students could
step out of the little dome and, with their naked eyes, see the stars
and planets they had just seen huger or brighter inside.

And there were some pretty things to see. Sullen, red Nergal
was always fascinating: it leered at you in the sky and awed you in
the telescope. Three of the asteroids were naked-eye objects, once
you knew where to look for them—if you had good eyes. The
corpses of the former flare stars were always worth looking at, just
to remind you to ponder about their mysteries. There were double
stars, a fair number of comets, a gas nebula lighted from within by
newborn stars—Pal Sorricaine loved to look at all of them and com-
municated his feeling to his students.

Nobody was using the little mirror when Viktor came
puffing up to the observatory—not in broad daylight. The class
wasn't even inside the little dome. There was a teaching machine,
its screen hooded against the sunlight, and a dozen or so people
were gathered around it, looking at the rainbow colors of a
Hertzsprung-Russell diagram of stellar types.

Viktor saw Reesa sitting there cross-legged on the spiky Newmanhome grass, sharing a blanket with Billy Stockbridge. That was displeasing; he hadn't really taken his mother's remarks seriously. He was no more pleased to see Jake Lundy in the class. Viktor didn't really like Jake Lundy—hadn't since they had first met, in the long-ago school days when Lundy was the older kid sometimes stuck with supervising the young ones, and something of a bully. It didn't help that Jake, a little older than Viktor, had managed to land one of the coveted jobs as *aircraft* pilot, instead of being stuck with a surface ship. It also happened to be true (as Viktor knew) that Jake Lundy was the father of Reesa's older child—not that that had anything to do with Viktor's feelings about the man, of course.

When Viktor approached the group his father paused in his lecture long enough to give him a combination of a welcoming nod and a peremptory gesture to take a seat. Viktor sat near enough to Reesa so that she could talk to him if she wanted to, yet far enough away that he wasn't obviously seeking conversation. She gave him a quick, absent smile and returned to the lesson.

Viktor's father wasn't looking well. Though his artificial limb was a high-tech device as close to the real thing as any machine could be, he limped as he moved around the teaching machine, and his voice was hoarse as he explained the natural sequence of star types Hertzsprung and Russell had described centuries earlier. It seemed to Viktor that the old man's hands were shaking, too. But he paid attention to the lecture, and when it was finished and Pal Sorricaine asked for questions, Viktor's hand shot up.

"What's this about space piloting?" he demanded.

The dozen students grinned tolerantly at him.

"If you'd stay around Homeport you'd know these things, Viktor," Pal said. "We'll have rocket fuel soon, from the gas-liquefying plants they're building for the freezers. The council decided weeks ago that as soon as *New Argosy* arrives we'll start space exploration again. So I volunteered to give a refresher course on astrophysics, for anyone who wants to try for astronaut training."

"Why astrophysics, though?" Viktor asked his father. "I mean, why not something useful, like navigation?" It seemed to him a natural and harmless question, but his father scowled.

Pal rubbed his lips. "It's my course, Viktor," he said, his voice hostile. "If you don't want to take it, go away."

Unexpectedly, a female voice spoke up. "But I think your son is right, Pal," the woman said, and stood up on the far side of the crowd. It was Ibtissam Khadek, looking older than Victor remembered her, and quite determined. "We know that your personal interest is in such things as theoretical cosmology and your so-called Sorricaine-Mtiga objects," she went on, looking around for support, "but for most of us here, what we want is to *go into space*. To explore this whole solar system, of which we know so little—and to do it now, please. In my case, before I am too old to be accepted for a ship's crew."

Pal Sorricaine looked astonished, and then resentful, and then surly. "There's nothing to keep you from starting a course of your own, Tiss," he pointed out.

The astronomer shook her head. "We shouldn't be competing," she said sweetly. "We should be working together, don't you think? For instance! When my grandfather first described this system, he of course marked Enki"—how like the woman, Viktor thought, to insist on calling familiar Newmanhome by its Babylonian name!—"as the most habitable planet, but he specifically listed the brown dwarf, Nergal, as the one most important to observe. It's our plain duty to take a good look at it, for the sake of science!"

"We're looking at Nergal all the time," Pal Sorricaine protested. "We've got millions of pictures. *Ark*'s instruments are covering it routinely."

"I am not speaking of *routine*," Khadek cried. "I am speaking of a dedicated *mission*."

"But why Nergal?" Jake Lundy put in. "For that matter, why don't we look at Nebo? I think that's even more interesting, because we all know it's been changing! Your grandfather said it had almost no water vapor in its atmosphere, but now it's so clouded we can hardly see the surface—why is that?"

"You are right," Tiss Khadek conceded graciously. "Of course we should do both. But, I think, Nergal first—after all, it is the first brown dwarf anyone has had the chance to observe."

Viktor started to open his mouth to get into the discussion, but Reesa's warm hand pulled him toward her. "Look what you've started!" she whispered, while the argument raged around them. "Why did you come here?"

"I've got as much right to be here as you do," he whispered hotly back, and then was compelled to add, "Anyway, I was looking for you. I, uh, I thought I'd spend a little time with Yan today. I mean, it's my birthday."

"Of course it is," she said testily. She looked at him closely, then nodded. "I'm going back to feed the kids as soon as this is over, then I'll bring them back up here for the fireworks and the dancing . . . if you want to come."

"All right," Viktor agreed—and then saw that his father had quelled the discussion and was looking at him dangerously.

"We're going on with the class now," Pal Sorricaine said loudly. "Anybody has anything to say on any other subject, we can take that up after the lesson. Now! Are there any questions about stellar evolution?"

Viktor walked his father back to their home—helped him, actually, because the old man's artificial leg was giving him trouble again, and besides he had disappeared into the dome for a moment by himself before he was willing to leave. Viktor didn't have to ask his father the reason. He could smell it on the old man's breath.

"Dad?" Viktor offered, halfway down. "I'm sorry if I messed up your class."

His father gave him a discouraged look. "That's all right," he panted gruffly. "Ouch!" He stopped to rub his thigh, then put a hand on Viktor's shoulder and limped on. "It's not you," he said. "It's that Tiss Khadek mostly. She keeps trying to get the whole bunch fired up about her pet Nergal." He winced. "Would you mind if we didn't talk right now? This is hard work—"

"Of course, Dad," Viktor said, but not happily. It was difficult, looking at this shrunken old man, to remember the strong man with the laughing blue eyes who had tossed him in his arms on *New Mayflower*. When at last they got to his parents' home, Pal Sorricaine sank wearily into a chair.

Viktor was shocked to see even more weariness on his mother's face. Nevertheless she greeted him joyously—put up her face to be kissed, told him he looked as though he wasn't eating enough, and

winked that there was a surprise waiting for him. He didn't have
to guess at the surprise. He knew his mother would have seen
the ship in dock and would long since have baked a cake for his
birthday.

But she was beginning to look tired and, well, almost *old*. When
he said something she said firmly it was just that she'd had a hard
day. The two new children drained a lot of her energy, coupled
with the demands of her job—it was a busy time for agronomists,
she told him. "Agronomists?" Viktor repeated, startled. "I thought
that was just your, you know, kind of hobby."

"It started out that way, Vik," she sighed. "But I've switched
over. I did have undergraduate courses, you know, and—well, feeding people seemed more important than building more machines.
And now, with new cultivars to clone and test every time someone
starts planning to plant a new microenvironment, they need all the
help they can get."

"And then she helps me, too," his father put in, looking slightly
recovered.

Viktor blinked. "Teaching your course?" he guessed, incredulous.

"No, of course not teaching my course. Except in a way,
maybe—I mean, she's been helping to download the data banks from
Ark and *Mayflower*. We've set up new storage by the power plants
and the freezers, so in case anything happens to those ships—"

"Nothing can happen to the ships," Viktor said, shocked.

"Something might," his father said firmly. "Then we'd be
screwed for fair. Do you know how long it would take to get everything retransmitted from Earth? But we've already got most of
the astrophysical files duplicated here," he finished, looking pleased
for the first time. "That was a big job. Do you know, I think that
calls for a drink."

And they had one . . . except that his father had two. And Viktor began to understand what put those worry lines on his mother's
face. It wasn't just hard work. What was aging her was worry about
her husband.

Viktor was glad enough for the little birthday party and the company of young Edwina and the two brats, but he was even more glad when he got away.

When he got back to the top of the hill it was dusk, and the dancing had already begun. Viktor searched the dancers. They were in a double circle of couples, men and women singing softly to themselves in Spanish as the three-piece fiddle-guitar-and-drum band played something with a Mexican lilt. It was a *corrido*, and Viktor saw Reesa in the inner circle, holding right hands at shoulder height with—hell, yes! He scowled. It was Billy Stockbridge again.

But Reesa was not the only young woman among the dancers. When the next tune started Viktor grabbed a pretty young tractor driver and whirled her through a square dance. And then he was caught up in the fun of the dancing itself. He hardly noticed when he found himself with Reesa as his partner, swinging her around wildly, her laughing and panting, leaning against his arm around her waist. They did the *krakowiak*—hop, click heels, *stamp*; they did the macho Greek dances and the slow Israeli ones. When Reesa sat out one dance to nurse the baby, Yan, Viktor didn't even miss her, though when it was over he came to where she was sitting on the blanket, the baby at her breast. It was only a little annoyance that Freddy Stockbridge was sitting there, too. Freddy wasn't dancing. He wasn't reading his prayer book, either, because it was too dark for that, but Viktor noticed with irritation that Freddy had put on a clerical collar for the occasion.

Reesa looked up at Viktor, her face flushed and happy. "They're going to start the fireworks in a minute," she said. "Why don't you sit with us? Freddy, go get us some wine."

Viktor eased himself down to the blanket beside her, watching the sleepy little mouth of his son sucking absentmindedly at Reesa's breast. He glanced after the disappearing Freddy.

"I thought priests were supposed to be celibate," he said.

"Mind your own business," Reesa told him. Then, relenting, she said, "I guess Freddy is. He just likes children. He's real good about baby-sitting for me."

"Doesn't take after his brother, then," Viktor observed, but the way Reesa's face tightened told him not to pursue the subject. Anyway, a pistol-shot sound in the air and a gasp from the crowd marked the first of the fireworks. They quieted to watch the display as Freddy came stumbling back with three cups of wine. Viktor helped Reesa cover his sleeping little son, tucking him in next to her already sound asleep toddler. Viktor was beginning to feel really good. The fireworks were brilliant and lovely to look at, under the warm Newmanhome sky. And then, when they were over, they did the last few dances, ending with the sweet, slow *Misirlou*. Misirlou means "beloved" in Greek. Perhaps that was why, when the last dance was over, Viktor looked around. Neither Jake Lundy nor Billy Stockbridge was nearby, so he offered quickly, "I'll help you get the kids home, if you want."

Reesa didn't object. Freddy looked annoyed but drifted away. The two of them shared the sleeping children, Viktor carrying the toddler and Reesa the baby, Yan, as they walked down the hill. They didn't speak for a while, and then Viktor remembered a question on his mind. "What's this astrophysics class all about?" he demanded.

"It's just what your father said it is," she said shortly. She looked at him with curiosity. "I noticed today you're all sunburned," she accused. "What do you do, lounge around on the deck all day to get that he-man tan for the girls? Do you want to wreck your skin?"

He refused to be diverted. "No, really," he insisted. "Do you think knowing how to tell a Wolf-Rayet star from an ordinary O is going to help you get to be a space pilot—twenty years from now?"

"It might," she said seriously. "And it might not be twenty years; *Argosy* has small spaceships ready to go, you know, and it's due pretty soon now."

"Sure, when *Argosy* lands," Viktor scoffed. It was what everybody said when they didn't have something they really wanted: it would certainly be somewhere in the third ship's limitless treasure of stores. "What makes you think they won't have their own pilots for their own ships?"

She shrugged. "We still have our own landers," she pointed out. "We'll have more fuel for them, once they get the freezers going. And anyway—" she hesitated, then plunged on. "Anyway, I think it's good for your father to be doing something. He's, uh, he's drinking a lot these days, you know."

"I do know," Viktor said stiffly. As an afterthought, he added, "It's his business."

Reesa didn't challenge that. They walked in silence for a moment, then Viktor said tentatively, "I thought if you weren't doing anything, later this evening—"

She stopped and studied him, shifting the sleeping baby from one shoulder to the other. "What is it, this is Wednesday so it must be Reesa's turn? Isn't your girlfriend on the ship keeping you happy?"

"I only said—"

"I know what you said." She started walking again, silent for a moment. Then, she said, "Well, why not? After all, it is your birthday."

It took eight days to pump the grain out of the ship's hold and reload it with the new cargo for the South Continent. Viktor had to be there for the last of it, because the last things winched aboard were fourteen pregnant cows and a wobbly but feisty bull calf. "Do cows get seasick?" Alice Begstine asked the handler.

The woman wiped her sweating forehead. "How do I know? Are you going to have rough weather?"

"I hope not, but you never know."

"Well, then you'll find out," the woman said grimly. "Anyway, you'd better lash them down if you do. They could fall and break their legs or something."

"It sounds like it's going to be a fun trip," Alice observed. And then, when they were actually putting out to sea and she was on the bridge next to Viktor, she said, "Shan was asking after you."

"Oh, yeah," Viktor said, concentrating on setting a course while the wind was fair. "I'm sorry about that. I meant to come and see him, but—how's he doing, anyway?"

"He's learning to talk," Alice informed him.

"That's wonderful," Viktor said, guilty but pleased. "Well, it's your watch. I think I'll look around below. And then I think I'll hit the teaching machines."

The revived talk about space travel, at least, had been an inter-

esting development of his leave, but on the whole it hadn't been
entirely a happy one. Viktor was beginning to worry a little about
his family. His mother was certainly working too hard, and his
father . . .

Well, Pal Sorricaine wasn't the man he had been on *New Mayflower* anymore. He was drinking again. It was because of the pain
of his missing leg, he said. But what Reesa said—not right away, but
reluctantly, and after keeping silence for a while, and then only
because she never lied to Viktor—was that the course in astrophysics
was a joke. Oh, the story about starting space travel again soon—
maybe—was true enough; the council had voted it a medium priority. But the real purpose of the course was simply to give Pal
Sorricaine something to do. Viktor himself had seen that the machines did most of the real teaching. They were far more patient
than Pal Sorricaine, and fairer. Especially with the younger students
who had never studied astrophysics before. The teaching machines
were not put off by teenage sulks, or cajoled by teenage flattery.
Probably the younger ones got something out of the course, but the
others—well, everybody liked Pal Sorricaine, and they were willing
to go to a little trouble to please him.

Viktor felt a small, lasting ache at the thought of his father being
humored.

And he felt a certain irritation with Reesa, too. Although she
had seemed happy enough for them to spend much of his time
ashore together, she hadn't seemed particularly excited by his attentions. Nor had she tried to conceal from him (that same damned
honesty!) that there were others more attentive, and more often
around.

All in all, he was glad to be back at sea.

Even that, though, wasn't as exciting as it once had
been. When Viktor had first shipped out, as soon as he was big
enough to do an adult's job, everything had been thrillingly new.
They hadn't just cruised back and forth, as though on tracks; they
had gone where, literally, no human had ever been before. They
visited islands that they populated with earthworms, insects, algae,
and flowering plants, as well as the seedlings that, they hoped, would

one day be great forests of oak and apple and pine. Then they returned to those islands, a few Newmanhome years later, to seed them with second generations of fish and birds and small mammals—and a few years after that, with a couple of pairs of foxes to keep the rabbits down, and sheep to start earning the island's keep. He was too young to have been involved in the spreading of trace minerals in the soils of some of the lands, so that Earthly crops could grow, but he helped dig out the muck where recurrent marsh flooding had drowned thousands of years of colonizing plants, creating a sort of mulch that was almost as good as guano. He was even part of an expedition a hundred kilometers down the coast, once, when an explorer broke a leg in the jungle and had to be rescued from deep, ferny, swampy tangles of Newmanhome's native vegetation.

All that was in Viktor's apprentice days. His current job was crewing one of the giant grain ships that fed the growing city on the North Continent from the new farms on the South. Food for Homeport's people could be grown nearer the city and a lot was. But clearing the tangled, ropy vegetation of that part of the North Continent was hard work. Worse, the stuff refused to stay cleared. The principal native vine was more tenacious than crabgrass or kudzu, and harder to kill. Its root systems went down a dozen meters and more, and the stuff was quite content to grow up right through a field of corn or soy from the vestiges of its roots.

At some point, the leadership council decided, a new city, or a dozen of them, would have to be planted in the hotter, wetter south. The location of their first town, Homeport, had been chosen at long range, from probe imaging and the hurried studies of the *Ark* officers as they were busy inserting themselves into orbit, and it had been a minor mistake. But, like many such mistakes, it perpetuated itself. Every new building that went up was one more inducement to stay there. The buildings couldn't easily be moved.

The grain could, easily enough. Great Ocean was generally placid, and the prevailing winds were strong enough to drive a grain ship's rotor sails without at the same time raising storm waves big enough to be a nuisance. Navigation was no problem. Viktor's navigating talents were largely wasted. There were no icebergs to collide with, because there wasn't any ice. There were few other ships, and hardly ever any nearby; there were very few reefs or shoals. In fact there was no bottom closer than three hundred meters for the next week's sailing. The signals from the derelict interstellar ships in orbit gave them accurate positions at all times, so between ports the crew was largely honorary.

So Viktor and his shipmates did what everybody on Newmanhome did when they had leisure time. They watched TV, most of it rebroadcast by the orbiting ships from transmissions from distant Earth. (That didn't make them homesick. Watching the stories about crime and violence and overcrowded cities made them grateful not to be there.) Or they made some more babies. Or they tuned in on the transmissions from the third ship, *New Argosy*, late because of the funding squabbles but now well on its way—and, oh so eagerly awaited! It held so many things they didn't have—grand pianos, and a submarine, and even a complete installation for making more antimatter with a prefabricated near-Sun solar-power satellite—and, wow, what they could do *then*!

Or they studied.

In Viktor's case, after hearing what the Homeport council had decided, study came first. He spent half his waking hours at the ship's teaching machine, going over and over the fundamentals of orbital transfer and astrogation and celestial mechanics. He didn't seriously believe he would ever get into space, even to help deploy the antimatter manufactury when it arrived. But even an outside chance was worth fighting for. And he even did some refresher studying on his father's particular interest, astrophysics and cosmology. It wouldn't ever be *important* to him, in any way. He was sure of that—wrong, as it turned out later, but *sure*. Nevertheless it was interesting.

The people of Newmanhome didn't usually think hard about being happy to be where they were; they had gotten used to it, even the ones who remembered anything else. It was as good a planet as they hoped, and better than they had feared. There was no such thing as "continental climate" on Newmanhome. The biggest continent was smaller than Australia and looked more like a fat question mark than a more or less symmetrical blob. There wasn't much in the way of seasons, either. They'd given up the idea of "months" in their new calendar; they divided the year into Winter, Spring,

Summer, and Fall, with fifty-odd days in each of the divisions, but there was less difference between Winter and Summer than between two successive weeks in most Earthly climates. An axial tilt of only six degrees and a nearly circular orbit disarmed the cycle of seasons; Newmanhome was more like Hawaii than like Chicago or Moscow.

The shorter day helped even things out weatherwise, too. The night didn't have time to cool down as much as on Earth, so extremes of temperature were moderated still more. And the Newmanhome day was close enough to Earth's twenty-four hours that even the people who were grown up when they landed had long since readjusted their diurnal rhythms.

There was plenty of native life on Newmanhome, but not a single native animal to compete with human beings and their stocks. There were things that almost seemed like animals, because they moved about during the day, but they sank roots at night. There were things that ate other things, like terrestrial saprophytes and carnivorous plants, but they all photosynthesized, as well.

Some of the plants were warm-blooded or warm-sapped— and some of the mobile eating things liked to eat the warm ones. That was as close to a danger as the colonists had found. If one of the free-ranging predators, particularly the marine ones, found a sleeping human being, it was likely enough to try to eat him. The predators fed by lancing the prey with hollow things like thorns and injecting digestive saps, then sucking back the resulting soup when it was done. The process didn't work on human beings. Their tissues resisted the lysing enzymes of the predator plants, and anyway after the first itching stab or two the human prey would certainly wake up and go somewhere else. But they could get a hell of a painful wound in the process, and sometimes people died.

Sometimes people died from other causes, too. They were a young population, there on Newmanhome, and deaths were rare. But they happened. Drowning. Accident. Even once or twice the great scandal of a murder and suicide in a quarrel. But Newmanhome was benign to its colonists. Certainly people wore out early from hard work, and there were always those handicapped older ones who had come out of cryonic suspension with a kind of freezer-burn that slowed them down, or limited their abilities, but otherwise people were pretty healthy. The only diseases they encountered were the ones they had brought with them, and years of selection, therapy, and prophylaxis had kept those diseases few.

Until the first week of Winter in the thirty-ninth Newmanhome year of the colony.

There was no warning of trouble.

The harvest was the most bountiful yet in the grain fields of South Continent. Viktor and his first mate, Alice Begstine, had had a good time while the ship was loading. They had borrowed a rol-ligon and gone exploring in South Continent's high country, be-yond the farm lands. The ship's cook, who was one of Alice's other part-time lovers, had elected to stay ashore that trip, so she and Viktor bunked together on the voyage, enjoying it, too—though Viktor still secretly fantasized about Marie-Claude sharing his bed. They even, halfway home, saw a Von Neumann nautilus swimming sturdily toward their port beside him, to turn itself in. It was one of the first to have accumulated enough metal to trigger its return reflexes. It looked to have at least fifty chambers, each one bigger than the one before it in its spiral shell. "It's got to be a ten-tonner," Alice guessed. Viktor couldn't doubt it. Ten tons of valuable heavy metal soaked up from the thermal springs at the bottom of Great Ocean—what was the point of mining, when you could send the roving Von Neumann automata out to do the job for you? And the holds bulging with grain. And the colony growing. And new lands being explored—why, things were really going *splendidly*!

So they thought, right up to the moment of landing at Home-port.

As Viktor's ship slid gently in to mate with the floating dock he saw his father standing there, waiting for him.

That was a surprise. As he finished the docking drill, Viktor saw with a critical eye that his father was freshly shaved, but his hair was shaggy; he wore a clean, pressed blouse, but the cuffs of his pants were mud stained, though the streets were dry. Viktor easily read the meaning of the signs.

His father had been drinking again.

The ship was lashed to the floating dock. The huge snout of the grain pipe swung over the deck, slipped down through the open hold, and began snuffling up the cargo. Viktor picked up his kit bag, slung it over his shoulder, and swung himself down to the dock. His father, standing right where he landed, said at once, "Your mother's sick."

Just like that. No "Hello, son," or even, "I've got some bad news for you." Just "Your mother's sick," and a thumb jerked to the waiting tandem bike.

Amelia Sorricaine-Memel was sick, all right. The first thing the doctors told him, as gently as they could—but they had very little time to be gentle or considerate just then—was that they were pretty sure she was dying.

It wasn't pneumonia or emphysema or the flu. It was something the surveyors had brought back from Continent Delta, way on the other side of the planet, just really being explored for the first time.

What they brought back was a mold. It had thrived there as a parasite on some of the warm algal organisms of the tidal flats, but it had found a new home in human lungs. For the algae of the littoral it was a benign enough parasite. All it did was slow down their growth a little. For humans it was worse. It killed.

Viktor's mother lived seventeen painful hours after he reached her bedside. She was wheezing and strangling for breath the whole time, even when they put a mask over her face to give her oxygen, even when they put her in a hyperbaric chamber under enough pressure to force the oxygen into her lungs. Even when they drenched the air she breathed with antifungals strong enough to threaten her life.

Probably the antifungals did threaten it. They probably took it, in fact, because when she died her face was pink again, instead of the cadaver blue of oxygen starvation. But she was just as dead.

Amelia Sorricaine-Memel wasn't the only one to die. Twenty-eight hundred of the colonists died in sixty days, just under half the population of Newmanhome, before the frantic biologists discovered—not a cure, no, but an antifungal agent that, sopped onto a gauze mask, killed the spores before they could get into the respiratory system. The agent smelled like rotting manure, but that was a small enough price to pay for the survival of human life on New-manhome.

It wasn't just human life that was at risk. All the carefully bred and preserved livestock—fish excepted, actually, but all the sheep, goats, cattle, dogs, horses, deer—had to be forcibly fitted with halters and masks of their own. They all fought it, but they survived—

All but the cats.

No one could make a cat leave a wet gauze mask in place over its mouth and nose. They maintained the cat tradition to the extinction of the species: the cat who has no master and acknowledges no law but its own, even if it dies for it. Die they did.

When Viktor got back to his parents' home he pushed open the door and stopped.

The place reeked of stale beer and vomit. His father was sprawled beside the bed, snoring raggedly, impossible to wake. He had fouled himself, and there were stains of urine and vomit on bed and floor. He had taken his artificial leg off and lay with it clasped in his arms, like a beloved woman.

It was not the first time Viktor had seen his father drunk, but it was a long way the worst. Viktor would not have believed that he could have felt such hatred for the old man. He did not fear that his father was dying. He almost wished it were true. He set his kit bag down on the table, pushing aside empty bottles, and stood over the drunken man, listening objectively to the rattling, choking sounds of the snores.

You dirty old bastard, he thought.

A shadow from the doorway made him turn, and there was Billy Stockbridge peering in, his mother behind him.

Even at that moment Viktor felt a tingling shock in his groin at the sight of Marie-Claude. She had cut her hair short since the last time he had seen her, and there was a certain soft thickening of the flesh under her chin that he didn't remember seeing before. She was wearing a short, thin dress that did nothing to flatter her—the kind housewives put on to clean their kitchens—and she was carrying a bucket and a mop.

Even with the hideous antifungal mask, she was very beautiful.
"Viktor," she said, "I didn't know you were here. I'm sorry
about your mother."

"But we've got to get your dad to the hospital," Billy added.

"They've got more important things to do than looking after
drunks," Viktor said contemptuously—and was startled to see the
quick flare of anger that twisted Billy Stockbridge's face. But it was
his mother who spoke, already by Pal Sorricaine's side, lifting an
eyelid with her thumb, feeling his sweating forehead.

"Viktor. Your father isn't just drunk. He's got acute alcohol
poisoning. He could die. Help Billy get him to the hospital."

What Viktor would not have done for his father he could not
refuse Marie-Claude. He pulled a blanket off his parents' bed and
rolled the old man into it. Billy helped, glowering. The filth was
already staining the blanket as Viktor picked Pal Sorricaine up and
threw him over his shoulder. The filth didn't matter. It was only
one more insult added to the rancor that was already overflowing.
"I'll be back," he said, and carried his father out the door, Billy
Stockbridge trailing glowering behind.

When Viktor got back from getting his father admitted—only to a pallet on the ground, because all the beds were full
of the dying—Marie-Claude had thrown open the windows, scrubbed
up the worst of the filth, and cleared off the litter of bottles and
dirty clothes. She had even made a pot of tea. She poured a cup for
Viktor as he sat down.

She seemed pale, silent, drawn, abstracted. But all she said was,
"Is your father going to be all right?"

Viktor shrugged. "They're treating him, anyway." Actually,
even the doctor who finally came to see them had had no hesitation
about admitting Pal Sorricaine, once he had felt his pulse. Lying on
the ground and wholly unaware, the snoring man had been washed,
bedded, and stuck with IVs to replenish his lost liquids and electro-
lytes before Viktor left. The doctor said it would be at least forty-
eight hours before Pal would be able to go home. (Strange that even
yet people said "forty-eight hours," as though it were a natural unit
of time.) "Billy wanted to stay with him a while," Viktor added.

Marie-Claude nodded in that weary, absent way, as though she were thinking about something else entirely—though with the antifungal mask covering most of her face there wasn't much he could tell about what she was thinking, anyway. "Billy is very fond of your father," she mentioned.

Viktor gaped at her. "For God's sake, why?"

She didn't seem surprised at the question. "Why shouldn't he be? Pal is a good man, Viktor. You're too hard on him. He's had trouble adjusting, and there's his leg, and then your mother's sickness . . ." She said it all flatly, like a comment on the weather. Her voice was as pallid as what he could see of her face.

There was something wrong with Marie-Claude. For a moment the natural fear flashed though his mind—*the sickness?*—but no, he reassured himself, it couldn't be that. The sick ones were unmistakable, the gasping struggle for air, the cyanosed complexion. None of that applied to Marie-Claude. Still, Viktor looked at her with concern.

"Are you all right?" he demanded.

She looked at him questioningly and then seemed to shake herself. She poured more tea for him, thoughtfully. "Nobody's all right now, are they? But I'll be fine." Then, without warning, she said, "Viktor. Why don't you marry Theresa McGann?"

There was a swallow of tea halfway down Viktor's throat. He gagged. "You talk like my mother," he got out, strangling.

"Then your mother talks sense to you. I'll speak for her, since she can't anymore. You ought to have a real family, not just leave a puppy here and there. Marry Theresa. Or somebody. Why not?"

"Because," he said—boldly, bitterly, "the only woman I want to marry will go to bed with anybody on Newmanhome, except me."

She looked at him in puzzlement.

Then, for the first time, he saw a crinkling at the corners of the eyes, just visible above the mask. She was almost smiling. She put her hand on his. "Dear, dear Viktor," she said with affection. "Do you have any idea how grand you've been for my morale, all these years?"

He snatched his hand away. "Damn you, don't *patronize* me!" he grated.

"I don't mean to," she said apologetically. She studied him thoughtfully for a moment. Then she closed her eyes, as though in resignation. When she opened them again she said, "Have you finished your tea? Then let's close the windows and lock the door. I'm a lot too old to marry you, Viktor. I'm too old for an affair with you, too, I mean for any long time. But if you really want us to make love—once—well, why not?"

Viktor didn't see Marie-Claude after that, not for a long time. For the whole next day he went around grinning to himself. He was just about the only person in the colony smiling that day. People looked at him with surprise and sometimes with anger. He was reliving every moment and touch of that wonderful copulation. Marie-Claude in bed was what he had been dreaming of since before even puberty, and the reality was not in any way a letdown. They had been careful with each other's gauze masks, kissing through them, with all their foul smell and taste, and in every other way they had been wild. She had responded to him with gasped and choked cries, and at the end, when she sobbed and cried out, she had dissolved into shaking tears.

Viktor was startled and worried and did not, just then, know why.

She didn't show up at the mass funerals when his mother, with forty-two others, was being put under the ground. (Even there Viktor could hardly help an invisible smile now and then, even while he cried.) That was just as well. There was a nasty—and completely unexpected—quarrel at the grave site. It concerned religion, of all things. The Moslems didn't want to have their dead buried with the unbelievers, and once the Moslems made that clear, some of the other sects began muttering, too. It took all of Captain Bu's bellowing to restore order. Then a rancorous emergency town meeting was called that night, people shouting each other through tears and gauze masks, before it was decided that future burials could be segregated by religion.

It was there that Freddy Stockbridge, coming up to offer a prayer for his mother for him, filled in the missing piece in the puzzle of Marie-Claude. Yes, she had been strangely abstracted that day. Her

own husband, that forgotten man, the man who, when Viktor remembered his existence at all, he had thought of with the contemptuous pity of the seducer for the cuckold—that man had himself
died only hours before Amelia Sorricaine-Memel.

Viktor had bedded the widow before the man's corpse was cold.

But Marie-Claude was true to her word. She didn't turn to Viktor to take her dead husband's place. She boarded a ship for Archipelago West as soon as one sailed. Months later Viktor heard that
she was marrying a molecular biologist bereft at the same time as
herself.

When Pal Sorricaine got out of the hospital he was
shaky and, beyond the gauze face mask, pale. He confronted his son
steadily enough, though. "I just couldn't handle it, Viktor," he said.

Viktor turned away from cleaning the house—the smaller children were back in their home again, and he had been the only one
to take care of them. He said to his father, just as steadily, "That's
crap. You've been a drunk for years. You've just been getting worse,
that's all."

His father flinched. "That's what I meant, Viktor. Your mother
dying was just the last straw. I haven't been able to handle my life
for a long time now. Being here—missing a leg—so much to do, and
not much that I'm able to do to help. Vik, I just don't feel like I've
got a *place* here."

Viktor studied his father. He had never seen him look so—was
the right word "defeated"? No, the word that fit best was "pointless." Pal Sorricaine did not seem to have any point or purpose to
his life.

Viktor lifted the lid of the stewpot and sniffed. Dinner could be
served when Edwina came back with the littler kids; it was ready
now. "Eat something," he growled, putting a plate in front of his
father. The man accepted instruction obediently, pushing his mask
aside for each spoonful of broth and meat and potatoes. Pal Sorricaine didn't seem to want to prolong the conversation. He simply
did as he was told, without comment.

To his son, that was scary. "But you've got your class," Viktor
said abruptly.

Pal shook his head, going on eating. "There's nothing left for me to teach them, Vik."

"But your observatory—"

"Viktor," his father said patiently, "every one of those kids can run the telescope as well as I can. Billy can run it better. He's been the one who's been commanding the *Mayflower* instruments for months." He began to look interested for the first time. "Billy's done a series of observations of Nebo that would make a doctoral dissertation for him back on Earth, Viktor. There are some pretty funny levels of high-energy radiation coming from around there— nothing I would have expected. Nothing I can account for, and, Viktor, I don't even know where to begin to look anymore. But Bill keeps working at it. He's very bright. You'd be interested in that, Vik; I'll ask Bill to show you. He's always eager to oblige. You know, he sort of took care of me when I was, well, under the weather."

"Eat your dinner," Viktor commanded sourly. He didn't want, for a whole complex of reasons, to hear any more about the virtues of Billy Stockbridge.

Because of the epidemic everything was delayed, disorganized, generally screwed up. Viktor's ship had unloaded in record time, but the cargo of machines and chemicals for the return trip was late. The ship's sailing was put off.

The day before it finally sailed Viktor looked up Reesa McGann. She had their son with them, as well as her toddler by Jake Lundy. As a matter of fact, there were twenty-two infants under her care, because she was trying her luck with a day-care job. "What happened to space piloting?" he asked.

She didn't even smile. It wasn't much of a joke; she didn't have to say that obviously there weren't going to be any space-piloting jobs around now because the epidemic had pushed everything back to the edge of bare survival.

Then, without at all planning it, he found himself saying, "Reesa, my mother told me just before she died that I ought to marry you. So did—someone else."

"Who else?" she asked curiously. When he didn't answer, she said, "They're right, of course. You ought to."

He blinked at her, surprised and amused. "Do you want me to?"

She thought that over for a moment while she propped a bottle for one of the younger ones under her care. Then she said, "Yes, no, and maybe. Yes, first: Screwing at random and making babies with different people is kind of kid stuff. There's a time to settle down, and both you and I are right about at that time. Then, no: You've been horny for Marie-Claude Petkin since you were in diapers yourself. There's no point thinking about marrying you until you get her off your mind."

Viktor flushed, half angry, half laughing. She stopped there. "You didn't tell me what the maybe was," he protested.

"Well, isn't that obvious? If you ever get over having the hots for Marie-Claude, then maybe I'll still be around. Give me a call if you do, okay?"

He grinned at her—unwilling to take the discussion seriously, trying to keep it light and jocular. "I have to be the one who calls? You won't call me?"

"Viktor," she said earnestly, "I've *been* calling you since we were both school kids. I just keep getting a busy signal."

It turned out Viktor was going to another funeral—Alice's older child had died, along with all those thousands, and so had her mother—and so, as it also turned out, he wasn't going to have a ready-made bunkmate that trip. Alice was going to stay home with Shan for a while.

The funeral was worse than the one the day before. The town meeting had settled very little when it had authorized separate burials for Moslems. Kittamur Haradi was a Moslem, all right, but he was a *Sunni*. He didn't want his late wife buried with the Shi'ites. So a separate, smaller ditch was dug for the second Moslem sect.

And then the community's chief working rabbi (there were only two) got the segregationist fever, declaring that Jewish burials should be in a place of their own, where a star of David could be erected.

Viktor couldn't see the sense of it. When the bodies were laid into their great, shallow pits they all looked much the same. At least, he thought, with what remained of his identification as a Christian who hadn't been to a service since the landing, the Catholics and all the Protestants, even the Quakers and Unitarians, had all raised no objection to a common grave for their dead.

Not then, anyway.

That night he let his father persuade him to come and see what Billy Stockbridge had been doing. It wasn't just that he thought it might be interesting, although he did; it was a way of keeping some sort of contact with the old man. Not making up, exactly. But not building the wall between them any higher, at least.

They didn't go to the observatory, they went to the little cubicle under the radio dish that Pal Sorricaine had begged for an astronomy center. But Billy wasn't there. "I don't know where he could have got to," Pal Sorricaine said, frowning. "Everything's so mixed up with all the deaths—I haven't really talked to him for weeks. Well, let's see what he's got. I think that's his current program that he left up. Let me take a look . . ."

He stumped over to the console and sat down to study the screen, first cursorily, then frowning.

"But this isn't Nebo," he said, scratching absently at his gauze mask with one hand, rubbing his stump with the other. "Look at this. Bill's been doing stellar spectrometry—lots of it. See here, he's been taking observations on a bunch of bright stars; here's Betelgeuse, here's Fomalhaut, here's— Wait a minute," he said suddenly. He scowled at the screen. "Look at that."

Viktor looked obediently, trying to remember what he knew about stellar spectra. What he mostly remembered was that you couldn't tell much just by glancing at them; you needed careful comparisons against standards to see anything meaningful. "Look at what?" he asked.

"The absorption lines are all mixed up," Pal Sorricaine complained. "Look at the hydrogen alphas! See, Bill's got two sets of spectra for each star, one's recent, the other's a year or two ago. Their frequency shifted! Not much; it could even be an instrument screwup . . ." He stared at the screen, gnawing his lip under the mask. Then he said, "No. Bill's a better observer than that. He wouldn't get them all wrong. Something systematic is going on."

Viktor said, not quite understanding, "Are all the stars screwed up?"

"No! Look at this nearby bunch—stars within five or six light-years. They haven't changed. But these more distant ones— But that's impossible!" he cried angrily.

"What's impossible?"

"*Look*, damn it! Here, everything in this direction is red-shifted— all these others are blued. And that couldn't happen, Viktor, not possibly. Unless—"

"Come on, Dad! Unless what?" Viktor demanded, angry and uneasy.

Pal Sorricaine shook his head. "Let's find Billy," he growled, and Viktor heard with alarm the worry in his father's voice.

They didn't find Billy Stockbridge. Billy found them. He was coming up the hill, very fast, when he saw them coming down. When Pal Sorricaine started his angry questioning, Billy just shook his head. "Come into the observatory," he said. "Let me show you."

And inside the little observers' room he sat down at the keypad without another word. "This is an old star photograph," he explained over his shoulder as a sky view appeared on the screen, a negative, black dots on a white background. "Now I'm superimposing one I just took." The number of stars suddenly doubled and then began to move about as Billy worked over the keypad. "Just a moment till I get them registered . . ." The stars abruptly coalesced, as far as Viktor could see, but Billy was busy setting up another program.

Then he leaned back as the image began to pulse, like a fast heartbeat, twice a second. "Now look," he ordered.

Viktor glanced at his father, silently staring at the screen with his brows screwed together in perplexity—or worry? "I am looking," Viktor said, annoyed. "I don't see anything, but—hey! Isn't that one jumping back and forth? And that one, too—and that over there . . ."

"My God," Pal Sorricaine said softly.

Billy nodded grimly. "In this segment of the sky I've found twenty-three stars that show movement on the blink comparator. As soon as I made those Doppler measurements I had to make an optical observation. The Dopplers were right. Look again, Viktor. Look at the ones on the edges of the screen. This one—" He put a finger on a large dot near the left edge. "—and this little one over here on the right. Wait a minute, I'll slow the blinks down."

And when he did, Viktor saw that as the dot on the left jumped left, the dot on the right jumped right. "They're all moving away from the middle!" he cried. And then, on second thought, "Or toward it?"

"Away is right," Billy told him soberly. "That's why I picked this frame to show you. The ones we see moving are the nearest stars—some of them, anyway—the ones with the largest parallax. They're all in motion."

Viktor stared at him in silent consternation. "But they can't be!"

And from behind him his father said, "You're right, Viktor. They're not moving. But somehow or other—and goddam rapidly, too—all of a sudden *we* are!"

CHAPTER 7

It was a pity that Pal Sorricaine never had any possible chance of meeting Wan-To, because of course Wan-To could have explained it all to him. Wan-To might even have been happy to discuss it, because he was pleased with his work.

After Wan-To, observing through his Einstein-Rosen-Podolsky pair, saw the first batch of stars begin to pick up speed, he paused to enjoy the spectacle. It was good work, he thought contentedly. It was also a very smart ruse de guerre. He was sure that if he had seen this happening, without warning, his first reaction would have been to zap every one of those stars. Immediately, without second thought. They were definitely unnatural.

His sibs were bound to do the same. They might try to figure out just what was causing it, but they were very unlikely to have any ERP setups near enough for quick study, and they wouldn't find his matter doppel. It would make little difference if they did. They would assume one of those stars held a fleeing Wan-To—or somebody—and they would zap them.

It was such a good ploy that he did it again. If it was a good strategy to set up one false target it would be even better to set up several.

That was no problem for him, but it was a somewhat boring prospect. However, he didn't have to do it *himself.* Anything that

Wan-To had ever done once he never had to do a second time, unless he wanted to for the fun of it—not when he could so easily make a copy of enough of himself to do the job. So he duplicated those parts of himself that were needed for that task, as a small "doppel" inside his own star, and instructed it to repeat the process with a few other groups of stars. The more the better, when it came to confusing his opponents; let them have a lot of things to worry about. Anyway, it was very little trouble. Making such copies of parts of himself was no harder for Wan-To than copying a computer file was for a human being. He didn't even bother to oversee his copy's work, so he didn't notice that one of the groups of stars included the star that held the planets that included the world humans had come to call Newmanhome.

Of course, it wouldn't have mattered to Wan-To if he had.

Then, for the first time in quite a while, Wan-To felt sufficiently at ease to think about relaxing for a bit. He wondered what was happening with his neighbors, and he was beginning to feel a little lonesome.

Not much had changed in his immediate vicinity. If a human astronomer had been sitting on the surface of Wan-To's G-3 star and gazing at the heavens—assuming the human could somehow have avoided flashing into a wisp of ions long enough to gaze at anything at all—he would have seen little change. He would have observed that most of the stars in Wan-To's sky were not perceptibly moving or changing color. For that matter, to the human observer it would have appeared that hardly any of them had flared into "Sorricaine-Mtiga objects," as so many had in fact been doing for the past few dozen Earth years; the human observer would have been woefully behind the news.

The reason that was so was that the human eye doesn't see anything but light. And light is bound by its limiting velocity of 186,000 miles a second. That's pretty slow—far too *dreadfully* slow for Wan-To's kind. Things were happening, all right, but a human observer would have had to wait a long time to find out what they were.

Wan-To, with his ERP pairs and his tachyons, was a lot better off, observationally speaking. He knew almost instantly what was happening many hundreds of light-years away. For example, he knew that nearly eighty stars had in fact been zapped by someone. He still didn't know who the someone was—well, the someones. He knew that more than one someone was involved, if only because he had zapped six of the stars himself, laying down a little probing fire of his own. He also knew that one or two of those random shots had come uncomfortably close to his own G-3, though he was pretty sure that was just an accident. He didn't guess at that. It was too important; he worked it out carefully. Wan-To had his own equivalent of chi-squared analysis, and the most rigorous interpretation of the positions of the flared stars he could make showed a highly random distribution.

The other thing Wan-To didn't know was whether anybody had been hit.

Wan-To did care about that, after his fashion. True, at least some of his neighbors seemed to be trying to kill him. But they were the only neighbors he had—not to mention that, in fact, they were in some sense his own flesh and blood.

Then he heard a signal he hadn't heard in some time. Someone was calling him.

When one of Wan-To's kind wanted to talk to another he simply activated the appropriate Einstein-Rosen-Podolsky cluster and announced his name—that is, he made the sound that passed for a name, among the plasma minds like Wan-To. They didn't make real sounds, of course. "Sound" is a matter of vibrations in the air, and certainly there was no gaseous atmosphere where any of them lived. But even in the interior of a star there are what are called acoustic phenomena—you might as well call them sounds, though no human ear could have heard them—and each one of Wan-To's siblings made a characteristic sound. There was Haigh-tik, who was actually (in a sense) Wan-To's first-born, and took after Wan-To a lot—friendly, deceitful, and very, very smart. There was Gorrrk (it was a sound rather like the cooing of a basso-profundo pigeon), and Hghumm (guttural white noise, like a cold engine finally starting), and poor, defective Wan-Wan-Wan, the dumbest of the lot, whose "name" was a little like the sound of a motorcyclist gunning his motor at a red light. Nobody paid much attention to Wan-Wan-Wan. Wan-To had made him late in his "parenthood," when he had become very cautious about how much of his own powers he passed on to his progeny, and poor Wan-Wan-Wan was pretty close to an idiot. There were eleven of them, all told, Wan-To himself included, and seven of them had tried to call him while he was busy setting his stars in motion.

Wan-To considered that fact. Very likely one (or more) of the seven was the one who was trying to kill him, calling to see if he was still alive.

But there were the three silent others to think about. They hadn't called. That might be even more significant. Perhaps they had been zapped; or perhaps they were the ones who were doing the zapping, lying low in the hope that the others would think they were gone.

What a pity it was, Wan-To thought ruefully, that it should always come to this in the end.

Restlessly he checked his sensors. Everything was going as planned. Five separate groups of stars, the smallest with only half a dozen members, the largest with well over a hundred, were already accelerating out of their positions in the sky, in random directions. (Let Haigh-tik try to figure *that* out, Wan-To thought gleefully.) They would be going pretty fast before long; his constructs tapped the energy of the stars themselves to drive them, converting their interior particles in gravitons to create attractors, even bending the curvature of space around them to isolate them and speed things up.

He wondered if Haigh-tik and the others would really assume that Wan-To himself was in one of those clusters, running away. That would be a useful deception—if it worked—but Haigh-tik in particular was too much like Wan-To himself to be fooled very long.

No, Wan-To thought regretfully, deception wouldn't work very long between Haigh-tik and himself. Sooner or later one of them would have to destroy the other.

It was a great pity, he told himself soberly. Then, for something to do, he sent out the pulses that would turn three more possible targets into seminovae.

It would have been so nice if they could all have lived together in peace . . .

But, things being as they were, he had to protect himself. Even if it meant blowing up every star in the galaxy but his own.

CHAPTER 8

When the engineers from the message center came after Pal Sorricaine to see if he could explain what was going wrong with their incoming transmissions from the third interstellar ship, the old man looked at them uncomprehendingly for a moment. Then he slapped his forehead and bugled like a hound. "Holy sanctified *Jesus*," he moaned. "I should've *guessed!*"

He hadn't, though. Neither had anyone else. With all the commotion and speculation and uneasy, scared excitement that the movements of the nearby stars had caused, no one had stopped to think that the arrival of the interstellar ship, *New Argosy*, might also be affected.

Affected it was.

True, the messages that were still coming in from *New Argosy* were normal enough, even cheerful. The ship was still in its deceleration phase, still a long way out. Therefore it would be the better part of a year before the comm center on Newmanhome would receive anything the third ship had to say about the sudden decision of a dozen stars and their orbiting bodies to begin running away.

The engineers hadn't expected to hear anything like that. They had expected that the incomings from *Argosy* would keep on their frequency lock, as they were supposed to do. The incoming messages didn't oblige.

They, too, were Doppler-shifted.

Nobody wanted to believe the probable explanation for that, but the mislock was systematic and increasing. They couldn't doubt it any more.

New Argosy was not a part of the volume of space that was theirs. Newmanhome was on the move. *Argosy* was not moving with it.

The scary part, the part that frizzled the nerves of the colonists, was that *New Argosy* didn't yet know what was happening. Their transmissions reported everything on course, no troubles at all, not even any more of those pesky, worrying flare stars—landfall at Newmanhome expected right on time!

But that was now impossible, since Newmanhome had become a moving target.

That was a personal matter for every colonist. *New Argosy* wasn't a mere astronomical object. It was something every one of them was waiting for. It was Santa Claus's bag, laden with gifts. *New Argosy* held *people*—more people than either of the first two ships had carried, a passenger list of three thousand more corpsicles, intended to be thawed out to join the first colonists on Newmanhome—many of them friends, colleagues, even relatives of those already there.

It also held *supplies.*

It was crammed full of things that had not been high enough priority to go into either *Ark* or *Mayflower*, but that the colonists wanted very much, all the same. It held grand pianos and violins, tubas and trumpets; it held a thousand new strains of flowering plants and about fifteen hundred species of birds, beasts, and arthropods that Newmanhome would never see without it. It held the wonderful solar-power satellite that was their only chance of making more antimatter to replenish the dwindling stores in orbit. It held the three small spacecraft that they could use to explore their system. Most of all, it held hope. What *New Argosy* contained was the promise of a future—the promise that the colonists on Newmanhome were not finally, *totally*, cut off from the Earth that had borne them . . .

And it was lost.

The colonists had to have a town meeting to talk it over. The meeting couldn't decide anything, of course—there weren't any useful decisions they could make. The meeting was just so that everyone could hear and say everything that could be said—and then, with the catharsis of getting all that out of their systems, get back to their real world—meaning Newmanhome, the only world they had left.

Although the plague had decimated Newmanhome's population, there were 3,300 people still alive. The only ones over the age of four not present there were the work crews in orbit, at sea, or in the small parties on South Continent and the other somewhat inhabited parts of the planet. Twenty-six hundred people gathered on the hill outside the town, with the loudspeakers relaying what was said to the fringes of the crowd.

They had set up a committee of twelve to put all the information together and make some kind of a report. Pal Sorricaine was on it, of course. So was Billy Stockbridge, and sick old Frances Mtiga (flown back specially from West Archipelago), and old (but far from sick or feeble) Captain Bu Wengzha. As soon as the committee had finished saying what everyone already knew, hands began to go up.

"If we can see that they're out of position, why can't the people on *Argosy?*" someone asked.

Pal Sorricaine stood up, tottering on his artificial leg; he hadn't been doing much drinking, in all the excitement, but he was showing signs of wear. "By now they probably can. Remember, they're still almost a light-year away. The messages we're getting from them were sent nearly two Newmanhome years ago."

Another hand, a woman from Delta: "But we notified them about what was going on, didn't we?"

"Of course we did!" Captain Bu replied. "But they haven't had time to receive the message yet. The speed of light is the same in all directions." He turned to the rest of the committee behind him, where Billy Stockbridge had said something. "What is it, Billy?"

Billy pointed. "It's my brother. He's busting to ask something."

There was Freddy Stockbridge in the front row, conspicuous in clerical garb; he had been studying for the priesthood long enough and, for lack of a handy pope or cardinal, had finally appointed himself ordained. He grabbed one of the roving microphones from an usher and shouted into it. "Can you tell us what is going on, really?"

Pal Sorricaine shrugged. "We've told you everything we can," he said. "The data is clear. Relative to the rest of the galaxy, our little local group is moving—and accelerating. It looks like some other groups are beginning to move in a different direction, too, but we're not as sure of that. As to *why* all this is happening—God knows."

And Freddy Stockbridge said strongly, "Yes, that's right. We don't know. But He does."

Viktor walked Reesa home from the meeting. She paused outside her house and gazed up at the stars. "They don't look any different to me," she said.

Viktor squinted up. "I can't see colors in stars most of the time anyway," he confessed. "They all look about alike, just bright spots. Anyway, we couldn't really tell the difference with the naked eye."

She shivered, although the night, like almost every Newman-home night, was muggily warm. "Let's tuck the kids in," she said.

It didn't take long. Viktor found himself attracted in a way that he wasn't used to by the sight of Reesa cuddling the baby, whispering to him, changing his diaper, and feeding him. The feeling wasn't sexual. He didn't *think* it was sexual, at least, although that was certainly there, too. It was just, well, appealing. "Taking care of kids is a lot of work," he said sympathetically when they were sitting outside again.

"It is for one person," she said—rather sharply, he thought. It made him suddenly uncomfortable.

"Well, if you want," he said awkwardly, "I guess I could take the baby now and then, I mean when I'm in port."

She shook her head. "That's no good for him. He needs a home. I think what I need is a husband."

Now Viktor was definitely ill at ease, not to say alarmed. "Husband? Really? Would you want to, uh, I mean, would you be satisfied to just make love to one guy for the rest of your life?"

"As in marriage?" She thought that over seriously for a moment, then turned and faced him squarely. "Is matrimonial fidelity important to you, Viktor?"

He was beginning to feel trapped. "I—" He hesitated, pondering what he was saying, and what it might mean. "I think so," he said at last.

"Well, I probably could," Reesa said. "Yes, I'm just about sure I could—if I were married, I mean."

It was quite true that they couldn't see any change in the color of the stars, not with the naked eye, but the changes were there nevertheless. In one direction starlight was blue-shifted, in the other red. And the shifts grew, week by week.

Pal Sorricaine had something to do now. He and Billy Stockbridge spent all their time poring over the spectrograms, checking every possible reference to anything that might bear on the subject in the datastores—coming up empty, but still driven to go on trying to figure out what the *hell* was happening to their little pocket of space.

The spectral shifts didn't affect the nearest of the stars; they had established that early on. There were about a dozen of those within a volume of space some six light-years across—including the burnt-out cinder of one of the old "Sorricaine-Mtiga" flares. Their spectrograms were unchanged. Newmanhome's own sun was nowhere near the center of that volume, but nearly on one edge—so Sorricaine was scathing in answering the colonists who (how superstition did feed on the unexpected!) muttered that it was their blasphemous temerity in colonizing across space that had somehow changed things.

No, it just had happened (somehow!) that a volume of space had disengaged itself from the rest of the galaxy. Either their little group of twelve stars and all their associated planets, moons, and orbiting junk was (somehow!) beginning to hurry in the general direction of the Virgo clusters . . . or the rest of the galaxy was (again somehow—no one could think of any mechanism that might make any of this happen) hurrying away from it.

Of course, all this was terrifying.

At least, it was terrifying if you let yourself think about it. It

was *impossible*. Fundamental natural law—law that was rock-solid at
the bottom of scientific knowledge, the elements of motion that had
been engraved in granite by Isaac Newton and confirmed by everybody since him—was simply being violated.

To think seriously about that was to realize that as a scientist
you knew nothing at all. Science was simply *wrong*.

But how could that be?

The people who lived on Newmanhome couldn't question *science*. Science was what had brought them there! They weren't Third
World peasants or stock-herders. They were chemists, engineers,
physicists, geneticists, mineralogists, agro-technicians, mathematicians, doctors, metallurgists—nearly every adult who had boarded
either of the two colony ships had had advanced degrees in some
scientific field, and every day they were earnestly passing on that
knowledge, and that mind-set, to their children.

The result was that there was a burning dichotomy in every
head on Newmanhome that simply could not be resolved.

The only way to survive it was not to think about it at all—as
long as they could manage that, anyway. After all, the rest of their
world was still behaving the way it should. True, there were still
those unexplained emissions from the scorched surface of the planet
Nebo, but Nebo was a long way away. On the surface of Newmanhome, in the orbiting hulks above it, everything stayed normal. The
crops flourished.

And, best news of all, the health teams finally found a micro-
organism that could flourish in the human system and destroy the
spores of the plague. So everyone's gauze masks came off.

But when the communications from *New Argosy* turned from
shock to panic, through forlorn hope to despairing realization that
it never would land on Newmanhome, because Newmanhome was
accelerating away from the ship faster than it could possibly hope
to catch up—then it all became very personal.

When Viktor and Reesa married at last—it was the 43d
of Spring in Colony Year 38—the bridal party was loud and happy
for the joyous occasion. But that night, out on their balcony for a
last sip of wine before they went to bed, Viktor gazed for a long

time at the stars. It was a clear night. They could see the spark that was *Mayflower* sliding across the southern horizon, on its umpty-thousandth orbit.

"Should we volunteer?" Viktor asked his bride.

She didn't have to ask him what he meant. She knew. The colony had at last considered itself strong enough to spare liquid-gas fuel for a rocket. Finally a new crew of volunteers would soon be going into space to relieve the weary orbiting crew, to let them after all these years come down and set foot on the planet they had crossed twenty-odd light-years of space to inhabit.

"Maybe next time. When the children are a little bigger," she said, her hand in his as they looked up. "Viktor? Do the stars look any different to you now?"

It was a question they went on asking each other. Viktor squinted thoughtfully at the constellations. He said at last, "I don't know. I don't think so."

Behind them little Yan came out on the balcony. His fingers were in his mouth, reaching with his other hand to clutch at Reesa's dress but with his eyes fixed on Viktor. Behind him his older half sister, Jake Lundy's daughter Tanya, was quietly playing. Yan wasn't used to seeing his parents together. He was hardly used to seeing Viktor at all, because, although Viktor had spent an hour or two, at least, with the child every time his ship was in port, Yan had seen more of a good many other men.

Viktor picked the boy up. Yan didn't resist, but he didn't let go of Reesa's skirt, either, rucking it up until, laughing, his mother pulled the little fingers loose.

"Why," Viktor said wonderingly to his son, "we're a family now, aren't we?"

Reesa studied his face. "Do you like being a family?" she asked—a serious questioner, wanting a trustworthy answer.

"Of course I do," Viktor said quickly, and then nodded twice to show he really meant it. "We're a *great* family. All of us," he added. "Yours and mine and ours—would you mind if we had Shan with us?"

"I wouldn't, but I think Alice wouldn't like it. Still, she's at sea a lot, and really she shouldn't be taking the boy along. He needs school." She stopped there, but in a way that suggested there was a sentence or two unsaid.

"What is it?" Viktor asked, puzzled.

She stroked Yan's small head. "I guess you aren't going to stop going to sea yourself," she said, not looking at him.

"No, why should I? It's my job, and—" Then a light broke over him. "Reesa, are you worried about me shipping out with Alice?"

"I'm not *worried*."

But she was certainly concerned. Viktor could see that clearly enough. "I suppose I could get a different ship," he offered, thinking that there were a lot of things involved in being a family that were going to take some getting used to.

"If you want to," she said.

He didn't say that the question was what *she* wanted; he had learned that much about being a family already. "That way I could be here when Alice was at sea some of the time, so it would make sense to have Shan with us," he pointed out.

"That would be good," she said, gazing at the stars. "Well, if you'll put Tanny back to bed—I've got to be a cow for the baby—I'll come in in a few minutes. We might as well consummate our marriage, again."

The life of a colony went on. When Viktor Sorricaine, honeymoon over, shipped out again for South Continent, he discovered some of the disadvantages of being a *family*. The ship's radio operator was an unattached young woman named Nureddin, and normally he would probably have expected to wind up in bed with her. Now it didn't seem right. By the time he got back to the colony he was gladder to see his wife than he had expected, even. She hadn't wasted any time. She was a quarter of a Newmanhome year pregnant by then, with a year and a bit still to go, her belly quite definitely rounded out, her movements a little clumsy—but not in bed.

If a person managed to put out of his mind some of the gnawing, unsettling questions about what the hell had *happened* to the outside universe, it was a pretty good time on Newmanhome. There were even some celebrations. Up in the hills over Homeport, in the growing complex by the geothermal power plant and the microwave rectennae, the big new cryonics freezers were completed at last. The first thing that meant was that now there was fuel for the long-idle landing craft, because the same gas-liquefying plants that kept the freezers cold could also manufacture liquid hydrogen and oxygen to fuel the little spacecraft.

That was a big plus—though Viktor had been disappointed to learn that he was not even on the shortlist of space pilots; there were too many others ahead of him. But it was a tempered joy, all the same. The freezers had not just been another job. They were a major philosophical commitment—no, damned near a *religious* commitment—to the future. They were built to last, and they were built *big*. They were mean to hold all the frozen specimens and tissue samples that were all the people on Newmanhome had left of horse-chestnut trees and ginkgos and aardvarks and Luna moths and salamanders. They were their best tie with old Earth, fully automatic, with power from the geothermal wells—also fully automatic—built to last a thousand years . . .

And now destined to remain largely empty for most of that time, because the great cargoes of frozen biological materials from *New Argosy* were never going to get there.

No wonder the celebration was short and not at all raucous.

There was other bad news, too. Ibtissam Khadek died that year, quite unexpectedly, still protesting that the colony should be investigating her grandfather's prize brown dwarf. Reesa's mother, Rosalind McGann, was having a bad time with her own health—no one seemed to be able to say what the problem was, exactly, except that it might be the long-delayed consequences of undetected internal "freezer burn."

And Pal Sorricaine had started drinking again.

Worse than that, Reesa told Viktor, he was making his own brew. There was plenty of native vegetation around, and it certainly fermented into alcohol readily enough, but it was stupid for anyone to drink it.

Viktor was alarmed. "What about the kids?" he asked worriedly.

"They're fine," Reesa said. "Edwina's quite a grown-up little lady now, you know. She and the boys are living with Sam and Sally Broad—they don't have any children of their own, though God knows they've tried hard enough." She hesitated. "Maybe you ought to go see them," she offered.

Viktor nodded. "I will," he said. "But first I'll talk to the old man. Not that I think he'll listen to me," he finished bitterly.

So Viktor went back to his parents' home early the next morning. His father was just getting up, and he listened to his son's fatherly advice without much patience. "What's the matter with you?" Viktor yelled at last. "Do you want to poison yourself? Don't you have anything to do with your life?"

Pal Sorricaine bent to tie his leg a little tighter. "It isn't that I don't have anything to do," he explained. "It's just that I don't know how to do the things I have to do. Nobody does. We're all stupid, Vik; we don't know what's going on. Not just about the fact that we're moving—Jesus, we don't even know what's happening on Nebo!"

"What about Nebo?" Viktor asked, distracted in spite of himself.

"I don't *know* what about Nebo! Have you seen any pictures of it lately? All those damned clouds! We can't see a thing now with the opticals."

"Well, clouds aren't so surprising," Viktor began.

"Don't you remember *anything*?" his father demanded angrily. "Nebo used to be bone-dry! Now—now I don't know where all that water vapor came from, and that's not the only thing. Something there is emitting a lot of high-energy radiation, and I don't know what it is, and I don't know why it's doing it."

"Does it have anything to do with, uh, with the fact that we're moving?"

"I don't know that, either! And did you see the new Doppler shifts? We're not only moving, we're *accelerating*." Pal looked wearier and more defeated than Viktor had ever seen him. "We're going to be getting up to a significant fraction of the speed of light soon, if this goes on. Do you know what that means?" he demanded.

"Why—" Viktor thought, then blinked as an idea came to him.

"Are you trying to tell me there might be relativistic effects? Will we be getting into time dilation, like on the *Mayflower* coming out here?"

"God knows!" his father cried triumphantly. "Certainly I don't! And I never will, because nobody *cares*." He licked his lips, avoiding Viktor's eyes. Then, defiantly, he got up and limped over to a cupboard to take out a bottle. As he poured himself a drink he said, "I can't help thinking there's a connection with Nebo. If I could get the goddamn town meeting to send a probe, we could find out something!" he grated. "But they don't want to spend the resources."

"That's a copout, Dad," Viktor said sternly. "I don't want to talk about spaceships, I want to talk about you. You're going to kill yourself if you don't leave that stuff alone."

His father grinned at him, his face gaunt and wolfish. "Get them to send a probe, and I'll stay sober and go on it," he promised.

"I can't do that. You know I can't."

"Then," his father said, "the next best thing you can do is mind your own business."

On Viktor's next voyage his family came along.

It was an experiment. Reesa was a qualified navigator herself, though somewhat rusty. Though the ship didn't need two navigators—it hardly needed one—there was always work for extra hands to do in supervising the rotor speed and double-checking the orbital position fixes against star-sighting . . . though, actually, when Reesa or Viktor took a sextant reading on a star they weren't as much thinking about whether their ship was in its proper place as whether the star was. Some of the parallax shifts were now detectable even with the sextant.

Alice Begstine had proved unexpectedly unwilling to turn Shan over to the newly married couple, so they left without him. They couldn't ship out together more than once or twice, they knew, because when the new baby came Reesa would want to stay on land for a season or so, at least. But it was worth trying, and as a matter of fact they all enjoyed it. Tanya was a touch seasick at first, but it was more psychological than real—Great Ocean behaved itself, as it usually did. The children roamed the ship. One of the crew was always glad to keep an eye on them and make sure Tanny spent her allotted hours at the ship's teaching machines. The baby was as happy on shipboard as anywhere else, and Reesa enjoyed the new experience. They basked in the sun; at South Continent they explored the hills and swam in the gentle surf. On the way back Viktor almost wished they could do it forever.

There was, of course, always in the back of their minds the worry about what the hell had happened to the universe.

It bothered even little Tanya, though mostly, of course, because she could see that the grown-ups were bothered by it. And when Viktor took his turn in tucking them in at night he was eager to do for Tanya what Pal had, so often, done for him. The stories he told her were about Earth, and the long voyage to Newmanhome, and the stars. On the last night before they landed he was standing with her on the deck outside the cook house where their dinner was simmering to completion, the rotors grumbling as they turned. Tanya squinted at the sunset they were watching and asked, "What makes the sun burn?"

"Don't look at it too long, Tanny," Viktor cautioned. "It's not good for your eyes. A lot of people had their sight damaged a few years ago, when everybody was—" He hesitated. He didn't want to finish the sentence: *When everybody was looking at the sun every few minutes, wondering if it was going to flare like so many of the other stars nearby, and burn them all up.* "When we were first on Newmanhome," he finished. "Now it's your bedtime."

"But what makes it burn anyway?" she persisted.

"It doesn't really *burn*, you know," he said. "Not like a fire burns. That's a chemical reaction. What the sun does is combine hydrogen atoms to make helium atoms."

Tanny said proudly, to show she understood. "You mean if I take some hydrogen out of the stove fuel tank, and—and what would I have to do then? To make that helium, I mean?"

"Well, you couldn't really. Not just like that. It takes a lot of energy to make protons—the proton is the heavy part of the hydrogen atom, the nucleus—to make protons stick together. They're positively charged, remember? And positive charges?"

"They push each other away," Tanny said with satisfaction.

"Exactly right, honey! So you need to *force* them into each other. That's hard to do. But inside a star like Earthsun, or our own sun—like any star, really—the star is so big that it squeezes and squeezes."

He hesitated, wondering how far it made sense to go in describing the CNO cycle to Tanya. But, gratifyingly, she seemed to be following every word. "So tell me, Daddy," she persisted.

He couldn't resist Jake Lundy's daughter when she called him that! "Well," he began, but looked up to see Reesa coming toward them, the baby in her arms, the unborn one making her belly stick out farther every day.

"It's almost dinnertime," she warned.

Viktor looked at his watch. "We've got a few minutes," he said. "I just put the vegetables on, but you can call the crew if you want to."

"Tell me first, Daddy," Tanya begged.

"Well," Viktor said, "there are some complications. I don't think we have time to explain them right now. But if you can make four protons stick together, and turn two of them into neutrons—you remember what a neutron is?"

Tanya said, careful of how she pronounced the hard words, "A neutron is a proton with an electron added."

"That's it. Then you have the nucleus of a helium atom. Two protons, two neutrons. Only, as it happens, the mass of the helium nucleus is a little less than the combined mass of four hydrogen nuclei. There's some mass left over—"

"I know!" Tanny cried. "*E* equals *m c* squared! The extra mass turns into energy!"

"Exactly," Viktor said with pleasure. "And that's what makes the sun burn. Now help me get dinner on the table."

As they reached the door she lifted her head. "Daddy? Will it ever stop?"

"You mean will the sun cool down? Not in our lifetimes," Viktor told her confidently, not knowing that he lied.

———————

So the voyage was absolutely perfect, right up until the end of it . . . but the end wasn't perfect.

It was horrible.

Probably Reesa should not have been trying to guide the grain nozzles into the holds while she had the baby in her arms. The dock operator was a new man; he couldn't get the nozzle into position; Reesa put the baby down to shove the recalcitrant nozzle.

She shoved too hard.

She lost her footing and tumbled. She only fell two or three meters, and it was onto the yielding grain—but that was enough. When Viktor frantically scrambled down after her she was moaning, and there was blood soaking into the top layers of grain.

They got her to the hospital in time to save the baby. It was was premature, of course, but a healthy young girl for all that; there was every chance the newborn would survive. And so would Reesa, but she would be a long time recovering.

Definitely, she would not be making the next voyage with her husband and the kids. When Reesa's mother came over, aching and complaining, she seemed to consider it all Viktor's fault, too. It was the first time he had thought of Roz McGann as a mother-in-law. He accepted all blame. "I shouldn't have let her do that," he admitted sadly. "Thank God she's going to be all right, anyway."

"God," Roz McGann sniffed. "What do you know about God?"

Viktor stared at the woman, feeling he had somehow missed the thread of the conversation. "What are you talking about?"

"I'm talking about God," she said firmly. "Why didn't you marry Reesa properly? In church? With a priest?"

Viktor blinked, astonished. "You mean with Freddy Stockbridge?"

"I mean *properly*. Why do you think we're having all these troubles, Viktor? We've turned away from religion. Now we're paying for it!"

Later on, walking away from the hospital in the moonless Newmanhome night, Viktor found himself perplexed. He knew, of course, that there had been a religious revival on Newmanhome—half a dozen of them, in fact. The Sunni Moslems and the Shi'ites hadn't stopped splintering when they broke into two groups; they schismed again over which way was East, and almost did it again over the calendar. (How could you set the time of that first sighting of the new moon that began Ramadan when there was no moon to sight?) The Baptists had refused to be ecumenical with the Unitarians; the Church of Rome had separated itself from Greek Orthodox and Episcopalian. Even Captain Bu had declared himself a born-again Christian, and every other soul on Newmanhome tragically doomed to eternal hellfire.

By the third year after the spectral shift there were twenty-eight separate religious establishments on Newmanhome, claiming fourteen hundred members—divided in everything, except in their unanimous distaste for the three thousand other colonists who belonged to no church at all.

When Viktor looked in on his father he found the old man sitting by himself in the doorway of his home, gazing at the sky—and drinking.

"Oh, *shit*," Viktor said, stopping short and scowling at his father.

His father looked up at him, unconcerned. "Have a drink," he said. "It isn't ropy vine, it's made out of potatoes. It won't kill you."

Viktor curtly refused the drink, but he sat down, watching his father with some puzzlement mixed in with the anger. The old man didn't really seem drunk. He seemed somber. Weary. Most of all he seemed abstracted, as though there were something on his mind that wouldn't go away. "Reesa's going to be all right, I think," Viktor volunteered—angrily, since Pal Sorricaine hadn't had the decency to ask.

His father nodded. "I know. I was at the hospital until they said she was out of danger. She's a good strong woman, Vik. You did a good thing when you married her."

Baffled, slightly mollified, too, Viktor said, "So you decided to come back here and get drunk to celebrate."

"Trying, anyway," Pal said cheerfully. "It isn't seeming to work."

"What *is* the matter with everybody?" Viktor exploded. "The whole town's going queer! I heard people fighting with each other over, for God's sake, whether there was one God or three! And nobody's got a smile on his face—"

"Do you know what day it is?"

"Hell, of course I do. It's the fifteenth of Winter, isn't it?"

"It's the day *New Argosy* was supposed to arrive," his father told him. "I wasn't the only one drinking last night. Everybody was feeling pretty lousy about it—only maybe I had more reason than most."

"Sure," Viktor said in disgust. "You've always got a reason. You can't figure out why the stars flare, you don't know what's happening on Nebo, you're all bent out of shape because of the spectral shifts—so you get drunk. Any reason's a good reason to get a load on, isn't it?"

"So I find it, yes," his father said comfortably.

"Oh, *hell*, Dad! What's the use of worrying about all those far-off things? Why can't you get yourself straight and live in the life we've got, instead of screwing yourself around about things a million kilometers away that really don't affect us here anyway?"

His father looked at him soberly and then poured himself another drink. "You don't know everything, Vik," he observed. "Do you know where Billy Stockbridge is?"

"Don't have a clue! Don't care. I'm talking about *you*."

"He's arranging for a town meeting tomorrow. We've got something to tell them, and I guess you'd say it really does affect us. We've been monitoring the insolation pretty carefully for about a month now, ever since Billy first saw something funny about it."

"What's funny?"

"I don't actually mean 'funny,'" his father said apologetically. "I'm afraid there isn't any fun in it at all. We decided not to say anything until we were absolutely sure; we didn't want everybody getting upset unless they absolutely had to—"

"Say anything about *what*, damn you?"

"About the insolation, Vik. It's dropping. The sun's radiating less heat and light every day. Pretty soon people will notice it. Pretty soon—"

He stopped and thought for a moment, then poured himself another drink.

"Pretty soon," he said, holding the glass up to look at it, "it's going to be getting cold around here."

CHAPTER 9

Although Wan-To was vastly more than any human, he did have some human traits—even some that some humans might have considered endearing. He took the same joys in a job well done as any human hobbyist.

So when he finished putting his star-moving project together, he took a little time to watch it run. It gave him pleasure to see how well his matter analogues had carried out their tasks. The star clusters he had selected were all in motion now, and picking up speed. Each of the stars involved was dimming slightly—naturally enough, as much of each star's energy was going into the manufacture of graviscalars rather than radiating away as light and heat. Each star carried with it its planets, moons, comets, and asteroids, all caught up in the graviscalar sweep. His five matter analogues were still there. He could talk to them and give them further instructions if he had any to give. But they had slowed to standby mode, waiting out the time until their program called on them to go into action again.

More than that, it was working! He saw with glee that his combative relatives had seen what he had wanted them to see and done just as he had planned for them to do. Of the five star groups Wan-To had sent on their way, two had already been zapped in toto by one or another of his colleagues, each single star torn apart. Two others were under attack. That amused Wan-To. Obviously some-

body had come to the desired conclusion that he was in one of those
fugitive stars, trying to make a getaway in that unlikely fashion.
Well, they would give that up by and by, he was sure. The systems
run by Doppels One and Four were now history, and those of
Doppels Three and Five were being hit—though not at all with the
first enthusiasm—and would no doubt soon be gone, as well.

The trouble was, he found that watching the project operate
was not nearly as interesting as making it in the first place—just like
any human hobbyist. Wan-To was beginning to feel bored.

And lonely.

When Wan-To couldn't stand the loneliness anymore,
the first one he called was Ftt. Ftt was a pretty safe opponent—if he
really was an opponent—because he wasn't all that powerful, or all
that smart. Wan-To had created him toward the end of his efforts
to make company for himself, by which time he had realized the
dangers of making exact copies. Of course, even the handicapped
ones might develop in ways he hadn't planned, but he didn't really
think there was much to fear from Ftt.

It didn't matter what he thought, in the event. There was no
answer from Ftt; not from him, and not from either of the other
two silent ones, either.

That gave Wan-To some pause. One of them, Pooketih, was
hardly more threatening than little Ftt. But the remaining one of
the silent group was Mromm, and he was something quite different.
Wan-To had made him second, right after he had made Haigh-tik,
and although he had begun to be cautious in how much of himself
he copied into his offspring, Mromm still had a lot of shrewdness
and powers not much less than Wan-To's own. Mromm was very
capable—almost as capable as Wan-To himself—of maintaining silence until he had a good target to aim at.

Wan-To was beginning to feel uneasy.

When he tried again it was to the dumbest and weakest of the
lot, Wan-Wan-Wan, and Wan-Wan-Wan didn't answer either. In his
case, Wan-To considered, it wasn't likely he was lying in wait.
Something had happened to him. Wan-Wan-Wan had tried calling
Wan-To, and if he didn't respond now the chances were very good

that Wan-Wan-Wan wasn't with them anymore. That angered Wan-To; who of his offspring would be mean enough to kill off poor Wan-Wan-Wan?

The answer was, any of them. Given a good reason, he would have done it himself.

Wan-To persevered—cautiously—and by and by he did get some responses.

But when he finished talking to the ones who responded, he knew very little more than before. Merrerret and Hghumm said they were shocked that anyone would do anything like *that*. So did Floom-eppit, Gorrrk, and Gghoom-ekki, but they added that they suspected Wan-To himself.

Of course, they all put their own individual personalities into what they said. They did have individual personalities. Wan-To had made them that way. He had randomized some of the traits he had given them—a sort of Monte Carlo process, familiar to Earthly mathematicians—and so Floom-eppit was a joker, Hghumm a tedious bore, Gorrrk, an unstoppable talker if you gave him the chance. It took Wan-To a long time to get rid of Gorrrk, and then he faced the one he was most worried about.

Haigh-tik was his first-born, and the one most like himself.

That didn't mean they were exactly the same. Even identical copies began to vary with time and the "chemistry" of the stars they inhabited; the dichotomy between nature and nurture was strong among Wan-To and his kind, just as on Earth. Wan-To was very cautious talking to Haigh-tik. After they had exchanged remarks on the flare stars (neither exactly accusing the other, but neither excluding the possibility, either), Haigh-tik offered:

"Have you noticed? Several groups of stars are moving."

"Oh, yes," Wan-To said smoothly. "I've been wondering what was going on."

"Yes," Haigh-tik said. There was silence for a moment, then he added, "All these things worry me. I'd hate it if we messed up this galaxy, too. I don't want to move. I really like it where I am."

"It's a nice star, then?" Wan-To asked, not missing a beat. "I know you like the big, hot ones."

"Why take a dwarf when you can have a giant?" Haigh-tik

responded, with the equivalent of a shrug. "They're much better. You have so much *space*. And so much *power*."

Wan-To gave the equivalent of a silent and unseen nod. He knew what Haigh-tik liked, all right. He had liked the same things himself, when he created Haigh-tik—before he had decided that moving to a fresh star every few million years, when the big, bright ones were bound to go unstable, was too much trouble. He offered, "But, tell me, Haigh-tik, are you sure you'll get out before it collapses? Those O types burn up all their hydrogen so fast, and then—"

"Who said anything about an O?" Haigh-tik sneered.

Wan-To's "heart" leaped with exultation, but he kept his tone level. "Any of the big, hot young ones—they can all trap you."

"Not this one," Haigh-tik boasted. "I've just moved into it; it's got a good long time yet. Longer," he added, in a tone that fell just short of being menacing, "than a lot of us are going to have, if all this sniping at each other doesn't stop."

As soon as they had "hung up," Wan-To, highly pleased, began a search of his star catalogue. What he was looking for was a star of the kind human astronomers called a "Wolf-Rayet"—even hotter and younger than an O—and the newest of that kind he could find.

Then, with a certain sentimental regret, he summoned his clouds of graviphotons and graviscalars and sent them swarming to the likeliest candidate. Poor Haigh-tik! But Wan-To was only doing what had to be done, he reassured himself.

If there was one thing that could frighten Wan-To it was the thought of his own extinction. Stars, galaxies, even the universe itself—they all had fixed lifetimes, and he could accept the loss of any of them with equanimity. If all of his comrades were blown up he could stand that, too—he could always hive off new sections of himself for company (being very careful about what powers the new ones had, this time).

He thought hard for a time about that unpleasant subject. Wan-To was a great student of astrophysics and cosmology. It wasn't an abstract science to him. It was the stuff his life was made of. He understood the physics of the great and small . . .

And he could foresee a time when things could begin to get quite unpleasant for him, even if he survived the present squabbles.

When that particular Wolf-Rayet star was history, Wan-To (metaphorically crossing his nonexistent "fingers") called Haigh-tik on the ERP communicator again. And was very disappointed when Haigh-tik answered.

Haigh-tik had lied to him about his star!

But Wan-To saw the humor of it, and was amused—yes, and a little proud of his first-born offspring, too.

And Pal Sorricaine got his wish. Earthly astronomers did, in fact, adopt the term "Sorricaine-Mtiga stars" to describe that class of anomalous objects . . . right up to the time when their own Sun became one.

CHAPTER 10

Quinn Sorricaine-McGann was not only the first "legitimate" child of Viktor and Reesa—they nicknamed her "Nab," for "Not a Bastard"—she was also the last. Most of Reesa made a complete recovery, but she could never have another child. But considering Newmanhome's prospective future as little Quinn was growing up, neither Reesa nor Viktor was sure they wanted another.

Newmanhome wasn't a paradise anymore. It was getting definitely colder. The growing season on South Continent had shortened, and that was the end of spring wheat and long-ripening soy. The uniform of the day had changed, even in the settlement: no more shorts and shirts all year around. It was sweaters and shoes, and if it had not been for the flood of hot geothermal water that came from the wells—more and more of them every year, as the colonists foresaw the increasing need for power as well as heat—their homes would have been chilly.

The skies at night were woefully changed. The stars had slid about the sky and changed color: In one direction they were definitely blue-white, in the other yellowish red, and in between there was a growing band of no stars at all, except for the handful that were traveling with them.

On Quinn's thirteenth birthday—she was then the equivalent of a healthy Earthly seven-year-old—her father was just returning from Christmas Island with a shipload of evacuees; the Archipelago wasn't fit for human beings anymore. He was anxious to be there for the birthday, but storms had delayed them. It was a nasty trip: high waves, three hundred refugees in space that really wasn't meant to hold more than a quarter of that, and most of them seasick most of the way. As he entered the harbor at Homeport snow was falling, and the whole city was covered in white.

He hurried to his house and found Quinn happily making a snowman, while the little girl's aunt, Edwina, stood by. Edwina was a grown-up young woman now, with a family of her own. They kissed, but Viktor was frowning. "I didn't expect to see you here," he said. After Edwina had married Billy Stockbridge, Pal's disciple, the two of them had emigrated to South Continent, where there was a need for workers in drilling geothermal wells.

"They closed the project down," Edwina said. "The way the weather's going, it wouldn't have been producing power in time to save any of the crops."

Viktor nodded soberly. South Continent had been the first part of Newmanhome's inhabited areas to feel the effects of the cooling sun. Winter came early. The vast farmlands were fertile as always, but when a killing frost came the farms died. "Where's Reesa?"

"Don't get too cold," Edwina called to Quinn and her own children, who nodded without looking up from their work. "Reesa? Oh, Jake came by for her a couple of hours ago. They're taking Father's refresher course; I expect Billy's there, too."

Viktor frowned. Of course, Jake Lundy had to be accorded some sort of status—would you call him a friend of the family? Well, of some parts of the family, since he was the father of one of Edwina's children, too. (The man was really excessively active, Viktor thought.) It was quite normal for him to come around to see his daughter, but Viktor hadn't know he was spending time with his daughter's mother again. "What refresher course?" he asked.

"Dad's course. The one he's giving on space piloting. No, not astrophysics this time; I said piloting. They're using the old trainers."

"For what?" Viktor demanded, astonished.

"What else could you use them for but practicing space piloting?" his sister asked witheringly. "Don't ask me, anyway. You'd know more about that sort of thing than I would, and it's just an idea of Dad's."

Her contemptuous tone made Viktor blink in surprise. Edwina had always been Daddy's girl. She had consistently taken Pal Sorricaine's side against Viktor—probably, Viktor believed, because she had been too little to be aware of what was going on when their mother died. He said, as tactfully as he could, "I thought you liked Dad's ideas—whatever this one is."

"It's not my business, is it?" she replied with a shrug. "I think the kids ought to come in now," she fretted. "Vik? We're going to have a birthday party for Quinn right at sundown—they ought to be back by then. But I'd really appreciate it if you could take the kids out of the way until then, so I can get things ready."

"Sure," Viktor said, still looking at her with that inquiring gaze.

She flushed and then said angrily, "Oh, what the hell. They can do what they want, but I don't have to like it. What's the point? What's happening is obviously Divine will!"

What Viktor really wanted to do was to find out what his father's "refresher course" was all about, but since it was Quinn's birthday, after all, that would have to wait. As a good father/uncle, he took Quinn and Edwina's three littler ones on a tour of his ship as she lay at dockside.

It was one of his better ideas. The children were thrilled. There were serious stinks in the passenger holds, where the work crews were doing their best to sluice them clean after the nasty voyage and only beginning to make a dent in the filth, but the bad smells only made the children giggle and complain. Then he took them down into the engine room, where the hydrogen turbines provided the force to spin the ship's rotors against the wind. That was a different kind of stink, oil and hot metal, and the big machines were very satisfying to look at for young children.

Viktor was having as good a time as the children were, but when he stopped to think he wasn't quite at ease. It wasn't so much that Reesa seemed to be getting unexpectedly friendly again with Jake Lundy—that was a minor irritation, sure, but Viktor wasn't really *jealous*. It wasn't even that the outlook for the colony was grim and getting worse; they had all had to factor that prospect into their lives long since. What was mostly on Viktor's mind was his younger sister, Edwina. It was getting obvious that Edwina was attracted to a new sort of cult that had grown up on Newmanhome. The cult wasn't exactly a religion. It wasn't any sort of conventional one, anyhow; it cut across the various sects. As far as Viktor could tell it was more mystical than religious: Its adherents seemed to believe that whatever had made the stars flare and then some of them move, and their own sun begin to dim, was, if not God, at least a supernatural power; and perhaps they shouldn't thwart it. Viktor knew it had made some stormy scenes in Edwina's marriage. Billy's point of view was that if they didn't thwart—whatever it was—they would all die; Edwina's seemed to be that if that was what the Divine wanted them to do, then that was all right, too.

It was not only the weather that was turning bad on Newmanhome. Everything else seemed to be going sour, too.

When he brought the kids back to Edwina's home Reesa was there before him, helping to set the table with paper favors. She wasn't alone. Billy, Pal Sorricaine, and Jake Lundy were in one corner of the living room, having a private drink. Reesa looked up and nodded to Viktor as he came in, but her attention went mostly to the children. "You go in and get cleaned up," she scolded her daughter. "You shouldn't be seeing any of this until it's ready, anyway." And then she lifted her lips to Viktor for a kiss.

It wasn't much of a kiss. He was aware of Jake Lundy gazing benignly at them and it made him uncomfortable. "Can I help?" he asked, as much to reproach the other men as to make a genuine offer of service.

"You already did by taking the kids off our hands," Reesa said absently, gazing around. "Oh, the presents!" she said, remembering. "I'll go home to get them. Take your coat off, Viktor. Billy'll give you a drink if you want it."

The drink was applejack with apple juice. When Viktor had one he looked challengingly at his father. Pal Sorricaine shook his head.

"Just the juice, Vik," he said, holding up his glass. "Taste it if you want to, but I can't afford to drink now. There's too much to do."

"What, exactly?" Viktor asked. "What's this about giving refresher courses in space navigation? Do you still think they'll let you take a ship to Nebo?"

"They should," his father told him seriously. "There's still anomalous radiation coming from there, and I'm positive it has something to do with what's happened—it started when everything else started, and that's no coincidence."

He paused to light a thin cigar. "But they won't, of course," he finished. He didn't have to say why; the subject had been debated at length. Most of the colonists thought it was a waste of scarce resources—*New Mayflower* couldn't be used, because it was their source of microwave energy, and even *New Ark* might be needed for something else, sometime. And a lot of the rest were filled with that silly antiscience feeling that had been growing—the "Divine will" people, like Edwina.

"What's going to happen," Billy Stockbridge said, "is that we're going to get some new fuel for the microwave generators. *Mayflower*'s antimatter is running out. We can't get along without the microwave power."

"But we're digging more geothermal shafts," Viktor objected.

Billy shrugged. "Maybe when all the shafts are down and the generators are installed we won't need microwave anymore, but that's years away. So we're going to cannibalize *Ark*." Viktor blinked at him uncomprehendingly. "For fuel," Billy explained. "*New Ark* still has some residual antimatter left over from its trip. We can tow *Ark* to meet *Mayflower* in orbit and transfer its fuel to add to *Mayflower*'s."

"Holy shit," Viktor said, his glass forgotten in his hand. But when he thought about it, it made sense, if one didn't mind taking risks. Certainly transferring the reserve fuel would be hard, dangerous work. They would be handling *Ark*'s highly lethal, extraordinarily touchy remaining antimatter store in ways that had never been intended—but if the project worked it would give Homeport extra years of life, even if the sun continued to cool.

He stared at his father. "Is that really going to happen?"

Pal Sorricaine nodded. "The project has already been approved.

We're making more oxy-hydrogen fuel for the old shuttle right now, and the ship's still operational. Of course, it hasn't been used for years, since the last crew rotation—"

Viktor didn't let him finish. "I want to go along," he declared.

"I thought you would," his father said mildly. "So do Captain Bu and Captain Rodericks—" New Ark's original commander on the long-ago voyage from Earth "—and, naturally, Billy and Jake and Reesa. But we'll need at least twenty volunteers. We'll be there at least six months, and then—"

"And then what?" Viktor demanded.

His father looked at him speculatively. Jake and Billy kept their eyes carefully averted. "And then," his father said, "maybe we can get around to other important things. Now here comes Reesa, so let's get this party started. Billy? Can you play "Happy Birthday" on your guitar?"

The launch was scary and bruising, but it got them there. Then the hard work started.

It was the first time in more than thirty Newmanhome years that Viktor had been inside New Mayflower. Muscles used to planet living had forgotten the skills of operating in microgravity. He bashed himself a dozen times against walls and ceilings before he learned to control his movements.

In the rush of landing, the colonists had not left a tidy ship, and the skeleton crews that had remained aboard to care for the MHD generators hadn't bothered to waste much time in cleaning up. Trash was everywhere outside the tiny space the crews had occupied. Broken bits of furnishings, discarded papers. Spoiled food. Even, in the freezer section, a dead horse, long mummified but still direly stinking if you came too close. The shuttle left a dozen of its crew there to start preparing Mayflower's fuel systems for replenishing. Then Viktor and fourteen others pushed off for the slow orbital drift around to Ark.

Down below, Newmanhome was spread out for them to see. It wasn't blue anymore. Most of it was white, and not all the white was cloud tops. The oceans nearest the pole had already begun to freeze over. Some mountain lakes were now glaciers, and there were immense storms over most of Great Ocean. Viktor and Reesa gazed down at the cloud tops where Homeport seemed to be in the process of being battered by another winter storm. The town had already begun digging in—it was easier to keep warm underground than in the vicious winds of the surface.

"I hope Edwina's keeping the kids covered up," Reesa murmured.

From behind them, Jake Lundy said comfortingly, "She's a good mother, Reesa, even if she's getting some strange ideas. And anyway, once we get this done there'll be plenty of energy—for a while, anyway."

When they entered *New Ark* it was even worse than *Mayflower* had been. Its crews had had no reason to leave a livable ship at all. The internal power generators still worked, supplied with the mere trickle of energy they needed from the tiny fraction of *Ark*'s store of antimatter that remained in the engines. So, for all those abandoned years, the ship had been kept—well, not warm, but at least above the freezing point. *Ark*'s freezers, with their untouched reserve supplies of organisms and cell cultures, were still in good shape. What was mostly missing was light. *Ark*'s colonists had thriftily removed nearly all the light tubes, along with everything else that could be cannibalized from the ship, for a more immediate use down below on Newmanhome. Even the station-keeping thrusters were still operational—everyone sighed with relief at that, because otherwise their task of transferring fuel would have been much harder.

Indeed, there was enough energy left in the main-drive fuel chamber and station-keepers to send *Ark* completely around its solar system—if anyone had wanted to do that.

When they fired up the drive for the rendezvous with *Mayflower* it didn't protest. It began pouring out its floods of plasma as though its engines had been last used only days before. *Ark* crept toward *Mayflower* in its orbit, and the work crews began the hard work of cutting up the interior bulkheads and carefully—oh, *very* carefully— beginning to dismantle the restraining magnets that held its antimatter fuel in place.

There was no room for error in that. If the antimatter had been allowed to brush against normal matter, even for a moment, even the barest touch, the resulting blast would have scattered all of it— and people on Newmanhome would have seen a major flare star in their sky, just before they were scorched blind in the blast.

So Captains Bu and Rodericks and the three surviving Engineer Officers from the two ships—Wilma Granczek had died giving birth to her fourth child on the Archipelago—began the precarious work of shifting the fuel.

It wasn't easy. When *Ark* was designed, no provision had been made for such a project. Of course, it wasn't only the fuel that had to be moved, it was the magnetic restraints that held it free of contact with anything else, and the steel shell that surrounded the captor fields, and the power source that kept the fields fed and working.

There was no way to move that sort of awkward mass through the ship's ports. They had to cut a hole in the side of *Ark*, to get the stuff out, while the other crew was cutting another just as big in the hull of *Mayflower* to insert it there.

Outside the ship, secured by cables, Viktor wielded the great plasma torch, Jake Lundy at his side.

He hadn't planned it that way. He didn't seek out Lundy's company. It was, he thought in an abstract way, just considering the possibilities, better to have Lundy out there with him than inside with, possibly, Reesa—though what they could have been doing, in the cramped confines of the livable part of *Ark* would hardly have been much, anyway. But he was getting really tired of Jake Lundy's company. It even crossed Viktor's mind for a moment that it wouldn't be awful, really, if Lundy's cables had somehow broken and the man had drifted helplessly away into space, never to return. He even thought, though not seriously—he told himself that of course it wasn't a serious thought—how easy it would be to misaim the plasma torch, now eating through the tough steel of the hull, to burn away Lundy's cables . . .

He didn't mean that, of course. He reassured himself that that was so. His marriage to Reesa was comfortable; they were used to each other; they shared a love for the kids, and the habits of a dozen years. In any case, he was never *jealous* concerning Reesa—as he had been, for instance, of the incomparable Marie-Claude Stockbridge.

To take his mind off such matters he gazed around. From outside the ship Viktor could see Newmanhome spread out below them. He didn't like to look there; the spreading white at the poles was ice—something that Newmanhome had never seen before. Looking at the fearsome skies was even worse. The sun was still the brightest object around, but woefully dimmer than before. The cherry coal of the brown dwarf, Nergal, was almost as bright, but the sun's other planets had dimmed with their primary. The eleven normal stars still shone as bright as ever. But there were so few of them! And the rest of the universe, separating itself into great colored clusters, red and blue, had changed into something wonderful and weird and worrying.

He was glad when their shift ended and they were back inside, though there wasn't much there to take comfort in, either. The shuttle had been too full of people to leave room for amenities— even for food; though fortunately *Ark*'s freezers still had their stocks of frozen spare animals. But one did get tired of eating armadillo, or bat, or goat . . .

When they had raped the side of *Ark* there was little to do until *Ark* completed its slow crawl toward its younger sister ship.

"We could have used the main drives," Captain Bu fretted.

"Don't need them!" Captain Rodericks said sharply. "There's plenty of power in the auxiliary thrusters. Anyway, this is *my* ship, Bu, and we'll do it my way."

"The slow way," Bu sneered.

"The *safe* way," Rodericks said resolutely. "Talk about something else!"

But the other things they had to talk about were not cheering. Word from Homeport was that the community was making progress in digging itself underground, where the soil would be their best insulation against the cooling winds; the clothing factories were doing their best to turn out parkas and gloves and wool hats, things that had never been needed on Newmanhome before.

They were cold inside the hulk of *Ark*, too. Bu wanted to cut off power to the freezer sections to use it to warm their little living quarters, but Captain Rodericks refused. His grounds were simple: "Some day we may need what's in those freezers. Anyway, it's *my ship*." So they huddled together, usually in the old control room, and spent their time watching *Mayflower* drift nearer and gazing, through screens and fiber-optic tubes, at the scary skies.

It was Furhet Gaza, the welding expert, who said, "Everybody! Look at those stars."

"What stars?" Reesa asked.

"Our own stars! The ones that aren't shifting. They aren't any dimmer, are they?"

"They don't look that way," Billy Stockbridge said cautiously. "What about it?"

"Well," Gaza said earnestly, "maybe we're making a big mistake. Maybe we shouldn't wreck our ships! Maybe we should get everybody back on board and head for one of them."

Billy Stockbridge gave him a look of disdain, but it was Captain Rodericks who said angrily, "That's stupid talk, Gaza! What you say is impossible. In the first place, there are too many people on Newmanhome now; we wouldn't all fit in what's left of this old ship. In the second place, how would we get everybody up here? We don't have a fleet of a thousand shuttles to carry them."

"It's worse than that, Captain," Billy Stockbridge put in.

He got a hostile look from Furhet Gaza. "Worse how?" Gaza demanded.

"We don't even know if those other stars have planets," Viktor offered, but Billy was shaking his head.

"That's not it, either. It doesn't matter if they do have planets; they wouldn't be any use to us. I've checked those stars. They're dimming, too. It's just that what we're seeing is the way they were up to six years ago, so they don't look much different—but they're different now, Gaza. And anyway—"

He stopped there. It was Captain Rodericks who said, "Anyway what, Stockbridge?"

Billy shrugged. "Anyway," he said, "we've got a better use for whatever fuel is left in the drive."

"You mean try to take the fuel out of the drive unit, too? But that's hard, Stockbridge; we've agreed that we'll just shift the reserves. That's where most of it is, anyway—enough to power *Ark*'s

generators for another five or ten years, with a little luck. We don't
need to make our job any harder than it is already."

Billy pursed his lips. "That's true." And that was all he said.

Outside of the endless work of cutting metal and preparing the fuel for the move, the biggest job was staying alive—
which meant scavenging for food in *Ark*'s freezers. Viktor went
with Jake Lundy as his partner when it was his turn. He didn't
think about reasons why; he simply volunteered his services, certainly not to forestall Reesa doing the same.

He still felt a certain tension in Lundy's presence, but Lundy
seemed quite at ease. He had done the food-scavenging bit before,
and was friendly and forgiving when Viktor tried to pull one of the
freezer drawers out and couldn't work the catch, not at all like the
ones he had seen on *Mayflower*. "Here, let an expert do it," Lundy
said amiably, showing what he meant with a quick twist and pull.

"That's fine," Viktor said sourly as the drawer slid easily out.
It did take an expert to handle *Ark*'s freezers, because in Viktor's
opinion they had been badly designed in the first place. *Mayflower*'s
had been a generation later, and a generation better. *Mayflower* had
sensibly kept the entire freezer section at temperatures between am-
bient and liquid gas, while *Ark* simply clustered drawers of freezer
compartments in chambers that looked like an Earthly morgue.

Viktor stood uselessly by while Lundy unsealed the drawer.
Clouds of white vapor came off the contents as he poked around
with the thick gloves. "Oh, shit, Viktor," he said in disgust. "Didn't
you check the labels? This stuff's no good, unless you expect us to
eat sperm samples from the small mammals."

"What labels?" Viktor demanded.

Lundy just gave him a patient look, then resealed the drawer
again. He ran his finger over the plaques on a couple of adjacent
drawers to rub the frost off, then said, "Here. This one might do.
It's got turtle eggs and, let's see, what's this? Some kind of fish, I
guess. Hold the sack for me while I pull them out."

Carefully he lifted out the plastic-sealed objects, unidentifiable
under the coating of frost already forming on them, and placed
them in the tote bag. "That'll do for now, I guess," he said when

the sack was half-full. He resealed the remaining contents of the drawer and turned, ready to leave, when he saw the way Viktor was looking at him. "Is something the matter?" he inquired politely.

Viktor hesitated. Then, without knowing in advance he was going to say it, he said, "Do you mind telling me what's going on?"

Lundy looked at him thoughtfully, then turned and absently rubbed the plaque on the door clean. "I don't know what you mean," he said.

"The hell you don't! I've asked Reesa, and she won't tell me a thing. Neither will Billy. But I know damn well there's some kind of secret! At first I thought—"

Viktor hesitated. He was unwilling to say that his first thought when he saw Reesa and Lundy whispering together had been the—well, not the *jealous* feeling that something was cooking between them, but certainly a lot of curiosity about just what it was they whispered about. He finished, "I thought all sorts of things, but none of them make sense."

"What sorts of things?"

"I don't know! That's why I'm asking!" And then he took a wild plunge into speculation. "Is it Nebo, by any chance? I know Billy's always had this idea that we had to go there. He got it from my father, of course. But it's crazy."

"Why do you think it's crazy?" Lundy asked, sounding interested and not at all defensive.

"Well—it just *is*. What could we do if we got there?"

"We could try to find out about those anomalous radiation readings, for one thing," Lundy said seriously.

"Why?"

"That," Lundy told him, for the first time looking strained, "is what people might want to go to Nebo to find out. I don't know what. I only know that something's going on there, and it might be important."

"But—" Viktor shook his head. "What would be the point? Even if the others would let you take *Ark* there, I mean? You can't see anything through the cloud cover."

"There's radar," Lundy pointed out. "And if that didn't settle anything, we could—" He hesitated, then finished, "We could always drop a party onto the surface of Nebo to find out."

"But—but—but our job is to transfer fuel to *Mayflower*, not go gallivanting off to satisfy somebody's curiosity!"

"We're doing that part of the job," Lundy pointed out. "Then, when it's done, we'll still have drive fuel in *Ark*. We can't transfer that! Once it's in the drive itself it's too dangerous. So when we've finished what we came for—then we can take a vote."

"On what? On taking *Ark* to Nebo?"

Lundy shrugged.

"And you've been planning this for—how long?" Viktor demanded.

"Since Reesa first suggested it," Lundy said simply. Reesa! Viktor stared at him with his mouth open. Lundy went on: "Now, the question is, are you going to keep your mouth shut about it until we've finished the fuel transfer?"

"I don't know," Viktor said wretchedly.

But, in the event, he did keep his mouth shut. He didn't say a word. He ate the food they had brought back—the fish turned out to be almost too bony to eat, but the turtle eggs, roasted, were delicious—and all the time he was watching his wife and wondering what other surprises were hidden inside that familiar head.

CHAPTER 11

The fifth of Wan-To's doppels did not have a real name. It wasn't important enough. When Wan-To addressed it at all it was simply as Matter Copy Number Five. Still, Five was fairly important to the remnants of the human race on Newmanhome, because it happened to be the one that had set up shop on the scorched little planet the people of Newmanhome called Nebo.

Although Five was certainly very tiny, primitive and stupid by Wan-To's standards, it was quite capable of doing everything Wan-To ordered it to do. It was even capable of figuring out how to do things Wan-To himself had never gone to the trouble of figuring out before.

There's a human story that describes that situation pretty well. Problem: A human army lieutenant has the task of erecting a thirty-foot flagpole when he only has a twenty-foot length of rope and no hoisting machines. How does he do it? Answer: He calls over his highest-ranking noncom and says, "Sergeant, put up that flagpole."

So when Five received its orders it exercised its built-in ingenuity to carry them out.

It had to start pretty much from scratch. It had no experience of this bizarre kind of environment (it had no experience at all, of course, except what Wan-To had implanted in its memories). It was not deterred by the odd qualities of this "planet" (solid matter! And an "atmosphere"! Five understood the concept of a gas well enough, but these particular gases were so incredibly cold—hardly more than eight or nine hundred Kelvin). Then, the task of manipulating matter all by itself was not really easy. There were so many *kinds* of matter. There were all those things called "elements" and all their molecular combinations and isotopic variations and interacting relationships. It was definitely a nasty job. But someone had to do it—Wan-To had so decreed.

The first thing Five had to do, starting with its control of magnetic and electrostatic forces, and its limited (but adequate) supply of gravitational particles, was simple excavation. It had to wrench out large quantities of matter—ill assorted, full of things Five didn't want at all—from the surface of the planet (and from some sources pretty far below the surface) for separation into the basic building blocks it needed; call them "ores." To separate the various kinds of useful things out of the ores, it invented what humans might have called a sort of mass spectrometer: vaporized matter passed through a sieve of forces that pulled out each separate atom, according to its weight and characteristics, and deposited them one at a time (but very rapidly!) in "storage bins" until such time as Five was ready to put them together in the combinations and shapes it needed. And it needed so many different shapes of matter! It needed antennae to locate and lock onto the various nearby stars it was meant to carry along. It needed chambers to contain the forces that would move them; it needed sensors to make sure they were moving properly; it needed a separate kind of antenna, just to keep in communication with its master, Wan-To.

And it needed them all in a hurry, because Wan-To was not patient. Wan-To took for granted that the doppel, Five, was moving as rapidly as possible. Five slaved to do so. It wasn't that it was afraid of punishment. The heart of an animal doesn't pump because it is afraid its master will be angry if it stops; it pumps because that is what it *does*.

When, rarely, Wan-To bothered to call up to check on progress Five was not fearful. It was only happy to report that it was doing its job.

When you came right down to it, all Five had to do, on a planet that had nothing, was to create an entire industrial complex. It took Five several weeks, but before the castings had quite cooled on the last of its guidance antennae it had already begun reaching out to all of its chosen eleven stars. It wasn't hard for Five—not for a near (if severely abridged) copy of Wan-To himself.

Five didn't like to question Wan-To. (Wan-To hadn't instructed it to ask questions, only to get the work done.) So Five had to make a number of decisions on its own. Wan-To's orders had been to accelerate this little group of stars. Well, that certainly meant to accelerate at least one planet with them—namely, the one he was on. But what about the other planets, satellites, and lesser things?

Five pondered that for a long time, then decided to play it safe and take everything. Of course, that made its job a little harder. Now there weren't just a dozen bodies to move. There were roughly half a million, it counted, including all the asteroids and comets big enough to bother with.

It was a daunting job, but Five was not daunted. Five was quite capable of doing all sorts of intricate and difficult things, only not very smart about what things to do.

From time to time Wan-To did communicate with his one surviving matter analogue. Five wasn't much company, but there were some good things about carrying on a conversation with it. The most important of them was that that kind of conversation was perfectly safe, because the thing was a dolt. It could never threaten Wan-To.

The bad side of that coin was that talking to the matter analogue was terribly boring. To begin with, it was boringly slow. The matter thing took forever to get a simple sentence out. Anyway, what could such a sluggish, rudimentary thing possibly have to say?

The answer to that was, "Not much."

At first, Wan-To had been mildly interested by the matter-copy's reports, especially the ones that were transmitted as "pictures." Wan-To wasn't much good at pictures. His perceptions operated in nine spatial dimensions (though, true, six of them were only vestiges), and a flat representation wasn't much good to him. Also, things with definite boundaries of any kind were scarce in Wan-To's experience, especially when they didn't flow or fluctuate. (How *stag-*

nant matter was!) It had been an interesting bit of puzzle solving for Wan-To to attach any meaning at all to the pictorial data the matter-copy turned in. Then, when he had gotten used to the ideas of "shapes" and "edges," the next question was, "What are all these 'solid' things good for?" Why were those great shiny arrays Five was building that swayed from horizon to horizon as the planet turned always pointing toward its little star? ("Energy accumulators," the matter-analogue informed its master—but how odd to be tapping energy from *outside* the star!) Why those spiraling shapes whose aims converged at a point far beyond the star's farthest planets? (They were the guides for the graviscalar flow that was pulling the whole group along.) Why the long square structure? or the domed ones? or the ones deep underground? (But you had to have them, Five humbly protested. They sheltered the matter machines that contained the forces that did the job. It was the way it was able to fulfill its mission.)

Of course, Wan-To had left the details of how to do the mission up to the matter-doppel's own judgment. Wan-To couldn't be bothered with such details. The matter-copy had been instructed to create a pit of gravitation for that star and its attendant bodies to fall into—endlessly—and it hadn't been told specifically how. The commissioned officer's instructions were just to do it, and do it the sergeant had.

That sort of entertainment palled quickly. After a few questions Wan-To began to tire of the answers. Just before Wan-To decided on cutting off communication with the doppel and looking for something more interesting, he asked the important question. "And the stars in your group? Have any survived?"

"Almost all," Five reported. "Two were damaged some time ago, but there have been no attacks since."

Wan-To didn't respond. That was as he had expected. He was just about to cut off, without of course bothering with any such politenesses as a good-bye, when the matter-copy gave its equivalent of a deferential cough. Humbly it told him that it had come across one little phenomenon it hadn't expected. Nothing in the datastores Wan-To had transferred to him had suggested that small bits of matter might organize themselves into aggregates that seemed to be—well, what else could you call it?—more or less *alive*.

For a long time after he had finished wringing out of the doppel every scrap of information it possessed about this new kind of "life," Wan-To lay in his plasma core, restlessly writhing, marveling at this interesting new thing. How very *odd*! From all the matter-copy had observed, these "living" things were quite small, quite rudimentary (human taxonomists would have called them mosses, bacteria, invertebrates, and a few flowering plants), and certainly quite trivial in any large sense.

So, of course, the relevant word was only "interesting." It certainly was not in any way *important*. There was surely no way that these things could possibly affect the lives of Wan-To or his like, ever.

Yet it was strange that in all his billions of years of life Wan-To had never come across such a thing before.

True, he rarely bothered with anything concerned with matter—what was the point? And true, he told himself justly, even Wan-To himself was fairly young, as far as his probable life expectancy went. It wasn't his fault. The universe itself was only about twice as old as Wan-To, though he had already determined that it would survive for a highly exponential number of times that long (and, if he was lucky, he would survive with it). Matter-life was naturally quite transitory. It was also rather new on the scene, he decided, for some quick "ball-park" (not that Wan-To knew anything of ball parks) calculations had suggested to him that it would take quite a while for this matter-life to arise by chance.

He saw how such a thing could happen, though. All it would take was some random combinations of particles that, purely by chance, turned out to have organizing and reproductive capacities.

It was probably not unlike the same random events that, he knew, had brought his own life into being.

———

Actually it had not been Wan-To himself that had been brought into being by those events, but his predecessors. That was an unimportant distinction, though. Wan-To's predecessor (being so solitary he hadn't bothered giving himself a name) had made a nearly exact copy of himself when he made Wan-To, and Wan-To had as many memories as his "father" did.

Which, in this case, was not very many. Apart from any other consideration, the proto-Wan-To hadn't been very smart then—well, he had been an infant, after all! His entire network had hardly amounted to more than two or three hundred billion particles altogether, and none of them fully integrated with the others as yet. But as he had grown over the eons to be very smart indeed, and, quite curious, he had spent a lot of thought in deducing how that event had had to be.

As his galaxy (the old one, the one Wan-To had left when it became uninhabitable) turned on its axis, the leading edge of one of its spiral arms passed through a "density wave," and a patch of ionized gases was compressed by the shock of contact.

That was just the beginning. It didn't create Wan-To's predecessor. It only made it possible for the next nearby event to do so.

That event came when a particular star of a rather rare kind came to the end of its hydrogen-burning life. It had been a very large star, so it used up its hydrogen quite quickly. Then, with most of its hydrogen turned into helium, it was running out of its best fusion fuel and destined for trouble.

The star could, to be sure, go on burning the helium into heavier elements still. But it took four hydrogen nuclei to make one helium, so when you got down to helium there was only a quarter as much fuel to begin with. Worse than that, helium burning doesn't yield as much energy. Energy was what that old star was beginning to run out of. Energy was what it needed to keep its shape, because it was only the pressure of the terrible heat from within that kept the immense pressure of its outer layers from collapsing into its core.

When the energy from the hydrogen at last ran out, it did collapse.

All that vast mass dropped—"like a stone," a human being might say, but much faster, and with far vaster impact, than any stone ever dropped on Earth. It struck the core, squeezing it from all directions at once. The core rebounded. Four-fifths of the mass of the star blasted itself into space in that great bursting, with floods of X rays and gammas and neutrinos, as well as ten-million-million-degree heat and blinding light; and as that furiously energetic mass raced through space it struck the already compacted mass of gas that was the womb that held the not-yet-existent precursor of Wan-To.

That was what Earthly astronomers would have called a "supernova." The humans, too, had wondered about how things began, and they had worked out that their own sun and most others had been born in that way. They rarely saw a real supernova, of course—especially not one in their own galaxy—because human beings didn't live long enough for that. But they knew that such events happened, over and over, hundreds of millions of times in each galaxy.

They did not, however, ordinarily give rise to anything like a Wan-To.

The supernova that gave birth to Wan-To's forebear was not any ordinary Type I or Type II. It was of the rare kind Earthly astronomers had named an "Urtrobin supernova," after the Soviet astronomer who had found the first of its kind in an obscure galaxy in the constellation Perseus. Urtrobin supernovae don't start with any ordinary supergiant star, a mere twenty or a hundred times as massive as the Earth's sun. What is required for an Urtrobin supernova is that very rare celestial object, a star that masses as much as two thousand suns put together.

There aren't many stars like that. A lot of Earthly astronomers refused to believe that any such overbloated body could ever form—at least, they refused until they began to calculate in the relativistic effects and saw that those did in fact make it possible. But when such a supermassive star collapses its explosion does not last for a mere matter of months. It takes as much as a year for it to reach peak brightness. Then it declines to obscurity only over a period of decades.

It was in just such a godlike hammer blow that Wan-To's ancestor's wisp of gas was squeezed and drenched. It was enough. The ancestor was born.

Such an event, affecting such a scarce collection of ionized gases, was very rare indeed in the universe. There could not have been very many such beings formed, not in all the dozen billion years since the Big Bang.

Indeed, Wan-To would have thought his unfortunate parent had been very likely the only one . . . if he had not observed the wreck of some distant galaxies and realized that creatures like himself must have done the wrecking.

He did not want his present galaxy wrecked. It was such a chore to move.

CHAPTER 12

It was a long trip to Nebo, a hundred and twenty hard days, tough times for any small group of people locked into each other's company. For Viktor the trip was grim.

Black worry began creeping over him as soon as they pulled out of Low Newmanhome Orbit. It got worse. First it was the radio; the surprised, then frantic, then furious calls began to come in from the surface. It got worse still when his sister Edwina got on to plead with him, worst of all when she turned the microphone over to little Tanya. That was pretty close to heartbreaking, the sweet, worried little voice, begging. "Mommy? Daddy Jake? Daddy Viktor? Won't you please come home?" It sent Reesa fleeing into a dark and empty cargo compartment, and when Viktor found her she was weeping uncontrollably. Then she closed up, would hardly talk at all. Not just Reesa, either. Everyone was having second thoughts; everyone was in a touchy, grouchy mood. By the time Captain Rodericks had inserted *Ark* into its parking orbit around Nebo and the lander was stocked and ready to take a crew down to the surface, hardly anyone was speaking to anyone else.

In Viktor's black cloud of worry he kept turning their decision over and over in his mind, asking himself the same nagging questions. Did the kids really need them at home? Well, of course they did, but . . . And did the *people* need them there, for that matter? Wasn't it, maybe, their *duty* to be there, sharing whatever came of

156

this unexpected, this *unexplained* new calamity that was (maybe) threatening the colony's very survival? Well, maybe that was so, but still . . .

But still what they were doing was *necessary*! They had to find out what was happening on Nebo! Didn't they?

And even if they didn't, if the whole thing was criminal folly, it was long too late to be asking any of those questions. They were committed.

The other part of Viktor's black cloud was the unhappy state of his relations with Reesa. Something had gone very wrong. In all those hundred and twenty days they did not make love once. True, there wasn't any privacy to speak of in the stripped-down ship. True, Captain Rodericks (who took as an article of faith that only a busy crew could possibly be a happy crew—however laughable it was to use the word "happy" in the present circumstances) had set up an elaborate routine of drills and practice emergencies, Captain Bu backing him up all the way, and everybody was exhausted most of the time. But Reesa hardly even *talked* to Viktor any more.

What made that particularly hard to accept was that there were people she did talk to, and one of them was Jake Lundy. So to all Viktor's doubts and discomforts there was added the thing he had never wanted to believe himself capable of. He was jealous.

Four people were to go down to the surface of Nebo in the ship's lander. No one volunteered. No one refused, either; they drew lots.

When Jake Lundy turned out to be one of the chosen ones— and Viktor and Reesa were not—Viktor didn't rejoice, exactly, but it certainly did not break his heart.

"We're going to be ready for anything," Captain Rodericks had decreed, and so they pretty nearly were. Contingency plans were made for everything anyone could imagine. Emergencies were invented. Ways of dealing with them were devised. Every day, sometimes more than once a day, without warning, there was a ship's drill. Over and over the crew rehearsed what to do in case of sudden air loss (helmets on, suits already in place), or power outage (standby batteries kept constantly recharged), or the sudden death or incapacitation of any crew member—backups for every job, everyone trained to do everything.

"Just what the hell do you think is going to happen?" Viktor demanded, tired past the point of tolerance.

Rodericks only shook his head and ordered, "Get on with it! Run that leak-patch drill again! The way you deal with emergencies is to plan ahead for them—then you can *survive*."

When they weren't doing make-work drills, they were stocking the lander for its indispensable job. That wasn't easy, because there was little left on old *Ark* to scavenge, but they stripped themselves bare to give the lander everything they could. Communications equipment. Recording equipment—Captain Bu even dismantled *Ark*'s old log, and made them stow it aboard the lander. Hot-weather clothing, cold-weather clothing—they could not be sure what they would find. Dried foods from the ship's ancient emergency rations. Fresh (well, recently unfrozen) food from the capsules on the cryonics deck. That was one of Viktor's principal tasks, salvaging everything that seemed edible from the old capsules (how quaint they were, and how unlike *Mayflower*'s! They were no more than pods, stacked on aisles that were no colder than any of the rest of the spaceship—what a wasteful way to design them!). Then they added plastic sacks of water, and flashlights, and Geiger counters, and infrared viewers, and cameras—everything anyone could think of that the resources of the old ship and the personal possessions of the crew could produce. It all went in. And, at the very end, even four rifles, too. Captain Rodericks himself had produced them out of a long-forgotten hoard—not because anyone on *Ark* really expected anything to shoot at, but because Captain Rodericks insisted.

And then they were there. The lander was stocked. There was nothing left to do but the launch.

For all that long voyage *Ark*'s sensors had been fixed on one target only, the planet they were about to invade. What the people aboard *Ark* saw of the surface of the mystery planet depended on how they looked at it. Through the fiber-optic links to the external telescopes there was very little to see. The cloud cover was in the way—featureless white by day, emptily black when they were in the nightside portion of their orbit around the planet—except for a few spots, where something bright beneath the clouds lighted them ruddily from below.

The instruments told them a lot more. They had long been detecting definite, large-scale emissions from the surface—gamma rays, X rays, radio static. The infrared sensors showed the clear-cut heat sources under the clouds. And radar was the most useful of all. The radar plot had grown more detailed with every day. The radar images were displayed as holograms, and they showed a variety of hard-edged structures. There were flat, broad things that looked almost like buildings. There were tulip-shaped things, like the horn on an old acoustic phonograph, all apparently oriented toward the dimming sun. There were ribbed metal shells like the carapace of a turtle, and those came in two varieties. Some had things like horn antennae nearby; others were surrounded by great spiky clusters of spiral metal, like Art Deco lightning rods.

None of the sensors detected anything moving. Nothing seemed to be in any physical action anywhere on the surface of Nebo. Captain Rodericks, defending his gift of weapons, argued that there had to be life of some kind there—how else to explain the machines? Could they have built themselves? But there was no sign of the kind of movement that one associated with life, especially of civilized, technological life—nothing like trucks, planes, trains—nothing like anything that might have held whoever it was who built the metal structures. For that matter, there was no sign of any living, moving thing at all.

All the same, when Viktor studied the radar he said, "Even if we don't see them, I guess you were right, Captain Rodericks. It stands to reason there's somebody down there." And then he added, "My father was right."

Captain Rodericks barked at him, "Your father was right about *what?* Do you know what those things are?"

Viktor looked up from the scan. "I don't *know* what they are," he said, keeping his temper, "but I can see what they're *doing*. My father always thought that Nebo and the astronomical events were connected. Obviously they are! Look at those antennae. They're all pointed right at the sun!"

Jake Lundy stood up. He glanced at Viktor, then walked over and studied the plot.

When he turned around he was smiling—not a happy smile, the small smile of relief of someone who has had his mind made up on a tough question. "I'd say that settles the first landing place. We check those things out."

On the next to the last orbit, they had a farewell dinner for the chosen four. It wasn't gourmet food. It all came out of the ancient cryonics stores of *Ark*, and it had been put there in the first place for its value as biological specimens, not for epicures. But they managed a sort of stew out of seed corn and a kind of hard, flat peas, and the main course was the last of a small breeding stock of dwarf sheep, roasted.

Captain Bu said a short, reverential grace. There was no wine. There was not much conversation, either. Once Bu looked up from stirring the stew around his plate and said, to no one in particular, "You know, the lander has to come back. Otherwise there won't be any way for us to get down to the surface of Newmanhome again."

Jake Lundy laughed. "What's the matter, Captain? Do you think they'll maroon you in *Ark*, for taking the ship?" But that was obviously what Bu did think. Jake shrugged and changed the subject. "It's a pity," he said deliberately, gnawing at a tiny chop, "that none of these strains will ever live on Newmanhome now."

And little Luo Fah, who also had drawn one of the four slips in the lottery, stood up. "I'm not hungry," she declared. "Do we have to wait for another whole orbit? Can't we launch the lander now?"

Then, all of a sudden, it was happening. The four got up. Some stretched. Some yawned. Some rubbed their chins, or shook hands with one or more of the others. Lundy, after a quick and noncommittal glance at Viktor, pulled Reesa to him and kissed her. (She wasn't the one who had started it—but she didn't resist at all, Viktor observed.) Then they filed slowly into the lander and sealed it down. Viktor and two others closed the inner seals and retreated to the control room, where Captain Rodericks was on the radio to the ship, his eyes glued to the course plot. The little dot that was *Ark* was creeping across the face of the planet Nebo. Captain Bu cleared his throat, looking around, and then began to pray aloud. "Dear Almighty God Who is all-seeing judge and eternal master of us all, I pray You care for these, our friends, who embark on this dangerous mission in Your service—"

"*Launch!*" Captain Rodericks cried. And the ship shook slightly, and the lander was gone.

On the radio speaker, Jake Lundy's voice unemotionally reported distance, altitude, and speed every few moments. On the navigation radar, the lander was a blip of bright red, paralleling their course but falling behind. As it passed out of the shadow of Nebo the optics picked it up, too, a glimmer of metal, dropping away into Nebo's air. Everyone was watching, Captain Rodericks hunched over his controls, Captain Bu with his eyes glued to the fiber-optic tubes, everyone else staring at the wall displays.

And as they stood there, Viktor felt Reesa's hand creep into his.

He didn't respond. He didn't pull away, but he left his hand limp and uncooperative in hers.

She removed it and turned to look at him. "Is something wrong?" she asked.

He was stubbornly mute. He didn't even look at her. He kept his eyes on the screen.

"Come on, Viktor," she said, her tone unfriendly. "Are you pissed because I kissed Jake Lundy good-bye?" She was scowling now. "He's going into real danger, damn it! I would've kissed Rodericks if it'd been him!"

Viktor allowed his gaze to turn to her. "Would you have been off in a corner whispering with Rodericks all this time, too?"

"Viktor! What the hell are you talking about? Are you jealous?"

"I thought you were my wife, not his," he said stiffly.

"I am your wife, damn you! I'm not your *possession*. But I'm your wife, all right!"

"A wife is supposed to be true to her husband," he pointed out. "You agreed to that."

"*Viktor!*" she blazed, flushed with anger. "What do you think we were doing? He wanted someone to talk to—who better than me? Oh, Viktor," she said, her voice thick, "you're a dirty, suspicious man. I don't want to talk about it now. I don't want to talk to you at all! We'll have to settle this later."

"We certainly will," Viktor said grimly. But he didn't know, neither of them knew, how much longer "later" was going to be . . .

A shout of shock and anger from Bu took their minds off the quarrel. "The lander! It's been hit!" he cried; and the others watching the wall screens were shouting, too—and then everything went bad at once.

The radio communications from the lander stopped in the middle of a sentence, and a vast warbling sound filled the speakers.

On the phosphor screen Viktor and Reesa watched in horror as, from the surface of the planet, an intolerably bright orange-red light winked at them—brighter than they had ever seen on a screen—so bright that the screen shut down in automatic self-defense.

And a shock shook the *Ark* as though it had been rammed by a truck.

Captain Bu, at the fiber-optic periscope, screamed in pain, as that intolerable brightness, unfiltered by electronics, struck his eyes. The metallic voice of the ship's warning system spoke up from behind Viktor: *Sensor lock lost. Sensor lock lost. Sensor* . . . At the same time, another machine voice, deeper and calmer, announced *Thruster controls inoperative* over and over, while still a third cried, *Systems malfunction!*

It seemed that every emergency system in *Ark* was announcing trouble at once. The crunching came again—then once more; and this time *Ark* itself jerked under them, sending them flying, while the last of the damage reporters cried, *Air pressure dropping!*

There was no doubt that was true. Viktor could hear the scream of escaping air from somewhere. His ears were popping. His lungs hurt until he exhaled, and then as he tried to breathe in he was gasping. There was a faint, frightening pressure behind his eyes.

Reesa turned from trying to help the moaning, blinded Captain Bu. "Something's shooting at us!" she gasped. "Oh, God! Those poor people down there! Jake'll never get back now!"

And even in the shock and terror of that moment Viktor heard her use his name.

"We ought to get into space suits," Viktor bawled, and then cursed himself. What space suits? They had all gone down to the surface with the landing party.

It was Captain Bu who best kept his head, in spite of terrible pain. He cupped his hands over his blasted eyes and shouted orders, instructions, and demands to be told what was going on.

There was a well-ordered drill for air-loss incidents. True, the drill assumed that the full ship's company would be present to slap on the sticky patches and trigger the airtight door closings. Also true, the drill had been set up for a wholly different *Ark*, one that had not existed for decades, an *Ark* with all its pieces still intact. In the shedding of so much of the ship, to burn in the antimatter reactors or simply to be paradropped to the surface of Newman-home, many storage spaces had been lost, or shifted around, and misplaced, and the unexpected strike from Nebo had completed the damage. The compartments where the sticktight patches were kept no longer existed.

And it no longer mattered, really. Patches wouldn't do the job. *Ark* had not merely been holed, it had been gouged through by the laserlike blasts from the surface of Nebo. The part of the hull where the optics had been mounted was gone, burned away entirely; the ship was as blind as Captain Bu himself. Thruster fuel had exploded in another place. The whole center keel of the ship was bent; airtight doors weren't airtight anymore. The only part that still maintained integrity—almost maintained it—was what was left of the old freezer compartment. Gasping in the rapidly thinning atmosphere, Reesa and Viktor tugged the blinded, moaning captain through the bulkhead hatch to the cryonics deck and dogged it shut.

"Wait!" Viktor cried. "What about Rodericks and the others?"

"Didn't you see? They're dead! Close that hatch!" Reesa shouted. And, when Viktor had it clamped, it was just in time. The air in the cryonics deck was thin, but at least its pressure remained steady.

"If those shots ever hit the antimatter . . ." Reesa whispered, and didn't finish.

She didn't have to. If whatever it was that was firing on them from the surface fired again, and if that shot were to strike the antimatter containment—then nothing else would count. There wasn't much antimatter left in *Ark*'s fuel chamber, but if what was there got loose *Ark* would become a mere haze of ions.

She turned to the blinded Bu, while Viktor prowled restlessly around the freezer compartment, looking for he knew not what. A weapon? But there was no one nearer than the surface of Nebo to fight. No one had dreamed that *Ark* might ever need long-range weapons.

And no one had dreamed, either, that anything on the surface of Nebo might try to kill them. Viktor wondered if anyone in the lander had survived. More likely, they were dead already—as he and Reesa and Bu were likely to be, at any moment.

Then a thought struck him. *Ark* did have one serious weapon, of course . . .

He bounded back to where Reesa was trying to find something to bind Bu Wangzha's burned-out eye sockets. "We could blow up the antimatter ourselves!" he cried.

Reesa turned and stared at him. "The radiation," he explained. "If we set the antimatter off, the radiation would burn half the planet clean!"

She was staring at him unbelievingly. But she didn't have to answer. Captain Bu spoke for her. "Let go of me, Reesa," he said, sounding quite normal. He sat up, his hands over his destroyed eyes. He breathed hard for a moment, and then said, "Viktor, don't be a fool. In the first place, we're cut off from the controls. There isn't any air there. And we shouldn't blow up the planet anyway."

Viktor averted his gaze from the horrible eye sockets. "At least we'd *hurt* them!" he said savagely.

Bu shook his sightless head. "We couldn't destroy the whole planet. The most we could do is prove that we're dangerous—and what if they then decide that the people on Newmanhome have to pay for our act? What chance would they have against something like those lasers?"

"What chance do they have now?" Viktor snarled.

"Not much," Bu said calmly, "but better than we have up here. The air won't last forever, and there's no way we can get out of here."

"So we're dead!" Viktor snapped.

Bu gazed at him with the sightless eyes. Viktor averted his gaze, but the captain's face was almost smiling. "If you're dead," he said, "you might as well be frozen."

"What?"

"The freezers are still working, aren't they? And even blind, I think I can get the two of you stowed away."

"Captain!" Reesa gasped. "No! What would happen to *you*?"

"Exactly what will happen to all of us if we do nothing," Captain Bu said comfortably. "Frozen, you have a chance to survive until—" He shrugged. "To survive for a while, anyway. Don't worry about me. It's a captain's job to be the last to leave—and anyway, I have faith, you see. The Lord promised salvation and eternal bliss in heaven. I know He was telling the truth." He grimaced against the pain, and then said in a businesslike way, "Now! You two get out the preparation boxes and the rest of the freezer equipment, and show me where everything is. If you start it, I think I can finish the job by touch."

"Are you sure?" Reesa began doubtfully, but Viktor caught her arm.

"If he can't, how are we worse off?" he demanded. "Here, Bu. This is the perfusor, these are the gas outlets . . . "

And he let the blind man do his job, fumblingly as he did, even while the hulk of the old ship shook every now and then with some new blow or some fresh excursion of the control rockets. It was the only chance they had—but he knew it was a forlorn hope. It was being done wrong, all wrong . . .

And it was wrong, a lot wronger still, when he opened his caked, sore eyes and looked up into the eyes of a red-haired woman in a black cowl. It wasn't until she said, "All right, Vik, can you stand up now?" that he realized she was his wife.

"You aren't Captain Bu," he told her.

"Of course not," she said, sobbing. "Oh, Viktor, wake up! Captain Bu's been dead for ages. Everybody has! It's been *four hundred years*."

CHAPTER 13

The slow approach of old *Ark* didn't frighten the matter-copy on Nebo. Still, caution was built into Five, and it watched the thing very carefully.

Five had plenty of time for watching. Once its little fleet of stars was well launched on its aimless flight—really aimless, because it was not *to* anywhere, simply *away*—Five had very little to do.

That wasn't a problem. Five didn't become bored. It was very good at doing nothing. It simply waited there on its slowly cooling little planet, observing the dimming of its star as the stellar energies were drained away into the gravitational particles that drove the cluster along. Five didn't have much in the way of "feelings," but what it did have was a sort of general sense of satisfaction in having accomplished the first part of its mission. It did, sometimes, wonder if there was meant to be a second part. For Five the act of "wondering" did not imply worry or speculation or fretting over possibilities; it was more like a self-regulating thermostat constantly checking the temperature of its process batch, or a stockbroker glancing over his stack of orders before leaving for the day, to make sure none remained unexecuted. Five was quite confident that if Wan-To wanted anything else from it, Wan-To would surely let it know.

All the same, it was, well, not "startled," but at least "alerted to action," when it detected the presence of an alien artifact approaching its planet.

Five knew what to do about it, of course. Its orders included the instruction to protect itself against any threat; so when the thing fired a piece of itself toward the planet's surface, Five simply readjusted some of its forces and fired high-temperature blasts of plasma at both the object in orbit and the smaller one entering the atmosphere. When it was sure neither was functioning any longer, Five deployed a small batch of graviphotons to move the larger object away from its presence—not far; just in a sort of elliptical orbit that would keep it out at arm's length.

That left the part that was already in Nebo's atmosphere.

It was obviously too small and too primitive to be dangerous anymore. Five caught the falling thing in a web of graviscalars and lowered it to the surface of Nebo for examination.

That was when Five discovered that the object was hollow—and that it contained several queer things that moved about on their own. They weren't metallic. They were composed of soft, wet compounds of carbon, and they made acoustic sounds to each other.

They seemed almost to be *alive.*

That was a bit of a problem for the little homunculus called Five. Its instructions had never foreseen any such bizarre situation as this. It almost wished it dared contact Wan-To for instructions.

That contact was a while in coming, because Five was not very frequently on Wan-To's mind.

Wan-To's mind was rather troubled, in fact. He didn't like to speak to his sibling/rivals, because there was always the risk of giving away some bit of strategic information to the wrong one. But he wanted *something* interesting to do.

His billions of years of boredom had caused him to produce a lot of entertainments, and one of them was just to wonder. In that way too he was very like the human beings he had never heard of: he was insatiably curious.

One of the things he wondered about (like the humans) was the universe he lived in. Wan-To was more fortunate than the humans in that way. He could see better than they, and he could see a lot farther.

Of course, Wan-To himself couldn't "see" diddly-squat outside his own star, because the close-packed ions and nuclear fragments of his core certainly didn't admit any light from outside. It would have been far easier to peek through sheets of lead than to see through that dense plasma.

When you think of it, though, human astronomers aren't much better off. The part of them that wonders is the human brain, and the brain can't see anything at all. It needs external organs—eyes—to trap the photons of light. Even the eyes don't really "see," any more than the antenna on your TV set "sees" Johnny Carson flipping his pencil at your screen. All the human eye does is record the presence or absence of photons on each of its rods and cones and pass on that information, by way of neurons and their synapses, to the part of the human brain called the visual cortex. That's where the images from the rods and cones are reconstituted into patterns, point by point. The "seeing" is a joint effort between the photon gatherers, the pattern recogniziers—and, finally, the cognitive parts of that wet lump of flabby cells the human being thinks with. So, in his own way, it was with Wan-To.

It should not be surprising that Wan-To's immensely greater brain could see immensely more.

Wan-To's eyes didn't look like any human's baby blues. They didn't look like anything much at all; they were simply the clouds of particles, sensitive to radiation of any kind, that floated outside the photosphere of his star.

Sometimes he worried about having them out there, because it was possible that a risk could be involved. The detector clouds were not a natural part of any star and it was just barely possible that one of his colleagues might find some way of detecting their presence . . . and thus of locating precious *him*. But the "eyes" were so frail and tenuous that they were not at all easy to spot. Anyway, Wan-To didn't have any choice, because he had to have the eyes—needed them for survival; after all, he had always to be watchful, for defense and for potential gain. So the small risk was worth taking. It brought the great gain of helping to ease his permanent itch of curiosity.

So Wan-To was quite happily employed, for long stretches of time, peering out at the great cosmic expanse all around him and trying to figure out what it all meant—very like those never-encountered humans.

Wan-To was not at all color-blind—not even as much so as all human beings are, by the physical limitations of their cells as well as by their habit of living at the bottom of a well of murky air. That is to say, he wasn't limited to the optical frequencies. His eyes saw all the electromagnetic radiation there was. The difference between X rays and heat was less to him than the difference humans perceive between orange and blue. As long as energy came in photons of any kind, Wan-To saw it.

That was particularly· useful to his inquiring mind because of the phenomenon of the redshift; because in the long run it was only the redshift that told him how far away, and how long ago, what he was seeing was.

Wan-To had realized that the universe was expanding long before Henrietta Leavitt and Arthur Eddington figured it out. He did it in the same way. He observed that the bright and dark lines in the light produced by ionizing elements in distant galaxies did not quite match the lines in the light from those nearer by.

Humans called those "Fraunhofer lines," and they moved downward with distance. Wan-To didn't call them that, of course, but he knew what they were. They were the light that a given element always produced at a given frequency when one of its electrons leaped to another orbit around the atomic nucleus. And he knew what the redshift meant. It was the Doppler effect (though he did not give it that name), caused by the fact that that particular object was moving away from him. The more it shifted, the faster the object was running away.

It had taken Wan-To very little time (oh, maybe a couple of million years—just the wink of an eye, really) to fill in all the gaps in his understanding and realize that the faster the objects moved the farther away they were; and thus that the universe was expanding! Everything was running away from everything else—everywhere!

And, as Wan-To also was aware that every time he looked at an object a billion light-years away he was also looking a billion years into the past, he understood that he was looking at a history of the universe.

The whole thing was arranged in shells layered around him, separated by time as well as space. What Wan-To saw nearby was galaxies more or less like his own. They contained billions of stars, and they had recognizable structures. Mostly they whirled slowly around their centers of gravity, like the spirals of M-31 in Andromeda. Some of them had fierce radiation sources at their cores, no doubt immense black holes. Some were relatively placid. But they were all, basically, pretty much alike.

But that was only true of the "recent" shell. Farther out it got different.

Around a redshift of 1 (say, at a time perhaps six billion years after the Big Bang, when the universe was only half its present size— about when Wan-To himself had been born, in fact) most galaxies seemed to have pretty well finished their burst of star formation. Farther and earlier, their gas clouds were still collapsing into the clumps that squeezed themselves into nuclear fusion and became stars.

At redshifts up to 3 lay quasars. That was where the galaxies themselves were being born. By redshift 3 all the objects were running away from him at nearly nine-tenths the speed of light, and it was getting to the point where nothing further was ever going to be seen because they were nearing the "optical limit"—the limit of distance and velocity at which the object was receding so fast that its light could never reach Wan-To at all. And the time he was seeing was getting close to the era of the Big Bang itself.

That was a very interesting region to Wan-To. It was there, in that farthest of the concentric shells of the universe, that he found the domain of the blue fuzzies—the tiny, faint, blue objects that must be newborn galaxies, tens of billions of them, so far away that even Wan-To's patient eyes could not resolve them into distinct shapes.

The blue fuzzies propounded any number of riddles to Wan-To's curious mind. The first, and the easiest to solve, was why the blue fuzzies were blue. Wan-To came up with the answer. The blue light he was seeing came from the brightest line produced by the hydrogen atom when it gets excited. (Sometimes this line was called the Lyman-alpha line, in honor of the human scientist who first studied it in detail—but not by Wan-To.) At its source, that line wasn't visible to human eyes at all; it was in the far ultraviolet. But at a redshift of 3 or 4 it wound up looking blue.

The biggest question was what lay beyond the blue fuzzies. And that, Wan-To recognized with annoyance, was something he could never discover by seeing it. Not just because of their distance, pushing right up against the optical limit. Most of all because there wouldn't be anything to see. Until the gas clouds that formed galaxies began to collapse they simply didn't radiate at all.

Wan-To writhed about in his warm, cozy core, very dissatisfied with the fact that natural law kept him from knowing *everything*. There should be some way! If not to see, then at least to *deduce*. There were all sorts of clues, he told himself, if only he had the wit to understand them—

The call that came in then broke his concentration.

What an annoyance! Especially as he certainly didn't want to talk to any of his siblings just then.

But then he realized, astonished, that the call wasn't from a sibling at all. It was from that contemptible, low-level intelligence, his Matter-Copy Number Five, which had had the incredible presumption to dare to call *him*.

It took even Wan-To's vast intellect a while to understand what Five was trying to tell him. No, Five insisted, the object it had destroyed was not one of those quaint, inanimate matter things like comets or asteroids. It was an *artifact*. It was *propelled*. It had its own energy source—which, Five had determined, came from something that was very rare indeed in the inanimate universe.

The artifact's energies were definitely derived from antimatter.

Antimatter! Wan-To was astonished. Even Wan-To had never personally experienced the presence of antimatter, though of course he had long since understood that it might exist and sometimes, rarely, did exist in small, very temporary quantities. But even that wasn't quite the most astonishing thing. Stranger still was Five's report that small, independent entities—*made of matter*—had come floating down to the surface of its planet in a container that the large artifact had launched. And they were still there.

Wan-To had long since forgotten any resentment he had had at Five's impudence in disturbing him. This new development was too interesting.

Of course, it wasn't *important*. There was no way such tiny, limited creatures could affect anything Wan-To was interested in. Not to mention that there was something about them that Wan-To found repellent, queer, *repulsive*. It was not easy for him to understand how they could be alive at all.

To be sure, humans would have had just as much trouble understanding Wan-To. The reasons would have been much the same, but reversed in sign. The perceptual universe of matter creatures like human beings was Newtonian; Wan-To's was relativistic and quantum-mechanical. The Newtonian world view was as instinctively alien to Wan-To as quantum mechanics was to a human, because he himself was a quantum-mechanical phenomenon. Not even the spookiest particles were strange to him, because they were what he was made up of and lived among. He could examine them all as easily as a human baby examines its fingers and toes—and in much the same way, with all of his senses, as an infant peers at them, and touches them, and flexes them, and does its best to put them into its mouth.

But when those same particles slowed down and bound their energies into quiescence—when they congealed into solid "matter"—he found them very distasteful indeed.

It struck him as quite odd that his matter-copy on Nebo didn't seem to share his distaste for those repellently *solid* things it had discovered there. Worse than that. There were the small, active ones that had presented themselves without warning on the surface of the planet, and the doppel admitted humbly that it was not actually destroying them, but was indeed apparently helping them survive.

"But you just told me that you damaged the object they came from," Wan-To said incredulously.

"Yes, that is so, and pushed it away from me, too," the doppel confirmed. "But that was because it contained antimatter, it generated forces which could have imperiled my assignment. These smaller ones are quite harmless."

"They are quite *useless*," Wan-To snapped. The doppel was deferentially silent. Wan-To mused for a moment, then said, "You are quite sure the object with the antimatter does not present any problem?"

"Oh, yes. It is now in an orbit which will keep it from this planet, and it has no capacity to change that orbit anymore." The doppel hesitated, then said humbly, "You have taught me to be curious. These 'living matter' things are of interest. Shall I continue to observe them?"

"Why not?" Wan-To said testily, and discontinued the conversation. The doppel was basically so *stupid*. Wan-To resolved never again to make a matter-copy of himself; they simply were no fun to talk to.

He wondered briefly why the doppel bothered with the things, then dismissed it.

It never occurred to Wan-To that even the doppel could be as hungry for some sort of companionship as himself. Wan-To had never heard of "pets."

But Wan-To's loneliness did not end, and when his core reverberated with the call of one of his least threatening "relatives," Pooketih, Wan-To answered. He said at once, "Tell me, Pooketih, have you ever encountered living beings made of matter?"

"No, never, Wan-To," Pooketih replied, but then, to Wan-To's surprise, he added, "But Floom-eppit has, I think. You could ask him."

Wan-To was silent for a moment. He knew that he couldn't ask Floom-eppit anything, because Floom-eppit had failed to respond to anyone's calls for some time—one of the early casualties, no doubt. "You tell me what Floom-eppit said," he ordered.

"I will try, Wan-To. It was only a mention, when we were discussing what was causing so many stars to explode. He said he had encountered living things made of matter in one of the solid objects around a star he had inhabited for a while. He said they made him uncomfortable, so he moved."

"Just *moved*?"

"Well," Pooketih said, "he then, of course, zapped that star. He thought them an annoyance, and it was easy to end that problem." Pooketih hesitated. "Wan-To," he said, "I have had a thought. Is it possible that when Floom-eppit zapped that star one of us thought it was a hostile act?"

"Who would be so silly?" Wan-To demanded, but he knew the answer.

So did Pooketih. "You made some of us quite silly, Wan-To," he pointed out. "Perhaps one of us thought some other of us was trying to kill him. Why should any of us think that, Wan-To?"

Wan-To considered how to answer that. It sounded like a serious question. Was there guile behind it?

He was not quite sure how much guile Pooketih possessed. Pooketih was certainly not one of the cleverest of Wan-To's tribe. By the time he created Pooketih, Wan-To had already noticed worrying signs of insolence from Haigh-tik and Gorrrk and Mromm. And insolence was the first stage of insurrection.

It was quite likely, Wan-To had decided even then, that one of these ages he would have to take measures against them. So when he made Pooketih and the later ones he cautiously withheld from them a good quarter of his knowledge and at least half of his competitive drive. (But maybe even half was still dangerously much?)

"There is nothing in the universe that can harm any of us, except each other," Wan-To said cautiously. "I suppose that the knowledge that you can be destroyed by somebody is likely to make you think of destroying him first—for a certain type of mind, I mean."

"Do I have that type of mind, Wan-To?"

"Not on purpose," Wan-To said glumly.

"Do you?"

Wan-To hesitated, almost considering telling Pooketih the truth. But caution vetoed that impulse. "I made you," he pointed out. "I made all of you, because I wanted your companionship. I would miss you if you were gone."

"You can make others," Pooketih said sadly.

That was too true to deny. Wan-To was silent. Pooketih went on unhappily, "It was so nice when you first generated my patterns. I knew so little! Everything you told me was a wonderful surprise. I remember your telling me what your own star was like, and how it differed from mine."

Wan-To was suddenly uneasy. "That was a different star," he said quickly. "I have moved since."

"Oh, yes, so have I, several times. But that was so interesting, Wan-To! I wish you could tell me again."

Now Wan-To was definitely uncomfortable. "I don't want to do that now," he said shortly.

"Then tell me something different," Pooketih pleaded. "Tell me—for instance, tell me why it is that some groups of stars have suddenly changed their courses and moved away from us."

Wan-To wasn't uneasy anymore. Now he was quite convinced that Pooketih was trying, in his silly, innocent way, to probe for information he should not have. Wan-To said deceitfully, "Ah, but wouldn't that be interesting to know, Pooketih? Perhaps you can find out. Try to do that, Pooketih, then you tell me!"

And then Wan-To terminated the conversation and paused to consider.

Was it possible that Pooketih was not wholly without guile after all?

It was with regret that Wan-To decided Pooketih must be slain. As it turned out, though, that wasn't easy to do, because Wan-To himself was not safe. When five consecutive stars of his own type flared, each with a stellar mass between .94 and 1.12, Wan-To began for the first time in his long life to be afraid.

The resemblance between those stars and his own could not be an accident. Some one of his copies had deduced enough of what Wan-To's home star was like to start a systematic campaign of destruction. Someone's searching fire was specifically directed at *him*.

The option of flight was always open to him. He could quit this star and move to another. He could choose an unlikely one, he thought; maybe a little red dwarf, or one of those short-lived Wolf-Rayet kind of things. Neither was attractive as a permanent home—the dwarf star too confining, the huge infant star too unstable. But that was exactly the reason why no one would look for him there.

But—getting there! That was the problem! It meant abandoning the concealment of his star and launching himself as a pure pattern of energy, as naked and unprotected as any molting Earthly crustacean, across the interstellar void. The danger would not last for long. He would not be easy to spot. There was a good chance that he could make the journey and be safely hidden before one of his sibs detected his presence. He calculated the odds on survival as at least a hundred to one.

That one chance in a hundred was too much to take. Especially, Wan-To thought with pleasure, as he had a few tricks still up his sleeve.

So for some little time Wan-To was quite busy. He was making another copy of himself.

Practice, Wan-To was sure, made perfect. This time he was going to make the exact person he intended, without any possibly dangerous traits. Also, he schemed, with certain memories carefully excised; this copy would never cause him any trouble.

In order to do all that, Wan-To had to scan every part of his memory stores. Copy a pattern here, strike one out there; it was a lot like an earthly computer expert trying to adapt a program for, say, air traffic control to become one for, perhaps, ballistic missile defense. It took a long time, for there were billions of years of memories in Wan-To's store, and during all that time Wan-To could not permit himself any interruptions at all. So he turned off most of his scanning systems, muted the attention calls from his relations, even shut down his communication with the doppel on the planet Nebo. (As it happened, this was too bad in some ways, but Wan-To didn't know that.) He devoted himself entirely to the construction of the new being, and when its patterns had been completed he activated it with pride and hope.

The new being stirred and looked around. "Who are you?" it asked. And, almost in the same moment, "More important, who am I?"

"I am Wan-To, whom you love and wish well," Wan-To told it. "Your name is also Wan-To."

"But we can't both have the same name! Can we?"

"We do, though," Wan-To informed him. "Of course, just between the two of us you should have a different name, otherwise it would be very confusing, wouldn't it? So, just for the two of us—let me see—yes, I think we will call you 'Traveler.' "

"That isn't a proper name," Traveler complained. "Does it mean I am going to go somewhere?"

"How clever you are," Wan-To said with pride. "Yes. You are going to leave this star and take up residence in another one, far away."

"Why?"

"Because no star is big enough for two like us," Wan-To explained. "Don't you feel cramped? I do. We'll be much happier when you have a star of your own."

Traveler thought that over for a time. "I don't feel happy at all," he said. "I feel very confused. Why is that, Wan-To? Why don't I remember why you made me?"

"You're still very young," Wan-To said promptly. "Naturally you are still learning. But to develop properly you will have to go to a star of your own, and you are going to do that right away."

"I am?" the copy wailed. "But, Wan-To, I'll be lonely!"

"Not at all!" Wan-To cried. "That's the best part, Traveler! See, as soon as you leave here you will activate your communications systems—do you know where they are?"

"Yes," the copy confirmed after a moment. "I've found them. Shall I do that now?"

"No, no!" Wan-To said hastily. "Not *now*! When you're on your *way*. You will call all your new friends, who are waiting to meet you—Haigh-tik and Pooketih and Mromm. You will simply say to them, 'Hello, this is Wan-To calling.' "

"Is that all I say?" the copy asked doubtfully.

"No," Wan-To said judiciously. "You will also want to tell them exactly where you are. That information you will also find in your stores if you look. And then—and this is the most important part, Traveler—then you will forget that I exist. You will *be* Wan-To."

"I don't know how to do that," the copy wailed.

"You don't have to," Wan-To assured him comfortably. "You'll find that I've already arranged that; once you leave this star you won't remember anything about it, or me. And then," he promised grandly, "your new friends will tell you everything you need to know. They will answer all your questions. Now go, Traveler. And I wish you a happy journey."

When Wan-To's last remaining sensor informed him of a vector boson blast a few light-years away, he began to feel more at ease. They had taken the decoy. The zapping of G-3 stars would stop.

Now all he had to do was wait until the others had wiped themselves out . . . perhaps, he thought, for quite a long time.

Like Viktor and Reesa, in another place and time, he did not then know just how long that time would be.

C H A P T E R 14

By the time Viktor got his eyes well open he almost wanted to close them again. Even the long, still sleep of the freezers was better than this madhouse! First it was Reesa, shaky, fearful, trying to explain things to him—

"We're about to land on Newmanhome. These people found us and thawed us out . . ."

And then it was a man in a kilt, bearded and belligerent. "If you want him landed, get him awake, do you hear me? There's no time to waste!"

And then there were "these people" themselves. He managed to pry his sticky eyelids apart far enough to see "these people" for himself. None were familiar. Every one was a stranger, and strange to look at. There was the tall, olive-skinned man who wore the kilt, bare-chested and bare-legged in spite of the chill. There was another man, beardless, with a page-boy bob of sparse blond hair, who wore a ragged red pullover that came down to his knees, showing something like red tights underneath. Reesa herself wore an all-black outfit, like jogging sweats—cottony-flannelly pants and blouse, with a cowl covering most of her face. Another woman had the same outfit, except that instead of being black her sweatsuit was striped gray and white, like a prison uniform. "Who are 'these people'?" Viktor croaked.

His wife's face disappeared, and the angry, hostile countenance

179

of a bearded man in the same all-blacks took her place. "I'm Mirian," the man said savagely, "and we've saved your worthless life. You've been frozen here for hundreds of years."

"I warned you we should have left them that way," called the woman in the prisoner stripes.

Mirian disregarded her. "You're awake," he told Viktor, "and you're coming down with us."

"Down?" Viktor murmured dazedly. "Down where?" But nobody was answering him. There were eight or ten people in the old cryonics deck, and they were all busily rigging one of the pods for a drop. Reesa came over to him, wobbly and worried, holding out a set of the black sweats.

"Put these on," she begged. "If you're not ready I think they'll just leave us here!"

"Leave us here?" Viktor blinked. "Then why did they bother to come to save us?"

There was a sudden bark of unfriendly laughter from the man who called himself Mirian. "Oh, we didn't come to get you. We need this ship. We didn't even know you were here till we opened this pod up, looking for something to eat."

"And we should've left them frozen," the woman in red insisted. "Now what are we going to do?"

"We're going to drop them," the man in the kilt said belligerently. "Mirian, too. He woke them up; he takes them away, before they get in our way anymore."

"Not me!" Mirian shouted. "I'm part of this team, Dorro!"

"You're dropping with them," the kilted man snapped, "because I say so, and I'm the captain."

"You Greats are all alike," the woman sneered, but she turned to finish rigging slings in the pod.

Viktor turned helplessly to his wife. She shook her head, helping him knot the drawstrings of his sweats. "They only woke me half an hour ago, Vik. I don't know much more than you do. They wanted *Ark*—I'm not sure if it's for the antimatter fuel, so they can replenish the generators on *Mayflower*, or maybe to use it to explore the rest of the solar system—"

"We of the People's Republic do not waste time in 'exploring,'" the man in the kilt said frostily.

"Well, whatever. And things aren't so good on Newmanhome anymore, they say—"

Viktor held up a hand, imploring. "I don't understand," he said.

"Ok, Viktor," his wife groaned. "Well, try this much, anyway. We're *alive*."

That at least could not be argued. As Viktor finished dressing he told himself that simply to be alive, against all odds, was wonderful in itself. Wonderful? No, close to miraculous—thawed without microwave, without the oxygenating perfusion liquid, only raw heat. But his parts seemed to work. He thought for a moment of dying, blinded Captain Bu, who had gladly given them a chance for life on the expectation of his own reward in heaven. Thank God for Bu's born-again Christianity, Viktor thought. Without that conviction of a heavenly reward he might not have been nearly so willing to be the one who died.

Then Viktor thought of a question. "What about Earth?" he asked fuzzily. "Haven't they sent more ships?"

Mirian turned around to gape at him. Then he laughed. "Earth!" he said, and the others were laughing, too.

Viktor looked at them in puzzlement. "Did I say something funny?" he asked plaintively.

Mirian tugged at his pale, fine beard, glancing around to see if anyone else would answer. Then he said gruffly, "We have heard nothing from Earth for hundreds of years. Come, get into the pod; it's time to launch. And forget Earth."

Forget Earth!

But that was impossible. As Viktor was trying to urge his creaking muscles into the contortions necessary to climb into the capsule, twist himself into his harness, and strap himself in, he was not only not forgetting, he was actually remembering again all the scenes that had stored themselves away in the back of his childhood memories. The waves breaking on the Pacific shore, the white clouds in the blue sky, the heat of the high desert, the redwoods—

The world. Could all that be *gone*?

Then he couldn't think for a moment, because the hatches were grinding closed and he felt the quick nudge as the capsule fell free from its mother ship. He saw there was a window. It was tiny, and in a poor position for him to look out of it. But he did catch a quick glimpse of what had to be the proud planet of Newman-home . . .

But it was different, terribly different! There were a few clouds, but they were hard to see, because almost everything was white. Great Ocean was a wide blue sea no longer. It was as icy as Earth's Arctic Ocean, and, as with the Arctic, there was no clear line between sea and shore. Everything, *everything*, was ice.

"Hold on for retrofire!" Mirian shouted.

The sudden hammer blow of the rockets bruised Viktor's unpracticed body. That was only the beginning. The buffeting of atmospheric reentry seemed to go on forever. Then it ended; and then they were just falling, swaying on their sail-film parachutes.

Viktor shut his eyes. They no longer stuck together when he blinked, but he could feel the incrustations at their edges, and the flakes of dirt and dead skin on his body. Everything was happening too fast. He hadn't quite gotten used to being fired at by—whatever it was—on the planet Nebo; this unexpected new situation was more than he could take in.

Something very bright penetrated even his closed lids.

He opened them just in time to see a spot of incandescent light swing around the interior of the capsule as it rocked. Everyone was averting their eyes. The very bright something had peered in, for just a second.

"My God," Viktor said wonderingly. "Was that the *sun?*"

Mirian turned to him fiercely. "The sun? No, of course not. Are you crazy?"

"Then what was it?" Viktor persisted.

Mirian stared at him for a moment. Then he shook his head. "I keep forgetting—you don't know anything at all, do you? It wasn't always there, they say." He swayed as the capsule bobbed in a strong gust of wind, nearing the ground. "Brace yourself for landing!" he yelled; and then, to Viktor, he said, "That bright thing—it was what they call the 'universe.'"

CHAPTER 15

As it turned out, the time before Wan-To felt secure again was a very long time indeed. An appallingly long time, when you consider that through all of it Wan-To did not dare speak to any of his colleagues.

It wasn't because he wasn't hungry for conversation. He was very nearly desperate. So desperate that he had split himself into fractions once or twice, for convenience in talking to himself. It wasn't satisfying, but he had gone on trying to pretend that the echo he was hearing was really intelligent talk—until he thought that was making him almost irrational. He stopped that. He would have tried almost anything by then, though. He even began to wish that he could at least still talk to the harmless, stupid Matter-Copy Number Five. But that had long ago stopped being possible. It wasn't the distance. Einstein-Rosen-Podolsky pairs ignored distance. It was the relativistic effects of the speed the doppel's plunging flight had begun to attain. At Five's velocity, so close now to c, the pair was no longer identical. Even if the ERP had worked, the conversation would have been hopeless, because time dilation had come into play—a moment of Doppel Five's time was tedious millennia for Wan-To and the rest of the universe—but that problem didn't arise, because the ERP was no longer operational at all, and that was the end of that. Wan-To did not expect ever to hear from that doppel again.

Then he began to have problems of another kind.

He observed that the core of his star was filling with ash.

That was something to worry about. The stuff wasn't really "ash" in the sense of the oxidized residue of a chemical combustion, naturally; it was a slurry of helium ions, the stuff that was left over when hydrogen fused. He regretted a little that he had picked a mainstream star slightly larger than the norm. Yes, you got more energy to play with when your home star was large, but it didn't last as long, either.

Still, who could have guessed that he would be *stuck* in the thing, a prisoner, afraid to venture out?

Now and then the Einstein-Rosen-Podolsky communicators called Wan-To's name. He never replied.

Wan-To hadn't replied to anyone for a long time. He was far too suspicious. He was convinced that any call was almost certainly a trick, just one of his adversaries hoping to find out if he was really dead. Wan-To was too wise a bunny to fall for Brer Fox's wiles.

He was also far from happy. For the first time in his life Wan-To began to feel trapped. His jolly little stellar home had become a prison, and his cell became less comfortable every day.

It wasn't getting smaller. Far from it. In fact, the star was entering its red giant phase. It had spent most of its young life turning hydrogen into helium, but now the central core was all helium ash, doing nothing at all but sitting there and waiting for the day when it could fuse into higher elements.

Meanwhile, the remaining hydrogen was in a thick, dense shell around the helium core. It was fusing faster than ever—producing more heat than ever—pressing ever more insistently on the mantle of thinner gases that surrounded it; and the mantle was bloating under the pressure.

Wan-To had never stayed inside a star as it left its main sequence before. He didn't like it.

To be sure, his physical safety was not in danger. Well, not in much danger, anyway—certainly not as much as risking a hurried flight of his own to another home. But the star had swelled immensely under the thrust of that inner shell of fusing hydrogen. If it had had planets, as Earth's Sun did, its outer fringes would have been past the orbit of Mars by now. It was a classical red giant, swollen as huge as Betelgeuse or Antares—beginning to decay.

Did that give Wan-To more room? Infuriatingly, it did not. His star's mass did not increase. There was no more matter to fill that enlarged volume than there had been when it was its proper, normal size. Indeed there was less, because it was beginning to fall apart. The outer reaches of the star were so distant from the core and so tenuous—by Earthly standards, in fact very close to a vacuum—that the radiation pressure from within was actually shoving the farthest gases away from the star entirely. Before long those outer regions would separate completely to form that useless shell of detached gases called a planetary nebula.

And Wan-To knew that then nothing but the core would remain for him to occupy. A miserable little white dwarf, no larger than an ordinary solid-matter planet like the Earth—far too cramped to be a suitable home for anyone like Wan-To!

For that matter, he was too crowded already. He dared not risk any part of his precious self in those wispy outer fringes. He was imprisoned in the remaining habitable parts of his star, and worst of all he was blind. Photon-blind, at least; he could still detect neutrinos and tachyons and a few other particles, because they reached inside the outer shells easily enough. But light couldn't, and neither could any other part of the electromagnetic spectrum, and his delicate external "eyes" had long since been swallowed up and ruined as his star swelled.

So Wan-To tossed and turned in the home that had become his prison, fretfully ignoring every call that came in. Each one, in fact, was a fresh annoyance, if not simply a trap.

Then a voice on the ERP pair called again, and this time it did not stop with his name. "Wan-To," it said, "this is Mromm. I am quite sure you are alive. I want to propose a bargain."

Wan-To paused, suspicious and worried. Mromm! After all these eons!

It was a great temptation to answer. He was tired of being lonely and imprisoned; and it was surely possible, at least *barely* possible, that Mromm's intentions were friendly.

It was also possible, however, that they were not. Wan-To did not reply.

The voice came again. "Wan-To, please speak to me. The object that Haigh-tik destroyed wasn't you, was it? You wouldn't let yourself be caught that way, I'm positive."

Wan-To thought furiously. So it was Haigh-tik who was the killer! Or, alternatively, Mromm who was hoping to make Wan-To think he was innocent?

Mromm's voice sighed. "Wan-To, this is foolish. All the others are dead now, or hiding. I think Pooketih, at least, is simply hiding, but that comes to the same thing—he wouldn't dare to do anything just now, because then you or I might find him. I don't think there is anybody else. Won't you please answer me?"

Wan-To forced himself to be still. All of his senses were at maximum alert as he tried to decode Mromm's hidden meanings—if indeed they were hidden; if it weren't perhaps true that he was telling the truth?

And then Mromm, sounding dejected, said, "All right, Wan-To, I won't insist you speak to me. Let me just tell you what I have to say. I'm going to leave this galaxy, Wan-To. It's getting very unpleasant now. Sooner or later Haigh-tik will come out again, and he'll be just trying to kill everybody else off all over again—if there are any of us left. So I'm going away. And what I want to say to you, Wan-To is—please let me go!"

To all of that Wan-To was listening with increasing pleasure and even the beginnings of hope. If it were true that Mromm was leaving this used-up galaxy (and that sounded like a good idea, even if it came from Mromm), and that Haigh-tik was holed up and out of action at least for the time being, and all the others were either dead or, like Pooketih, terminally stupid . . .

"I'm going to take the chance, Wan-To," Mromm decided. "Even if you don't answer, I'm going. I'll never bother you again.

But please, Wan-To remember! I'm *part of you*. You *made* me! Please be kind . . ."

But by then Wan-To had long stopped listening to Mromm's foolish babble. He recognized a chance to escape when he saw it— and that meant he had to act *now*.

And so Wan-To left another galaxy behind. His objective this time was much farther away. Even as a pattern of tachyons, traveling many times faster than light, it would take a long time to reach it.

But that was all right; he had got away.

While Wan-To was in transit his thoughts were blurry and unclear; he would not be fully himself again until he reached the new galaxy and selected a proper star and used its energies to build the full majesty of himself anew. But, in his cloudy way, he was quite happy.

True, it was too bad that it had been necessary to destroy poor, trusting Mromm as soon as he left the shelter of his star, but Wan-To couldn't take chances, could he? And it meant he would be lonely for a long time—at least until he assured himself that any future copies of himself he might make for company would never, ever threaten him again.

But at least he would be *safe*.

And, countless thousands of light-years away, traveling far faster than Wan-To and in a completely different direction, the doppel on Nebo at last gave up hope of instructions from its master.

What a tragedy that Wan-To had not anticipated the presence of these strange matter-creatures! It meant that the doppel itself had to make the decision on what to do about them. And the doppel was not, after all, very smart.

CHAPTER 16

Having a new life, even on the icy and starveling Newmanhome of 432 A.L., was purely wonderful—or should have been. It did have certain lacks.

The lack Viktor most felt was of Reesa, kept away from him except for the odd fugitive glimpse. He missed her. He thought of all the things he would like to talk over with her. He had imaginary conversations with her, which mostly had to do with his complaints about the food, the housing, most of all the job they had assigned him to. (It did not occur to him, even in his fantasies, to tell her simply that he loved her.) And it was almost like talking to her really, because he was easily able to imagine her responses to his complaints:

"Quit bitching, Viktor. We were *dead*. Everything after that is a big plus."

And when he pointed out that they hadn't really been *dead* dead, just *frozen* dead:

"That's dead enough for me. Dead for *four hundred years*. Remember that, Viktor. Maybe things will get better later. Maybe we'll even get a room to have for our own."

"Maybe they'll even take me off the shit detail," Viktor muttered bitterly to himself, "but I wouldn't bet on when."

But it wasn't really as good as talking to the real Reesa would have been, and besides the words that stuck in his mind were *four hundred years.* Even though they were Newmanhome years—no matter how you calculated it, it was two Earthly centuries. Half a dozen human generations—several human *lifetimes!* Except for Reesa herself, everyone he had ever known was long since dead, gone, moldered, and forgotten. He would never come back to friends, for every friend was dead—the ones he would miss, the ones he had loved, even the ones he was quite willing to spare—like Jake Lundy, now presumably a pinch of dust somewhere on the surface of the planet Nebo. It didn't matter who: they were absent. Every relationship he had ever had was over. Every conversation he had ever intended would have to be left forever unsaid. Everyone who had made up the furnishings of his life was—history.

He could never go back to them—least of all, to his family.

That thought was the worst of all. It brought Viktor a sharp interior pain that made him grunt. (The others working on the shit detail looked at him curiously.) He would never see Yan or Shan again, or Tanya. Or little Quinn. They had all grown and aged and died hundreds of years before. They were *gone,* and nowhere in the universe was there anyone to fill the empty space their loss had left in his life.

To be alive when everyone who mattered to you was dead, Viktor realized morosely, was not unlike being dead yourself.

With all that to weigh on him, the inconveniences of his present existence should have seemed quite trivial. They didn't, though.

Viktor knew, of course, that he hadn't been singled out, particularly, for a hard life. Everyone had a hard life now. There weren't any easy ones. Newmanhome was completely frozen over; the few thousand surviving human beings struggled for a threadbare existence in tunnels in the ground; *everyone's* life was a struggle and a hopeless yearning for something better.

But these people certainly hadn't singled Viktor and Reesa out for any favors, either. The two unplanned and undesired new mouths to feed got the worst of housing, food—and, most of all, employment.

In other times it would have been different; weren't they *special?*

As Viktor worked crankily on his aptly named shit detail he reflected on the injustice of it all. They should have been celebrities. When the early European sea explorers had brought savages home to show off to their crowned heads and dabblers in science—people like Hawaiians and Tongans, bushmen and Amerindians from the Virginia coast—at least the bewildered aboriginals had had the pleasure of being the centers of fascinated attention. They were sources of entertainment for their hosts. Everyone crowded to see them.

That kind of life wasn't all pleasure, of course. The savages had to get used to being poked and prodded, gawked at and questioned. They had no more privacy than zoo creatures. But then, if they were lucky, months or years later, stuffed with foods that made them sick, taught the civilized vices of gambling and getting drunk, and, luckiest of all, if they hadn't acquired tuberculosis or the pox along the way—then, perhaps, they were allowed to return to their homes a world away.

Viktor and Reesa were not that lucky. There was nothing amiable in the greetings they received; and, of course, they had no home to return to.

More accurately, they *were* home. The tunnels and caves their captors lived in were on the same site as the town of Homeport they had left. Most of them were, anyway. The central common halls, the power plant with its endless trickle of geothermal heat, the freezers it fed—they were all on the hillside that had been just beginning to be covered with houses when Newmanhome's sun had begun to dim. The largest of the underground "towns"—the one belonging to the sect they called the Holy Apocalyptic Catholic Church of the Great Transporter—was under what had once been downtown Homeport. The Great Transporters weren't the only more or less independent tribe (or nation, or religion—anyway, a separate enclave that these paltry few had insisted on subdividing themselves into). Allahabad and the Reformers were along the shore, due west of the old town. The Peeps (actually they called themselves the People's Republic, and what their religion was exactly Viktor could not really tell) had even dug their warrens out under what had once been the bay, though now it was solid ice from bottom to top.

It wasn't the geography that had changed for Reesa and Viktor. It was their home itself, the world they had lived in, that was gone.

The tunnel dwellers didn't waste light on the mushroom farm—that was one of the big reasons for raising mushrooms—and when Viktor reported for work he stumbled around in the stinking dark until his eyes adjusted.

He hated the job. He had every reason to, but he had no choice about it. No one on (or under) Newmanhome was unemployed. Everyone had work, for long hours of every day—well, every day but one. They did get days off now and then. The Greats would not work on Sundays, the Reforms on Saturdays, the people from Allahabad on Fridays—these because their religions forbade it; and the Peeps had elected to consider Tuesday their day off because, although they had no comprehensible religion of their own, they had an obsessive need to make sure none of the others had any privileges they could not share.

Viktor and Reesa were special cases. As soon as it was determined that they not only were not members of any of the four sects (and, indeed, had never heard of them before their freezing), they were put in the newly invented category of stateless persons who were entitled to no days off at all. And the jobs they got were the jobs no adult wanted.

Viktor had thought his boredom on *Ark*'s long flight to Nebo was pretty close to intolerable. Now he looked back on it almost with longing, for his job on the "shit detail" was a good deal worse.

It wasn't only labor that wasn't wasted on Newmanhome. Nothing else was, either, not even excrement. When any person in the settlement had to relieve himself he followed strict procedures: Urine went into one vat, feces into another. The urine was processed to use its urea for nitrogen fertilizer for the underground crops. The feces became the most important constituent of the soil the crops were grown on.

Viktor got in on the ground floor. He was assigned to the unlovely task of spreading the fresh dung in a dark, unbearably malodorous cavern, where mushrooms grew on its surface and worms and dung beetles mined it for their nourishment. He wasn't alone in the job. Reesa wasn't with him, of course—they were kept mostly separate until such time as the Four-Power Council should decide their fate—but there were four other laborers assigned, one from each of the sects . . . and none of them older than Newmanhome twenty-two. Mooni-bet and Alcar, respectively Moslem from Alla-habad and Reformer from the quarrelsome, allegedly Protestant-Christian sect, harvested worms and beetles to feed the chickens in the breeder pens—it meant scurrying around on top of the peatlike layers of excrement and scooping the little living things up with slitted spoonlike tools. Mordi, the Great Transporter girl, and Van-dot, the boy from the People's Republic, harvested mushrooms, which was easier still. And that left Viktor the hard labor of shov-eling. The fresh loads of dung had to be spread onto the fields for the mushrooms to grow on. When they had produced a few crops and had aged enough to be fit for fertilizing other things, those sections had to be shoveled into wheeled vats, to be taken and mixed with soil for the lighted grain-growing caverns.

It wasn't the work that Viktor minded most, not even the stink and the hostility of the children he worked with. It was not *know-ing*—not knowing so many things! He didn't know where Reesa was, he didn't know what the blindingly bright thing they called the "universe" was. (Though he was beginning to have some very strange suspicions about that; relativistic effects were at work.) On a more immediate level, he didn't even know what was being de-cided about his and Reesa's future, and none of his co-workers wanted to talk.

It wasn't just him. They didn't even speak to each other very often. The hostility among the adults of the four sects was shared by the children, who worked in silent, disagreeable concentration. But children are children, and can't stay silent forever.

The worms and dung beetles and mushrooms they harvested had to be carried out to the chicken farms or the food depots. One day when three of the children were away from the excrement chamber, dragging their hoppers of harvest to their destinations, the young girl from Allahabad ventured close to Viktor, looking up into his face.

"Hello," he said, forcing a smile. "I'm Viktor. Which one are you?"

"I'm Mooni-bet," she said, glancing fearfully at the doorway. Then she whispered, "Is it true? Were you really on old Earth? Did you actually see *Mecca*?"

Viktor stared at her, startled. "Mecca? No, of course not. I remember California pretty well, and maybe even a little of Poland—
but I was as young as you when I left. And, until we left Earth, I
didn't get to do much traveling."

She stared at him, wide-eyed. "You saw *California*? Where the
movie stars and the *oil sheikhs* lived?"

"I don't remember any sheikhs or movie stars," Viktor said,
amused, almost touched by the girl's naïveté. "I mean, except on
television—but I suppose you have the old tapes of that kind of
thing, anyway."

"We do not look at graven images," the girl said sadly. "Not
counting sometimes when we're working in the bean fields, anyway—the Greats have screens there, but we're supposed to turn
away from them."

She had stopped her bug catching and was just standing there,
gazing curiously at him. Viktor rested on his spade, aware of a
chance that might not come again. "Tell me, Mooni-bet, do you
know where my wife is working?" She shook her head. "Or
whether they are going to give us a room of our own?"

"That is in the hands of the Four-Power Council," she explained. "You must ask your supervisor."

"I've asked him," Viktor said grumpily. His supervisor was the
Great Transporter named Mirian. Mirian was not a communicative
man, and he seemed to resent Viktor, probably as one more nasty
chore added to his burden. "He just tells me to wait."

"Of course he does. That is right. The Four-Power Council will
perhaps discuss your situation when they meet."

"And when will that be?"

"Oh, they meet all the time," she informed him. "Except holidays, I mean—they meet on Mondays, Wednesdays, and Thursdays.
But when they will come to your case I do not know. They have
much to discuss about important questions, for both the Peeps and
the Reforms are now on overload." She lowered her voice to a
whisper as she spoke, looking around as though she were discussing
something naughty. "I do not understand about that, but all is in
the hands of Allah."

"Oh, sure," Viktor agreed. Then, as she started to turn away, he tried to prolong the contact. "Mooni-bet? Tell me one other thing, if you will. That very bright thing in the sky—"

"The universe, yes," she said, nodding encouragingly.

"That's what I mean. Why do you call it the universe?"

"It's its name, isn't it? The muezzins call it that," she told him. "I don't know why. I thought the universe was all around us, but they say that is no longer true."

He blinked at her. "No longer true?"

The girl shook her head. "I don't know what that means, only it is what we bow to in devotions. They say old Earth is there, along with everything else." She paused, then added helpfully, "My father said when he was a boy it was much brighter. I don't know what that means, either, only—" She broke off, then turned away. Over her shoulder she whispered, "They're coming back! Don't talk to me anymore, please!"

"Why not?" he demanded. "Can't we talk while we work?"

"We *don't*," she whispered, looking agonizedly toward the returning workers.

"But I do," he said, smiling.

The three returning children stopped in the doorway, scandalized. The boy in the kilts of the People's Republic called menacingly, "I will report this!"

Viktor shrugged. "What is there to report, Vandot? I am simply talking; I have not been ordered to be silent, after all. If you don't want to listen, then don't listen. But I've been on Earth, and I am going to talk about what Earth was like, long ago, when I was young . . ."

And he did, shoveling the dung, while the mushroom cutters and beetle collectors lingered near him at their work. They glanced at each other diffidently, conscious that they were certainly bending the rules, if not breaking them outright; Mordi, the Great Transporter girl, was particularly uneasy, because she was the one from Viktor's own commune. But they were listening, all right. How could they help it? For Viktor was telling them about the traffic jams in the cities, the surf at Malibu, about flying in supersonic jets that crossed oceans in an hour. And about the experience of flying from star to star, when *Mayflower* was whole and mighty. And about life on the colony when *Mayflower* landed, and sailing across Great

Ocean in warm sunshine, and walking in the sun on a green meadow . . .

And by and by they began to talk, too. After all, they were only children.

Even slaves have to eat, and finally Vandot announced that the workday was done. Because Mordi had an errand to run Viktor followed the little girl, Mooni-bet, back through the tunnels to the caverns of the Great Transporters. She was nervous there, among the hostile black-shrouded enemies of her people. She was glad to abandon him at the entrance to the grown-up dining hall, disappearing to hurry to her own tunnels; and when Viktor entered he found his supervisor, Mirian, just coming in. The man looked glum. That didn't discourage Viktor; it seemed to be Mirian's normal expression. Viktor turned to face him. "I've been asking about that bright spot you called the universe," he said, "but the kids I work with don't seem to know much about it. Can I ask—"

He didn't finish, because Mirian gave him an unfriendly look. "No," Mirian said, crossing himself.

"No what?" Viktor asked plaintively.

"No, we do not discuss that subject here. I know nothing about it. I wish to know nothing about it."

"All right," Viktor said, suddenly angry, "then tell me what you do know about. When can my wife and I have a room of our own?"

Mirian stared at him belligerently. "A room of your own!" he repeated, raising his voice sarcastically so others could hear. "He wants a room of his own!"

"But I have a right to that much!" Viktor protested. "I don't even know where Reesa is—"

"She is housed with the Moslems in Allahabad, since they are not on overload just now," Mirian informed him.

"Of course, I know that, but what I want to know—"

"What you want to know is none of your business! In any case, I don't want to talk to you about it—not until the Four-Power Council issues its orders, certainly."

"Why do you have to be so nasty?"

"What right do you have to complain?" Mirian snapped angrily. "You owe us your life! And I am paying for my charity in reviving you!"

Viktor was puzzled. "Paying how?" he asked.

"I should be up on that ship, doing my proper work! But because they blame me for reviving you, they sent me back down to this miserable—" He stopped there, looking around to see if anyone had heard his complaints. Then he closed his mouth with a snap and turned away. He squeezed between two others on a bench, conspicuously leaving no room for Viktor to join him.

When Viktor sat down at another table the strangers next to him were equally unwilling to talk. Viktor sighed and devoted himself to his stew of corn and beans. At least, he reflected, the children had given him a pretty good idea of the polity and customs of this new Newmanhome. The four sects did work together on common needs. The chambers of the Four-Power Council were common and kept separate from the living quarters of the sects. So were the food-producing caves, or most of them—Allahabad insisted on growing its chickens and gerbils separately, for dietary reasons, and the People's Republic chose not to share the grain and bean fields of the others. (They weren't really "fields," of course. They were stretches of tunnels where artificial light fed plants that were hydroponically grown; and the austere diet of the Peeps was even less varied, and even less tasty, than the meals of the other three communities.) The freezer caves, where they had long before stored the animals they could no longer afford to keep alive, were also common, though there wasn't much food in them anymore. (The children didn't want to talk about the freezers, for reasons Viktor didn't at first understand.) The geothermal power plant was common, along with the datastores. All four communities shared their benefits and their responsibilities—though there weren't many responsibilities, since the original builders had done good work. The four factions had no choice about maintaining their common possessions, of course; if the power plant failed they would all be dead in a day.

But for most of their lives the sects stayed firmly apart. Great Transporters married Great Transporters, Moslems Moslems. The citizens of the People's Republic married no one, because they didn't believe in marriage, but they made love (on occasions directed by their leaders) only with their own. And all four communities tried their best not to have too many babies, all in their own ways, because there was barely food enough and heat enough and living space enough for the twenty-two hundred human beings already alive on (or, rather, under the surface of) Newmanhome.

Of course, their ways of keeping the population down differed from community to community. When Viktor found out about them he was startled, not to say repelled. The Reformers and the Moslems practiced nonprocreative sex—frequently homosex. The People's Republic did their best at abstinence, with males and females housed firmly apart except on designated nights, when a couple who had deserved well of the state were allowed to do well with each other. And the Great Transporters, so to speak, attacked the problem from the other end. Their religion forbade them to take life—well, except in war, of course. For that reason they didn't use contraception, nor did they practice abortion; they had babies, lots of babies, and when they pruned their populations it was among the adults—at least, mostly among the *near* adults, anyway; if a Great Transporter child managed to survive his rebellious adolescence he had a fair chance of a natural death, sixty or seventy Newmanhome years later.

What the Great Transporters did was dispose of their criminals, and they had a lot of criminals. In their community there were two hundred and eighty statutory crimes punishable by their supreme penalty—it came to about one crime for every two persons in the community, and the sentence was passed frequently.

Of course, the sentence wasn't death. Not exactly, anyway. Execution was another of the life-taking sins that was prohibited. They had a better way. They put their criminals in the freezer.

It was fortunate for the Great Transporters that there was so much unused freezer space. The freezers had been big to begin with. Then they had been further enlarged when Newmanhome began to get too cold to support outside life, and tens of thousands of cattle and other livestock were slaughtered and frozen. The freezers had their own independent, long-lasting lines to the geothermal power plant; they were fully automatic and would last for the ages.

But that was one more of the many sources of friction among the communities, because the Greats were rapidly filling them up.

The four communities rubbed abrasively against each other in plenty of other ways. The Great Transporters hated to see even unbelievers profane their Sabbath. The Moslems lost their tempers when they saw anyone drinking alcohol; the Peeps were constantly irate about the wasteful, sinful "luxuries" of the other three groups, while the Reformers simply hated everyone else.

That was where the work of the Four-Power Council came in. They usually made sure that the frictions were kept minor. The system worked pretty well. They had not fought a real war for nearly eighteen years.

Viktor slept badly that night, in his barracks with forty other unattached male Greats sniffling and snoring and muttering in their sleep all around him, and the next day at his loathsome job was no better than the last.

Even the children seemed to have second thoughts about their undisciplined behavior of the day before. When Viktor asked Moonibet if she had seen Reesa the girl hung her head. She looked worriedly to see if anyone was listening, then whispered, "We are on overload now, Viktor. She has been moved to the Peeps."

And then, when Viktor tried to ask Vandot, the boy from the People's Republic snapped at him. "We are here to work, not to chatter like religious fanatics."

"Watch your mouth!" the girl from the Reformers snarled at him.

"I only say what is true," Vandot muttered. "In any case, I know nothing of your wife, Viktor. It is not my business. Nor is it yours; because your duty is to pay us all back for reviving you from—" He hesitated, not willing to say the word. "For reviving you," he finished. "Now get to work."

Viktor didn't answer that. It wasn't because he had been ordered by a child. He hadn't quite figured out what an answer to that sort of remark ought to be. It was true that he was alive. That is to say, his heart pumped, his eyes saw, his bowels moved. Even his genital organs were still in working condition, at least he thought they would be if he were allowed to be with Reesa long enough, in enough privacy, to test them out.

But was that really a "life"?

It was certainly a kind of life, but Viktor could not believe that it was the only life he was ever going to have again. It was not at all *his* life.

His life had been on a very different Newmanhome, with very different friends, family, and job. Especially job. Viktor Sorricaine's job had never been simply the thing he put hours into in order to keep himself fed. Viktor's job had been his profession. His *position*. His skills. It was the thing he could organize his life around, the thing he *was*. And Viktor Sorricaine could not recognize himself as a shoveler of human dung. He was a trained pilot! More than that, he was at least an amateur, thanks to his father's endless lecturing, of such things as astrophysics—the very person these people needed to investigate this eerie ghost in the sky that they called the universe. That was what Viktor Sorricaine was . . .

From which it followed that this chilly, weary dung shoveler wasn't the real Viktor Sorricaine, and this life was not *his*.

And when Mooni-bet came near him again in her gathering of dung beetles, he spoke to her, not keeping his voice down. "I do have a complaint, Mooni-bet," he told her. "I'm being wasted here. I have skills that ought to be used."

The girl looked at him desperately. "Please," she whispered, looking over her shoulder.

"But it's important," Viktor insisted. "That thing they call the universe. It needs to be understood, and I have scientific training—"

"Be still!" the Peeps boy cried, coming up to them. "You are interfering with the work!"

"Anyone can do this work," Viktor said reasonably, refraining from pointing out that it was a task that even silly children could handle. Obviously.

"We *all* must work," Vandot cried, his shrill boy's voice almost cracking. He rubbed his hands nervously on his smeared kilt, staring around at the others in the gloom. Mordi, the Great Transporter girl, averted her eyes, but when she glanced toward Viktor her look was almost guilty. Vandot asserted his righteous young masculinity. "The most important thing is survival," the boy declared. "And the most important part of that is food. Shut up and get those beds prepared!"

Survival, Viktor thought bleakly. True enough. That seemed to be the central rule of the game.

It was natural enough that the social structure for these people had to bend to conform. Their rigid ways were a pattern for survival. Earth's Eskimos, in their far milder climate, had developed unusual social institutions of their own to deal with the brutal facts of their lives. True, the Eskimos had solved the problem in a different way—without rigid laws and stern central government, without punishment (and these people were absolutely *devoted* to punishment)—but then the Eskimos had started from a different position. They hadn't had long-ingrained traditions of certain kinds of governments and religions to try to preserve. They came into their harsh new environment without the baggage of any real government or religion at all.

The people of this new Newmanhome, in Viktor's eyes, were both authoritarian in government and fanatic in religion. So they lived their dreary, deprived, regimented lives in the caverns under the ice crags that had once been the city of Newmanhome. They had a few things going for them—fortunately, because otherwise they could not have survived at all. The most important one was that, although their sun had gone pale, the fires inside the planet still burned as hot as ever. The geothermal wells produced heat to keep their warrens livable, and even power enough to run their little factories (not to mention their freezers). The supply was not at all lavish. There certainly wasn't enough energy to be had to keep Newmanhome's tens of thousands of people alive . . .

But then there weren't that many people left alive anymore. Not on Newmanhome. Not anywhere.

When, grudgingly, Vandot allowed that work was through for the day, Viktor tried to scrape some of the filth off his hands. He looked around for Mordi, expecting to walk back to the

Greats residence together, but she had already left the growing cavern.

What a drag, Viktor thought irritably. He was fairly sure he could find his way by himself, but there was no reason she couldn't have waited for him . . .

She had.

She was standing outside the cavern, looking both frightened and resolute, and next to her was his supervisor, Mirian.

"You simply won't cooperate, will you?" Mirian said angrily. "What Mordi reported was true. You not only don't do your own job, you interfere with the others."

Viktor gave the girl a reproachful look. She shrugged disdainfully and turned to leave. "All right," Viktor said, "you've made your point. Now let's get something to eat."

"Eat!" the supervisor growled. "We'll be lucky if we eat at all this night, you've seen to that. I've got to bring you to the Four-Power Council for a hearing. Come on!"

There wasn't any use questioning Mirian when the man didn't want to talk. Viktor tried anyway, of course. He wasn't surprised when Mirian simply shook his head and pointed toward a rack of parkas.

That was the first Viktor had known that they were going outside.

And then, as they battled their way across the hummocks in the teeth of a freezing gale, he looked up and saw the thing that had puzzled him most: the "universe." It was like a sun, but it was immensely brighter than any sun, a pure, blue-white point in the sky that seared his eyes.

He tried to imagine how their little group of stars could possibly have been flung so fast, so far, that they were catching up with the light from every body in the universe. They had to be moving almost at the velocity of light itself! If only there were someone to ask, someone to talk to . . .

But while they were in the open it was too cold to talk, and then, when they were in the separate cavern that housed the meetings of the Four-Power Council, Viktor almost forgot his questions about the strange thing. For an unexpected joy was waiting for him.

Reesa was there.

It was the first time they had been together in the two weeks since landing, and as Viktor saw her sitting there, in the bare, cramped waiting room, with her People's Republic "hosts" watchful on either side, he felt a sudden, unanticipated rush of longing, pleasure and—what was it? He thought it over, as he held her in his arms, while the Peeps grumbled menacingly, and decided it was simply love.

He understood that with wonder. It was a novel thought for him. Reesa had been his wife, of course. She had been a comfort, a pleasure, a partner—she had been a useful adjunct to his life in many ways; but he had never before realized that he had somehow grown to center his life around her in the classical tradition of monogamous love. That sort of romantic fixation had been reserved for Marie-Claude Stockbridge.

It was a surprise to Viktor to realize that he had not even thought of Marie-Claude since they had come back to life in this icy hell.

"Are you all right?" he whispered into his wife's fine, warm-smelling hair.

"I'm fine," she said. "I've been tending the gerbils and the chickens—you wouldn't believe what they feed them! Bugs and worms and—"

"Oh, I believe, all right," Victor assured her, hesitating at the choice: tell her about his own work, or tell her about the startling new truth he was bursting to share? He released her, looking at her consideringly. She didn't *look* fine. She looked careworn.

Nevertheless, the impulse to tell the truth won out. "That bright spot we saw—the universe? Do you know what it means? It means that somehow—God! I can't imagine how!—our whole solar system and some of the others nearby are rushing through space at relativistic speeds! We're traveling so fast we're actually sort of catching up with the light ahead of us! And—" He paused, blinking at the expression on her face. "What's the matter?" he demanded.

"Go on, Viktor," she said encouragingly. "You were saying about the stars that are moving at nearly light speed—ours and eleven others, right?"

He stared at her. "You *knew* that?"

"The Peeps told me, yes," she said. "They say it's been like that for three hundred years, almost, except that it used to be brighter than it is now."

"Well, *shit*," he said angrily. "If these people knew that, why wouldn't the Greats tell me?"

She looked at him absently for a moment. Then she nodded. "I forgot you were with the Greats," she said. "They don't believe in it. I mean, they don't believe in asking questions about *why*. They go by their Bible. If there's anything that isn't in the Third Testament, they don't want to discuss it at all."

"But—" he began, and then stopped. What was there to say? He was fuming inside, but there was no point in burdening Reesa with his anger against these people and their folly, especially when she herself was staring unhappily into space.

It took that long for Viktor to realize there was something else on his wife's mind.

"What is it?" he demanded. "Are the Peeps giving you a hard time?"

She looked at him in surprise. "No harder than anyone else, really."

"Then what's the matter with you?"

She looked at him blankly, then shook her head. "It's just—" She hesitated. Then, looking away, she finished. "It's just that I keep—wondering, Viktor."

"Wondering about what?"

"I wonder if Quinn had a happy life," she said, and would say no more.

It was a long, silent time before the door to the council chamber opened, and Mirian came out.

He came over to them. "You are granted asylum," he said grudgingly. "The council has just made its decision."

"But—but—but I thought we'd appear before them!" Viktor exclaimed.

Mirian looked at him curiously. "Why would the council want you to do that? What could you tell them that they don't already know, from the transcripts of your questioning?"

"I wanted to talk about the universe!" Viktor shouted. "My father was an astrophysicist—I learned from him! The way that thing looks in the sky has to mean that our whole group of stars is traveling very close to the speed of light, and I want to help to figure out *why*!"

Mirian looked suddenly gray. "Shut your face," he hissed, glancing around. "Do you want the freezer again? Most of us are on overload now, you know—if the orbital power plant doesn't start working soon there'll be a hell of a big freezing bee! No, count your blessings, Viktor. The council thinks you two might be helpful in launching the rockets for the fuel transfer—that's a break you don't deserve. Don't screw it up by talking blasphemy!"

CHAPTER 17

$\mathbf{W}$an-To's first few thousand years in the galaxy that was his new home went like the twinkling of an eye, and he was busy all the time. There was so much to do!

None of it was really *difficult* for him, of course. There was nothing he hadn't done many times before—this was, after all, his twentieth or thirtieth star, not to mention that he was now on his third galaxy. He had had plenty of practice, and so he knew exactly what to do first and precisely how to do it.

The first two things were to sniff out every corner of his star and to rebuild his external eyes. That didn't take very long. A century or two, and he was already at home. Wan-To had chosen an F-9 star this time—a little bigger and brighter than most of those he had preferred before, but he felt he deserved the extra energy, which was to say the extra comfort.

Then, of course, he had to check out the rest of this new galaxy. That necessarily took quite a lot longer. It meant creating a few thousand Einstein-Rosen-Podolsky pairs and sending them off to other parts of the galaxy, so he could keep an eye on everything that was going on in the new territory he had claimed.

Wan-To couldn't help feeling a certain tension during that period. After all, a galaxy is a big place. The one he had chosen had nearly four hundred billion stars, with a well-defined spiral structure—a pretty desirable neighborhood, and how could he be sure that some undesirable element didn't lurk somewhere in it?

But as the reports from his widespread ERPs began to arrive, they all came up empty. As far as he could tell, which was pretty far, every object in this galaxy was simply obeying the dumb natural laws of physics. There were no unwelcome signs of tampering. No unexplained patterns in the photospheres of any of the several billion stars he was able to examine in detail, no radiation coming in to any of his sensors that wasn't explained by the brute force of natural processes.

Wan-To began to relax. He had found a safe new home! Like any ancient mountain man, coming across a verdant Appalachian valley for the first time, he saw that it was his to clear and plant and harvest and *own*, and he might easily, like one of them, have said, *This is the place.*

He was *secure.*

It was only after he was well settled in, with all his sensors deployed and all their reports reassuring, that it occurred to Wan-To to ask the next question:

Secure for *what?*

Wan-To mused over that question for a long time. He was not religious. The thought of a "religion" had never crossed Wan-To's mind, not once in all the billions of years since he had first become aware that he was alive. Wan-To could not possibly believe in a god, since Wan-To, to all intents and purposes, was the most omnipotent and eternal god he could have imagined.

Nevertheless, there were occasional troubling questions of that sort that passed through Wan-To's vast mind. A human philosopher might have called them theological. The most difficult one—it was hard for Wan-To even to frame it—was whether there was any *purpose* in his existence.

Naturally, Wan-To was well aware of one overriding purpose of a kind—self-preservation, the one imperative that governed all of Wan-To's plans and actions. Nothing was ever going to change that; but once it occurred to him to ask what he was preserving himself *for* he could not quite see an answer.

The troubling question kept coming back to him.

Perhaps it was just that Wan-To was passing through what humans called "a mid-life crisis." If so, it had come upon him early. Wan-To wasn't anywhere near middle-aged. He was hardly past the adolescence of his immensely long span of existence, for he wasn't then much more than twelve or fifteen billion years old.

Wan-To didn't spend all his time brooding over the meaning of it all. He had plenty to do. Just investigating every corner of his new galaxy, first to seek possible enemies, finally just to know it, took quite a while—there were, after all, those four hundred billion stars, spread over some trillions of cubic light-years of space. Over a period of a few millions of years he studied the data coming from the Einstein-Rosen-Podolsky pairs he had planted at strategic locations in the arms, in the core, in the halo, everywhere in the galaxy that looked interesting. A lot of it was interesting indeed—coalescing gas clouds heavy with the approaching birth of new stars, supergiants exploding into density waves that impregnated other clouds, black holes, neutron stars . . . He had seen them all before, of course, but each one was just a little different, and generally intensely interesting.

Then that permanent itch of curiosity that needed always to be scratched drove his investigations farther into space. His galaxy was his own, uncontested; but Wan-To well understood that one little galaxy was very small stuff indeed in the vast scale of the expanding universe.

When he looked out on the distant rest of the universe he could not see that it had changed much in the few billion years of his investigations. There was a certain tendency for the distant blue fuzzies to turn greenish—they were farther away now, and receding relatively faster. And he saw that some of the older galaxies, even a few quite nearby, were beginning to show signs of senile decay. They were shrinking and losing mass—"evaporating" is the word that would have occurred to a human being. Wan-To understood the process very well. When any two stars happened to wander close to each other in their galactic orbits—as was bound to happen, time and again, in eternity—they interacted gravitationally. There was a transfer of kinetic energy. One picked up a little velocity, the other lost some. Statistically, over the long lifetime of a galaxy some of those stars would keep on adding speed and others would lose some—the faster-moving ones would sooner or later be flung clear out of their parent galaxy, while the slower ones would spiral hopelessly down toward collapse in the center, forming mammoth black holes. Such a process didn't happen *rapidly*—not in a mere few billion years, that was to say.

But Wan-To could see the process going on, and it made him wonder uneasily about his future.

He wished he had someone to talk to about all these things.

He wished, in fact, that he had someone to talk to about anything. He was getting really lonesome.

He brought himself up sharply every time he came to that point in his thinking, because he knew what the perils were of creating company for himself . . .

But in the long run he could not help himself. He succumbed. It was inevitable. Even Adam hadn't been able to stand the solitude of Eden forever.

Wan-To reminded himself that, whatever else they might be, any new copies of himself first and foremost had to be *safe*. He wanted no one, ever, sniping at him from ambush again.

So the first playmate he created in his new galaxy was stringently edited, with every character trait that led toward independence of action carefully censored out, and an unswervable devotion to himself tailored in. He omitted all the information that made it possible to use the gravitational forces that could wreck stars; he blotted out the parts that led to such emotions as anger and jealousy and pride. He made the new copy, most of all, *content*.

His newest copy was only a shadow of himself, really. It wasn't much smarter than his almost forgotten doppel, Matter-Copy Number Five. It didn't have enough personality to deserve a real name. Wan-To called it "Happy."

Happy was certainly happy. Happy took everything in stride. If Wan-To snapped at him, Happy replied with soothing burbles of good-natured sound—you might almost call them "giggles." When Wan-To was in a bad mood, Happy blithely ignored it.

Since one of the things Wan-To wanted from his dream companions was sympathy, he tried again. The new one was as dumb and feckless as Happy, and as impotent to cause trouble, but it was designed to *care* about Wan-To; he named it "Kind."

Within the next few thousand millennia Wan-To had created for himself a "Funny" and a "Sweet" and a "Sympathetic" and even a "Motherly"—Wan-To didn't call it exactly that, of course, because he had no idea of "mothers"; but if it had been human it would have clucked over him and fretted when he fretted and every day made him chicken soup.

So for a while Wan-To was no longer alone. But they weren't real company. They were idiots.

He was surrounded by a dozen cheerfully babbling children— sweet, obedient, charming . . .

Stupid.

No matter how much a parent loves his little ones, there comes a time when he wishes they would grow up . . . and Wan-To realized ruefully that he had made that impossible for his new flock. He was almost tempted to make a few more, with just a *trifle* more of independence and agressiveness . . .

But self-preservation always intervened.

Then he got his first real surprise.

One of his widespread Einstein-Rosen-Podolsky pairs reported peculiar behavior on the part of a star in its neighborhood. The thing had *flared.*

Well, that in itself wasn't very interesting. Stars were flaring somewhere in his galaxy all the time; it was a thing that some stars did. But this one was different. *Frighteningly* different. It wasn't behaving in the normal fashion of any proper flare star, but very much the way Wan-To and his earlier family had caused in their jolly little war of brothers. It was what Earthly astronomers had briefly called a "Sorricaine-Mtiga object"—

And it was not natural.

For a moment Wan-To felt stark terror. Had some of the others survived and sought him out here? Had some of his new brood somehow, impossibly, managed to break through their programming? Was there a *threat?*

If it was, it was not from any of his children. He queried each one of them, sternly, carefully, and their innocently wondering replies were convincing. "Oh, no, Wan-To, *I* haven't destroyed any stars. How could I? I don't know *how*." And, "We *wouldn't* do anything like that, Wan-To, you wouldn't *let* us."

Nevertheless another star flared.

The alternative possibility was even more frightening. Could one of that old crew of ingrates have followed him here? But there were no signs of it—none of any intelligence in any of the four hundred billion stars of his new galaxy. Not even a whisper of tachyon transmission, not anywhere.

As a last, baffled resort, it occurred to Wan-To to check some of the planets in systems near the flared stars . . . and what he then found was the most incredible thing of all.

There were *artifacts* there! On *planets*! There were planets where energy was being released, sometimes quite a lot of it, in forms and with modulations that were never natural!

There was alien life in his galaxy, and it was made of solid *matter*.

For the first time in many millions of years Wan-To thought of his lost doppel on the little planet he had sent speeding off into infinity. That had told him of solid-matter life, too, and he had dismissed it. But what was going on here was something else. These— creatures—were using quite high-order forces. If they could flare stars, then they knew how to manipulate the vector bosons that controlled gravity. And that meant that they might someday threaten Wan-To.

There was only one thing to do about that. Horrified, Wan-To did what any householder would do when he discovered loathsome pests in his backyard. It was a job for an exterminator.

It was only when Wan-To had made quite sure that none of those pesky little things survived that he thought of his lost doppel again. His good humor recovered, he thought with amusement of the way the doppel had tolerated them.

Well, if it had, Wan-To thought, it probably by now had learned the error of its ways.

———————

But in fact the doppel hadn't.

It had been a long time for the doppel to be out of contact with Wan-To—not nearly as long, in its time-dilated frame of reference, as it had been for Wan-To himself, of course, but still long enough. It had been quite long enough for the doppel to realize, with a real sense of loss, that there weren't ever going to be any fresh orders from its master.

The doppel had no way of communicating with Wan-To's murderous rivals, either. Even if they hadn't been cut off by the relativistic effects of the system's all-but-light velocity just as Wan-To himself had, Five had no Einstein-Rosen-Podolsky mechanisms for reaching them anyway. Wan-To had made sure of that. In fact, there was not any intelligent being, anywhere within the range of the doppel's senses, at all—except for those few strange solid-matter creatures it had permitted to live (for a while) on the surface of its planet.

The doppel certainly had very little in common with such rude entities. But they were *there*, and even a doppel can get lonesome.

It was for that reason that Five had permitted the survivors among the creatures that fell out of the destroyed *Ark* to reach the surface of Nebo without being annihilated. One of them, unfortunately, had gotten seriously broken when Five bashed its container, but there were three others.

In its first casual "glance" Five saw that there was nothing about the three surviving little monsters that constituted any kind of a threat. If they had been a little more technologically advanced—if they had carried with them any of that worrisome antimatter that the ship held, or any kind of weaponry more advanced than mere chemistry—then they would have died before they touched ground.

Five was not very intelligent, but it was smart enough to be assured that these things represented no danger at all.

Well, then, what did they represent?

When Five reported them to its master, Wan-To's response was not very helpful. Wan-To didn't tell it what to do about them. Wan-To left the matter discretionary.

So Five did what it was best equipped to do. It studied the things.

From the point of view of little Luo Fah, the first in the landing party whom Five chose to examine, that process was terrifying, agonizing, and fatal. Luo had hardly stepped out of the lander, mask pumping oxygen into her faceplate, pistol at the ready, when she was snatched brutally into the air and—well—disassembled. The clothes, the gun, and the air mask were the first to go, as Five methodically dismantled its curious little specimen to see what it was all about. There was stark fear and a lot of pain as things were wrenched off her with little concern for what they did to her clutching fingers and resisting limbs. The next part was far worse, but fortunately for Luo she didn't feel it. She was dead by the time the interior of her body was opened up for study.

The other two in the team were luckier—for a while.

One specimen had been enough for Five to deduce, roughly, how these things worked. They had a chemical basis, it perceived. They required an influx of gases (it didn't call the process "breathing," but it understood the necessity from the distress Luo had exhibited when it took her mask away). So it determined simply to observe the others for a while.

Five was cautious, of course. When it detected electromagnetic radiation, definitely patterned in nonnatural ways, coming from something inside the lander it could not permit that—who knew what the purpose of it was? So it destroyed the lander's radio transmitter with one quick, controlled bolt. That was bad luck for the man who happened to be the one transmitting, because the blast burned his face quite horribly. But it wasn't quite as bad for Jake Lundy, because Five then perceived that it had to be more careful with these things.

Five did not exactly have emotions. What Five had was orders. They were the commandments written in stone. They could not be violated . . . but what a pity that they hadn't included instructions for dealing with these solid-matter creatures and their artifacts.

Five also had a good deal of resourcefulness. What it didn't know it was quite capable of trying to learn. It was always possible, it reasoned, that at some time Wan-To would call again and would want to be fully informed about these unexpected visitors.

So it permitted those two to live. They were fascinating to

watch. Five was fascinated to observe, as the burn victim's wounds slowly began to heal, that they seemed to have some sort of built-in repair systems, like Five itself. (But then why hadn't the two earlier ones managed to put themselves back together?) As Five learned more and more about their needs it even provided them with the kinds of air they seemed to want—the kinds, at least, that they kept inside their vehicle. When it deduced they also needed water—by observing how carefully they measured it out to each other in captivity—it made them some water. When it discovered they needed "food"—which took quite a while longer, and the two survivors were cadaverous by the time Five got to that point—that was harder, but Five had of course long since investigated the chemistry of the things the specimens had eaten, and of the excrement they insisted on carrying outside and burying. It was no impossible task for Five to create a range of organic materials to offer them; and some, in fact, they did seem to be willing to "eat."

Unfortunately for Jake and his one surviving companion, that was pretty late in the game.

Five saw that things were going badly for its specimens. They were moving slower and more feebly. Sometimes they hardly moved at all for long periods. They spent a lot of time making sound vibrations to each other, but those slowed and became less frequent with time, too, as did their peculiar habit of, one at a time, making those same sound vibrations to a kind of metallic instrument. (Naturally Five investigated the instrument, but it seemed to do nothing more than make magnetic analogues of those vibrations on a spool of metal ribbon, so it returned the thing to them only slightly damaged.)

Five wondered why they didn't copy themselves, so as to have new, young beings of their sort to carry on for them. It thought that would be nice. That would provide a permanent stock of such playthings; Five could investigate them in detail, over a long period of time, offering them all kinds of challenges and rewards to see what they would do.

Disappointingly, the time came when the second of them stopped moving entirely, and as the body began to bloat Five reluctantly conceded that its specimens had died. And they hadn't ever copied themselves!

Five could not understand at all. It had never occurred to the doppel that they were both male.

A little while later—oh, a few hundred years—when the specimens were long dissolved into uninteresting dust, Five got another surprise.

When the doppel had not heard from Wan-To for all that time, because the relativistic shift had decoupled its Einstein-Rosen-Podolsky pair, it began to wonder if it should not try some other kind of communication. Or, more important, whether Wan-To was trying to call it, say, by means of tachyons.

So it began listening more intently on the tachyon frequencies, then even on the unlikely electromagnetic ones. It heard nothing—nothing, at least, from any stellar source anywhere, except for the endless hiss of hydrogen and the chatter of carbon monoxide and the mutterings from all the other excited molecules in the stellar photospheres and gas clouds—nothing that was *artificial*.

Until it realized that there was, in fact, a quite definitely artifactual signal beginning to come in now and then on the radio frequencies. It closely resembled the one that had caused it to destroy the lander's radio—and it came from Five's own solar system.

In fact, it came from a *planet*. That was astonishing to Five. A human being would not have been more surprised if a tree had spoken to him.

Of course, the doppel had no idea what messages were being conveyed by these bizarre signals, but once it had located their source it took a closer look in the optical frequencies, and what it saw gave it a start.

The hulk of the ship it had blasted was beginning to move under its own power again. It was being hijacked!

In that moment of discovery, Five came very close to again unleashing the forces that had destroyed *Ark* in the first place. If it had been a human, its fingers would have been on the button. Since Five was only a matter doppel it had no fingers; but the generators which produced the X-ray laser began to glow and build up to full power.

But they didn't fire.

Five withheld the command. It couldn't make up its mind what to do. If only Wan-To could be asked for instructions!

Fretfully Five ran over its instructions. There was nothing useful in them about solid-matter beings. All Five was ordered to do, really, was to snatch this group of stars out of its neighborhood and fly it away. It had done that. And it had no useful further instructions.

Five tried to do what its program had never intended it for; it tried to decide on its own if its instructions had some sort of built-in termination. The energies of the stars themselves kept pushing them faster and faster, by always lesser increments of velocity, right up against that limiting velocity of light itself.

Should Five allow them to go on accelerating forever? Trying to accelerate, at least—the rate of acceleration was always dropping now, asymptotically to be sure, but converging toward c itself.

If not, when should Five stop it? If it stopped, what should it do then?

Five had no answers to those questions. It would have to use its own discretion, perhaps—but if it guessed wrong, Wan-To might be angry.

Five was desperate, but not desperate enough to risk that. Not yet.

CHAPTER 18

Because the plan to revive *Mayflower's* MHD-microwave generators had originated with the Great Transporters, it was a Great Transporter woman named Tortee who was in charge. When Viktor and Reesa reported to her room she was waiting for them. Not patiently.

Tortee turned out to be incongruously fat, and that was astonishing to Viktor. How could anyone get that much to eat in this mob of the underfed? She was lying back on a chaise longue, blankets wrapped over her plump legs, and she glared at them suspiciously. "Who are you? Where's that silly little bitch with the tea?" she demanded. "Never mind. Where were we? Oh, yes," she remembered, sounding spiteful, "what they want to do is to try to start up the orbiting power generator again. Do you know what I'm talking about?"

"Of course, Tortee," Reesa said, causing Viktor to look at her sharply. Her tone had been admiring and deferential. Even soapy.

"Well, it's a waste," Tortee grumbled. "What they want us to do is take the little bit of fuel that's left in *Ark* and transfer it to *Mayflower*, turn it into electricity, beam it down. It's crazy."

"I guess so," Viktor said slowly. Following his wife's lead, he was doing his best to be agreeable to the old woman—Reesa's eyes were on him, to remind him. Still, the plan didn't sound entirely crazy to him. It wasn't that different from what he had helped do a few hundred years before. But Tortee was the boss of the project that had got him off the shit detail, and he didn't want to argue with her—especially not here in her own room, with view screens and computer terminals all around her. Terminals meant *data*. He coveted that room—not least for its huge, wide bed.

"No, that's really crazy," Tortee was insisting. "Think! We'd have to rebuild the rectenna in the first place; they tore that down long ago for the metal—and what would we have to tear down now for metal to rebuild it? Then there's the problem of transferring fuel from the engine accumulators in one ship to the generators in another. That's a lot harder than what you did back in the old days, Viktor. Then you only had to move the whole reserve fuel storage unit, right? And that was dangerous enough, but this means taking the *drive* apart. I've studied the plans. A million things can go wrong—and everything's a lot older now, so the chances of an accident are a lot worse."

"Well, that's true enough," Reesa put in, looking warningly at Viktor. "I'm surprised the containment didn't give out already and blow the whole ship up."

"And then even if it succeeded," the old woman went on, "what would we have? Enough fuel for maybe ten years of power transmission, then we're back where we started. Total waste!"

"*Terrible* waste," Reesa agreed.

"Oh, you don't know," Tortee said moodily. "You don't have any *idea* how much this is costing us—we don't have resources to spare here, you know! And meanwhile . . ." She looked around conspiratorially. "And meanwhile there's a perfectly good planet waiting out there for us, with plenty of warmth and water and air—"

Viktor cleared his throat. "You mean Nebo, I guess, is that right? But there's also something on Nebo that shoots at us, Tortee."

She glared at him dangerously. "Are you saying you don't support my project?" Viktor was silent. "Answer me! I thought I could trust you—you were one of those who went there, centuries ago!"

"That was a matter of scientific investigation," Viktor explained.

"Scientific investigation! You went there just because you were *curious?*"

"What better reason could there be?"

"Because Nebo is *habitable* now!" Tortee cried. "At least, we think it may be—and this planet isn't, not any more. Viktor!" She studied him suspiciously for a moment. "Do you want to be back on the shit detail?" she demanded suddenly.

"No, no, not at all!" Viktor said hastily. Reesa was giving him that look again, and he knew when to surrender. Still, he was beginning to suspect that the new assignment might not altogether be a blessing. He might find himself wishing he were back enjoying the comparatively relaxed conversation with the children in the mushroom cave, because he was beginning to be convinced that his new boss, Tortee, was a certifiable nut. "The only thing that's worrying me," he said, feeling his way, "is what are we going to do about the part of Nebo that shoots at us? Nebo's not exactly *inviting* us to come down and start living there. It's been pretty good at keeping us out."

"Anything worth having," Tortee said firmly, "is worth fighting for. I've thought all that out. We can patch *Ark* with what's left of *Mayflower*, then all we have to do is put in some weapons."

"But—" Viktor began, meaning to finish the sentence by stating the certain fact that neither he nor Reesa knew anything about installing weapons in a spaceship; he didn't get the chance. Reesa was in ahead of him.

"Right, Tortee. That's our first job," she said quickly. "We'll have to have help, of course; I expect there's somebody who can assist in designing rockets that can be launched from orbit. And we'll need to know what the targets are; you have survey tapes to show where the attacks came from, I guess?"

"Of course," the old woman said with pride. "I've had the instruments on *Mayflower* surveying every inch of Nebo, and I have the readings Mirian brought down with you. I can pinpoint exactly where they fired on you. There were three places; I've got them marked. I'm sure we can deal with that, and—what is it, Viktor?"

"The instruments," Viktor said. "What do they say about that bright thing you call the universe?"

The old woman looked at him silently for a dangerous moment. "What do you want to know that for?"

Viktor blinked at her. It wasn't that he couldn't answer the question; he simply could not understand why she asked it. "Why, because—because it's there, Tortee! That's what science is all about, isn't it? Trying to understand what's going on?"

"What science is about," Tortee proclaimed, "is making life better for everybody. That's what you should be thinking about. Not just *theories*. Idle curiosity is the devil's work; your job is to make this project succeed!"

She was looking not only angry but definitely dissatisfied with Viktor Sorricaine now. Fortunately the door opened then and a little girl staggered in with a tray. Although it was heavy laden—a pot of steaming tea, a platter of cookies, and one of sliced bread with what looked like actual butter on it—there was only one cup. The girl quailed under the imprecations Tortee hurled at her and retreated as fast as she could, but the old woman was already greedily cramming sweet biscuits into her mouth.

"There is one other thing," Reesa said, while Tortee's mouth was full. Tortee didn't try to speak; she only raised an eyebrow at Reesa, still chewing.

"We should find a better place for us to live," Reesa explained. "It would be better if we could be near you—for the work I mean. And so if you could have them give us a room of our own here—"

"Impossible!" the woman sputtered, crumbs falling onto the tray on her lap. "The Peeps would never agree to it. Dear Freddy, woman! Don't you know how suspicious they are already? If we tried to move you in here they'd tell everybody that that just proved that the Greats were plotting to seize the ship for themselves—not that they aren't saying it already, of course."

"Oh, of course," Reesa said, nodding as though the woman's babbling made perfect sense. "Here, let me pour some more tea for you."

She gave Viktor a quick, meaningful glance which stirred him into action. He jumped gallantly forward to hold the tray while Reesa filled Tortee's cup. The old woman watched critically, a slice of buttered bread ready in one hand, then seized the cup and sipped it cautiously.

"That's better," she said. "Now, what were we talking about?"

"You explained to us why it's impossible for us to move into this sector permanently," Reesa said. "You made it very clear; thank you, Tortee. Still, I do have to come here every day to work with you, of course. I suppose that Viktor and I might have the use of some workroom together—so we could do our jobs without disturbing you?"

"Ha!" the old woman said. Her eyes were suddenly gleaming. "I thought that was what it was about. What kind of room did you have in mind for your jobs? One with a bed, maybe?"

"Nothing like that," Viktor said, instinctively trying to shut the door on this invasion of his privacy; but Reesa was also speaking.

"*Exactly* like that, if we possibly could, Tortee," she said sweetly. "I knew you would understand."

"Ha," the old woman said again, eyeing them. Then she shifted her weight to a more comfortable position and grinned. "Why not? I'm going to work you harder than you've ever worked before, and I don't mind paying a little extra for good work. Is this room more or less what you had in mind? Because I'm going to report to the council this afternoon, and I'll be gone at least three hours."

She gazed at Reesa, who only smiled, nodding her head. The old woman licked crumbs off her fingers as she nodded back. Then she looked wistfully at her bed. "It won't do that old thing any harm to have somebody getting a little use out of it for a change— but I'm warning you! Be sure you change the sheets before I come back."

Tortee did not only have a private bedroom, she had a private bath. With their first passion spent, Reesa's second priority was a hot soak in the shallow metal tub. Viktor lay relaxed against the pillows while he waited his turn, nibbling on the staling bread and butter Tortee had left behind, listening to the faint splashing sounds from his wife's tub. Thoughtfully he considered his existence. Things had begun to look up a little, no doubt of that. It was certainly fine to be off the shit detail. It was even finer to have a job that made some sense for a person with his skills, and finer still to have had a nice warm bed to share with his nice, warm wife—in actual privacy!

There was no reason, really, why he should feel discontented.

The funny thing was that, all the same, he did. They were both alive—and reasonably secure for at least the near future—but what, he asked himself, were they alive *for?*

It was as disconcerting for Viktor as it had been for Wan-To to step back and look at his life like that. It made him wonder what the point was.

Viktor could not help feeling that there had to be *some* kind of point, or at least purpose, to it. After all, he had come close enough to losing his life often enough. He counted up: Three times frozen, three times successfully thawed without harm. He had taken three good cuts at those 180-to-1 odds; in fact, as far as the third time was concerned, you couldn't really figure any realistic odds at all. They might have floated in space forever without being found, if it hadn't been for someone coveting the old interstellar ship enough to spend prodigally of scarce resources to get it—and for Mirian succumbing to one of the few generous impulses in an ungenerous world when he revived them.

For what purpose? When you survived so much for so long, shouldn't there be a *reason?*

It couldn't be just to shovel excrement, or, as Reesa had been doing, breeding cockroaches in offal to feed fish. Could it be to help Tortee in her plan? Because if that was it, Viktor told himself skeptically, whoever arranged purposes had picked a loser this time: there was no *way* old *Ark* could be turned into the kind of space battleship that could win a firefight with whatever it was on the planet of Nebo that killed people.

On the other hand—

On the other hand, Tortee was gone, and Tortee's computers were right there in the room with him.

There might be a purpose to his life, after all! Galvanized at the thought, Viktor leaped out of bed.

When, minutes, later, Reesa came shivering back into the bedroom skimpily wrapped in a towel, he hardly looked up.

She stopped abruptly, astonished. "Viktor! What are you doing with those machines?"

He glanced at her blankly. "What do you think I'm doing? That woman's got a data linkage—all the data banks from *Ark* and *May-fllower*, the copies are still intact! Now I'm looking for later stuff, trying to find out what kind of research anyone's done on that fireball they call the universe."

"Are you out of your mind?" she demanded. "We can't push Tortee too hard, Viktor. If you use her things without permis-sion . . ."

He focused on her, his expression suddenly wrathful. Then, slowly, he relaxed. "Oh, hell," he said. "You're right, of course. But, my God, Reesa, this is the most important thing that ever happened! Just from the little bit I've been able to dig up so far, I'm pretty sure my first guess was right. Somehow or other, we've been picking up speed. *Lots* of speed; nearly the velocity of light! And that fireball is the universe, all right, but we're traveling so fast that all the light from it is concentrated in front of us!"

"Yes, Viktor. I see how important that is to you. But the most important thing is to stay on Tortee's good side," Reesa said firmly.

"Oh, Christ," Viktor said in disgust. "She's loopy, you know. She isn't even doing what the council ordered—they think they're going to get power out of *Ark*, and she wants to send it out to fight a war!"

Reesa was practicing patience. "Dear Viktor, that's their busi-ness, not ours. They told us to work for her, so we'll do what she tells us to do."

"Even if she's out of her mind? And—" He suddenly noticed that Reesa was shivering. "Hey," he said. "don't catch pneumonia on me!"

She pulled the towel tighter around her, looking demure. "Shall I get dressed?" she asked, but the mere fact that she had asked determined the answer; and, besides, he was suddenly aware that he was even barer than she, and equally cold.

"Well, not right away," he said. "Why don't you—we, I mean— why don't we get back under the covers for a while?"

"Let's just remember we have to leave time to change the sheets," Reesa said practically; but then, when they were under the covers, spooned back to front with his arm over her, she waited for him to move or to speak. He didn't.

"You're thinking about that fireball," she said into the pillow.

"I can't help it, Reesa. I—I wish I'd paid more attention to my father when I had the chance. He would have known more about it. This would have been the most interesting thing in the world to him."

"I never doubted it was interesting, Viktor," Reesa said gently, "and I understand how you feel about solving it."

"It's not just like solving a puzzle! It's important to everybody. It has something to do with what's going on on Nebo, too, I'm sure of it!"

"That's possible, Viktor. I don't see how, but I'm willing to believe it. All the same, Vik, I wouldn't try to convince Tortee, if I were you. All Tortee wants is to get Ark flying again, with guns blazing. And she's got troubles of her own. She's the one who wants to colonize Nebo, and she's got the Great Catholics behind her— but whether they'll stay that way depends on how fast she can show some kind of results. And the others—well, the Peeps are the ones who talked the council into trying to use the fuel for microwave power, and there's talk in Allahabad that colonizing another planet's a good enough idea, but it shouldn't be Nebo."

"Where then?" Viktor asked, startled.

"They're not very clear on that. Some of them think that since Ark's an interstellar ship basically they should try another star. Others have ideas about the moons of Nergal—they claim there ought to be enough heat from the brown dwarf to make something possible."

"Shades of Tiss Khadek," Viktor said, thinking. "Well, maybe that ought to be investigated, too. But that fireball—"

"Viktor, Viktor," his wife said gently. "If you play your cards right you'll have plenty of chances to see what you can find out about the fireball. In your spare time. When Tortee isn't looking. But don't push it, because she doesn't want to hear."

"I know, but—"

"Viktor. Did you know that both the Reforms and Allahabad are on overload, and the Peeps would be, too, if they hadn't been lucky enough to lose six or seven people last week? That means the whole colony has more people than they're allowed. So last week in Allahabad they froze three people for profaning shrines, and they're still eleven over their proper number."

"Profaning shrines! My God, Reesa, what kind of people are we living with?"

"We're living with people on the edge of starvation, Viktor. That's what you have to remember. All the time." She hesitated. "Do you know what else I heard? Some of the Peeps don't think even the freezers should be kept going. They're revolutionary idealists—they think they are, anyway—and they've got some pretty nasty ideas. They think they might as well thaw out some of the freezers without reviving them." She paused.

Viktor blinked at the back of her neck. "Why would they do that?" he demanded.

"Fodder," she said briefly. "Protein sources. To feed to the chickens and the gerbils, to turn the corpses into useful food."

"My *God*!" Viktor repeated, appalled.

"So go slow, my darling, please." She was silent for a moment, reaching up to put her hand over his as it cupped her breast. Then she said, "Viktor? Now that I'm all sweet and clean, do you think you'd like to get me all sweated up one more time while we still have the use of the bed?"

And of course that was the best idea she'd had yet . . . only at the end of it, when she was shuddering and moaning, there was a timbre to the sounds his wife made that reached through to Viktor, even at the peak of his own orgasm.

He had heard sounds like those before.

Not from Reesa. He had heard them from Marie-Claude in their one coupling, when her husband had died. Like Marie-Claude, Reesa was weeping even as they made love.

She didn't say anything in words. Neither did he. Only, when they were dressed again and making up the old woman's bed afresh, she stopped and looked at him. "We have to make the best of things, Viktor," she said harshly.

"Yes," Viktor agreed; and that was the end of it. Neither of them needed to mention the names of lost Shan and Yan and Tanya, and little Quinn.

Making the best of things wasn't easy. In this starved world there was hardly a "best" to aim for.

The project they were on promised more problems than rewards. Viktor had known all along that Tortee's plans were going to be exceedingly difficult. He hadn't known just how close they were going to be to outright impossible.

To begin with, there was the task of repairing *Ark* from what was left of *Mayflower*. How were they going to manage that? They didn't have an orbiting shipyard to do it in; they didn't have the big tools to do the job; they didn't have the shuttles to launch the tools they did have into orbit. They didn't even have the plans of the ships to work from. Those records might still be in the files somewhere, the stored data fiches that no one had looked at for a hundred years; but it would take a hundred years more, Viktor estimated, to find them again.

What he did have was a vast collection of pictures of the old interstellar ships, which Tortee had had taken from orbit, scaled, and computerized so that at least you could take some rough dimensions from them and hope the parts would fit where you wanted them to. Of course, no one expected a neat job. In space a few wrinkles or bumps made no difference—you didn't have to streamline a spaceship. All it had to do was hold its air and stay together under acceleration.

Assuming somehow they could deal with that, the harder job was still ahead of them: Invading hostile Nebo itself.

Tortee's promise was good there. She had provided them with a detailed mosaic of Nebo's surface, with fine-scale blowups of all the areas where the lasers (were they really lasers? The things that jolted foreign spaceships, anyway) were based.

Reesa was the one who converted all of Tortee's photos into three-dimensional plans for the computer to display. Tortee had good programs, painfully salvaged and restored from the ancient vaults. Viktor had seen most of the pictures before: the great, tulip-shaped horn antennae, the spiral things that had to be some other kind of antenna (or perhaps a sort of waveguide for some sort of discharge?). He even saw, with a shock, a familiar shape near one of the clusters that magnification revealed to be the wreck of *Ark*'s lander.

There was no sign of bodies anywhere near the lander. There was no sign of anything alive there, either, or anywhere else on Nebo.

After a week of hard work Viktor began to believe that targeting those conspicuous artifacts might indeed be possible after all. But after you targeted them, what were you going to hit them with?

That was when Tortee delivered on another promise. She had undertaken to find someone who knew something about rocket weaponry, and when she produced him Viktor was astonished to see that it was Mirian.

Viktor met Reesa as she came in from the Peeps' chambers, and the two of them went hand in hand to the workroom next to Tortee's. Mirian was waiting for them, nervously stroking his pale beard. "Listen, Viktor," he said at once, "I didn't give you any breaks before, you know? I'm sorry about that. Things were tough for me. I hope you won't hold it against me."

"Yeah?" Viktor said, not committing himself.

"I mean it," Mirian said earnestly. "I don't blame you if you're mad, but, see, I need this job. Working in the freezers . . ." He looked embarrassed. "Well, when they send you there to work what they're saying is, 'Watch it, fellow, or you'll be *inside* them before you know it.' So this is a big chance for me. I'll do my best for you. I swear I will."

"I'm not the one you have to worry about; Tortee's in charge," Viktor said uncomfortably.

Reesa was more practical. "Do you know anything about space weapons?" she asked.

"I know as much as anybody else does," Mirian told her, and managed a grin. Which was to say, Viktor realized as the man began describing his ideas, not very much at all. There was not much call for long-range weaponry in this frozen-over world; there weren't any long-range targets. When the sects fought among themselves it was mostly with clubs and knives, and the big terror weapon was a hand grenade.

Still, grenades meant explosives; and once you had explosives you could put a bunch of them in a warhead and mount it on a rocket. There was nothing intrinsically hard about building a rocket, either—the ancient Chinese had done it when most of the world still lived in mud huts. The hard part was guidance.

But, Mirian explained eagerly, guidance only meant cannibalizing instrumentation from *Ark* and *Mayflower* and the surviving lander shuttles. In the long retreat from near-Nebo, while Reesa and Viktor had still been slumbering undiscovered in the freezer pods, Mirian had put in weeks in a space suit, roaming the old ship, investigating the resources it still provided, and planning a revengeful return. "We can do it," he promised. "Honest to Fred we can!"

"At least," Reesa said practically, "we can see if we can. If it's possible at all—"

"It *has* to be!" Mirian cried.

Viktor's doubts did not diminish as the days went on. He had a very clear memory of the jolting blows *Ark* had suffered. The idea of taking on that sort of technology with the improvised firecracker rockets Mirian was trying to build was ludicrous.

Now and then, in the privacy of pillow talk with his wife, Viktor expressed his doubts. The rest of the time he kept his mouth shut. Yet, grudgingly, he admitted to himself that whatever these people lacked in wisdom or manners they made up in courage. Nothing was easy for them. Even food was so scarce that the storehouses were tiny: food didn't need to be stored for long when Sunday's harvest was Wednesday's memory. The 2,350 inhabitants of the four colonies lived on a marginal 2,200 calories a day—yet that added up to five million calories that had to be supplied each day. So many kilograms of chicken, frogs, rabbits, and fish; so many metric tons of grains, tubers, and pulses; so many cubic meters of leafy vegetables and fruits. The vegetables were not very leafy, nor were the fruits the handsome, unblemished objects Viktor remembered from his childhood supermarkets. But there was just so much you could do about growing things in caverns under the ice. Viktor's "shit detail" mushroom farm had supplied only a tiny fraction of that everyday crush of provender, but every tiny fraction was urgently needed. The alternative was overload—and if overload wasn't checked the next step was starvation.

Still they had managed to refurbish an old chemical rocket and send it clear to Nebo's orbit, board old *Ark*, and get it going again. The old interstellar ship had been at the aphelion of its stretched-out orbit of the time. They had not risked coming close to the faceless enemy on Nebo—yet they had stolen old *Ark* away from him. Whoever he was.

Viktor disliked these people very much. All the same, there was a faint touch of admiration coloring his contempt.

Even Mirian turned out to be quite human as they worked together. The man was a lot younger than Viktor had thought. Mirian was only thirty-nine—in Newmanhome years, at that; the equivalent of an Earthly college kid. That surprised Viktor. He seemed much too young to have volunteered for the mission on Nebo. Yet it also turned out that Mirian was married and had even left a child behind when he took off for the long mission. "But of course I volunteered, Viktor," he explained. "The Greats were pretty close to overload, and when I got caught—"

"Caught at what?" Viktor asked, guessing that the girl had turned up pregnant and Mirian had had to marry. But it wasn't that.

Mirian looked shamefaced, picking at his beard. "They charged me with theft. Said I'd eaten some of the community's honey. Well, I did," he conceded, "but it was only a few drips in a broken comb. It probably would have been just wasted otherwise. So they said they wouldn't prosecute if I volunteered for Nebo duty." He looked around apprehensively and lowered his voice. "It was Tortee's honey," he whispered. "She was the one who said I had to choose between the ship or the freezer."

"Tortee seems to have a lot of authority," Viktor commented.

"You'd better say that! She's—well, listen. How old do you think she is?"

Viktor shrugged. "Maybe a hundred and twenty?" Newmanhome years, of course, but none of these people had ever counted in anything else.

"Try seventy-five," Mirian chortled, enjoying Viktor's astonishment—why, the woman was Reesa's age! "That's right. She could still be having babies, except her husband's in the freezer—he worked there, and they caught him making a fire to keep warm. So she just eats, instead of, you know, being with a *man*. And—"

He stopped, looking suddenly frightened. "Oh, I thought I heard her coming," he said. "Listen, we'd better get to work. Now, we've got these fuel canisters; we can use them for the body of the rockets . . ."

The people on Newmanhome had a fair supply of explosives. They needed them now and then. When the ice moved, as it unpredictably did, glacier lips had to be blasted to keep them from burying what was left of Homeport too deep to survive.

But explosives were too dangerous to be freely available; half a dozen little wars among the sects had proved that. The explosives plant was located three kilometers away, heavily guarded by a fully armed squad from each of the sects, and the shuttle that would someday take people back up to *Ark* and *Mayflower* was within its perimeter, guarded just as heavily.

Viktor eagerly accepted the chance to go outside to visit the launch site. It was the Peeps' day off, so Reesa was obliged to stay idle with the others in the warrens of the People's Republic, but Viktor and three others, one from each but the Peeps sect, struggled into extra layers of clothing topped with sheepskins; an electrically warmed mesh covered his mouth and nose, and a visor was over his eyes. Even so, that first Arctic-plus blast that struck him soaked through the furs and the four layers of garments in moments, leaving him shaking as he toiled after the other four to the place where stronger, colder men were tanking up the lander shuttle with liquid oxygen and alcohol.

At least the winds were only winds. They did not drive blizzards of snow against the struggling men and women. The winds couldn't do that; snow almost never fell anymore. The air of Newmanhome had been squeezed skin-cracking dry, for there were no longer any warm oceans anywhere on the planet to steam water vapor into the air so that it could come down somewhere else as rain or snow. There wasn't any somewhere else when the whole planet was frozen over.

Squinting against the blast, Viktor could see the dark, cold sky.

It was not anything like the skies he had known before. The shrunken sun gave little heat. Even the dozen stars that were left were themselves, Viktor was almost sure, dimmer than they had been.

And then, as Newmanhome turned, red Nergal appeared, as bloodily scarlet-bright as ever. Minutes later that great puzzle, "the universe," burst eye-blindingly white over the horizon. Viktor gazed at it and sighed.

If only his father had lived to see. If only these people were willing to try to understand! If only—

He felt Mirian tapping him on the shoulder. Viktor looked where the younger man was pointing, up toward that same eastern horizon. "Yes, the universe," Viktor said eagerly through the mesh. "I've been thinking—"

Mirian looked suddenly fearful. "Hey, not that!" he cried over the sound of the wind. "Please don't talk about *that*! I meant over there, next to it."

Squinting through the mesh, Viktor saw what Mirian was calling his attention to. It was a faint spot of light, barely visible as it moved down toward its setting: *Ark*, in its low orbit, moving toward its final rendezvous with *Mayflower*.

Viktor stared at it. The time was getting close. When *Ark* and *Mayflower* were linked together the lander would be launched, and then it would all start.

He was suddenly coldly certain that Tortee was going to order him onto the shuttle. And he didn't want to go.

When they were back in the dining hall again Mirian was charged up with optimism. "We're going to do it," he told Viktor positively. "We've got crews trained for repair all ready; they'll be taking off for *Ark* in a couple of weeks, and then—"

"And then," Viktor said, as gently as possible, "we have to hope that they can get the ship habitable again; and that these rockets will work; and that that little bit of antimatter left in *Ark*'s drive will hold out long enough to ferry people back and forth."

Mirian paused, a spoonful of the stew of corn and beans halfway to his mouth. "Don't talk like that, Viktor," he begged.

Viktor shrugged and remembered to smile. He was beginning to thaw out after his long run outside, and even the meatless-day stew tasted good. The important thing, he told himself, wasn't that this harebrained project should work, it was only that people could *believe* that it might. Even a false hope was better than no hope at all.

"I do wish," he said, "that we had some more antimatter. We could do a lot with more power. Even maybe build some lasers or something—something better than—" He stopped himself from saying what he had been about to say about the feeble rockets Mirian was putting together. "It was pretty nice when we had Earth technology going for us," he said wistfully.

"Is it true that you people actually *made* this antimatter stuff?" Mirian asked enviously.

"Not me. Not here—but, back on Earth, sure. They made all kinds of things, Mirian. Why, back on Earth . . ."

Mirian wasn't the only one listening as Viktor reminisced about the wonders of the planet he had left as a child. A woman across the table put in, "You mean you just walked around? *Outside?* Without even any clothes on? And things just grew out in the open?"

"It was like that here on Newmanhome, too," Viktor reassured her.

"And they didn't worry about—" She paused, looked around, and lowered her voice. "—like, overload?"

Viktor gave her a superior smile. He knew he was rubbing salt in wounds, but he couldn't help it. "If you mean killing people because there are too many to feed, no. Not ever. Fact, they *wanted* more people. Everybody was supposed to have all the children they could. Reesa and I had four," he boasted, unwilling to try the explanation of what was meant by "Reesa and I" and the divided parentage of the children . . .

The children.

Viktor lost the thread of what he was saying. Suddenly the cooling stew and the smells of the densely packed dining hall stopped being pleasant. The children! And he would never see any of them again.

Viktor excused himself and stumbled away to the jakes. He didn't have to urinate. He just didn't want anyone to see, in case he had to cry.

When he got back Mirian gave him a quick, hooded look and went on talking about his experiences as a freezer guard. "They've got all kinds of stuff in there," he was saying. "You wouldn't believe all of it. There's one whole chamber that's full of frozen sperm and ova, animals that they brought from Earth and never started up here. Whales! Termites! Chimpanzees—"

"What's a termite?" the woman across the table asked, but she was looking at Viktor.

Viktor did his best. "It's a kind of an insect, I think. They used to worry about them eating the wood in their houses in California. And a chimpanzee's like a monkey—I think," he added honestly, because all he remembered of chimpanzees was that he had seen a lot of almost human-looking primates one day at the San Diego Zoo, and he had been more impressed by the terrible way they smelled than by his father's lectures on which was which.

There was silence for a moment. Then Mirian put in, "We saw *Ark* when we were outside. Only it was near the fireball, so we couldn't get a really good look at it."

Viktor saw that everyone looked a little embarrassed when Mirian mentioned the fireball. Yet the man had brought it up; it was as good a chance as any to probe. "About that fireball," he began.

Conversation stopped. Everyone's eyes were on him, and every mouth was closed. Even Mirian was looking suspiciously at him.

The hell with them, Viktor thought. "I know what that fireball is," he announced. "It's a foreshortened view of the universe. Somehow, I don't know how, we've been accelerated so fast that we're catching up with all the light from everywhere."

Silence. No response at all. Then Mirian swallowed and said, "Maybe we should be getting back to work, Viktor."

But the woman across the table reached out to touch his arm.

"What are you telling us, Viktor?" she asked. "How could that happen?"

"I don't have the faintest idea," he said bitterly. "Something is pulling us. Or pushing us, maybe, but I don't know any forces that could do that. Anyway our planet, and the sun, and all the other planets around it, and a few other stars are all being pulled along very fast by *something*."

"What do you mean, 'something'? Do you mean by God?" the woman asked, crossing herself. "Freddy didn't say anything about that!"

"No, not God," Viktor said hastily. "It doesn't have anything to do with God, of course. It's some natural force, probably—or, well—" He stopped, angry at these people and even more at himself.

He hadn't stopped in time. "Are you saying the Great Transporter isn't God?" the woman demanded. An old man down the table stood up, his white mustaches quivering.

"I don't like this kind of talk!" he announced. "I'm going back to work!"

And Mirian, glowering as he led Viktor away from the table, warned, "You have to watch what you say, man! I'm as tolerant as the next fellow, you know that—but you don't want a charge of heresy and corruption of faith, do you?"

This day, Viktor thought gloomily, was not going well at all.

It did not occur to him that it was capable of getting a lot worse.

He was hunched over the keyboard when Tortee came back to her room. He cleared the screen quickly, but not quickly enough: She had caught a glimpse of the spectral analysis display. "What's that, Viktor?" she demanded ominously. "Have you finished the repair plans?"

"Almost done, Tortee," he said with a false smile, keeping his anger inside. "I'll have them for you this afternoon."

"I want them *now*! I've got a meeting with the Four-Power Repair Committee, and I need to show them what has to be done to the *Ark*. What've you been doing? No," she said forcefully as he opened his mouth, "I want to know what you were *really* doing. Show me that screen again!"

"But, really, Tortee," he began, and then knew it was no use. Sullenly he keyed in the file name and watched as the damning spectrum flashed on the board.

The old woman might have been a religious bigot, but she was not a scientific fool. She recognized the patterns at once. "You're checking spectra," she announced, "and I can guess what that's a spectrum of. Viktor, I don't know what to do with you. You've been openly talking religious error—" He started to speak again, startled, but she overrode him. "Don't deny it! Do you think people don't report to me? Half a dozen people heard you in the dining hall today! And you're wasting working time with your immoral habits. I can't put up with this. Do you have anything to say for yourself?"

"I'm only trying to find out the truth about what's going on!" Viktor cried hotly.

"The *truth*," Tortee said icily, "has long since been revealed to us. Blessed Freddy set it down for all to see in His Third Testament, and that's the only truth that matters. I forbid you ever to speak of this subject again." He was astonished to see that she was really angry. Her pudgy face was squeezed into a scowl. "Don't try my patience too far, Viktor! I don't want to have to punish you. You wouldn't like it." She stared at him for a moment, then added as an afterthought, "You can forget about using my room for your personal pleasure again, too. Now get out of here! You and Mirian are wanted at the shuttle. They're almost ready to fuel up for the first repair crew."

It could have been worse, Viktor thought sourly. Reesa was right. He had gone farther with Tortee—well, with all these superstition-ridden, mule-stubborn people—than was sensible.

For that matter, sending him out to the freezer complex was punishment in itself. It was late. There was little chance they would be able to get back before dark, and no one wanted to be outside when even the feeble heat of sun and star burst were gone.

Mirian did his best to hurry the workers at the liquid-gas plant along. It wasn't hard to do, because the fuel detail wanted to be back by nightfall, too. Working at top speed, he and Viktor checked the fuel manifests, inspected the tanks' seals, and agreed that it was all in order. But the haste was all in vain, because then they were shunted over to the cryonics caves to wait. Their four-power escort hadn't shown up on time.

"Oh, hell," Mirian groaned, pulling unhappily at his beard. "We'll never get back before dark."

"I'm sorry, Mirian," Viktor said. "I think I got Tortee mad at me."

"You *think* you did! Oh, Viktor, just shut up. Every time you open your mouth you make more trouble!" And he slumped down against a wall and closed his eyes, refusing to speak.

Absently Viktor strolled around the chilly cave, glancing at the tunnels that led off from the central chamber. Inside each tunnel was row on row of capsules. Each one held a human body—convicted "criminals" mostly—with crosses for the Greats and the Reforms, crescents for the Moslems, and five-pointed stars for the Peeps. Those were the fruits of overload, Viktor knew, and dourly thought that the chances were good that he would be joining them if he didn't learn to keep his mouth shut.

By the time the escort arrived Viktor had made up his mind. He would never say a blasphemous word again. He would follow Reesa's example. He would do his best to please Tortee and to make her hopeless plan work.

He couldn't wait to see Reesa to tell her about his resolve.

It was almost dark by the time the two of them and their escort were stumbling through the freezing gale back to the dwelling tunnels. The fireball "universe" had already set, and the sun was nearly at the horizon; it was definitely getting too cold to be out of doors.

Mirian glanced at Viktor, then made a gesture of reconciliation. He pointed to the horizon. There was *Mayflower*, a hand's-span north of the setting sun. The old ship was just beginning to climb up the sky from the west in its hundred-minute orbit, with *Ark* still out of sight below and behind it.

Mirian put his head next to Viktor's and bawled, over the noise of the wind, "It won't be so bad, Viktor. Once they get the repairs going Tortee will be easier to get along with, you'll see."

"I hope so," Viktor shouted back, and bent his head, squinting against the cold as he trudged along. Easier to get along with! That wouldn't be hard, he thought resentfully. He slipped on a slanting block of ice, cursed, caught himself—

And heard a strange moaning sound from Mirian.

Viktor looked up quickly. Out of the corner of his eye he caught a quick flicker of light. Startled, he stared up. It was *Mayflower*, suddenly shining bright, almost as suddenly darkening again.

"What is it, Mirian?" he cried.

But Mirian didn't know. No one knew, until they had toiled back inside the tunnels again and the word from Tortee's instruments had spread like wildfire.

The sudden brightening of *Mayflower* had been only reflected light from another, hidden source. And that source—

It had been the worst disaster imaginable.

Ark had blown up.

Fortunately for the people on Newmanhome, *Ark* had still been below the horizon when it happened. It wasn't a chemical explosion that had blasted the old ship into ions, not even a nuke: it was the annihilation of matter and antimatter, pounds of mass converted into energy in the twinkling of an eye, in accordance with the old formula: $e = mc^2$. That hemisphere directly under *Ark* had received a sudden flood of radiation like an instant flare from the heart of a star.

There was nothing living on that part of Newmanhome. That was fortunate. For, of course, anything that had been alive in the face of that terrible blast would have stopped living at once.

The skeleton crew on *Mayflower* were less fortunate. Even through the thick skin of the spaceship, they had received more radiation than the human body was meant to experience in a lifetime.

And Tortee was weeping hysterically in her room. She refused to see Viktor at all. She let Mirian in for only a moment, and when he came out he was looking very grave.

"It's over," Mirian told Viktor mournfully. "If we don't have *Ark* we don't have a working drive. We can't build a rocket ship big enough to attack the planet."

"No, of course not," Viktor agreed, dazed, wishing Reesa were there. "What happened?"

"Aw, who knows?" Mirian said despondently. "Tortee thinks it was the Peeps. She thinks they were so set on getting microwave power that they started fooling around with the drive—to keep us from using it again, you know? And it just went off." He stopped for a moment, gazing at Viktor with an ambiguous expression. Then he said, "I've been thinking, Viktor. You've had a pretty good run for your money."

Viktor blinked, not seeing the connection. "I have?"

"I mean," Mirian explained, "you were born on *Earth*. Good Freddy, Viktor, that makes you just about the oldest person in the world."

"I guess it does," Viktor said grudgingly. That was an interesting thought, but not the kind that reconciled you to anything.

"So when the council decides . . ." Mirian left it hanging there. Victor looked at him in puzzlement.

"What is there to decide? You said yourself, the project's over."

"I don't mean the project, I mean about you, Viktor. Tortee won't stand up for you anymore, not after this. Not after—well, you know," he said awkwardly, "we're always pressed for living space here."

"What are you talking about?" Viktor demanded, losing patience. "Are you saying I have to go live with the Peeps or something, like Reesa?"

"Oh, no, not with the Peeps. And I suppose they might keep Reesa on. But you, Viktor—well," he said fairly, "it's not like *death*. We don't *kill* people. That's against the Commandments. And, who knows, somebody, sometime—there's always the chance that someday someone will thaw you out of the freezer."

CHAPTER 19

By the time Wan-To had worn out his hundreth star he began to get uneasy again. It wasn't that he was fearing attack from his long-gone siblings, for that had not happened in many hundreds of billions of years. He certainly wasn't worrying about the matter-creatures his long-forgotten Matter-Copy Number Five had reported. No, what was bothering Wan-To was that he couldn't help noticing that his neighborhood was going downhill.

It was no longer a prime, desirable place to be. Most of the stars in this galaxy of his were aging, and everything was getting rather shabby.

Of course, with four hundred billion stars to choose from, he wasn't really *out* of living space. There were even a few late-generation stars of his favorite kind, type G—like Earth's long-gone sun, for Wan-To's taste in stars was very like that of the human race, in many ways. When the one he was in was showing signs of bloat, since he definitely didn't want to sit through the transformation to red giant again, he picked out the best of the available Gs and made the move.

His latest home was a G0, a good, clean star. It was brighter and bigger than most, though Wan-To found after he had moved in that it had a faintly annoying taste of metals—naturally enough, since it had been formed out of gas clouds that had already been through a star or two.

Little annoyances like that weren't really important. But the star wasn't ideal, either, and Wan-To didn't see why he should be uncomfortable in his own home. He thought about alternatives. He always had the option of moving into a different stellar type, of course—say, an elderly K, or even a little red M. He knew Ms well; that was the kind of star in which Wan-To, long since, had installed his childish companions. He had certainly done that for the children's own good (because those stars were really long-lived and stable), but it was also, to be perfectly truthful, partly for Wan-To's own sake, because those smaller stars gave the children less energy to support their constant babble.

That was what was wrong with the long-lived stars, right there. They had less *energy*.

That ruled them out for Wan-To, who couldn't see why he should cut back on his own life-style, no matter what. But he could see, not very far ahead, a time when there just wouldn't be any new G-type stars left.

After some thought, the solution occurred to Wan-To. It was simple enough once he had thought of it.

If this galaxy, and most of the others, had grown past the age of frequent star formation by natural processes, why should that be a problem? There was always Wan-To, with his mastery of *un*natural processes, to help things along!

So he found a nice, clean gas cloud out in the galactic halo and set to work. It was simple enough. All he had to do was prod at it with a flux of gravitons, graviphotons, and graviscalars, judiciously applied in all the right places, to speed its condensation. Then he blew up a few heavy stars nearby, timing their rhythmic pulses to encourage some of the gas-cloud material to fall together in stars. He knew exactly what to do. After all, he had seen it happen often enough over the last billions of years! Once you got a density wave going, with a radiative-shock compression factor of a hundred to one or so, the gas clouds couldn't help becoming stars.

True, it would take some millions of years for them to settle down, but he had lots of time. True, he had to deplete the energies of many thousands of otherwise healthy nearby stars to get the process going . . . but what were a few thousand unimportant stars to Wan-To?

Whatever else he did, Wan-To was always careful to keep an eye on the galaxy he had left behind him—the old Milky Way, which he had fled when it turned into a battleground. He wondered if any of his colleagues had survived. He had spotted the star he had escaped from early in his observations—it had been no more than a ruin by then, its greenish planetary nebula already breaking up into wisps of meaningless gas, its helium-burning shell detached from the carbon and oxygen core, the core itself now no more than a white dwarf with a density of tons per cubic inch.

It looked like an abandoned home, and it was. No one could possibly have moved into that after he left, Wan-To was sure. Pretty sure. But he kept an eye on it, and on all the other stars that he suspected might once have sheltered one of his kind.

They were all ruins now, too. Possibly his siblings had all killed each other off? Possibly Mromm had been the last there was, and Wan-To needn't have run away after all?

"Possibly" wasn't good enough. Whatever else Wan-To did, he was never going back to *that* galaxy.

But was that enough? Was staying away from the competitors he knew about going keep him safe from possible unknown others?

Wan-To wasn't a bit sure of that. It struck him as a wonder that he had never met another like himself, apart from the copies he had made. That seemed statistically improbable to him. In this old universe, how could he be *the only one*? If natural forces had accidentally brought his unfortunate progenitor to life way back in the universe's infancy—when it was no more than four or five billion years old, imagine!—didn't it stand to reason that that accident might have been repeated somewhere since then?

But no other ever showed up . . . and, on balance, that was fine with Wan-To.

Wan-To had pretty much accepted the fact that he would be alone for all of that remaining long eternity that stretched ahead—not counting, of course, the sweet but boring babble of the children.

He didn't like the loneliness, though. He wished he were wise enough to create equals who could not ever become competitors. He was almost sure that there ought to be a way to do it. But he didn't know the way, and he refused to take the chance.

Of course, it never occurred to Wan-To that these solid-matter pests who kept developing every few hundred million years or so could be *company*. They were simply too far beneath him. (Imagine a human being buddying up with a spirochete!)

They were interesting, after a fashion. It entertained Wan-To to see how "matter-life" kept trying to amount to something, eon after eon, on this planet or that.

After the first few he had learned that the things usually started as "organisms"—that was not his word, of course, but the concept he had in mind was of creatures that metabolized oxygen and were composed largely of complex carbon compounds, which was pretty much the same thing. Lots of planets developed "organisms," but only a very few permitted their organic life to reach the stage of being able to interfere with the physical world. Sometimes the amusing little things did that very well. Sometimes they did it almost as well as Wan-To himself, for quite often they learned such skills as how to fission uranium and fuse hydrogen, and they very often sooner or later managed to build strange little metallic shells in which they ventured into space. A few exceptional races even succeeded in taming the subatomic particles Wan-To himself employed, neutrinos and quarks and graviscalars.

But none of them went beyond that; and none of them stayed at that point.

To Wan-To's surprise, they seemed to be a self-limiting phenomenon.

Wan-To didn't realize that at first. So the first half-dozen times an organic race got that far Wan-To simply gathered his forces and obliterated them, people, planets, star, and all.

Then he got more curious, and thus more daring. He withheld his hand for a while to see what would happen—of course, always poised to destroy them the moment they became a threat, or even became aware of his existence.

What he discovered, perplexingly, was that that point never came. That was a strange and somewhat repellent thing about these little solid-matter creatures: Not long after they became able to wield significant forces, they invariably used them to destroy themselves.

Wan-To thought wryly that they weren't much smarter than

his own kind. Not *as* smart, in fact. For, of Wan-To's kind, at least Wan-To himself had managed to stay alive, while of all the matter-creatures he had ever heard of or encountered, every one, he thought, was long since extinct.

In this, of course, he was quite wrong.

The doppel called Five could have corrected Wan-To, if there had been any way left for Five to reach his master.

The doppel was no longer entirely sure that it *wanted* to reach Wan-To anymore, because it wasn't sure that Wan-To would approve of what it had done. Five hadn't *disobeyed* any orders. But it had taken the liberty of trying to guess what Wan-To's orders would have been, if Wan-To had thought to give them, and so, after a long, long time pushing ever nearer to the speed of light, it had reversed the thrust of its impellers.

Five, along with all its flock of stars and orbiting bodies, was slowing down.

That was very daring of Five, and Five knew it. Of course, it took as long to slow down as it did to accelerate to that all-but-light velocity in the first place. Five had plenty of time to reconsider its rash action. But Five wasn't built that way. It was built to do only what its master wanted, or what it thought Wan-To wanted.

In that long deceleration Five was aware of the activities of the matter-creatures that had attacked it—or that it had attacked, whichever way one chose to look at it. The things were quiet enough for a while. Then Five noticed that they were putting artifacts into space again. None of the things came very near Nebo, so it didn't have to take any action. Actually, it saw with interest, most of the artifacts seemed to head out farther into the solar system. That was fine with Five. Let them do what they liked around the brown dwarf, as long as they didn't come near Nebo.

And then, when the deceleration had slowed enough so that the great light flare that had been all the light of the universe should have resolved itself into a surrounding sphere of stars and galaxies again . . . it *didn't.*

Five was filled with what a human would have described as

terror. Things were not the way they should be! The universe had become very strange!

The doppel thought long and hard, and saw only one way out for it.

First it summoned up all its strength to create a flood of low-energy, high-velocity tachyons. It impressed on them a message, keyed to Wan-To's own preferred tachyon band. It shut down almost all of its equipment to divert the energies left into broadcasting that message, over and over.

Five had no idea whether Wan-To would ever receive that last somber message. It was not even sure that Wan-To still existed anywhere, and certainly Five didn't have even a hint of a clue as to where that "anywhere" in this suddenly immensely scattered universe might be.

Then Five did the only thing left for it to do.

If Five could not serve Wan-To, there was no reason for it to exist any longer. Maybe, even, if it had served Wan-To badly (as it feared), it no longer *deserved* to exist.

So when all its accumulated energy had been used up and its last message had gone out, Five, in its equivalent of an agony of shame, performed its equivalent of ritual suicide. It shut itself off.

CHAPTER 20

Viktor knew he was waking up when he discovered that he was dreaming—there are no dreams in the brain of a corpsicle. What he was dreaming was about flying, and about pain.

The pain was very definite and unpleasant. It was not a nice dream, and he was glad, though very fuzzy in his mind, when he woke up.

Viktor was aware that he was definitely awake then, because when he tried to open his eyes, they were stuck. He had to strain to squint out of them. "Mom?" he asked of the thin, amused woman who was leaning over him. "Mom, are we there yet?"

He realized right away that that was foolish of him. The woman definitely wasn't his mother—wasn't anything like his mother, really. She was very tall and painfully thin, and she had great, round eyes. Viktor saw the eyes quite clearly, although he was having some annoying trouble in seeing anything else. His own eyes did not seem to want to focus clearly, and his head ... his head hurt like *hell*.

The woman turned and said something quick, liquid, and murmurous. It was not in any language Viktor knew, although parts of it came close to making sense—as English might have sounded, perhaps, if it been cooed by pigeons. She was speaking to someone Viktor could not see very well. Then she reached down and touched the side of Viktor's head, as though pointing something out to the unseen person.

It was probably a gentle touch, but it didn't feel that way. It told Viktor right away his dream of pain had not been entirely a dream.

The woman's touch exploded through his head like a hammer blow, dizzying him. He jerked away from that probing finger—and found that the dream of flying was not altogether an illusion, either. He moved so easily, with so little force dragging at his body, that he knew that he couldn't be on Newmanhome. In fact, he couldn't be on any planet at all; he didn't weigh enough.

Viktor let himself fall gently back, hazily pondering the problem. The woman and the other person—a man's voice, not so much cooing as harshly gargling the sounds—were carrying on a conversation in the language that Viktor could not quite comprehend. If he wasn't on a planet, he thought, he was probably on a ship. What ship? Not *Ark*, certainly; there was nothing left of *Ark* but droplets of condensed metal, if any of *Ark* was left at all. Not old *Mayflower*, either, he was sure of that. There was nothing on *Mayflower* like this amber-walled room with its soft clouds of pastel light drifting across the ceiling. Some things looked somewhat familiar—the thing he was lying on, for instance. It was very much like the shallow pan that corpsicles were thawed in, and he caught a quick glimpse of several others like it in the room. They were occupied. There was a human body in each, and warming radiation flooding down on them: he was not the only person being brought back to life, he thought, pleased with his cleverness at observing that.

But where was all this happening?

And what was *hurting* him so much? As the explosion of pain in his skull dwindled again he became aware of two other hurting places—a mean, burning sensation in his right leg below the knee, and a sharper, smaller, but still very painful, hurt in his buttock. None of it made any sense to Viktor. Nothing else did, either. "Sense" was beyond him; he was dazed, confused, disoriented, and he was even having trouble *remembering*. On all the evidence, he was quite sure he had just been thawed out from a time in the freezer. But he remembered, or thought he remembered, that he had been frozen before. More than once, he thought, and which time was this? He reasoned that it couldn't have been the times when he was facing a long interstellar flight, because he had been a child then.

He wasn't a child anymore, of course. Was he? And who was this woman, who was now coaxing him to lie down again?

The name "Reesa" crossed his foggy mind, but he didn't think this woman was she—whoever "Reesa" was.

He shook his head to try to dispel the confusion. That turned out to be a bad mistake; the pain burst through him again. But he felt the need to demonstrate his wakeful competence at once, like someone waked in the middle of the night by the telephone who instantly protests he wasn't asleep. He licked his lips, getting ready to speak.

"I don't feel very well," he said, forming the sentence with care.

Funnily, the words didn't come out right. It was more like an animal growl than a voice. He discovered that his throat, too, was extraordinarily sore.

The woman looked amused again and gestured to the man with her in the room. The man, Viktor saw, was quite normal-looking— neither as wraithfully thin nor as tall—but he wore what the woman wore, a sort of gossamer gown. He turned out to be quite strong. He pushed Viktor back down, holding him so that the woman could do something to him again.

The woman leaned close to Viktor. With her came a fragrance half like flowers, half like distant wood smoke.

Her nearness made Viktor suddenly aware that he was quite naked. The woman didn't seem to notice, or at least to care. She peered into his eyes. She touched the base of his throat with an instrument that glittered like metal but was soft and warm to the touch, while she studied a tiny, dancing firework display of color at the instrument's base.

Then she pulled down his lower lip. Instinctively he tried to twist his head away—again that explosion of pain!—but the man in the filmy gown gripped his head roughly, holding it immobile while the woman touched the damp, tender inside of Viktor's lip with some other kind of thing, and Viktor went quickly and helplessly to sleep.

When he woke up again he was alone in the room. Even the other resuscitation pans were empty.

His head still hurt, but the other pains were gone—well, not gone entirely, but now they were only little annoyances rather than agony. When he sat up he saw that his right calf, from knee to ankle, was encased in some sort of a pale pink sausagelike contrivance. He puzzled over that for a while, poking at it with a finger. He didn't understand it. He didn't understand much of anything at all; everything seemed so *complicated*. The way he felt, he thought, was almost like being drunk.

He tried to recollect how he had got here. There was a memory of being told he had to go back in the freezer . . .

Yes, that was true, he was pretty sure. It wasn't a comforting thought, though. He had a vague memory about freezing, something that someone had told him—was her name Wanda?—long before. It did not do to be frozen too many times. That he was sure of, though what it meant was very unclear.

He heard a man's voice growling something from the doorway, and when he looked around it was the fellow in the gown, looking at him. "You're awake," the man said—wonderfully, in words that Viktor understood. "Stay there. I'll see if Nrina wants to look at you."

Viktor made himself sit up. At least some questions were beginning to be clear. For some reason these people had decided to revive him from cryonic suspension. All right, he could understand that. He wondered how long he had been in the freezer this time. It couldn't be a matter of centuries again, of course. He simply would not accept that. But it had been long enough, at least, for the Reforms, or whoever's turn it was at the power plant detail this time, to get a little decent heat in the freezatorium. (But hadn't he just decided he wasn't in the freezatorium anymore? He wasn't sure.) And, if these people actually were Reforms, or if they were any other sect from frozen Newmanhome for that matter, they'd certainly changed their mode of dress. The man was taking off the filmy robe, and under it he wore nothing but a kind of kilt. Then, when the impossibly thin woman came back, Viktor observed that the gown she was wearing was the kind of clothing one wore for decoration or for modesty—well, no, not for modesty either, he thought; but certainly not for keeping out the cold. The thing was a long white smock, almost transparent, and he could clearly see that there was nothing much under it.

The woman looked different, though. She seemed to be more fretful and tired than when he had first seen her, as though she had been working hard, and the silky, gossamer gown was soiled with new spots of blood.

When he shifted position to look at her he thought to look down at himself, and was suddenly ashamed of his nakedness. Then, twisting for a better look, he saw that there was a wound on his right buttock. That was where one of the pains he had almost forgotten had come from. It wasn't an insect bite, but a sort of stab wound in the flesh. Someone had put some soft, rubbery film over it, transparent, almost invisible. The film peeled away easily when he poked at it, and under the dressing the wound was still oozing blood.

The skinny woman pushed his hand away, clucking reprovingly at him.

The man came over and firmly pressed the padding back in place. "Damn it! Leave it alone, can't you?" he said irritably. "Now sit still. Nrina's got to examine you to see if there's any more freezer burn, so you just let her do it, all right? I've got to check on the others."

Viktor puzzled earnestly over all of that. He understood all the words, though they had a strange quality, as though they had come from afar. But whatever was wrong with Viktor's head kept him from putting them together to make any kind of coherent picture. "Freezer burn—" Viktor began, but the man was already gone.

Lacking any better alternatives that he could see, Viktor did as he was told. He let the woman peer into his eyes, touch him in all sorts of personal places with her shiny instruments with their rainbow lights, lift up a corner of the pale pink sausage on his leg and peer under it, and finally replace it, looking satisfied. She patted his head—so gently, this time, that it didn't send him into a blaze of new pain.

Then she beckoned him to follow her.

He tried. He did his best, but his best wasn't very good. The right side of his head felt numb, and his right leg wouldn't support him, even in the astonishingly light gravity of the place they were in. She had to let him lean on her as they walked—it was more like gliding in a dream; like getting about in a spaceship under micro-drive—through an amber-walled corridor, to their first stop.

The first stop was a tiny room containing an amber, glassy bowl in which water gently whirled. Viktor identified it easily enough: a toilet.

Viktor had not forgotten that he was quite naked, though the woman didn't seem interested in that fact. Neither did she watch him while, embarrassed, he relieved himself, nor on the other hand did she specially look away. The second stop was a shower. He looked at it doubtfully. He wasn't sure how to make it work, and he wasn't sure he could stand alone in it.

When he tried it, the leg, at least, was feeling stronger. The woman turned the shower on for him. He limped inside, bracing himself against the soft, shiny wall of the cubicle. As the gentle, warm cascade began to pour over him it was so relaxing that he found that he was actually enjoying it.

When Viktor came out of the shower the woman handed him a round, soft towel for drying himself. "Thank you," he said hoarsely, rubbing his face.

The woman looked pleased, as though at a dog that had given an appreciative *woof*. But when he pointed at the dressings on leg and hip, trying to ask if they had been harmed by the shower, she only shrugged, either uncomprehending or just not interested in his question.

The third stop they made was stranger and a lot less pleasant.

The woman abandoned him in another room, to the care of a different man. This one was almost as skinny as herself, though he did have some strangely knotted muscles—whereas the woman's calves were like pencils and she had no visible biceps at all. The man gestured Viktor to a seat in something that looked like a dentist's chair.

When Viktor sat down as ordered, the arms of the thing quite suddenly swung out and wrapped themselves around him. He couldn't move. At the same time something else slipped around his head and gripped it as in a vise. It wasn't painful, but it wasn't resistible, either. Then the man approached Viktor with a different kind of a glittery instrument.

He touched it to Viktor's forehead.

This metallic thing wasn't soft at all. It bit into the flesh of Viktor's forehead and stung like a wasp. Viktor shouted in surprise and tried to struggle. That was no use. He was held fast. When the man took the instrument away the spot itched terribly, like a bee sting; but then the man sprayed the spot where he had been working with a different kind of metallic thing. The itching stopped at once, and the man touched something that caused the chair to release Viktor.

That ruled out the cloudy theory Viktor had just begun to formulate provisionally, that these people had thawed him out for the purpose of a little recreational torture. Then the man led him, stepping in long, gentle, high-rising paces, to another chamber, where he shoved Viktor inside and closed the door behind him.

Viktor looked around him. He was in a room with a number of flimsy-looking chairs (perhaps a waiting room?) and a kind of glass-topped desk (but it showed no other signs of being an office). Glassware and some metallic things sat under a mirror that was set against one wall, but it wasn't, as far as Viktor could decide, a laboratory.

He was not alone in it. Three other men, as naked as Viktor himself, were sitting uneasily in the frail chairs, talking to each other in worried, low tones. One of the men was black, one short and pale. The third was also pale but taller than Viktor and hugely built; and all three had the human-scale bodily form Viktor was used to, not the famine-victim limbs and structure of the woman who had thawed him out.

As Viktor came in, all three of the men looked quickly up at him with a fearful sort of suspicion in their eyes. Then their expressions cleared quickly, as though they had recognized him.

Well, they couldn't have. Viktor knew that. He was quite sure they were all total strangers to him; but then he saw that each of them bore a bright blue device tattooed on their foreheads, and in the wall mirror he caught a glimpse of the same design on his own.

It was an elliptical border enclosing some hen-scratchings that might have been numbers or words.

It was that tattoo that they had recognized. They all wore the same brand. So they were all in the same boat—whatever that boat was.

The tall man got up, offering a hand to shake. "Welcome to the party," he said, in the quick, rough English of the quarreling sects of frozen Newmanhome. "What did you get the freeze for?"

Viktor puzzled over the meaning of what the man had just said to him, rubbing the mark on his forehead absently. When he had put it together, through the cloud that seemed to pervade his mind, he rehearsed for a moment, then managed a full sentence. "They just didn't like me," he croaked.

"Mary!" the black one said. "When did they start doing it for *that*? I got my own freeze in three eighty-six, but at least I had a trial. They said it was for unauthorized parenting. Well, it was just her word against mine, but what could I do? Jeren here was frozen for drunkenness, and Mescro got it for thievery—"

The short, pale man cut in, scowling. "Watch your mouth, Korelto! I didn't *steal* anything. I just made a mistake and went through the meal line twice—it could've happened to anybody when they were on overload!"

"Does it matter?" The black man smiled. "Only it looks to me as though things must've got really bad by the time they froze you—uh—"

It took Viktor a moment to realize he was being asked his name. "Ah, Viktor," he got out.

The black man—Korelto?—looked at him searchingly, then glanced at his companions. "Are you all right?" he asked.

"He's a dummy," the short one named Mescro declared.

"Aw, no," the big one said. He looked down at the floor, as though abashed at his own temerity in trying to contradict the other. "He's just, you know, mixed up." He looked up appealingly at Viktor, then at the doorway. "Isn't that true, Manett?" he asked.

The man who had been in the thawing-out room stood there, gazing at them without pleasure. "No, Jeren, he's a dummy, all right," Manett confirmed. "Nrina says he's got freezer burn. Looks like it got his leg and his brain. But he'll do for what Nrina wants him for."

There was a satisfied, challenging look on his face that made the black man ask worriedly, "What's that, Manett?"

"That's what you're about to find out, guys," Manett said, with the pleasure of an old hand breaking in the new recruits. "It's time for you to pay for your thawing out."

"Pay how?" the little thief named Mescro demanded. "And what's going on, anyway?"

Manett pursed his lips thoughtfully. "Well, I'm willing to clue you in first," he said, hiking himself up on one of the benches to lecture. "Only don't interrupt, because you've got to earn your pay in a few minutes; Nrina's waiting for the stuff. Let's see. My name's Manett, I told you that, and I'm your boss. That's the most important thing you have to remember. It means you do everything I tell you, understand that? You'll be seeing a lot of me for a while. Then, next thing, probably you'll want to know the date. All right. It's the forty-fourth of Summer, in the year forty-two hundred and fifty-one A.L." There were gasps at that—Viktor was only one of the ones gasping—but Manett quelled it with a frown and went on. "Next: What's going to happen to you? Nothing bad. You'll be all right. Don't worry about that. You'll stay here for a few days, as long as Nrina wants you. You'll have to start learning the language while you're here, but that's pretty easy. You'll see. Then you'll go to live in another habitat, probably—I don't know which one—"

"Hey!" Korelto interrupted. "Hold on a minute! What's a habitat?"

Manett gave him a mean look. "Didn't I tell you not to interrupt? *This* is a habitat. What you're living in now. Anyway, what happens when you leave here I don't exactly know—I've never been on any habitat but this one, but Dekkaduk and Nrina say you'll be okay. You might as well believe them—you don't have any other choice, do you? Anyway, right after you do what you're here for we'll get something to eat and then I'll have more time, all right? Now," he said, standing up, "it's time to earn your pay. So will you get up, all of you, and go over there and take one of those specimen bottles each? And then, what you do, you each jack off into it, and be sure you don't spill a drop."

The fuzziness in Viktor's brain wasn't altogether a disadvantage right then, he thought. The thing he was told to do was degrading, and it made him feel ashamed and angry. If he had felt really *sober* he would have been twice as humiliated at what he was made to do.

But he did it. So did all three of the others, as startled as Viktor at the bizarre orders. They grumbled and tried to joke while they did it, but the jokes were resentful and nobody laughed.

Viktor was still trying to sort out the dreamy maze in his mind. There were so many questions! It was hard even to form them, but some stood out. For one: What was "freezer burn"? Viktor knew he'd heard the words before, and he knew they meant something bad. He just didn't know what. He knew that he could have asked the others, but he wasn't ready to do that—wasn't ready to hear the answer, perhaps.

Then there was that other big question. When Manett told them the date, was he joking?

It couldn't really be nearly *four thousand years* since he'd last been alive. Could it?

He cursed the fogginess in his brain then. He wanted to *think*. There were things he had forgotten, and he wanted them back! The things he did remember were fragmentary and unsatisfying . . .

They weren't pleasing, either.

He did remember, cloudily, waking up from a different freezing—had it been in old *Ark*? (He did remember the old interstellar ship *Ark*, though the memory was peculiarly fragmentary. It was almost as though there had been two different ships.) That time it had been a terrible shock. To have learned that everyone he had known was four hundred Newmanhome years dead had been numbing.

But at least then he had recognized the sensation. He had known that he felt numb.

To find out that another four thousand years, nearly, had passed while he lay as a lump of dreamless and unfeeling ice—why, it felt like nothing at all. He didn't feel pain. He didn't even feel the numbness. He didn't *feel* at all.

When they had embarrassedly made their donations of sperm, the trusty named Manett showed them to their quarters. Food was waiting for them, fresh fruits and things like meat patties and things like little cakes—and things Viktor could hardly recognize at all, some cold, some hot, some tasting nasty to his untrained palate.

"You're on your own time now," Manett announced. "You have to start learning to talk to these people pretty soon, but right now all you have to do is eat."

The tall man named Jeren cleared his throat and whispered apologetically, "Do we get paid for this?"

"Paid! Holy Freddy, man! Don't you think you got paid already, just by being taken out of the freezer?" Then Manett paused to think it over. "Actually, that's a tough question," he admitted. "I can't say I exactly understand the money system here, but there is one, I guess. No, you don't get paid. Whatever it costs for your food and all that probably gets charged to Nrina's laboratory somehow. If you want anything else, forget it. You can't afford it."

Mescro pricked up his ears. "What can't we afford?" he asked.

"Different things," Manett said, scowling. "Don't bother me with that kind of stuff now. Now, you all look like you've got enough jism stored up to squeeze out a sample four or five times a day for Nrina, so we're going to do you one more time before you go to sleep—but for right now you better get started learning the language."

"Aw, wait a minute," Korelto objected. "We haven't even finished eating yet!"

"Well, snap it up," Manett growled. But he was enjoying his role as mentor and straw boss, and when they insisted on asking him more questions, endless questions, through mouths stuffed with food, he tolerantly gave them answers.

Viktor wasn't one of the questioners. He ate in silence, trying to follow what was being said, missing most of it. Could it really be true that his brain had been damaged by "freezer burn"? It was certain that something had happened; the talk rolled over him, too fast to follow, too hard to understand. Then a familiar word caught his attention: the black man, Korelto, asking, "Where are we? It isn't Newmanhome, is it?"

"Hell, no. I told you that. It's a habitat."

"You mean another planet? Maybe Nebo?"

Manett gave him an incredulous stare. "Nebo? Don't you know

what it's like on Nebo? We never go near Nebo—it's hot as hell, and people get hurt there!"

Viktor frowned, puzzled. He had been close enough to Nebo to know that it couldn't be called "hot" anymore—not after the weakening of the sun's output. Still, he supposed, in comparison with the system's frozen-over other planets . . .

But Manett wasn't waiting for the next question. "You want to know where we are?" he asked. "I'll show you." And he got up from the table and walked over to one of those glass-topped things that looked like desks. "Come on over," he called, scowling over a thing like a keypad in one corner of it. "Just a minute . . ."

They were all clustered around it as Manett hit a key. The glass turned misty, then cleared again.

"There's old Nergal," Manett said, proud of his success in getting the thing to work.

Viktor yelped. So did the other three. They were looking straight down onto something immense and redly glowing, like a bed of mottled coals.

Viktor couldn't help himself. He reached out blindly and caught the arm of the big man named Jeren. Jeren was shaking, too, but he held to Viktor as they all stared down. Viktor felt himself falling into that glowing hell—no, not falling, exactly; what he felt was that ruddy Nergal was swimming up toward him, drowning him.

Manett's voice came to him from far away. "That's what they call the brown dwarf. They moved here while the sun was cold, and we're living in a habitat around it. A habitat is kind of like a big spaceship, you know? Only it doesn't go anywhere, it just stays in orbit. That's where everybody's been living for the last few thousand years, when it was so cold before the old sun came back."

"The sun came back?" one of the others cried out, astonished, but Viktor hardly heard. He was staring down, transfixed. He knew, *part* of him knew, that he wasn't really being swallowed by that glowing pyre; it was, he told himself, only part of the "freezer burn," the numbness in his head that was like a gauze scrim slipped between himself and the world. But he could feel himself swaying.

"Hey," he heard Jeren's worried voice say. "Something's wrong with this guy."

Manett's face appeared before Viktor. He looked disgusted. "You're relapsing," he accused. "You'd better get to bed."

Viktor tried to focus on him and failed. "All right, Daddy," Viktor said.

When he woke again his throat felt less like sandpaper, but his other parts were worse. Nor was his mind much clearer. He had a confused memory of being wakened and ordered to masturbate again into one of the soft, crystalline plastic vials, and of men's voices around him when he slept, but it was all hopelessly cloudy.

The voices were still going on. He lay trying to follow what they were talking about, with his eyes closed. Manett's voice drowned out the others. He was saying smugly, "You know what they want. They want you to jerk off into bottles. That's why they brought you up here, for sperm. It's like cross-breeding animals, you know? They've been out here for thousands of years and they want to get some lost genes back into the pool. Oh, it isn't just you guys. There are a couple of dozen of us real men around in one habitat or another that they've thawed out already. Not counting the stiffs—there's maybe a hundred of those stashed away in Nrina's cryonics place, waiting until she needs them."

"Is that where we were?" somebody asked.

"In the freezer? Of course that's where you were, where else? Nrina thaws out a few guys at a time for samples, then mostly they get sent away when she's through with them. But I stay here. I'm the only one on this habitat permanently. Nrina kept me to help her out, you know?"

Viktor heard a leering, sycophantic chuckle from one of the others. It sounded like Mescro. Then Manett's voice picked up again. "They collect a batch of corpsicles from the freezers on Newman-home and bring them here. Nrina takes cell samples from each, then she thaws out the ones that look interesting. You know that jab on your asses?" Viktor remembered the bandage clearly enough. "Well, that's where she gouged out a piece to get a DNA sample."

"I don't remember that part," one of the others objected—Jeren, Viktor thought.

" 'Course not. How could you? You were frozen—that's why it made such a big hole." Manett pulled down the waistband of his skirt to display the spot on his own hip where only a puckered little dimple still showed. "Don't worry, it heals up. Then after she checks the sample out, if your genes look interesting, she thaws you out and turns you over to me."

"Is that why they tattooed us, to show we're like gene donors?" Korelto asked.

Manett laughed. "You think they need a tattoo to show that? Don't you see what they look like—skinny as skeletons? No, they can tell that much just by looking at us. That mark," he said, sounding prideful, "is kind of a like a *warning*, you know? It tells all the women that we're still potent sperm donors. All the other males around here have that stuff turned off as soon as their balls start working. They can make love, all right—believe me, it's one of their favorite things! But they don't produce sperm. The women don't want to get pregnant, you know."

"But if they don't get pregnant, then how—"

"You mean babies? Sure they have babies, only they do it in a test tube, like. That's what Nrina does in her laboratory. They match up the sperm and the ovum in a kind of an incubator and they carry it to term, and when the baby's ready they pull it out and put it in a nursery. Listen, these people don't do *anything* that hurts. Or even makes them sweat—except for fun," he added, grinning. "Don't worry about it. If they ever decide they've got enough of your DNA they'll fix you, too, and then they'll take the mark off your forehead and you can plow right in."

Jeren, who was somewhat slow of thought, had just gotten to the question that interested him. "Wait a minute," he said. "Are you saying that, you know, some of these women might want to . . ."

Manett looked smug. "Has happened," he announced.

"Even the cute one that thawed us out?"

Manett scowled. "Never mind about her," he said darkly. "Change the subject."

"Sure, Manett," Mescro said, grinning. "Only I notice you don't have the tattoo any more, and I was just wondering—"

"I said change the subject!" Manett roared. And then, as he saw

Viktor trying to sit up, he said, "Oh, look, sleeping beauty's awake. What do you want, Viktor?"

"Well," Viktor said, trying to get the words out in spite of the sudden, almost breathless feeling that had hit him, "is it all men? I mean, if these people are so hungry for different genetic traits, don't they thaw out women, too?"

"Hell, no. Why would they do that? They don't really use the sperm, you know. It's just easy for them to work with, so they just extract the gene fragments they want, and then they mix them up with other strains to get the kind of genes they need for—for whatever they need them for, anyway. That's not my department. Nrina's told me all about that, but I guess I didn't listen. Anyway, that," he said, preening himself, "is one way we have an advantage over the women. We guys can produce a million sperms a day. Women can maybe do one ovum a month, if they're lucky, so if they want genes from a female they just do it the hard way, from tissue samples." He peered in a friendly manner at Viktor, who wasn't smiling. "What's the matter, you afraid you can't make your million a day?"

Viktor shook himself. "I—no. Nothing," he said.

But it hadn't really been nothing. It had been a quick flare-up of unexpected and quite unjustified hope, quickly blighted. No. There was no point in hoping along those lines.

Because that one little corner of his mind had suddenly come clear, like the desk that had showed him Nergal, and he had remembered Reesa.

For the next few days of Viktor's new life he thought of Reesa almost constantly—while he was falling asleep, while he was just coming awake, while he was donating his sperm samples, while he was eating, while he was trying to learn the new language— all the time. But he could think of her only as you think of the dead. Of the long dead, at that.

He wondered, in an abstracted sort of way, if Reesa had had a happy life after his freezing. He wondered if she had missed him, or if she had reconciled herself sooner or later to his loss and, say, married someone else. Someone like Mirian, perhaps. She would have been a prized sort of wife for a Great Catholic, Viktor thought, because she was quite capable of being sexually active but no longer of complicating his life by becoming pregnant.

He told himself that he hoped she had married. He hoped she'd been happy—as happy as anyone could be in that world, anyway.

He didn't go so far as to hope she hadn't missed him. And he did miss her, certainly he did. But it was a sort of remote, somehow well-aged pain. As soon as he had heard the present date he had almost felt the quick, irrevocable shifting of gears in his mind. That history was *ancient*.

No one could mourn for four thousand years.

The curtain had come down on the first two acts of his life. He was just beginning Act Three.

It might not be the life he wanted . . . but it was the only life he had left.

Viktor forced himself to plunge into studying the language of these frail, remarkable people who had brought him back to life. It wasn't easy. The fog around his brain made everything difficult, but there was help for him.

The biggest help was the desks.

They were actually like his old teaching machines, he saw. They provided him with hours on end of conversation with the image of a friendly, helpful, wise teacher talking to him from the desk.

The teacher was certainly not *real*. Viktor knew that; it was a computer-generated, three-dimensional picture, and the fact that it looked like an amiable (if exceptionally skinny) young man did not deceive him. It was real enough to correct his accent, straighten out his grammar, and provide him with the translation of every word and thought he needed.

The others who had been revived with him were, of course, busy at the same thing. Only Jeren, the gentle giant, was finding the process as hard as Viktor. Jeren was not a bright man. It wasn't freezer burn in Jeren's case. The man had just been born with a few slow linkages in his brain. Even with the cobwebs that cluttered his own mind, Viktor was far quicker than Jeren.

All the same, it was Jeren who became Viktor's friend.

The little weasel Mescro was too busy trying to make a friend of Manett to pay attention to anyone who had no power, and he had attached Korelto to himself. It was Jeren who helped Viktor when he stumbled, Jeren who brought Viktor food in those first days when Viktor was too weak, or too dazed, to get up for it. He stood chastely by Viktor, eyes averted, while Viktor performed the rite of masturbation, and helped him back to bed when he was done. And he sat by Viktor, talking when Viktor felt like talking, silently watching while Viktor dozed.

Jeren was a big man—taller than Viktor, far taller than most of the people of Newmanhome's Ice Age. He was solid, too, a hulking bear of a man, with a voice that was deep but so soft it was almost inaudible. He seemed to try to stay out of everyone's way. When he spoke to anyone he averted his eyes, so as not to challenge the other person.

With all of Viktor's own problems, there was something about Jeren that made Viktor feel sorry for him—or feel contemptuous of him. Why would such a big man try so hard to efface himself? Only because he felt somehow small—and if a man thinks himself small, who is anyone else to say he isn't?

Viktor never succeeded in reconciling himself to what he had to do to earn his keep—most of all, because there was almost always someone there with him while he did it. Usually the person was Manett. The man seemed to enjoy humiliating his crew of sperm donors, and Viktor more than the others, it appeared. If there had ever been anything about sex that Viktor disliked, it was trying to perform in the morning, but Manett was adamant. "Do your job," he ordered. "Then you eat. Then you get back to studying the language, and don't argue with me!" So, minutes after awakening every day, Viktor was standing in the sperm-donation cubicle, trying to think erotic.

What made it even more difficult was that sometimes Nrina, the woman who had supervised his thawing, followed him into the chamber. Viktor hated it when she stood behind him, because for some reason she had taken to watching with evident interest. Viktor glared confusedly at her. What he could see through her transparent, open-meshed smock stirred something inside him, all right, but it wasn't enough. He appealed to Manett. "I don't like her being here. It makes me—uh—it *interferes*."

Manett guffawed and translated. The woman replied politely. Viktor thought he could almost understand what she was saying now, in her husky, sweet voice, but he was glad when Manett translated anyway.

Manett didn't seem glad. He spoke sourly, as though he didn't like what he was saying. "She says she likes watching you, so go ahead."

"I don't think I *can*."

"What's that got to do with it? She—wait a minute." He listened to Nrina and then, glowering, addressed Viktor again. "She wants to know if you were really born on Old Earth."

"Of course I was. I told you." And then, turning to the woman, Viktor said haltingly in her own language, "This is true, yes."

"Get on with it!" Manett ordered, looking angry. "Or would you rather go back in the freezer?"

But the woman was laughing. She paused to say something to Manett and turned to leave the room. Manett looked annoyed. "Do it and then come out," he ordered. "And then Nrina says to hurry up and finish learning the language. She wants to talk to you."

The language wasn't as hard as Viktor had first feared. A long time had passed, but there were still English words embedded in their vocabularies, or at least the ghosts of the words. The difference was far less than that between the language of his own day—whatever you took that day to be—and that of Beowulf. The vowel sounds had changed. The words were sometimes clipped and sometimes slurred, and there were many hundreds of wholly new words to learn, words that Viktor had never heard before because the things they referred to had never existed before. But within a week he could understand some of what Nrina was saying to Manett, and before long he could speak to her directly.

The "desk" teaching machines were marvelous tutors—and a good deal more. The desk was not simply for teaching. It did that function very well, but it was also an atlas, and an encyclopedia, and a patient tutor, repeating the same thing over and over again as long as Viktor wanted it, until Viktor's slowly recovering brain could absorb it.

It was especially fine as a picture book. Even though Viktor's brain was still fogged part of the time, and his memory sketchy almost always, he could follow what the machines told him about his new world he was living in. The human population of Newmanhome had not only recovered from its ice age (though not on Newmanhome), it had flourished madly. There were three hundred million people alive now, and they lived very well. Most of them were in what an earlier human would have called O'Neill habitats, and those were various but uniformly fine. Some were like an ancient English countryside, with trees and flowering plants and hedgerows; animals like rabbits and foxes lived in the wooded parts; songbirds and hummingbirds flew in their air. Some were like cities a mile through, with ten million people huddled together. Some were quite strange—there was even a wilderness habitat here and there with grizzly bears and tigers, jungles and forests, even great slow waterfalls. Viktor discovered that not everyone lived on the habitats. A few preferred to live on Nergal's natural moons, now terraformed and quite comfortable. Most people tried to spend a little time on one of them now and then. It was a form of sport for them, moving about in a real gravity field, though a tiny one. They did it to keep their bodies in shape.

Considering how their bodies had stretched out in those scores of generations in micro- or low gravity, they did that very well. As Viktor caught occasional glimpses of other inhabitants of the place, he could easily see that that was true. The people of this place didn't wear much in the way of clothing—a cache-sex, a simple strip of cloth that covered their sexual organs and the cleft between their buttocks, was good enough for most practical purposes. Sometimes they wore a bit more. When Nrina was busy in her laboratory she wore a smock to keep the messes off her body, and sometimes she wore other things, just for the prettiness of them. Women wore nothing on their breasts, most of the time. They didn't need to. In the gentle gravity of the habitat the breasts didn't sag.

The other side of that coin was that the males were less macho than Viktor was used to—*much* less.

The males were not much bigger than the women. Not much stronger, either, Viktor thought; large muscles weren't needed where they lived. (The man, Dekkaduk, from Nrina's laboratory turned out to be a puzzling exception.) Particularly since none of them did much physical labor. Compared to them, Viktor was a giant. He was bigger than most of his reawakened colleagues in the sperm banks, for that matter, since the Newmanhome of their time had not provided its children with a generous diet, and certainly never any fresh air.

When Viktor began to explore outside the immediate confines of Nrina's laboratory he encountered still more strangers. He even tried speaking to some of them now and again, for language practice, but he was wary. When he looked at them, he did not fail to see that they were looking at him as well, and with just as much speculative interest. He thought that the branding on the forehead was probably a useful precaution. Some of the glances from females were frankly sexual, and Viktor appreciated that very much . . . the memory of Reesa slowly fading from his mind.

Some of the sexually charged looks, however, were from people who were definitely male, and about that Viktor was far less pleased.

By the time Viktor could make himself understood to people like Nrina his life had fallen into a routine. He ate when food was offered. He slept when he was tired. He made his required four donations of sperm each day—a little surprised at himself, and not unpleased: after all, he was pretty nearly a middle-aged man now! And between times, all the time, he tried to learn this world he was in.

Of course, Viktor was not the only newcomer in the habitat. Jeren, Mescro, and Korelto were as innocent as himself, and two of them, at least, were curious. (Jeren wasn't. Jeren took what came without complaint or question. His main interest was in following Viktor around.) But those three had an advantage Viktor didn't share. All the things they wanted to know Manett, the veteran of more than eight months ahead of them out of the freezer, already knew—and told them. But it seemed that Manett just didn't like talking to Viktor.

For some reason, Viktor could not guess why, Manett had taken a dislike to him. More than a dislike. Viktor pondered, without resolving, the curious idea he had formed that sometimes, when he caught Manett's eyes on him, the expression in them looked almost like fear.

Then Nrina called him in for another examination.

When Viktor greeted her, careful with his pronunciation, the woman looked pleased, but she just waved him to a table. There she did all the things she had already done to Viktor—touched his head with various instruments, studied the polychrome readings, and felt the part just above his temple that had hurt so badly, looking satisfied when he said it hurt no more.

"Your leg, then," she said, speaking slowly so that he could understand. He raised it obediently to the table, and she touched a buzzing rod to the dressing.

The pink sausage fell neatly open. Viktor looked, and smelled, and squinted his eyes shut, trying not to be sick. A big piece of his calf was *gone*. What was left stank of dead meat and decay.

Nrina didn't seem to mind. She bent close to study it, by eye and with more of the instruments that flashed rainbow colors for her. Then, satisfied, she sprayed it with something that felt like nothing at all, but quickly dissipated the terrible odor and left the exposed raw meat covered with a film of metallic gold. She pressed the two halves of the wrapping back together and sat down facing Viktor, her knees hugged to her breast, regarding him.

When she spoke to Viktor it was slowly, a word at a time. "You have . . . suffered . . . damage . . . from improper freezing. For . . . a long time. Do you understand?" He nodded. "So . . . there are two things. Your leg. It will . . . I think . . . be all right . . . in a season. It will . . . heal completely."

"That is good," Viktor said.

She nodded seriously. "The brain . . . I do not know."

Viktor blinked at her. "What?"

"I have . . . inserted . . . additional material . . . in your brain . . . to replace . . . what was lost. It may take. I think it has . . . partly."

"*Partly?*"

"Perhaps more. We must wait."

"I have been waiting," he said bitterly.

She studied him thoughtfully for a moment. Then, smiling, she said, "You will . . . wait some more. Now go. You will help Manett. You must learn . . . to do his work."

Manett was waiting for Viktor outside the examination room, and his expression was even more dour than usual. When Viktor asked him what Nrina had meant, Manett flared up. "It means she's going to give you my *job*, damn your hide!" he rasped. "Come on. I'll show you what to do—but just don't *talk* to me!" And he led the way to the outermost shell of the habitat, where the wraithlike but oddly muscled man who had tattooed Viktor in the first place was waiting impatiently for them.

The man wasn't wearing a filmy robe now; he was dressed in shiny, copper-colored things like overalls, which covered everything from neck to feet, and he had a hood of the same material in his hand. "This is Dekkaduk," Manett said, short and surly. "Get dressed."

Dekkaduk looked at him inquiringly, but didn't say anything either. He waited while Viktor struggled into the same sort of garment. It was light and flexible, but it felt metallic. Still, it was elastic, too, because it slid over the sausage around Viktor's lower leg easily enough.

"Now," Dekkaduk said, "we go inside." He was speaking the language of the habitat people. Because Viktor was concentrating on what he was doing it took a moment for him to understand. Manett helped him along with a shove.

"Dekkaduk said *move*," he snapped. "Get your damn hood on!"

Then Viktor found out what his job was. All three of them donned their hoods, then crowded all together into a tiny cubicle; Manett pulled the outer door closed—it was thick but light—and opened a door on the other side.

Immediately the transparent front of Viktor's hood clouded over and he felt a stinging cold. A moment later he could feel Manett roughly poking at his back, doing something that resulted first in a faint click, then a hiss. The icy cold of the suit warmed; warm air began to flow through the hood. Gradually the frosted inside of the faceplate began to clear.

Viktor could see Manett's face bending toward his, and through the two visors he could see the man's look of sour satisfaction. When Manett spoke Viktor could see his lips move, but the voice came from inside the hood, right next to his ear. "You're all hooked up," Manett announced. "Now let's shift some stiffs."

And so they did. For an hour or more. Warm inside their heated suits, with their warmed air supply from the cables that connected them to sockets in the wall; and the stiffs they moved were corpsicles from the cryonics chambers on Newmanhome.

What Manett and Viktor did was the hard work—pulling out the old capsules, opening them to show the frozen bodies inside. The air in the freezer must have been searingly dry, for no frost had collected on either capsules or bodies. Some were facedown, and they were the easiest; all Viktor or Manett had to do was to pull or cut away the hard-frozen fabric over the hip and then stand aside while Dekkaduk thrust a triangle-bladed instrument into each patch of rock-hard flesh to gouge out a tiny sample. The ones who had been frozen faceup were more difficult. They had to be lifted out, or at least turned to one side, so that Dekkaduk could get at them; and then Viktor could see the frozen faces. Some were almost as though only asleep. Some were contorted. Some seemed to be silently screaming.

Then they slid the capsules back—each marked with its star or cross or crescent. Viktor was glad when it was over, because it was frightening to look on the corpsicles and know that not long before he had been just like them—and not very far in the future, maybe, might well be back there again.

Back in his own study room, as he leaned over the teaching desk, he blew on his fingers. They weren't really cold. It was his soul that was cold. He thought it would never be warm again.

But as he talked to his unreal mentor in the desk he began to forget the freezer. "What shall we study today, Viktor?" the simulacrum greeted him. "It is up to you to choose."

"Thank you," Viktor said, aware that he was thanking no one real. "Can you show me some more pictures, please?"

"Of course. Incidentally, your accent is getting much better. But what pictures would you like to see?"

"Well," Viktor said, "I used to be interested in astronomy. Can you show me what the skies look like now? I mean, not just Nergal, but everything?"

"Of course," the tutor said. "Perhaps it would be best to display it as a surround." It disappeared from the desk, and at once an image sprang up all around Viktor. The image blotted out everything but itself, and it was almost all black. "You are looking," the disembodied voice went on, "at every astronomical object that is visible from your present position. The habitats have been omitted." Indeed, Viktor saw, there was the glowing cinder of Nergal. There, behind Viktor, the sun blazed—not very bright, he thought, but then they were much farther away than Newmanhome; perhaps it really had regained all of its luminosity. A couple of quite bright things had perceptible disks—some of Nergal's moons, no doubt. He picked out a few smaller, bright objects—stars and a couple of planets . . .

Apart from that, nothing.

Nothing? Viktor sat up straight, staring around at the sparsely featured sky. "But where's the *universe?*" he cried.

"You are referring to the optical concentration that was visible for some time," the calm, disembodied voice said. "That began to dim one thousand three hundred years ago, Viktor, and by eight hundred years ago, it was no longer detectable at all. What you see *is* the universe, Viktor. There isn't anything else."

And then, with a sickening certainty, Viktor at last began to believe. It had indeed been four thousand years.

Two days later what Manett said came true. When Viktor and the others started toward the room with the sample tubes, ready to do their work of filling them, Manett appeared. He looked angry and frightened at the same time. "Forget it," he said. "Nrina says she's got enough from you guys. We—" He swallowed. "We're leaving. All but Viktor, he stays here."

"Leaving for where?" Korelto demanded, startled.

Mescro looked searchingly at his mentor's face. "You've been fired," he guessed accusingly.

"Shut up, Mescro!" Manett snarled. "Let's go. There's a bus waiting."

"But—but—" Jeren cried, blinking as he tried to take the new situation in, "but we need to get *ready!*"

"For what? You've got nothing to pack," Manett said cruelly. "Come on. Not you," he added to Viktor, with poison in his voice. "Nrina wants to see you. Now."

And thus, without warning, they were gone. Only Jeren tarried to shake Viktor's hand sadly and to say good-bye. Viktor wasn't even allowed to follow them to their "bus."

Nrina was in the corridor, and she beckoned him to follow her. She was wearing a filmy rainbow-colored thing that might once have been called a negligee. It veiled, without hiding, the fact that under it she wore nothing at all, not even the cache-sex. Viktor averted his eyes, because there was something he really wanted to ask the woman, and her scanty attire made it difficult.

"It is very interesting to me that you were born on Old Earth," she told him seriously as they walked. "Here, this is my home. You may come in."

He followed her uneasily through a doorway. When they were inside she clapped her hands, and it closed behind them. It was not a large room, but it was prettily festooned with growing things, and there was a scent of flowers in the air. There was one of those desk things, of course, and soft pillows thrown about. The only other large bit of furniture in the room was a soft, cup-shaped thing, like the cap of a mushroom turned upside down.

It looked very much like a bed.

Nrina sat on the edge of the cup-shaped thing, which was large enough for her to stretch out in easily. She looked at Viktor appraisingly before she spoke. "Have you any questions for me, Viktor?" she asked.

Indeed he had—many, and a number that he didn't quite want to ask. He fumbled. "I did—I did want to know something, Nrina. Is my, uh, my brain severely damaged?"

"Severely?" She thought for a moment. "No, I would not say

'severely,' " she said at last. "Much of your memory has come back, has it not? Perhaps more will. The damage may not be permanent."

"*May* not!"

She shrugged—it was a graceful movement, but with the extreme slimness of her body it made Viktor think of a snake slowly writhing in its coils. "What difference does that make?"

"It make a great difference to me!"

She thought that over, looking at him carefully. Then she smiled. "But it makes none to me, Viktor," she pointed out. And she lay back on the bed, still smiling at him, but now with a wholly different expression.

He felt himself responding. Instinctively his hand went to the brand on his forehead.

"Oh," she said, reaching out with her own hand to take his, "that is all right, Viktor. I have fixed myself so that I cannot be fertilized. But I do want to know, I want very much to know, how you people from Old Earth made love."

CHAPTER 21

$\mathbf{B}$y now the universe was getting pretty old, and Wan-To was very nearly the age of the universe. There was a redeeming feature to that, though, because the older Wan-To got, the longer it took for him to become older still.

That wasn't because of the relativistic effect of time dilation. It had nothing to do with the velocity of his motion. It was only a matter of energy supply. Wan-To was living on a starvation diet, and it had made him very *slow*.

When Wan-To was young or middle-aged—or even quite elderly, say when he had reached the age of a few hundred billion years—he aged quickly because he did *everything* quickly. Wan-To was a plasma person. It was the flashing pace of nuclear fusion that drove his metabolism; changes of state happened at the speed of the creation and destruction of virtual particles, winking in and out of existence as vacuum fluctuations.

That was how it had been, once.

It wasn't that way anymore. Wan-To was almost blind now. He could not spare the energy for all those external eyes—but it didn't much matter, because what was there to see in this sparse, dark, cold universe? He did keep a tiny "ear" open for the sounds of possible communication—though even "possible," he knew, was stretching it. Who was there to communicate?

Wan-To's physical condition in itself was awful. (How awful just to have a "physical" condition at all!) He was trapped. He was embedded in a nearly solid mass, like a man buried in sand up to his neck. It wasn't impossible for him to move. It was only very difficult, and painful, and agonizingly slow.

He could have left. He could have cut himself loose from this corpse of a star to seek another. But there weren't any others better than the one he was in.

The wonderful quick, bright phase of his existence was so far in the past that Wan-To hardly remembered it. (His memory, too, was a function of how much energy he had to spare for it. A lot of memory was, so to speak, shut down—"on standby," one might say, to hoard what powers he had available.) The kind of energies to support that sort of life had disappeared. There wasn't any nuclear fusion anymore, not anywhere in the universe as far as Wan-To could see or imagine. Every fusible element had long since fused, every fissionable one had fissed.

And so the stars had gone out.

All of them. Every last one. Stars were history; and history, now, had run for so many endless eons that even Wan-To no longer kept count of the time. But time passed anyway, and now the universe had lived for more than ten thousand million million million million million million years.

That was a number without much meaning even to Wan-To. A human would have written it as the number 1 followed by forty zeroes—10,000,000,000,000,000,000,000,000,000,000,000,000,000 years. He wouldn't have understood it, either, but he could have juggled numbers around to give an idea of what it meant. He might, for instance, have said that if the entire age of the universe at the time when the human race first started thinking seriously about it— everything from the Big Bang to, say, the twentieth century on Earth—had been only *one second*, then on the same scale its present age was coming right up on something like fifty thousand billion billion years . . .

And, of course, that number wouldn't have meant much, either, except that anyone could see it was a very, very long time.

If Wan-To had been of a philosophical bent, he might have said to himself something consoling, like, At least I've had a good run for my money. Or, You only live once—but if you do it right, once is enough.

Wan-To was not that philosophical. He was not at all willing to go gladly into that long, dark night. He would have resisted it with all his force . . . if he had known a way to do it . . . and if he had had enough force to be worth talking about to resist it with.

Time was when Wan-To had hurled stars about in all the vigor of his mighty youth—had even made stars, out of clouds of dust— had even made himself a new galaxy or two, when all the ones in sight were beginning to dim toward extinction. He remembered that much, at least, because it gave him pleasure to mull over in his mind the wonderful, primordial, galaxy-sized clouds that he had caused to collapse and to begin to spin and to twinkle with billions of stars coming to life. Nothing in the universe was more powerful than Wan-To had been then, creator and destroyer of galaxies!

That had been a brave time!

But that time was long gone. In ten-to-the-fortieth-power years, most things are long gone.

What had happened in that long, long stretch of years?

The answer to that is simple.

Everything had happened.

The last of the galaxies had formed and evaporated and died. The last of the new stars had formed eternities before, as the last huge gas cloud shuddered into motion as a compressibility wave jolted it and caused it to crash together to form a new star. There couldn't be any new stars anymore. There might still be a vagrant wisp of dust here and there, but gravitational attraction wasn't strong enough to make it coalesce. That wasn't because anything had happened to gravity itself. It was just a matter of the law of inverse squares—after all, the universe was still expanding. It could not make more matter of energy, but it kept right on making more space. As the universe expanded, it cooled—there was more and more of it every second, and so the remnant heat was diluted more and more. And so everything was farther and farther away from everything else, so far that the distances were quite meaningless.

The last of the big, bright stars had long since gone supernova; the last of the Sol types had gone supergiant and turned into a white dwarf; all of those profligate wastrels of energy had long since burned themselves out. The red dwarfs had a somewhat longer run for their money. They were the smallest and longest-lived of those furnaces of nuclear fusion that were called stars, but then they had gone, too. The last of them had long before burned itself to a lump of iron, warmed by the only energy source that was left, the terminally slow decay of the protons themselves.

Proton decay! It hurt Wan-To's pride to have to live by so feeble an energy source as proton decay.

The only good thing about it was that it lasted a long time. When a proton decays, two up quarks and one down quark turn into a positron (which goes off and annihilates the first electron it comes across) and a quark-antiquark pair (which is to say a meson). The meson doesn't matter to anyone after that. The positron-electron annihilation produces heat—a *little* heat.

And all this happened very slowly. If the average life span of a proton was—well, let's not play the big number game anymore; let's just say it's a kazillion years—that didn't mean every proton in the universe would expire on the tick of that moment. That was *average*. Mathematics showed that the "half-life" of the proton should then be about seven-tenths of a kazillion.

By then Wan-To would be in even more straitened circumstances, with half the protons gone. In another such period half the remainder would be gone, and then half of that remainder.

The time was in sight, Wan-To saw with gloom, when there would just not be enough whole protons in any one cadaver of a star to keep him warm.

The word "warm" is an exaggeration. No human would have thought one of those hard, dead lumps very warm; the highest temperature proton decay could attain for it was less than a dozen degrees above absolute zero.

And that was when, after everything had happened, everything *stopped* happening, because there wasn't enough energy anywhere to drive events.

A few degrees above absolute zero wasn't what Wan-To considered warm, either, but it was all there was left for him. The solid matter he had once despised—the iron corpse that was all that was left of his last star—was the only home he could find.

It had not been easy for Wan-To to adapt to such a horrid environment. It had only been possible at all by resigning himself to the loss of most of his functions, and the slowing down of all there were left. Now the milliseconds of Wan-To's life dragged for thousands of years.

That was quite fast enough, in one way, for there wasn't much left for Wan-To to do—except to contemplate the fact that his future had no future except eternity. He wasn't even good at contemplating anymore, for his mind was fuzzy from deprivation. (Fuzzier even than that of the person who was almost as old as he was, Viktor Sorricaine.) That was just as well, because in his moments of clarity Wan-To realized that nothing was ever going to get better for him. All that would happen would be that the clinker he lived in would slowly, slowly cool even further, until there was no energy at all left to keep him alive.

And the horrible part of that was that it would go on for-ever . . . or close enough . . . for so long that even his present age would seem only a moment, before the last proton expired and he was finally dead.

Nothing but a miracle could change his hopeless certain destiny.

Wan-To didn't believe in miracles.

A miracle had to come from *somewhere*, and Wan-To could see no place in the doddering, dying universe where a miracle might still be born. Of course, he had long since forgotten the dozen stars he had hurled out of that ancient galaxy at so vast a speed that time, for that little system, had almost stopped.

CHAPTER 22

If it were not for the odd, bleak flashes of memory that sometimes cut through the fog in Viktor's brain—memories of Reesa that came and went, painful while they were there; memories of the children long dust, which left a dismal sense of hopeless loss— if it weren't for those things, Viktor might easily have thought this third act of his life close to the best.

To be sure, it was just a *touch* humiliating. Never once had Viktor imagined that his main career would be in sexually servicing a skinny, seven-foot woman with huge eyes. Yet it had its compensations. As the recognized lover of Nrina, Viktor became a privileged person.

He wasn't a "husband," of course. The only "rights" he had over Nrina were to share her bed, sometimes, her company—when she wasn't working; when she wasn't doing something else that she didn't wish to share with him. The basic job he had been thawed out for in the first place, as donator of sperm for her collection of useful genetic materials, no longer existed for him. Nrina explained that she had all the samples she needed for future genetic engineering. She now had better employment for that particular function. His only present responsibility was to give her pleasure. All of which added up to the fact that he was—

He didn't like to say it explicitly, but there was an old and unflattering expression for what he was. He was *kept*.

When Manett told him, with all that surly resentment, that Nrina had decreed Viktor was to take over his job, Viktor had thought it meant supervising the next batch of thawed-out sperm donors. But when, tentatively, Viktor asked Nrina when they were going to do the thawing she looked at him in surprise. "Oh, not *now*, Viktor," she said, stroking his shoulder affectionately. "First Dekkaduk and I must run the DNA assays on them, to see which are worth the trouble of thawing, don't you see? And we have much other work to do. Important work. Orders to fill, with deadlines which we must meet. No, it will be weeks at least, perhaps a whole season, before we are ready to acquire more material. But now—are you hungry? No? Then why don't we go to my bed again?" And he understood that what had once been Manett's main job was indeed now his.

Nrina's life wasn't his, though. Even her home wasn't really his; Viktor was surprised (and, on reflection, not very pleased) to find that the private chamber she had first taken him to was only a sort of guest room. Nrina's own home was far larger, and very much more complex and beautiful. It had one big room with a "transparent" ceiling—well, it wasn't always transparent, because Nrina could turn it off when she chose, and then it was only a sort of pattern of shifting, nebulous, luminous, multicolored pastel clouds. (And it wasn't *really* transparent, being only a sort of huge TV screen that showed the outside universe.) In the center of the room a cloudy sphere, as tall as Viktor's head, showed shapes in milky pastel light, though most of the room's illumination came from the gently glowing walls. (Nrina's people didn't seem to like harsh lighting.)

Then there was another room, quite small, but large enough for their needs. It held her own bed. That one looked terribly flimsy to Viktor; it was cantilevered out from the wall, and it did not look to Viktor as though it was built to stand very vigorous activity in it. (He was wrong about that, he discovered. The habitat's low gravity helped.) There wasn't any kitchen, exactly. There was a room with a cupboard that was a sort of a freezer and fridge, and another that was a sort of a microwave oven. (That was all they needed.

These people, Viktor found, didn't ever fry or broil anything—especially not hunks of dead animal flesh.) That was where Viktor ate most of the time—Nrina sometimes, too, though often enough she was off somewhere else, with whom Viktor never knew. That was not a problem in any practical way. There was always plenty to eat. Once Viktor learned how to handle the heating apparatus he always found stews and porridges and soups and hashes ready in the fridge, and sherberts in the freezer, and any number of different kinds of fresh fruits—always fresh, always perfect, too; though some of them were wholly unfamiliar to Viktor, and a few were perfectly foul to his taste. He wondered who replenished them. Certainly not Nrina!

Nor was Viktor idle. Not *really* idle, he told himself, he was in fact very busy learning about this new life he had been given. He had the freedom to roam where he would on the habitat. He used that freedom, too, except when his leg was hurting too badly. That wasn't often, anymore, but there were days when the pain was acute all day long. Then it hurt all the time, when it wasn't itching; sometimes it both itched, like a bad sunburn, and hurt, like a new scald.

Those days weren't a total waste, because he could spend them hunched over the communicator desk, learning all he could. But when the leg was no more than mildly annoying, he preferred to walk around.

You couldn't see much of the habitat at any one time, because everything was *inside*. There weren't many large open spaces. There certainly wasn't ever any sky, for a ceiling was never very far overhead. Strangely, much of the place was *bent*. The longest corridors were straight as laser beams, but the ones at right angles to them had perceptible upward curves.

The place was like a rolled-up version of—well, of Homeport, say. Of any city spread out on its land, except that this one had been rolled around and joined in a kind of tube. Everything Viktor saw was in the outer skin of that tube. That was why those transverse hallways were always curved. Viktor discovered that if he went all the way around one—it wasn't really far, a twenty-minute walk at most when his leg wasn't bothering him—he would come right back to his starting point.

What was in the middle? Machinery, Nrina told him when he

asked her. They were lying together in her cantilevered bed, nibbling on sweet little plums, both quite relaxed. The machinery, she said, was all different kinds. The core of the habitat was where they kept the air cleaners (to filter out the wastes and replenish the oxygen), and the temperature regulators, and the generators for electrical energy, and the communications equipment, and the data machine files—and, in short, everything that was needed to make the habitat comfortably habitable. All tidily out of sight. She yawned, pitching a plum pit on the floor and nestling cozily close to him.

But Viktor was wide awake. It was all a wonder to him. Technologically wonderful, of course, but also wonderful to think of starved, poverty-stricken refugees from old Newmanhome building all these things—enough of them to hold three hundred million people!

"Well, they didn't build them all at once, Viktor," Nrina pointed out reasonably, stretching her long, slim legs ("slim" now to Viktor's mind—no longer "skinny") and yawning again. "Once they got a good start it was easy enough. There were plenty of asteroids to mine for materials, and Nergal gave off a lot of heat, as long as you got close enough to it. Of course, now that the sun's back in business we wouldn't need to stay around Nergal anymore—but why would we bother to move?"

"Well, to a planet," Viktor began. "Newmanhome, for instance. They say it's warmed up now—"

"Planets!" she scoffed. "Planets are *nasty*. Certainly, now that Newmanhome is pretty well thawed out people can *survive* there, but who would want to?"

I would, Viktor thought, but he wasn't sure he meant it, so all he said was, "Some people might."

"Some silly people do," she admitted. "There are a few odd ones who seem to enjoy poking through the old records, and of course we need someone to pick over the freezers to find whatever organisms are left that might supply useful DNA. I don't call that living, Viktor." And she went on to explain why it certainly wasn't any kind of life she could stand for herself. The *gravity*! Why, on Newmanhome they had to move around in wheelchairs most of the time, even if they'd taken the muscle-building and calcium-binding treatments that would let them stand it at all. (As, it turned out, Dekkaduk had—thus those incongruous knots of muscle.) That much gravity certainly wasn't good for anybody. Not to mention the *discomfort*. No, it wasn't at all the kind of life she personally could tolerate.

And then, stroking his thigh, she interrupted herself. "Hold still a minute, Viktor," she ordered, leaning over to poke at his leg. "Does that feel all right?"

He craned his neck to peer at the pink sausage casing. "I guess so. I almost forget it's there." But reminded, he was aware of the smell. The wrapping was porous, to let the wound breathe as it healed, and odors did leak out.

Nrina didn't seem to mind them. "I'd better take another look," she decided. And then, "Oh, no, I'm meeting Kotlenny; well, Dekkaduk can do it. Go over and tell him to give you an examination."

Dekkaduk was waiting for him when Viktor got to the examining room. His expression was hostile.

It was no worse than Viktor had expected. Dekkaduk did not seem to be a friendly man. Their first meeting had been when Dekkaduk had tattooed the fertility warning on Viktor's forehead; all right, that was just a duty, and if it had been painful probably that couldn't be helped. But ever since the time they had taken DNA samples from Nrina's copsicles, along with the departed Manett, Dekkaduk had given every sign of despising the man from Old Earth.

"Ouch!" Viktor exclaimed, as Dekkaduk peeled the dressing off his leg. (That might not have been on purpose. Still, removing the dressing didn't hurt when Nrina did it.) Then as the full aroma of the healing wound floated to his nostrils, Dekkaduk muttered furiously to himself and ostentatiously turned the room's ventilation higher. (Well, it did stink. But that much? Nrina didn't appear to find the smell intolerable, after all.)

Dekkaduk hurt him (Viktor kept count) eight different times in the course of a two-minute examination. Even the healing, cleaning spray he used to cover the pink new flesh stung bitterly (Nrina's hadn't), and when he was through and the leg was rebandaged Dekkaduk simply said, "You're healing. Go away now."

Viktor went. Once away from Dekkaduk's touch the leg hardly hurt at all anymore. As he strolled along the corridor he was thinking of possible explanations for the man's hostility. It could, of course, be just his nature. Dekkaduk might simply have interests of his own and regard this rude survivor from prehistoric ages, Viktor Sorricaine, as an irritating irrelevance.

But there was another possibility that Viktor thought likely. What if Dekkaduk were not only Nrina's assistant, but her lover? More likely ex-lover—and jealous. It was a quite plausible theory, Viktor thought. It was even one that gave him a certain amount of satisfaction, because there was enough rude, prehistoric carnality in Viktor's genetic predispositions to allow him to enjoy beating out another male for a mate.

He had been walking without paying much attention to where he was going. He passed other people from time to time. Some he had met before, even spoken to; he was beginning to be on nodding terms, at least, with some of Nrina's neighbors, and as he got used to the stretched-out, willowy shapes of these people he began to notice individual differences.

At first they had all looked alike, like members of some famine-stricken basketball team. Then he began to distinguish among them. Some were darker than others. Hair color varied from so pale and fine that it seemed almost transparent to coarse strands like charcoal-colored knitting wool. Both men and women might have facial hair, though women's was usually only a pair of narrow sideburns. Quite a few of the people struck Viktor as downright ugly—noses that were splayed, hooked or reduced to the size of a shirt button; teeth that seemed too big for their mouths, or, in one particular case, a woman with vampire incisors that lay against her lower lip. (She had seemed more willing to be friendly than most. Viktor had not encouraged her.)

On Newmanhome, at least on the fat, rich Newmanhome of his youth, Viktor would have wondered why these people hadn't had orthodonistry or plastic surgery. Here he wondered even more, because those traits had to be *on purpose*. Some parents had gone to some genetic engineer like Nrina and *chosen* that receding chin, those pendulous ears for their child.

As Viktor strolled, idle and aimless, he saw the vampire-toothed woman coming toward him.

She was even taller than Nrina and—in the same ethereal way as Nrina, of course—quite as pretty. (Not counting those disconcerting teeth, of course.) The woman had let Viktor clearly know that strange, big-muscled primitives out of the freezatorium were in some ways quite interesting—though she had looked regretfully at the tattoo on his forehead. But Viktor only nodded to her now. It wasn't that his fertility was a serious problem. If Nrina had some kind of contraception, this other woman could probably manage it, too, but that meant a different kind of problem.

Kept men, Viktor was nearly sure, were expected to be faithful to their keepers.

He was quite a bit farther away from Nrina's area than he remembered going before. Ahead of him the corridor suddenly widened to an open space. There was a little pond, and around it were patches of growing things.

It was a farm.

Nrina had told him there was a farm on the habitat, though he'd never seen it before. It was really very pleasant. It wasn't at all like any farm on ancient Newmanhome, because of the funny way it bent, pond and all, and the fact that the "sky" was almost within touching distance over his head. But there were growing things there. He recognized some of them as having been in Nrina's locker, and was pleased to bend down and pick a—tomato? Something that tasted like a tomato, anyway, although it was a deep purple in color.

It occurred to him that it was possible these plants belonged to someone.

He looked around. There was no one in sight. He ate the tomato, nibbling around the stem, and tossed the little green remnant to the ground as he strolled. That was curious, too, he observed, for the ground wasn't really ground. This was no plowed half acre of somebody's produce garden; the tomato vines grew out of long, bulkheaded rows of something that was paler and spongier than any earth Viktor had ever seen, and between the rows were immaculately swept footpaths.

Someone kept this farm extraordinarily neat.

Then Viktor caught a glimpse of one of the "someones."

He was at the far end of the open space, and as he turned to go back he saw some dark-skinned person at the edge of the pond. He didn't actually see the whole person. The pond, and the land around it, had curved up until they were almost hidden by the bulge of the ceiling between. (So strange to look at! One wondered why the pond didn't spill out.) What Viktor saw was someone's feet, seemingly wearing dark, furry boots, and someone's hands tipping a sort of bucket into the lake.

Immediately the surface of the pond at that point began to erupt into little spouts and fountains. Fish were feeding there. Pleased with the discovery, Viktor started back in that direction.

The fish feeder was faster than he. By the time he got to where he could see the whole other end of the farm enclosure there was no one there. But the splashes he had seen were definitely fish feeding. They were still swirling around, just under the surface of the water, rising to snap at little bits of something edible floating where the fish attendant had left them.

It would be nice, Viktor thought, to feed the fish himself some time. Feeling at ease after his stroll, he went back to Nrina's home and busied himself with the teacher desk, awaiting her return from her laboratory.

She was later than Viktor expected, but he didn't mind. His unreal mentor of the desk hardly ever had to correct his grammar anymore, but remained ready to help whenever Viktor got stuck. That wasn't often. As Viktor gained skills he gained confidence. Apart from the fact that it taught him things he wanted to learn, just playing with the desk was fun; it was like an immensely complicated video game with real rewards for winning.

It was beyond his competence, or his mentor's aid, to access the kind of cosmological data he really wanted. Simple astronomy was easy enough, though. With the mentor assisting, Viktor got a look at each of the stars that had accompanied their own sun through space; they had all been given names, but the names rolled off his mind. Then he looked at their own planets, one by one . . . and then he struck oil.

With the mentor's help Viktor got a sort of travelogue of the mysterious planet of Nebo. Someone had done a flyby and deployed a robot shuttle. The shuttle didn't land. It simply skimmed through the atmosphere of Nebo, taking pictures of the great metal objects that Viktor had seen from space. It seemed that its handlers had been interested in two particular areas. In one there was a protruding edge of worn metal that Viktor thought might have been what was left of *Ark*'s lander; there was nothing else of interest nearby. The other was in very bad shape. The buildings seemed to have been blown up by some powerful explosion; but what that was about, too, Viktor could not learn.

Viktor stopped for a moment, listening. "Nrina?" he called. He thought he'd heard a sound somewhere in the other room, but it wasn't repeated and he went back to the desk.

Then Viktor switched views. "Habitats," he commanded, and his mentor provided him with the fact that there were more than eight hundred of them circling sullen, swollen Nergal. Then there were the natural moons human beings had colonized: Mary, Joseph, Mohammed, and Gautama were the important ones. (Sudden thrill almost of nostalgia: so some of the religious differences of frozen Newmanhome had persisted even here!)

Then he switched again, to study the other planets once more. Nothing had changed on most of them. Ishtar was still Ishtar, Marduk Marduk—gas giants with nothing much to recommend them— and Ninih, of course, was still too small and too far from the primary to be of interest to anybody. He stared briefly at the surface of ruddy Nergal (nothing much to look at but storms of superheated gases), then turned to the planet that mattered most to him: old, almost abandoned Newmanhome.

He caught his breath.

Newmanhome had changed again. It was reborn, all rolling seas, empty meadows, and young forests where the ice had gone—but it was not the Newmanhome he had lived on. It was *scarred*. During the glaciation all the planet's liquid water had been ice, covering the continents. As it melted, it formed huge meltwater lakes, blocked by ice dams. When the dams broke through, great torrents had scoured out scablands all the way to the sea.

There was no trace left that Viktor could find of the docks for the ocean-going ships or the town. True, in the hills near where he thought Homeport might have been, trying to translate the desk's coordinate system into his familiar navigation numbers, there was a cluster of buildings. But whether that was related to the old city he could not say.

This time he definitely heard the sound, and he could tell that it came from the kitchen.

"Who's there?" he cried. He heard the freezer door close, but there was no other answer. Puzzled, Viktor went to the food room.

Someone was leaving through the other door—hastily, as though not wanting to be seen. Viktor stood there, blinking. The bowls had been refilled with fresh fruit. The scatter of used dishes he had left was gone.

So that, he thought dazedly, was how the housework got done. But how peculiar that it was done by someone squatter and broader than himself, wearing a grizzled gray fur coat.

Half an hour later Nrina came back, to be greeted by his questions. "Yes, of course," she said, surprised he should ask. "Naturally we have someone to do things like that. Who would do them, otherwise? You saw one of the gillies."

"Gillies?" Viktor repeated, and then blinked as he connected the sound of the word with the glimpses he had caught. "Do you mean *gorillas*?"

"They're called 'gillies,' Viktor," Nrina said impatiently. "I don't know the word 'gorilla.' They are related to humans but without much intelligence—normally. Of course, we have modified them to be somewhat brighter—and quite a lot less belligerent and strong. Even so, they can't speak."

"You *modified* them?" he repeated.

"From genetic materials we found in the freezers, yes. Why not? Did you think I only made human beings?"

"I didn't know what you made," he said. He sounded aggrieved even to his own ears. He must have sounded so to Nrina, because she looked at him seriously for a moment.

Then she laughed. "Well," she said, "why don't I show you? Would you like to watch me work?"

Nrina was a creature shaper. Viktor began to realize that this woman was a major VIP, a star, famous through the habitats. She was remarkable even among the small number of greatly respected people who designed living architectures. The gorilla menials had come from their labs. So had the food animals and plants; so had the gorgeous and bizarre-smelling blossoms that decorated the spaces of their lives. Although their biggest business was making babies to order, she and her assistant, Dekkaduk, could make almost anything.

Dekkaduk was not pleased at Viktor's visit. He insisted that Viktor wear the gauzy robe over his cache-sex, and then fussily demanded he wear a hat, too. "Who knows what parasites might be in that disgusting fur on his head?" Dekkaduk demanded. He was nearly bald himself.

"Why, Dekkaduk," Nrina said, laughing, "probably about the same sorts of things as in my own hair. By now." Dekkaduk flushed furiously.

Nevertheless, Viktor wore the cap.

When Dekkaduk considered Viktor sufficiently sanitary, he turned away, glowering, and started work. He used the desk keypad to set up a large picture on the wall screen. It was a three-D representation of a young woman. She looked something like Nrina, but her hair was cocoa where Nrina's was butter, and her eyes were closer set. "Who is she?" Viktor asked politely, and Dekkaduk glared at him.

"You must not talk to us while we are working," he scolded. "But I will answer this question for you. She is no one. She hasn't been born yet. This is only what her parents want her to look like, and so we will arrange it. Now don't ask more questions until we are through."

So Viktor watched the image of the child who was not only not yet born but not even conceived, as Nrina and Dekkaduk matched the DNA strings that would produce that height, that color of eye, that taper of finger and that delicate arch of foot. That part of the process was not interesting for Viktor to watch, simply because he could not follow what was happening. Under the holographic image was a changing display of symbols and numbers—specifications, Viktor supposed, though he couldn't read them. No doubt they had to do with not only external appearances but nerve structures and disposition and . . . well, who knew what characteristics these people would want in a child?

But whatever the desire was, Nrina could supply it. She had no problem preparing the genetic blueprint that filled the order, and then it was only a matter of cutting and splicing and matching in.

The things they did were not merely a matter of surface appearance. They weren't even *mostly* surface appearance. The most important thing they built into every new baby was health.

There were all kinds of hereditary traits that had to be added or deleted or simply changed around a little. The effect was vast. The boys who came from Nrina's laboratory would never lose their virility or develop that benign prostatic hyperplasia called "old men's disease." The girls, however long they lived, would never acquire the "widow's hump" of osteoporosis. Bad genes were repaired on the spot.

Single-gene disorders were the easiest to deal with, of course. They came in three main kinds. There was the kind where a bad gene from either parent made the trouble; the recessive (or homozygous) kind where there wasn't any trouble unless it came from both parents; and the X-linked recessives that affected only males. All Nrina had to do with such conditions was a little repair work. If there was something wrong with the Apo B, C, and E genes Nrina made it right—and reduced the risk of a future coronary. If the hypoxanthine-guanine phosphoribosyltransferase gene was defective, a good one was patched in, and the child would not have Lesch-Nyhan disease. Codon 12 of the c-K-*ras* gene could be supplemented with a single nucleotide, and therefore went the risk of most pancreatic carcinomas and a lot of the colorectal ones, too. So Nrina's handmade children were exempt from many of the ills the flesh was (otherwise) heir to. No child born of their laboratory would

ever have Epstein-Barr, or sickle-cell anemia, familial hypercholes-
terolemia, Huntington's disease, hemophilia, or any other of the
hereditary nasties. Their arteries shrugged cholesterol away. Their
digestive tracts contained no appendix; there were no tonsils in their
throats.

For that reason Nrina knew very little of surgery. In some ways
her grasp of medical science was centuries behind old Earth's—or
even Newmanhome's. Dealing with Viktor's freezer-ulcerated leg
was about as far as they could go. No one in Nrina's world was
competent to cut out a lung or chop a hole in a side for a colostomy
bag. No one ever needed such things. Oh, they did die—sooner or
later. But usually later; and usually because they were simply wearing out; and almost always because they knew that death was coming and chose not to stay around for the final decay.

When they had finished with the day's production Viktor paused
as he slipped out of his cloak. "Could you do anything you wanted
to to them?" he asked. "I mean, could you give a baby six toes? Or
two heads?"

Dekkaduk gave him an unforgiving look. "Thank you," he said,
"for reminding us how primitive you are. Of course we could, but
we never would. Who would want it?"

Even Nrina sighed. "Sometimes you are almost *too* odd, Viktor," she complained.

When Nrina at last pronounced Viktor's brain as
cloudless as it was likely to get ("You will not remember everything, Viktor, and you will seem to remember some things that
never really happened . . . but only a little, I think"), he began to
think seriously about his future.

The big question, of course, was what future did he have in this
place?

Reason told Viktor that the fact that he had any future at all
was a great, big plus. He took some comfort from that. Anyway,
he didn't need a lot of comforting, for making love to Nrina was a
grand aspirin for all aches of the soul. Sometimes his trick memory
would throw up a sudden misplaced image. Then he found himself
thinking of lost Reesa, with a kind of melancholy ache that nothing

was ever going to heal. That didn't last, and meanwhile Nrina was there. She was willing and adventurous in bed, and when they were not making love she was—well, much of the time—affectionate, kind, and friendly.

It was true that she was simply not *interested* in some of the things that mattered to Viktor. The mystery of what had happened to the universe, for instance. Of course, she pointed out, there should be plenty of material on just about everything somewhere in the teaching files, if Viktor wanted to use them. He could even use her own desk, she added—when she wasn't using it herself, of course. When Viktor complained that the mentor didn't seem able to turn up the really interesting stuff, Nrina even took time to try to instruct him in some of the desk's refinements.

The desk really was a desk—sort of. At least, it looked like a kind of old-fashioned draftsman's table. It was a broad, flat rectangle, tipped at an angle, with a kneeling stool before it and a kind of keypad in the lower left-hand corner. The symbols on the keys meant nothing at all to Viktor, but Nrina, leaning gently over his shoulder and smelling sweetly of her unusual perfume and herself, showed him how to work the pads. "Can you read the letters, at least?" she asked.

"No. Well, maybe. I think so," he said, squinting. "Some of them, anyway." The written language had not changed a great deal, but it had become phonetic; the alphabet had eleven new letters. Nrina rapidly scrolled down to "cosmology," after getting Viktor to try spelling it in the new alphabet.

Nothing appeared in the screen.

"That is quite strange," she said. "Perhaps we're spelling it wrong." But though they tried half a dozen different ways, the desk obstinately refused them all. Nor was it any more help with "time dilation" or "relativistic effects" or even "quantum mechanics."

"What a pity," Nrina sighed. "We must be doing something wrong."

"Thanks," Viktor said glumly.

"Oh, don't be unhappy," she said, cajoling. Then she brightened. "There are other things you can do," she said. "Have you ever tried calling anyone? A person, I mean? I have to call Pelly anyway. Here, let me show you how to call."

"You mean like a telephone?"

"What is 'telephone'? Never mind, I'll show you." She tapped the keypad, got a scroll, stopped it at that name, and tapped the name. As Viktor opened his mouth she said quickly, "This is my personal directory—there's also a general one which I will show you how to use, but I don't use the big one when I don't have to. Would you? Wait a minute, here he is."

The desk went pale and opaque; on the black space on the wall behind it the face of a man formed pumpkin fat, with a pumpkin smile. "Pelly?" Nrina said. "Yes, of course, it's Nrina. This is my friend Viktor—you saw him before, of course."

"Of course, but he was frozen then," the pumpkin grinned. "Hello, Viktor."

"Hello," Viktor said, since it seemed to be expected of him.

Nrina went right on. "Your gillies are ready," she told the man. "And a couple of the donors want to go back. When will you leave?"

"Six days," the man said. "How many gillies?"

"Twenty-two, fourteen of them female. I hope I'll see you before you go?"

"I hope so. Nice meeting you—I mean alive, Viktor," Pelly said, and was gone.

"You see how it works? You can call anyone that way. Anyone in our orbits, anyway—it's harder when they're in space or on New-manhome. Then you have to allow for transmission time, you see."

But Viktor had no one to call. "What did he mean when he said he saw me when I was frozen?" he asked.

"That's *Pelly*," she explained. "He pilots spaceships. He's the one who brought you and the others back from Newmanhome." Then she said, remembering, "Oh, yes. He's been to Nebo, too. If you're so interested in it, you can ask him about it if we see him."

With the clues Nrina had given him, Viktor managed to work the directory himself. The desk gave more than a "phone number." It told him about Pelly: space captain; resident, generally, of Moon Gautama, but most of the time somewhere between the orbiting habitats and the other planets of the system.

He was poring over the views of Nebo again when Nrina came back, surprised to see him still bent over the desk. "Still at it, Viktor? But I'm tired; I'd like to rest now." And she glanced toward the bed.

"There are a lot of things I still want to know, Nrina," he said obstinately. "About Pelly, for instance. Why is he so fat?"

"So he can get around on Newmanhome, of course," Nrina explained. "He has to have supplements to build up his muscles—"

"Steroids?" Viktor guessed.

Nrina looked pleased. "Well, something like that, yes. And calcium binders so his bones won't break too easily, and all sorts of other things. You've seen how Dekkaduk looks? And he's only been to Newmanhome a few times, collecting specimens—" She looked embarrassed. "Bringing back people for me, I mean."

"Like me."

"Well, yes, of course like you. Anyway, Pelly goes there all the time. It makes him look *gross*, of course, which is why I would never— Oh, Viktor, I didn't mean it that way. After all, you were *born* like that."

He let that pass. "And did Pelly really land on Nebo?"

"You mean in person? Certainly not. No one has done that for many years."

"But people *have* landed there?"

Nrina sighed. "Yes, certainly. Several times."

"But not anymore?"

"Viktor," she said sensibly, "of course not. What would be the point? There's air, but it's foul; the heat is awful. And the gravity crushes you to walk there, Viktor—well, not you, no, but any normal person. It's much stronger than on a Moon. It's almost as bad as Newmanhome, but at least Newmanhome has a decent *climate*."

"But Nrina! There may be people on Nebo. Some of my own friends landed there—"

"Yes, and never came back. I know. You told me," Nrina said. "Isn't that a good enough reason to stay away?"

"But somebody made those machines. Not human, no."

"There's no one there. We've looked. Just the old machines."

"And have the machines been investigated scientifically?"

She frowned. "I don't know what you mean by 'scientifically.'

Some people were interested in them, yes. They even brought some small things back to study—I remember Pelly had a piece of metal he showed me once."

Viktor inhaled sharply. "Can I see the things? Are they in a museum?"

But Nrina only laughed when he tried to explain what a museum was like, from his fading memories of the Los Angeles Art Museum and the La Brea Tar Pits. "Keep all those dirty things around? But why, Viktor? No one should keep trash. We'd just be choking on our own old worn-out things! No, I'm sure they were studied at the time. No doubt there are assay reports and probably pictures of them somewhere—you can use the desk to see what they look like, and I think a few people like Pelly might have a few little bits for curios. But we certainly don't have a place where we keep such things, and besides—"

She looked suddenly harsh, almost as though both frightened and angry. "Besides," she finished, "those hideous metal things are *dangerous*. That's why no one lands there anymore. People got *killed* there!"

And then, reluctantly, she went to the desk and showed him what had happened, more than a century before. A ship landing on Nebo. People coming out of it, grotesque in metallized film suits to keep out the heat and helmets to give them air to breathe; they approached one of the mauve pyramids, half-buried in the shifting sands of Nebo. They were trying to drill a way in—

And then it exploded.

Of the pyramid itself nothing at all was left; it simply was vaporized. No more of the people. A few fragments of nearby objects, blasted in the explosion, littered the sands.

When he looked up he saw that Nrina had averted her eyes. "Turn it off," she ordered. "Those people were *killed*."

He surrendered. She came closer, smiling down at him. "That's better," she said softly, leaning against his shoulder.

He didn't resist. He didn't encourage her either. "All right, Nrina, I see what happened, but it doesn't tell me anything. What *are* those machines?"

"But no one knows that, Viktor," she said patiently. "And it isn't very interesting."

"It is to me! I want to know what they were there for—who built them—how they work. All this 'what' stuff is very interesting, of course, but can't I ever find out a 'why'?"

"Why what, Viktor?" she asked kindly, stroking his stubbly cheek. "Wouldn't you like to grow a beard? Most men do, if they can."

"No, I don't want to grow a beard. Please don't change the subject. I mean I want to know why things happen—the theoretical explanation behind the things I see."

"I don't think those words mean anything," she said, frowning. "I understand 'theory,' of course. That is the background of genetics, the rules that tell us what to expect when, for instance, we strip a certain nucleotide out of a gene and patch in another."

"Yes, exactly! That's what I mean! What I'm looking for is something on astronomical theory."

Nrina shook her head. "I have never heard of any 'astronomical' theories, Viktor."

When Viktor came home from a ramble Nrina was waiting for him. "I have something to show you," she said mysteriously, pleased with herself. "Come into my room."

There she surprised him. She opened a compartment in the wall. It revealed itself as a little cage, with something moving beyond the wire mesh. Nrina reached into it and drew out something tiny and soft.

It moved comfortably in her hand. "Tell me, Viktor," she said, hesitating as though worried at what his answer might be. "Have you ever seen one of these things before?"

"Of course I have!" He let her give him the furry little thing. "It's a kitten!"

"Exactly," she said triumphantly, observing as he stroked its fur. "Does it enjoy that?" she inquired.

"Most cats do. Where did you get it? I thought they were extinct!"

She looked gratified. "Indeed they were," she said, graciously acknowledging the remarkable nature of her feat. "I made it. There were some frozen specimens of feline sperm Pelly found when he brought you back." Experimentally she stroked the kitten as Viktor had done. Viktor could hear nothing, but the nerve endings of his hand informed him of the creature's silent, tiny purr. "It's always a worry," she said, "when you don't have any female genetic material for a new species. Oh, it's easy enough to structure an artificial ovum, but when the animal is something you've never seen before you have to wonder if you've got it exactly right."

Viktor stroked the soft, wriggly little thing and handed it back to her. "I'd say that looks like the rightest little kitten I've ever seen," he pronounced.

She accepted the compliment gracefully. "I'm going to give it to a little boy I know." Carefully she returned it to its cage, closing the door.

Viktor shook his head, marveling. "I knew you designed children. I knew you created intelligent gorillas—"

"Gillies, Viktor."

"—intelligent gillies for servants. I didn't know you could make just about anything you could imagine."

She considered that for a moment. "Oh, not anything," she decided. "Some things are physically impossible—or, anyway, I could make them, but they wouldn't survive. But this is the most interesting part of my work, Viktor. It's why anyone bothers to go to Newmanhome, really. There's a whole biota in those freezers on Newmanhome, you know. We don't know half of what's there. Even when there's a label we can't always be sure of what's inside, because they got pretty sloppy about keeping records for a while. So when I have a chance I match up sperm and ova—when I can— or find some related genetic material that I can tinker into being cross-fertile. Like this."

"Do you sell them, like a pet store?"

"I don't know what a pet store is, and I certainly don't 'sell' them, any more than I sell the babies. If someone wants them I get credit for my time." She sighed. "It doesn't always work. Sometimes I can't find a match or even make one; a lot of the specimens are spoiled, and it's terribly hard to reconstitute them. And then, even when we do get an interesting neonate, we can't always feed

them. Especially the invertebrates; some of them are really special-
ized in diet, they just won't eat what we try to give them. So they
die." She grinned. "Babies are a lot easier."

That was probably true, Viktor reflected, since the real human
fetuses never appeared in Nrina's laboratory as born babies. Gesta-
tion and birthing weren't her problems. What she produced was a
neat little plastic box, thermally opaque so it didn't need either
warming or cooling for forty-eight hours or so, containing a fertilized ovum and enough nutrient fluid to keep it alive until the proud
parents could put it in their own incubator. "Don't you ever want
to see the real babies?" Viktor asked her curiously.

"What for?" Nrina asked, surprised at the question. "Babies are
very messy creatures, Viktor. Oh, I like to hear how they turn out
and I'm always glad to get pictures of them—every artist wants to
see how his work turns out. But the only ones I ever wanted to be
around for more than a day were my own." Then she was surprised
again at the expression on his face. "Didn't you know? I've had two
children. One of them was just a favor to her father, so I didn't
keep her very long. He wanted something to remember me by, you
see. Her name's Oclane and, let's see, she must be fourteen or fifteen
by now. She's on Moon Joseph, but she comes to visit me sometimes. She's a pretty little girl. Very bright, of course. I think she
looks a lot like me."

"I didn't know," Viktor said, hastily revising his internal image
of Nrina. He had thought of her as many things, but never as a
mother—not even as one of those mothers of the present new-fangled
variety, who picked out specifications for their offspring and never
went through the uncouth bother of pregnancy. Then he remembered her words. "You said you had two children. What about the
other one?"

She laughed. "But you know him very well, Viktor. Who did
you think Dekkaduk was?"

The next time Viktor saw Dekkaduk he looked at the
man with new interest. Dekkaduk did, Viktor decided, more or less
resemble Nrina—but then, all these people resembled each other to
his eyes, in the same way that all Westerners looked alike to most

Chinese. What Dekkaduk didn't look like at all was anyone young enough to be a child of Nrina's.

There was an answer to that, too: Viktor realized he had no idea at all of Nrina's age. She could have been a youthful, good-looking forty—Newmanhome years, of course. She could equally well have been a very well preserved hundred or more. None of these people ever looked *old*.

In bed she was definitely ageless.

Viktor took much pleasure in that part of their intimacy. Still, there were times when he felt a kind of submerged resentment that his main reason for living was to provide a little sexual excitement for a woman he hardly knew. There were even times when he remembered that he had once had a wife. Then, sometimes, a gloom descended over him that was like the suffocating withdrawal of all air, like all the light in the world going out at once.

But there were other times that were not gloomy at all. Nrina was a splendid aspirin for all those passing aches of the soul.

Apart from all her other virtues, Nrina was deeply fascinated with Viktor's body. It wasn't just sex she wanted from him. She wanted to prod and squeeze and feel his archaic flesh, though of course she often wanted sex, too. She could be happy for half an hour at a time as they lay naked together, experiencing the flexing of his muscles. Not just his biceps, but his forearm, his thigh, his neck, all the muscles he could flex at all, while she held her hand on them to feel them swell. "And they're *natural*, Viktor, truly?"

Grunting. "Of course they're natural. Only please, Nrina, don't squeeze so hard on my sore leg."

"Oh, of course." And then a moment later, "And this hair here? Did everyone have it in your time?" But Viktor had always been ticklish in the armpits, and of course that ticklishness led to tickling back, which led to other things. Or she would minutely inspect the brownish spots on the back of his hand, touching them gently in case they were painful. "What are they, Viktor?" she asked, stretching behind her to reach for something he could not see.

"We call them freckles," he grinned. "Although—well, maybe those are a little more than just freckles. People get them when they get older. They're what we call 'age spots' then. They're perfectly natural—hey! Ouch!" But she had been too quick for him, jabbing the back of his hand with the sharp little metal probe she had pulled from nowhere.

"Don't make such a fuss," she ordered, carefully putting her cell sample away. "Here, let me kiss it."

And then, after a little study in her laboratory, she told him they were simply degenerated collagen. "I could clear those spots up for you if you wanted me to, Viktor," she offered.

He reached out to touch her body, not naked this time, but with only the flimsy gauze and the cache-sex to modify it. She turned comfortably beside him, taking her ease on a fluff of airy pillows beside him. Her skin was quite flawless. "Do they offend you?" he asked.

"Of course not! Your body does not offend me!"

"Then why don't we just leave them alone?" And wryly Viktor reflected that this was a strange relationship, in which she was almost entirely absorbed in his body, while he was desperate for everything that was in her mind.

Her body she let him have almost any time he chose—usually she chose first, in fact. Her mind was another matter. Viktor didn't feel that Nrina closed him out, or went out of her way to keep information from him. It was simply that so many of the things he wanted to know bored her. "Yes, yes, Viktor," she would sigh, while he was thumping excitedly on the desk screen. "I see what you are showing me. There used to be more stars."

"Many more!" he would answer, scowling at the impoverished sky below him. But she would yawn, and perhaps put her hand in a place that made him pay attention to other things again. What was thrillingly, even frighteningly, strange to Viktor was only the natural order of things to Nrina. It was as if someone from Tahiti had seen snow for the first time: The Eskimos wouldn't have understood his feelings.

When Nrina came back from her lab and found Viktor absorbed over the desk she was tolerant about it, usually. She stripped off her robe and sat beside him. He could certainly feel bare body touching bare body, but it did not keep him from concentrating on the desk instead of the touch of flesh. "It's nice that you have an interest," Nrina observed philosophically.

He tried again. "Nrina, I'm certain that some very strange things have happened. Don't you want to know about them? Don't you even *wonder?*"

"It's not my line of work, Viktor," she said, looking slightly ruffled.

He said in bafflement, "The universe has died around us. We've been kidnapped. Time stopped for us—"

She was yawning. "Yes, I know. The other savages—sorry, Viktor. The other people from the freezer talk about that sometimes, too. They call it 'God the Transporter' or some such thing. A silly superstition! As if there were some supernatural being who moved stars around just for fun!"

"Then what is the explanation?"

"It doesn't *need* an explanation. It just *is.*" She shrugged. "It just isn't a very interesting subject, Viktor. No one really cares except— Oh, wait a minute," she said, suddenly sitting up and looking pleased. "I almost forgot Frit!"

Viktor blinked up at her. "What's a frit?" he asked.

"Frit isn't a what, he's a who. Frit and Forta. I designed their son for them. They're old friends of mine. Matter of fact, it's Balit—that's their boy—who I made that kitten for; he'll be twenty soon, and it's time for his coming-of-age presents." She thought for a moment, then nodded. "Yes, I'm sure Frit knows all about that sort of thing. He'd be interested in you, probably. And he and Forta have been together nearly thirty years now, and we still keep in touch."

Viktor sat up straight. He had the tingling, electrical feeling that all at once, without his having anticipated it at all, a goal for his life had been given to him. "How can I reach this Frit?" he demanded.

She looked doubtful. "Well, he's very busy, but I suppose you could call him up," she said, then suddenly brightened. "I know!" she cried. "Why don't we go to Balit's party?"

"Balit's party?"

"Balit's Frit's son. They live on Moon Mary. No, wait a minute," she corrected herself. "They do live on Mary, but I think they told me they're having the party on Frit's family's habitat." She nodded to herself as the details of her inspiration were coming clear to her. "Dekkaduk can handle things here for a couple of days. It would be a nice trip for you, and I ought to take Pelly's gillies there anyway—that's where his ship is. And I'm sure they'd be glad to have us, and then you can talk to Frit all you want." She gave Viktor's thigh a decisive pat, pleased with her idea. "We'll do it! And don't ask me any more questions now, Viktor. Just believe me, it'll be fun!"

CHAPTER 23

Reminiscing is a recreation for the elderly. It is what people do when they have outlived all their other occupations—people like Wan-To.

Elderly human beings at least have bodily functions to use up some hours. They have to eat, use the toilet, maybe even hoist themselves into their wheelchairs and complain to those around them. Wan-To didn't have even those ways of passing the time. Wan-To didn't just have very little else to do, he had *nothing* else to do. In the exhausted, depleted, moribund universe that Wan-To lived in he not only didn't need to do anything to keep on living, he had nothing much in the way of limbs, powers, or effectors to do anything with. His mind still worked—quite clearly, in fact, though at a depressingly slow speed. But everything stayed within his mind. He didn't have any useful appendages anymore to convert any of his mind's impulses into action.

All that being so, Wan-To was lucky he had so much to reminisce about.

He certainly did have a lot of memories. If there had been a contest to see which single being, among all the universe's inhabitants in all the endless eons of its existence, had the most in the way of stored-up memories to take out and chew over, Wan-To would have been the incontestable winner. If your mind remains clear, and

Wan-To's had, you can remember a lot out of a lifetime of ten-to-the-fortieth years.

Ten to the fortieth power years . . . and maybe much more still to come. That was one of the things Wan-To had to think about, for there still was at least one decision he sooner or later would have to make.

That was going to be a very hard decision. Because it was so very hard he preferred not to think about it. (There was, after all, positively no hurry at all.) What Wan-To liked to think about—the only thing that could be described as a pleasure that he still had left—was the days when he had had all the power any being could ever have desired.

Ah, those long-gone days! Days when he carelessly deployed the energies of stars on the whim of a moment—without a care for the future, without penalty for his spendthrift ways! When he cruised at will from star to star, from galaxy to galaxy (wistfully he remembered how wonderful it was to enter a virgin galaxy, bright with billions upon billions of unoccupied stars, and all his!) When he lived off copies of himself for companionship and battled joyfully against them for survival when they turned against him! (Even the frights and worries of those days were tenderly recalled now.) Wan-To remembered lolling on the surface of a star, taking his ease in the cool luxury of its six or seven thousand degrees (and he'd thought that *cool!*) . . . and swimming through the star's unimaginably dense core . . . and frolicking in the corona, temperature now up to a couple million degrees, soaked with X rays, dashing out as far as ten million miles from the star's surface to the corona's fringe and then happily plunging back.

He remembered the fun (and challenges—oh, he relished remembering the challenges!) when he had created those little copies of himself, Haigh-tik and Mromm and poor, silly Wan-Wan-Wan—and Kind and Happy and all the others he had made; he even remembered, though not very well, the terribly stupid matter-copies he had made, like Five. (He didn't actually remember Five as an individual, to be sure. Five had not been important to him—just then.)

What he remembered was *living*. And though it gave him a sort of melancholy joy to remember, the knowledge that he would never have such times again made him almost despair.

It was only when he was close to despair that he could force himself to think about that other thing, the one about which he would sooner or later have to make a decision. It concerned the only things in the universe that had ever really frightened Wan-To—because there was so much about them that even he had never been able to understand:

Black holes.

There lay the choice that ultimately Wan-To would have to make. Not right away, to be sure—*nothing* ever had to be "right away" in this dreary eternity—but sooner or later, for the sake of survival.

A black hole might very well give him his best chance for really long-term survival.

Wan-To wasn't sure he quite wanted to survive on those terms. He did not care for black holes. The locked-in singularities where a star once had been—and then collapsed up itself and pulled space in around it—were about the only sorts of objects in the universe Wan-To had never investigated in person. He hoped he would never have to. They were *scary*.

The frightening thing about black holes was that inside them the laws of the universe—the laws that Wan-To understood so well—did not apply, because black holes were no longer really parts of the universe. They had seceded from it.

It was easy enough to get inside a black hole—in fact, the problem sometimes was to avoid falling into one. Once or twice Wan-To had to exert himself to steer away from one's neighborhood. But getting in was a purely one-way trip. Once inside, you couldn't get out again. Even light was stuck there.

That wasn't because the immense gravitational field of the black hole pulled light back down to its surface, as, say, the gravity of a planet like the Earth pulls a thrown ball back down. Wan-To knew better than that. Wan-To was quite aware that light *can't* slow down; that's why c is invariant. The reason even light couldn't escape was simply because the gravity of the black hole wrapped space around

it—bent it—so that the light orbited around it eternally, within the
Schwarzschild radius of the black hole, as planets orbit around
a sun.

But the exact mechanism that caught and held anything that
wandered by in those cosmic traps wasn't really what mattered to
Wan-To. What mattered was that once you were inside, you couldn't
get out again *ever*—not light, not matter. Not even Wan-To himself.

The things were *terrifying*.

Nevertheless, they had their virtues, Wan-To told himself. One
of those virtues was that a good-sized black hole, say even one of as
little as three or four solar masses, would continue its existence for
a *long* time.

That was not just a very long time, like Wan-To's present age
of ten-to-the-fortieth years. It was a long *long* time: ten-to-the-sixty-
sixth years, anyway.

Those are numbers that few human beings can ever grasp. Even
Wan-To had trouble working with them. Ordinary arithmetic isn't
meant for such numbers. But what they means was that if Wan-To
were to take the plunge so that he could live as long as one of those
fair-sized black holes—

Which is to say, for 1,000,000,000,000,000,000,000,000,000,000,
000,000,000,000,000,000,000,000,000,000,000,000 years—

And if you subtracted from that his present lifetime (which was
to say, the present age of the universe, because by now they were
pretty much the same number)—

Which amounted to 10,000,000,000,000,000,000,000,000,000,
000,000,000,000 years—

If, then, he succeeded in living as long as that black hole continued to radiate energy, he had still to look forward to—

Another 999,999,999,999,999,999,999,999,990,000,000,000,000,
000,000,000,000,000,000,000,000,000 years of existence. If such numbers meant anything at all, even to Wan-To.

And if, of course, you could call that "existence."

Because that radiated "energy" from the black hole wasn't really
very energetic at all. Such a black hole didn't begin to radiate in the
first place until the mean temperature of the universe—what was
called the "background radiation" when human beings first discovered it in their silly little microwave dishes, back in the twentieth

century—had dropped to the very low value of one ten-millionth of one degree above absolute zero. It was only at that temperature that the black hole would begin to radiate.

That was very feeble warmth indeed.

Wan-To knew dismally that he could manage to survive, more or less, even with that sort of input—but he did not like the idea at all.

The only thing was that he didn't see any better alternative . . .

Until he became aware that the tiny tick his few remaining sensors had registered some time earlier was, strangely enough, a sudden and wholly unidentified flux of tachyons.

CHAPTER 24

Nrina was flushed and excited as they boarded the bus. "It's going to be a nice party," she was saying. She seemed younger than Viktor had ever seen her, happily making sure her packages were stored and that Viktor got a window seat. "Have you got the cat? Please, don't let go of it. We'll have a couple of velocity changes, and we don't want it flying around and hitting some other passenger in the face. You don't get spacesick, do you?"

Viktor Sorricaine, who was fairly sure he was the oldest living space pilot in the known universe, didn't dignify that with an answer. "How far are we going?" he asked as he settled himself into the soft webbing of the seat, carefully adjusting the belt so that it didn't squeeze the restless little kitten on his lap. The dark-haired man across the aisle was staring at the little animal.

"Not far. Frit's family lives on a fabrication habitat; they make things. It's two or three levels down, but it's less than a quarter-orbit away. It'll take about two hours to get there."

Two hours! A spaceflight of only two hours? But he had picked up on something else she had said. "Is it a family party? I'm not family," he objected.

She looked at him in surprise. "That doesn't matter. I am. Sort of, anyway. They'll certainly be glad to have you; there are always guests at this kind of party—" She stopped to nod to a young-looking woman who was strolling languidly through the bus, glancing to see that everyone was strapped in. "That's the driver," Nrina informed him as the woman passed. "We'll be leaving in a moment now." The driver seated herself in the front of the bus, before a broad screen. Casually she pulled a board of pale lights and twinkling colors down into her lap, glancing over it for a moment. Then she touched the control that closed the entrance hatch behind them, and Nrina said, "Here we go, Viktor. Don't let go of the cat."

Then they were in space. In *space*!

Viktor was thrilled by the feel of the bus launching itself free of the habitat. It wasn't violent. The launch was no more than a gentle thrust against the back of the webbing, a quarter-gravity at most. Viktor found himself grinning in pleasure, though he felt Nrina, beside him, shifting uncomfortably in her seat. Absently, Viktor patted her knee with his free hand. (Under his other hand, the kitten didn't seem to mind the acceleration at all. It was actually purring.)

Considered as a spaceship, the bus was—a bus. Even the old Newmanhome lander shuttles had been twice its size, but then they necessarily had to be; they had to carry the fuel and rockets capable of fighting a planet's gravity. The bus had no such needs. All it needed were air and room for its dozen or so passengers, and engines enough to push it along through interorbital space.

Just outside Viktor's window, it seemed, was the smoldering, bloody face of the brown dwarf, Nergal. The planet was less than a hundred thousand miles below them, almost hurting his eyes until Nrina indulgently leaned over him and darkened the polarization. Nergal-light wasn't like bright sunshine, it looked *hot*—though only visible light came through the polarization, with the infrared frequencies screened out.

The word for it was "baleful."

As the ship rotated Nergal slid away, and Viktor got a look at the habitat they had just left: A length of sewer pipe, half a mile long, spinning in stately slow motion, with odds and ends of junk hanging from it. Some of the appendages were the great mirrors that caught Nergal's hot radiation and funneled it into the magnetohydrodynamic generators that gave them the power they needed to run the habitat. Some were probably communications gear; more were things Viktor could not even guess at.

Then that was gone, too, and Viktor turned to find Nrina looking at him with interest. "You're excited, aren't you?" she asked, placing her hand over his.

"I guess I am," he admitted. "Oh, Nrina, it's so good to be in space again! That's what I dreamed about when I was a boy— Look, there's another ship!" he cried as something the size of a family car slid rapidly past, only a mile or two away.

Nrina glanced briefly at the thing. "It's just a cargo drone, probably nobody on it." Then, reassuringly, she said, "This is quite safe, you know, Viktor."

But it wasn't safety that was on his mind, it was the glandular excitement of being *in space*. Viktor stared longingly at the nearly empty black sky.

It was so terribly *black*. So very little was left of the familiar sky. Without Nergal or the distant sun, there was nothing to see but an occasional glint—a distant habitat, perhaps, or another ship— and one or two more distant things: the surviving stars.

That was it.

The familiar spread of constellations that had always been there—*always*—simply did not exist anymore.

Viktor shivered. He had never felt so alone.

Chatter beside him reminded him that he wasn't alone at all. Nrina had taken the kitten from him and was feeding it with a little object like a baby bottle, while half a dozen other passengers were clustered around in admiration, braced awkwardly against the mild thrust of the ship. "Yes, it is called a 'cat,' " Nrina was explaining. "No, they've been extinct for ages. Yes, it's the only one of its kind now—I just finished it—but if it lives I think I'll make a mate for it. No, they aren't wild animals. People used to have them in their houses all the time. Didn't they, Viktor?" she appealed.

"What? Oh, yes, they make great pets," Viktor confirmed, recalled to reality. "They do have claws, though. And they needed to be housebroken."

That led to more questions (What were "claws"? What was "housebroken"? Could they be trained to do useful things, like gillies?) until the driver broke up the party. "Everyone get back to his seat, please," she called. "We'll be matching orbit with the target in a moment."

As the little ship swerved Viktor saw what was waiting for them. This new habitat was also cylindrical—no doubt because that was the best shape for an orbiting people container—but along its perimeter were a dozen rosettes of air hatches where odd-looking little ships had attached themselves. "They're raw-materials gatherers," Nrina explained when he asked. "This is a manufacturing habitat, didn't I tell you? That's what Frit's family does, manufacturing. Those things—I suppose you've never seen them before—they are set loose here. Then they go out to the asteroids and so on to grow and reproduce themselves and bring back metals and things to use—"

Viktor felt a start of recognition. "Like Von Neumann machines?" he asked, remembering the ore-collecting nautiloids that he had encountered so often in the seas of Newmanhome.

"I don't know what those are, but—oh, look! That must be Pelly's ship!"

And Viktor forgot the Von Neumanns, because as the habitat rotated under them he saw what Nrina was pointing to. Yes, that was a *ship*, a *real* spaceship, hugged to the shell of the habitat. The ship had to be nearly a thousand feet long by itself, and it in turn had hugged to its own shell a lander larger than their bus. He stared at it longingly. That was more like it! A man could take pride in piloting a ship like that . . .

"Maybe Pelly will be at the party," Nrina said with pleasure. "Anyway, we'll be getting out in a minute, Viktor. Do you want to take the cat?" She passed the kitten to him and then, leaning past him, looked with disfavor at the habitat. "It doesn't look like much, does it? It's so big. It has to be, I suppose, because they do all sorts of industrial things there. I don't think anyone would live there if they didn't have to. Still, it's quite nice on the inside, anyway. You'll see."

What she said was true. On the inside the factory habitat was nice, very much so, but it took Viktor a while to find that out.

Its design was not like the one they had come from. It was almost a reversal of Nrina's, in fact. Instead of a shell of dwelling places surrounding a core of machinery, this habitat's machinery was all in the outer shell. The passengers exited the bus into a noisy, steel-walled cavern, with the thumping, grinding sounds of distant industrial production coming from somewhere not far on the other side of the wall. Then Viktor and Nrina and the kitten took a fast little elevator, and when they emerged Viktor saw that the whole heart of the cylinder was a vast open space. Great trees grew along the inside of the rim, all queerly straining up toward the axis of the cylinder. There a glowing rodlike thing stretched from end to end to give them light. The whole place was almost like a vast park, rolled around to join itself.

It was a teetery, vertiginous place to be, for the ground beneath Viktor's feet curved up past the glowing central rod to become the sky over his head. Nothing fell on him, of course. Viktor knew perfectly well that nothing could, because the rotation of the habitat pasted those distant upside-down trees and people as firmly to their "ground" as he was pasted to his. All the same, he was less uneasy when he avoided looking up. There were plenty of other things to see. There were brooks and ponds. There were beds of flowering plants, and farm patches. There were even herds of what looked like sheep and cattle, grazing on the meadows that bent up to join on the far side of the habitat. There were people, too, many people, going about their business or simply strolling and enjoying the park.

Viktor realized that something was missing from the bizarre scene: buildings. There were none in sight. It seemed that no one lived on the surface of this interior shell; their homes, their offices or workshops or whatever, were all inside the shell, "underground," so to speak, with only entranceways visible on the surface—like the one they had come out of, rising direct from the bus dock.

"Ah, yes," Nrina said as she got her bearings. She pointed to a round pond a hundred yards away—just far enough along the curve of the shell to make Viktor uneasy again, because the water looked as though it really ought to be spilling over out of its bed. "Sit there on that bench," she commanded. The bench was in a trellis of something like grapevines. "Let me have the cat—we don't want Balit to

see it yet. Then you just stay there while I find the others and check
the operating room." She was gone before he could ask her what
in the world she wanted an "operating room" for.

As Viktor sat, the quivers in his stomach began to settle down.
The air was warm enough to be friendly but not oppressive; there
was a gentle, steady breeze, perhaps from the rotation of the cylinder. A fair number of people were in sight, though none close
enough to Viktor to talk to. Near the round pond there was a grassy
meadow, where twelve or fourteen adults and children were flying
huge bright, many-colored kites, laughing and shouting as they
played the fluttery things in the steady breeze.

Of course, like everyone else Viktor encountered these days,
they were just about naked—breechclouts, yes, they all had those,
and a few wore gauzy cloaks, or even hats; but that was it. And
they were having fun. They weren't just flying the kites for the sake
of watching them dart and wheel in the sky. They were in a contest.
The kite flyers were fighting one kite against another. Some of the
players were children, most were fully grown, and all of them were
screaming in excitement as they tried to use the sharp edges of their
own kite tails and cords to cut someone else's down.

Between Viktor and the kite flyers was a sort of garden. Some
pale, long fruit was being harvested—maybe a kind of cucumber?
Viktor thought. And a crew of dwarfish, hairy "gillies" was moving
along the rows to pick the ripe fruit. They seemed to Viktor larger,
or at least squatter, than the ones he had seen before. As Viktor
watched, one of them glanced around, then crammed one of the
fruits into its own mouth. When it saw Viktor watching, it winked
at him in embarrassment.

So even the gillies had privileges here. He found the thought
reassuring. It emboldened him to pick a few grapes off the vines he
was sitting under. They were not very sweet, but they were deliciously cool on his tongue.

When Nrina came back she was not alone.

Half a dozen or more other men and women came milling out
of the entranceway with her, all next door to naked, of course, and
all chuckling to each other and looking anticipatory. They were all
strangers to Viktor—almost all, anyway, though one exceptionally

stocky, round-faced man looked vaguely familiar. Viktor was surprised to see that all of them were carrying things that looked like baseball bats, for what reason he could not guess.

Nrina introduced him all around. "This is Viktor," she said proudly. "He was actually born on *Earth*! And this is Wollet, Viktor, and this is his daughter Gren. This is Velota and this Mangry—Frit's father and mother, you know—and Forta's sisters, Wilp and Mrust; this is Pallik over here; and do you remember Pelly?"

Recognition dawned. "I do," he said. "I saw your ship as we were coming in. How are you, Pelly?"

The man looked agreeable but surprised. "I'm very well, of course. Why do you ask?"

Nrina laughed and interrupted, sparing Viktor the trouble of finding an answer. "That's how they used to talk on Old Earth," she explained. "Viktor's really quite civilized, though. Not like some of the others."

They didn't shake hands, either, Viktor discovered, although several of them did hug in greeting, and one of the men kissed his cheek. Which one, Viktor could not have said. Of all the dozen names Viktor had been given he retained none, though the other party guests all seemed to know each other.

Then Nrina handed him one of the clubs. He almost dropped it—not because it was heavy, but for the opposite reason. The bat was made of a sort of rigid foam, strong and soft to the touch, that weighed almost nothing.

A soft *thwack* across his own back made him jump and whirl: It was the little girl—Gren?—giggling as she swung at him again. He fended the attack off with his own club, careful not to hit the girl—the blow hadn't hurt at all, but he was very unsure of just what was going on. Her father—Wollet?—nodded approvingly, grinning as he took practice swings with his own club. "We'll give it to them, all right," he exulted. "Where are they, Nrina? Let's go!"

"Hold the club behind your back, you ass," she commanded, laughing at him. "You too, Viktor. We don't want them to see what we're doing, do we? Frit said they'd be watching the kite battles—yes, there they are! Oh, and look at Balit—isn't he a perfect little doll?"

It was Wollet's turn. "If you don't shut up they'll hear us," he warned, and led the way to where two men and a young boy were watching the battling kites, their backs to the group with the clubs. The boy certainly was nice-looking—slim, pale-haired; the equivalent of an Earthly ten-year-old, with the promise of good adult looks in the bones of his face. Viktor frowned. Another puzzle! On the boy's pretty young forehead there was exactly the same blue tattoo as Viktor wore himself. But he had no opportunity to ask about it, for the others were all shushing each other as they moved closer. Although the boy was doggedly staring at the bobbing kites, he was also stealing glances around in every direction, as though suspecting something, until one of the men with him leaned down and, smiling, whispered in his ear. Then Balit stopped looking around. Still, the body language of the way he stood showed that he was tensed up for—what?

There were other spectators, who glanced from Balit to the approaching group, with expressions of amused tolerance. The two men with Balit kept their eyes steadfastly on the kites in the sky. As they approached, Viktor saw that one of the men was as tall as himself, though as slightly built as all these people; he had both mustaches and a beard, all waxed or sprayed or some-other-how swept out in majestic and improbable long curves. The other man, smaller and even more delicately built, had one hand on the boy's head and the other tucked into the hand of his companion. His beard was far shorter and less conspicuous—but, all the same, it was definitely a beard.

Suddenly confused, Viktor whispered to Nrina, "Who are those two guys?"

"Frit and Forta, of course. Balit's parents."

"Oh. For a minute I thought they were both men."

"They *are* both men, Viktor. Do be quiet!"

"Oh," Viktor said again, feeling his eyes beginning to bulge. One more surprise! He could have expected almost anything of these people, but what he had not expected at all was that Balit's parents should both be male.

Then things got even more surprising. "Now we attack! Show no quarter!" Nrina shouted joyously, and her whole band began to run toward the little family, waving their clubs. "Don't you dare try to resist!" Nrina ordered ferociously, thwacking the taller man happily across his shoulder with the harmless bat. "We've come to steal your child and you dare not try to stop us!"

But both the men, laughing, were already resisting. They whirled around, pulling soft clubs of their own out of the waistbands of their breechclouts and defending themselves vigorously against the combined attack of Nrina's band of marauders. A couple of blows hit Viktor, who was blinking in confusion as he was thrust into the middle of the fracas. Of course, the clubs didn't hurt. It was almost like being hit with a helium-filled balloon; the foam-light clubs were incapable of hurting anyone; and there was no doubt of the out-come—it was two against a dozen, after all. The bystanders were cheering and egging both sides on, as the outnumbered parents slowly fell back, leaving the boy standing tense and smiling anx-iously behind them.

"Pick him up, Viktor," Nrina commanded, laughing breath-lessly in pursuit. "Go on, do it! You're much stronger than any of us, so you can be the one to carry him away!"

What made Viktor follow her order was that the boy seemed to acquiesce. He moved toward Viktor, smiling tentatively and holding out his arms.

And so Viktor Sorricaine, four thousand years out of his time, found himself in the act of kidnapping a child on a manmade habitat that circled the brown dwarf, Nergal. Well, why not? he thought wryly. Nothing else made sense! Why should this?

The band of kidnappers broke off their battle and flocked after Viktor, shouting in triumph while the despoiled parents watched proudly after them. The whole abducting mob hurried into one of the entranceways. Then Nrina told Viktor to put the boy down. "I'll take care of him from now on," she said indulgently. "Did you meet Viktor, Balit? He was frozen for a long time, you know. He was actually on Old Earth—imagine! He'll tell you all about it at the party, I'm sure."

"Hello, Viktor," the boy said politely, and then looked plain-tively at Nrina. "Is it going to hurt, Aunt Nrina?"

"Hurt? Of *course* it won't hurt, Balit," she scolded indulgently. "It'll take five minutes, that's all. Then it will all be over. And besides, you'll be asleep while I'm doing it. Now, come to the operating room—and, oh, I've got the most wonderful coming-of-age present for you!"

An hour later the party was in full swing. Balit was sitting on a kind of throne on top of the buffet table, a glass of wine in his hand, Nrina's gift purring gently in his lap, and a garland of flowers on his head, while his captors and his parents and several dozen other people who had shown up from nowhere drank and ate and joked and sang and congratulated Balit on his new status as a man.

Viktor had never seen a young boy look more pleased, though he noticed that Balit did from time to time surreptitiously reach down to touch his genitals, as though to make sure they were still there.

They were. As good as new. It was simply that through Nrina's quick and expert minor surgery, they were no longer capable of producing live sperm. "It's what every male does when he gets close to puberty," Wollet explained heartily, refilling Viktor's glass. "That way he doesn't have to worry about, you know, making someone really—what was the word?—yes, *pregnant*." He gazed fondly at his daughter, who was teasingly stroking the kitten in Balit's lap—and a little of Balit, too. "It makes the girls a little jealous," Wollet said. "They have a coming-of-age party, too, of course, but they don't have the jolly old fighting and the kidnapping and the carrying away, and that's what makes this kind of party so special. Don't you agree?"

"Oh, yes," Viktor said politely. "Uh, Wollet? That mark on the boy's forehead . . ."

"The fertility mark, yes. What about it? Oh, I see you've got one, too. Well, Balit shouldn't have intercourse now for a few weeks, you know, until any live sperm in his tract dissipate, then they'll take the brand off. Hasn't Nrina told you all this? I guess she would do you, too, if you asked her to—I mean, now that you're not donating anymore. Oh, here comes Pelly!"

Viktor was not at his best, greeting the bloated-looking space captain; he was not used to the fact that everyone he met seemed to know all about the state of his genital systems. All he could say was, in a rush, "Pelly, I really want to talk to you—"

"About Nebo. I know," the man growled good-naturedly. "Nrina warned me you would. Let's get out of this noise, though. Suppose we pick up a couple of drinks, and then we can go over there and sit by the edge of the pond."

It wasn't just Nebo that Viktor wanted to talk about, but Pelly was easy. He seemed almost to admire Viktor—well, naturally enough, he explained. "You, Viktor—you've really *traveled*! All the way from Old Earth—all I've ever done is cruise around this little system."

So it wasn't just the fizzy, faintly tart, mildly fruity drinks they were putting away that made Viktor feel good. He had become used to being a curiosity, but it had been a long, long time since he had felt himself *admired*. He glanced back at the coming-of-age party, which was increasing and multiplying as random passersby came by and joined in and stayed. Nrina was showing Balit how to feed the kitten out of the improvised bottle she had made; Frit, from the top of the banquet table, was declaiming a poem.

"Nrina said you had some artifacts you'd picked up from Nebo," Viktor said.

Pelly shook his head. "Oh, no, not me. I mean, I didn't pick the things up personally—I've never landed on Nebo, and I never will. But I do have this thing—I carry it around to show people." He fumbled in his pouch and handed Viktor a bit of something that was metal-bright, but a pale lavender in color.

Viktor turned the thing over. It was astonishingly light, for metal: a rod about the size of his finger, tapering to round at one end, the other end cracked and jagged. "Is it hollow?" he asked, hefting it.

"No. It's what you see. And don't ask me what it's for, because I don't know." Pelly restored it to his pouch, then had a change of mind. "I know, I'll give it to Balit for a coming-of-age present! There are plenty more of these things—not here, of course, but on Newmanhome." He peered keenly at Viktor and the moon face split in a smile. "I'm going back there in a few days, you know."

"Really? To Newmanhome?"

"To tell the truth," Pelly admitted, "I'm looking forward to it. I'm generally happier on the ship than I am here—maybe because I'm pure, you know. I mean," he explained, "nobody tinkered with my genes before I was born. Not much, anyway, outside of, you know, getting rid of genetic diseases and that sort of thing. I probably wouldn't even have needed the muscle builders and things to be on Newmanhome, except for growing up on a habitat—but I was always a lot heavier than the other boys."

"I didn't know there were any like you anymore," Viktor said.

"There aren't many. Maybe that's why I like space. Maybe I take after the ones who originally came here, you know. You've seen their ships! Can you imagine the courage of them— What's the matter?"

"I haven't seen those ships. I wish I could."

"Oh, but that's easy enough," Pelly said, grinning. From his shoulder bag he pulled out a flat board, glassy-topped, like the teaching desks. He touched the tiny keypad. "There it is," he said ruefully. "Pathetic, isn't it?"

Viktor bent over to study the picture. "Pathetic" was the right word—a single hydroxy-propelled rocket, tiny in the screen but certainly not very large in any case. It was orbiting with ruddy Nergal huge below it, and as Pelly manipulated the keypad to move the scene forward in time the ship was joined by another, and another— more than a dozen in all, linking together in a sprawling mess of nested spaceships. Viktor could see years of history happening in minutes as the ships deployed solar mirrors and began to reshape themselves. "That was the first habitat," Pelly told him. "Altogether only eight hundred people made it to Nergal—that was all they could build ships for; the rest, I guess, just stayed there and died. Things got better when they began constructing real habitats out of asteroidal material, but for a long time they damn near starved. Then, once there was some sort of plague, and most of the ones around then died of that." He swept his arm around the scene about them. "Did you know that all of us are descended from exactly ninety-one people? That's all that were left after the plague. But then it began to get better." He flicked off the screen and looked at Viktor, seeming a little abashed. "Does all this bore you?"

"Oh, *no!*" Viktor cried. "Honestly, Pelly, it's what I've been trying to find out ever since Nrina thawed me out! Listen, what about the time-dilation effect?"

Pelly blinked politely. "I beg your pardon?"

"The *basic* question, I mean. The reason all this happened in the first place—the way our little group of stars took off at relativistic speeds. I've been trying to figure it out. The only thing I can think is that we were traveling so fast that time dilation took over—for a *long* time, Pelly, I can't even guess how long—long enough so that all the stars went through their life cycles and died while we were traveling." Viktor stopped, because Pelly's eyes were beginning to glaze.

"Oh, yes," Pelly said, beginning to fidget as he glanced around. "Nrina said you said things like that."

"But don't you see? It's all linked together! The structures on Nebo, the Sorricaine-Mtiga objects, the foreshortening of the optical universe, the absence of all stellar objects but a handful now—"

"Viktor," Pelly said, his voice good-natured enough but also quite definite, "I'm a space pilot, not a poet. Ask me anything about practical matters and I'm happy to talk as long as you like. But this—this—this sort of, well, *mystical* stuff, it's just not what I'm interested in. Anyway," he finished, holding up his empty glass, "we need refills now, don't we? And they're beginning to dance again—what say we join them?"

It took two more glasses of the mild, bubbly stuff before Viktor was ready to accept defeat. Ah, well, he told himself, it was too much to hope for real understanding from any of these people. All they cared about, obviously, was having fun.

But halfway through the second glass fun began to seem worth having even to someone on whom, alone, the burden of solving the riddle of the universe seemed to rest. Nrina was leading an open circle of scores of people, dancing around the guest of honor's throne, laughing. She waved to Viktor to join them.

Why not? He swallowed the rest of the drink. Then he trotted to the line and took over Nrina's position.

The fizzy drink probably had something to do with that. Viktor wasn't in the habit of taking over a lead spot among strangers. Especially when, in this thistledown gravity, his steps were balloonlike rather than the macho stomps he liked best. Nevertheless, everyone followed as he led them, patiently but firmly, in a sort of loose, watered-down Hine Ma Tov—leaving out the tricky Yemeni figures, just step-bend and running steps, until everyone in the line had grasped it and was laughing and out of breath.

"That was nice," Nrina told him breathlessly, throwing her arms around him at the end. "Kiss, Viktor!" And while they were kissing the proud father came up to them, beaming.

"Viktor! I didn't know you were a dancer." And before Viktor had a chance to be modest, the man was rushing on. "I'm Frit. I'm so glad Nrina brought you. We haven't had a chance to meet, but I wanted to thank you for helping with Balit's party." He squeezed Viktor's arm. "Imagine! None of his friends ever had a person from *Earth* carry them away! He'll be the envy of his whole cohort."

"It was nothing," Viktor said graciously. Nrina patted his shoulder affectionately and strolled away. Viktor hardly noticed. He was staring in fascination at Frit's mustaches. At close range they were even more of a marvel; they extended beyond his shoulders on both sides, and although Viktor was sure he had seen one of them bent in the mock scuffle it was now repaired and stood as proudly as before. They did not at all match Frit's hair, either. At a distance Viktor had thought the man was wearing a white cap, but it was actually close-cropped white kinks, like the standard image of an old Pullman porter, though Frit's skin was alabaster.

"You must meet Forta," Frit went on, beckoning to the—well, Viktor thought, I guess you would say to the other father, though how all that worked out he couldn't imagine. "This is Viktor, dear," Frit told his mate. "Nrina says he's very interested in the stars and all."

"Yes, she told me," Forta said, demurely offering his shoulder to hug. "Do you know what we should do, Frit? We should ask Viktor to come and stay with us for a while. Balit already asked me if we could; he was just thrilled at being kidnapped by somebody from Old Earth! I know Balit would love to show him off to his friends—"

"Yes, dear," Frit said tolerantly. "But what would Viktor think of that? We can't expect him to spend his time with a bunch of kids."

Viktor blinked, then said, suddenly hopeful, "I'd really like to talk to you about what's happened to the universe. If I wouldn't be any burden—"

"Burden?" Forta echoed. "No, certainly you wouldn't be a burden; we'd love to have you come home with us. And—" He hesitated, then grinned modestly. "—since you're interested in dancing, shall I dance for you now? Frit's just finished a new poem in honor of Balit's coming of age—it's about growth and maturity—and I've done the dance accompaniment."

"Please do," Viktor said. He was completely out of it, really. He was wholly confused about what had been going on and what was to come. But he was game. He didn't, after all, have many other options.

CHAPTER 25

When Wan-To became aware that a fresh burst of tachyons had struck his receptors, he did not respond very quickly. (He didn't do *anything* very quickly these days.) It took him a while to switch from one mode of activity to another.

Torpidly, almost groaning in protest, he bestirred himself to see what this latest batch of tachyons was like. Naturally, his detectors had recorded them in case he wanted to examine them in detail—though that was probably hardly worth the trouble. Or wouldn't have been, if he had had anything more worthwhile to do.

Wan-To was not excited about the event. He had lost the habit of excitement, in this dead universe where there was no light, no X rays, no cosmic rays, no anything but the distant purring, popping sound of the protons of his own star as they gave up the ghost. Even so, it wasn't unusual for batches of stray radiation of one kind or another to reach him. Infrequent, yes—everything was infrequent these days. But not startling. Such things were simply the showers of particles that were the ghosts of some immense stellar catastrophes from long ago—from the time when any immense event could still happen, in this moribund universe.

But this time . . . This time . . .

This time it was the most exciting thing that had happened to Wan-To in a very long time indeed. Although he could hardly believe it at first, he was soon certain that this was no random burst of particles. It was a *message*.

It was a wonder that Wan-To could read the message at all. The coded pulses were of the very lowest-energy tachyons—therefore almost the fastest of all—and yet they had taken a long time to reach him (so vast had the always-expanding universe become, in ten to the fortieth years). They had to have been transmitted with considerable power, too. Wan-To knew this to be true not merely because of the distance they had traveled, but because he observed that the tachyons had not been transmitted in a tight, economical beam. They had been *broadcast*.

Broadcast! So the sender hadn't known where he was! But they were definitely meant for Wan-To—the opening pulses said so.

That fact was as much of a thrill to Wan-To as the first ecstatic sight of a sail on the horizon to any shipwrecked mariner. Impossible though it was to believe, even now, in this terminal coma of the universe, there was someone somewhere who had something to *say* to him.

But what was this message?

To find that out was a labor requiring much energy out of Wan-To's slender store, as well as a great deal of long, hard concentration. The message had come in very fast. The whole burst had taken only a matter of seconds, and it had been many ages since Wan-To had been able to operate at that speed. He had almost forgotten what it was like to do things at the speed of nuclear reactions. In order to interpret the message at all, he had to slow it down by orders of magnitude and ponder its meaning bit by bit.

Then, too, although the message had been stored automatically for examination at his own pace, the poverty of Wan-To's resources meant that even the basic storage was sketchy. Some sections of the message seemed to be missing. Some of the content was doubtful. Wan-To found it necessary to reactivate large parts of his "mind" from inactive storage to help in puzzling out what the message meant, and that in itself was a considerable drain on his meager strength.

But, in the final analysis, he didn't need to read it all. The signature alone was enough to tell him nearly all there was to know.

It had come from that long-forgotten idiot, the one he had charged with sending a little flock of stars on a wild-goose chase—Matter-Copy Number Five.

Five's stars were still alive.

Those long-ago stars had been careening through space so fast that time dilation had frozen them nearly immobile. They had not aged. They hadn't rotted into decay with the rest of the universe.

In a universe where everything else had decayed into stagnant death, they were still young . . . and bursting with *power!*

CHAPTER 26

$\mathbf{M}$oon Mary was a natural moon—well, a formerly natural moon, now terraformed and made lovely. Along with the myriad habitats it orbited around the brown dwarf, Nergal. "Forta needs a moon's gravity," Frit explained on the way. "Dancers have to have a lot of muscles, you know! If he can dance here he can dance anywhere—well, not on a *planet*, or anything like *that*, but on any of the other moons or the habitats. The exercise will be good for your leg while it heals, too."

"Besides, we've got a lot of data in our store," Forta put in hospitably. "I'm sure you'll find all sorts of interesting things in it."

And Balit said with excitement, "Look over there, Viktor! That's Moon Mary. Watch how we come in—oh, Viktor, I do love being in *space!*"

Viktor did watch. It was worth watching. They didn't simply "land." Moon Mary was not left wide open to the universe; it couldn't be, since it didn't have enough gravitation to hold a breathable air. To land, their little ship had to slide through an opening that appeared magically in the atmosphere-holding, radiation-shielding forcefield that kept the people who lived on Moon Mary safe.

As soon as Viktor stood up his bad leg told him he wasn't in habitat minigravity any more. It hurt when he put his weight on it. He winced.

But this was more like it! It wasn't a habitat, it was practically a *planet*. The buildings stuck up on the surface, as they ought to; and there was a real *sky*.

Actually the sky wasn't real at all, for if you had subtracted the force shield what remained would have been terrible. The shield diminished the intensity of the ruddy glow of Nergal. It might also, Viktor thought critically at first, have diminished their capacity to extract "solar" energy from Nergal, but it turned out they didn't need that. Moon Mary was packed with geothermal energy, easily extracted through steam wells. The satellite was so close to its primary, immense Nergal, that it was under constant gravitational flexing and stress from Nergal's great mass, and so its interior was constantly being heated by friction, compression, and strain.

Of course, experience had taught Viktor that there was a black lining to every silver cloud. He found what the bad side of Moon Mary's geothermal activity was very quickly. They were hardly out of the spaceport when Viktor felt the ground shudder beneath him. Balit giggled. Forta smiled tolerantly, and Frit explained, "Just an earthquake, Viktor. We have them all the time."

"But we're used to them," Forta added. "Truly, there's no danger."

When Viktor saw that his hosts lived in a pencil-thin tower thirty stories high, he swallowed. They took a glass-walled elevator, which slid rapidly up the outside of the tower, letting him see just how far they were soaring above the hard ground. In the elevator he swallowed again, and was glad when it slowed gently to their floor and Forta politely opened the door for him.

Once inside their apartment everything was reassuringly stable. They seemed to have the whole floor to themselves. All the rooms except the sanitary facilities were outside rooms—which meant they had curved walls and large windows looking out on the parklike gardens outside, with red Nergal hanging huge over half the sky. He allowed them to point out the room that would be his, and he kept Forta and Balit company as they pulled meals out of their freezer and set the table—until another sudden shiver of the whole structure made him grab for the back of a chair.

"You'll get used to it, Viktor," Balit said, trying not to show amusement. "We're quite safe here."

"All our buildings are designed for this sort of thing," Forta added.

It took a while for Viktor to believe it, but it was true enough. Of course, he knew that the problem of earthquakes had even been solved back on Earth itself, in the pre-Toyota Japan of the nineteenth century and earlier. Since earthquakes could knock buildings down, you didn't want any building that might fall on you and crush you to death. Those early Japanese found a satisfactory solution for their time: Build everything out of the flimsiest material you can find—and don't smoke in bed.

But when the twentieth century came along those lessons didn't apply anymore. Technological man had possessions. A home needed to be a place to store the possessions, as well as a place to sleep and eat. Preindustrial Japan had handled that by having as few possessions as possible, and those light and sturdy. Their grandchildren, however, lived in Toyota-, Sony-, Nissan-Japan, and they wanted more. They wanted to own a large number of tangible things, even if they were large and heavy. They wanted homes that could house their washer-dryers, stereos, Jacuzzis, king-sized beds with innerspring mattresses, radar ovens, food processors, and VCRs. They wanted flush toilets. They wanted built-in garages and electronic stoves.

All those new wants made hard work for the architects. Plumbing? Well, yes, but water intakes and sewage outlets meant underground networks of pipes and conduits that could rupture in even a moderate quake. They wanted high rises, which meant elevators and some very heavy structural members that could fall on the inhabitants unless built with sophisticated skill and attention to the harmonics of the natural frequencies of earthquake shocks. Paper and bamboo went out. Sprung, flexible steel, prestressed concrete, and curtain walls came in.

By the time the people on Moon Mary began to build in earnest, all those old lessons were learned over again.

To be sure, those latter-day architects were helped a great deal by Mary's light gravity. There simply didn't have to be that much mass involved in support columns. They were helped even more by high technology. Chips replaced tangles of wire. Transformable walls served as windows or temperature control devices. Water recycling saved a lot of plumbing, and what couldn't be avoided was flexible and tough. When, during Viktor's first night on Moon Mary, he woke to find the whole building swaying, he was the only one in it who jumped out of bed. Everyone else slept right through, even young Balit, and the next morning they laughed at him for his fears.

They laughed quite politely, though. They were always polite. "Helpful" was another thing—they did their best, but to Viktor's crushed surprise they had little help to give.

These people, whom Nrina had touted to him as the most knowledgeable alive, didn't even know the *vocabulary* of astrophysical research! "Spectroscopy," Frit said, sounding the word out. "Spec—*tross*—k'pee. That's a really pretty word, Viktor! I must use it in a poem. And it means something about finding out what a star is like?"

"It means measuring the bands of light and dark in a spectrum from a star, so that you can identify all the elements and ions present," Viktor said darkly, gazing at the man who had been advertised to know all these things.

"Ions! Spectrum! Oh, Viktor," Frit said with delight, "you're just *full* of wonderful words I can use. Forta? Come in here, please. We're going to find some 'spectroscopy' in our files for dear Viktor!"

But, as it turned out, they didn't.

They couldn't, or not in any easy way, at least. Between the two of them, Frit and Forta managed to get their data-retrieval desks to turn up several hundred references to one astronomical term or another. But "spectroscope" was not among them. Neither was "spectroscopy," nor even the field terms "cosmology" or "astrophysics." True, there were long lists of citations under such promising words as "nova" and "supernova" and "black hole" and even "Hertzsprung-Russell diagram." But, when tracked down, all the references were to plays, paintings, musical compositions, poems (some by Frit himself), and dances, frequently by Forta.

"It's only programmed for the things we're really interested in," Forta apologized.

Viktor couldn't believe their failure. He was the only disappointed person, though. Frit and Forta were enthralled.

"Great Transporter!" Forta cried in delight. "I didn't know we had this sort of material here! Perhaps it's from Balit's school files—but see here, Frit! Isn't this *beautiful?*" He was looking at a five-hundred-year-old painting of the Hertzsprung-Russell diagram. "I can't think why people have let this be forgotten! What do you think, Frit? All these star colors! For a new dance! Don't you think they'd look marvelous in my costume?"

Frit patted his mate's arm fondly, but he was peering at the diagram on the desk. "I don't think I know what it means," he admitted.

"It shows the slope of the mass-luminosity relation," Viktor explained. "You can see how stars develop, and their color depends on the temperature of the photosphere, anywhere from red through yellow and white to blue."

"Exactly!" Forta cried, hardly listening. "I will dance the aging of a star. See, I'll start out *big*—" He mimicked being *big*, lifting his shoulder, puffing his cheeks, arcing his arms up and before him. "And then the lighting will be blue, then greenish, then yellow and smaller, for a long time—is that right, Viktor?—then *big* again, and red!"

"You'll be lovely," Frit said with pride. He smiled at their son, politely silent as the grown-ups talked. "Don't you think Forta could make a lovely star dance?"

"He always does," Balit said loyally, but keeping his eyes on Viktor.

Forta sighed. "But I'm afraid we're not giving our friend Viktor what he wants. There just isn't much of that sort of thing in the current files."

Viktor pricked up his ears. "Are there others?"

"Of course there's always the old data banks on Newman-home," Frit said, looking surprised. "Only they aren't very convenient, you know. Because they're *old*. And they aren't *here*."

"Can I access them?" Viktor demanded.

Frit looked at him with the expression of a host whose guest has just requested a bigger bedroom, or a rare brand of tea. "I'm not sure if I know how you could do that," he said, thoughtfully. "Forta?"

"I suppose it's *possible*, Viktor," Forta said doubtfully. "They go back a long time, though, all the way back to when everybody still lived on Newmanhome. When we built the habitats, thousands of years ago, everything was shiny new, you know, and the data-retrieval systems were all redesigned. The ones we use now aren't really compatible with the ones on Newmanhome, and besides, there's hardly anyone there."

"On Newmanhome?" Viktor repeated.

Forta nodded. "It's a nasty place to live, with everything weighing so much. People don't like to go there—except funny ones like Pelly," he added laughingly. "So the old records might as well not exist, don't you see?"

Balit, watching their guest with concern, squirmed away from his parent's fondly patting hand. "We do have the paintings, Viktor," the boy piped up.

And when Viktor looked inquiringly at Balit's parents, Forta said with pride, "Yes, of course. There are some wonderful paintings of the star burst, for instance. It was still in the sky, oh, up to six or eight hundred years ago. Then it just gradually began to fade, and then the sun came back."

"That must have been an exciting time," Frit said wistfully. "Of course, we weren't born then."

Forta thought that over. "I don't know if I'd say 'exciting,' exactly. I know people did talk about it, quite a lot, once they noticed it. And there was the art. I remember my mother taking me to—whose performance was it? I think it was Danglord's—yes, that's what it was. It was a dance play about the sun returning. I was just a child, hadn't even had my coming-of-age party yet, but—" He smiled bashfully at Viktor. "It was certainly important to *me*. I think Danglord's play was what made up my mind to be a dancer myself."

As the family's guest expert on the care and feeding of primitive organisms, it was Viktor who had to show them how to thaw out a little of the frozen cat-milk substitute Nrina had made for them, and how to hold a bottle so the kitten could drink out of it. "She'll be eating solid food soon," he promised. "Then she won't be so much trouble. Meanwhile, what have you done about a cat box?"

Then he had to explain what a cat box was for, and help them improvise one out of a tray from the cooking room, and fill it with soil from the garden, and show them how to put the little animal in it and stroke her and encourage her until she finally did what she was put there to do.

At least he was useful for something, Viktor thought.

After a final glass of wine Frit escorted him to their guest room. "It's not actually a *guest* room," Frit explained, showing Viktor where the sanitary facilities were and the drawers to store his clothes. "It's going to be Balit's room, now that he's liberated—but of course he's happy to have you use it for your stay," Frit added hastily.

"I don't like to put him out," Viktor said politely.

"You aren't putting anyone out! No, we *want* you here, dear Viktor. In fact, it was Balit's idea. He'll stay in his own old room, where he's quite content. But this one, you see," Frit added with pride, "is an *adult* room. You'll have your own desk—you can use it as much as you like, of course. I think you'll be quite comfortable," he finished, looking around like any hostess. Then he grinned, a little embarrassed. "Well, I don't see any harm in telling you. We're going to be redecorating Balit's old room. We've ordered another baby from Nrina. She'll be a little girl—we're going to call her Ginga—and of course she won't be born for a long time yet, so Balit will be quite all right in that room."

It wasn't until Frit was long gone and Viktor had undressed and climbed into the soft, warm bed that it occurred to him that he should have said "Congratulations."

The ground shook again that night. Viktor woke, startled, to find something warm and soft near his toes. It mewed in protest when he moved.

He got up, grinning, and stroked the kitten back to sleep as he sat on the edge of his bed, thinking. Alone in the bedroom, Viktor admitted to himself that he was a little uncomfortable. He knew why.

He wasn't really easy in his mind to be moving into a house of gays.

Viktor was quite certain that he was not at all prejudiced against homosexuals. He'd known plenty of them, one time or another. He'd worked with them, shipped with them—they weren't any different than anybody else, he considered, except in that one particular way. But that way wasn't anyone's business but their own, and certainly it didn't matter in any real sense as long as you didn't get *involved* with them.

The trouble was, *living* with them seemed to be getting pretty involved.

It reassured Viktor that the household didn't seem much different than any other. Forta and Frit had their own bedroom. Balit had his; Viktor had the one Balit would graduate into. Nothing was, well, *bizarre* about the household. Not really. If Forta would sometimes kiss the back of Frit's neck as he passed behind his chair, and if Frit would slip an arm around Forta's waist while they stood together—well, they did love each other, didn't they?

What was most important, neither of them showed any indication at all of loving Viktor. Not that way, anyway.

The boy, Balit, almost did. He certainly acted loving, but there wasn't anything sexual about it. Balit sat next to Viktor when they ate their meals, and kept Viktor company while he fruitlessly hunted for what he never found on the information machines. It was Balit who marked which foods and drinks Viktor seemed to enjoy and made sure there were more of them at the next meal. He always seemed to be there, watching Viktor, whenever he was not asleep or at school.

"It's a kind of hero worship," Forta explained. The dancer was working at his bar, stretching those long, slim legs even longer, with one eye on the kitten waking on the floor between them. Viktor realized with surprise that Forta was *being* a cat. "This will work, I think," Forta said with pleasure, giving it up as the kitten curled up to drowse again. "What were we saying? Oh, yes. Please don't let Balit bother you. But the thing is that you were the one who actually carried him away for his freeing ceremony; that's a big thing for a young boy."

"He's no trouble at all," Viktor protested. "I like having him around."

"Well, it's obvious he likes you." Forta sighed. "I mean, he likes you as a person, not just because of what you did. As a matter of fact—" Forta hesitated, then smiled. "Actually, Balit wondered if he could ask you to come to his school. If you wouldn't mind. He'd like to show you off. I know it wouldn't be much fun for you, spending an hour or two with a bunch of little kids staring and asking you all kinds of questions—but you can't blame them, Viktor. You *were* born on Old Earth. They aren't likely to see anybody like you again."

"I'd be glad to," Viktor promised.

The school was no more than a hundred yards from Balit's home, in the middle of a grove of broad-leafed trees that hung with fruit and blossoms interchangeably. (There weren't any seasons on Moon Mary. Plants grew and bloomed when they felt like it, not when the weather changed. The weather never changed.) Red Nergal hung in the eastern sky, where it always hung in their position on Moon Mary's surface. At their distance it loomed no larger than Earth's moon, but Viktor could feel the heat from it. And in the west was one bright star. "There used to be thousands and thousands of stars," Viktor told the boy, who nodded in solemn appreciation.

"Things must have been so much nicer then," he sighed. "We go in there, Viktor. That's the door to my class."

It wasn't much of a door—Moon Mary's buildings did not have very strong walls, since they didn't need them to keep out cold or heat; it was light, pierced wood, as might have been in Earth's old tropics, and it opened to Balit's touch.

It wasn't much of a class, either—eight kids, mostly girls—and it didn't seem to be exactly a classroom. It looked rather like the guest lounge of a small motel at first, a bedroom-sized chamber with hassocks and couches strewn before a collection of child-sized teaching desks, but as Balit led Viktor in the room darkened.

"We'll have to wait a minute," Balit apologized. "They're starting a viewing. I don't know what it is, though—" And then, all around the children, a scene sprang into life, three-dimensional, seeming natural size, full color. "Oh, look, Viktor! They're doing it specially for you! They're showing Old Earth!"

If it was really Earth, it was not an Earth Viktor recognized. He seemed to be standing on a sort of traffic island in the middle of a large street, and it was by no means empty. Thousands, literally *thousands*, of people were riding bicycles toward him in a dense swarm that spilt in two just before they reached him, and came together again on the other side. They wore almost uniform costumes—white shirts, dark blue trousers—and they were almost all male. And *Oriental*. There was no sound, but to one side was a huge marble building set in a sort of park, and on the other what looked like a hotel and office buildings.

"I don't know where this is supposed to be," Viktor apologized.

Balit looked embarrassed. "But they *said* it was Earth," he complained. "Wait a minute." He bent to whisper to the little girl nearest him. "Yes, this is Earth, all right. It is a place called Beijing, around the year one thousand nine hundred sixty, old style."

"I was never in Beijing," Viktor said. "And anyway—" He stopped there. What was the use of telling these children that they were not off by a mere few thousand miles, but by several centuries? He settled for, "It's very nice, though. But can we turn it off?"

Then Viktor had the floor. The teacher sat there smiling, leaving it all to the children to ask questions, and that they did. About Old Earth. (People rode *horses*? If they made love did they really have babies out of their *bodies*? And what, for heaven's sake, was a "storm"?) About the Sorricaine-Mtiga objects (Oh, they must have been exciting to see!), and about his near-death in orbit around Nebo (Something tried to *kill* you? Really take away your *life*?), and about Newmanhome and the Big Bang and the reasons why there were so few stars anymore anywhere in the sky.

That was where Viktor began to wax really eloquent, until Balit, speaking for all of them, said gravely, "Yes, we see, Viktor. The stars that blew up, the sun going dim, the changes on Nebo, the disappearance of all the other stars—we see that as they all happened at the same time, or close enough, they must be connected. But how?"

And all Viktor could say was, "I wish I knew."

That night Balit was telling his parents excitedly about the hit Viktor had made with his classmates. "Viktor was almost *killed* by those things on Nebo," the boy said, thrilled. "Frit? Can I go to Nebo sometime?"

"What, and get killed?" Frit teased.

Forta was stretching and bending at his bar, but he panted, "No one goes to Nebo, Balit, dear. It's worse than Newmanhome! You couldn't even stand up there."

"Pelly can," the boy objected. "He gets injections, and then he's almost as strong as Viktor."

Frit looked shocked. "Balit! No. Those injections *destroy* your figure. Do you want to bloat those pretty legs so they look like *balloons*? No offense," he added hastily, catching Viktor's eye. "But, Balit, you couldn't ever really dance that way, you know."

"I might not want to be a dancer, Frit," his son told him.

Forta straightened up abruptly in the middle of a long stretch. He blinked worriedly at his son. "Well, of course," he began, "what you do in your adult life is entirely up to you. Neither Frit nor I would think of trying to prevent you from anything you really wanted to do, once you were grown—"

"But I am grown," Balit told him seriously. "It's almost time for me to have the mark off my forehead. Then I could even marry if I wanted to."

Frit cleared his throat. "Yes, of course," he said, tugging at one of his mustaches. "However—"

He paused there, looking at Viktor in a way Viktor understood at once. A guest must not involve himself in family affairs.

"I think I'll go back to my desk," he said.

But what he wanted was not there. Viktor began to think that nothing he found was going to scratch his itch of curiosity. The more he found, the more he realized there was not much to find on the subjects he cared about.

There was plenty in the files on the history of the human race after the Reforms had put him back in the freezer. They had had a war about the destruction of *Ark*, of course—each sect blaming the other. They had (as Viktor counted them up) a war every two or three years anyway, on one pretext or another. It was easy enough to see why they were so combative. Viktor could imagine the lives of the bare few thousand of them, near starving in their icy caves, wounded by events that they had never expected and that they could not explain—there was no future for them. Of all the things they lacked, the one in shortest supply was hope.

It was astonishing to Viktor that they had somehow found the resources and the will to dispatch a handful of rickety, improvised ships to Nergal. That was heroic. It was very nearly superhuman; it meant long years of savage discipline, starving themselves and denying themselves for that one last, supreme effort. He marveled at their progress since then—now so many teeming millions, living in such luxury! It wasn't the numbers that made him wonder, of course. The increase was not surprising, since they'd had several thousand years to do it in. You only have to double a population ten times—ten generations will do it easily, if there's plenty of food and no saber-toothed tigers to keep the surplus down—to multiply it by a thousand.

Nor was it surprising that in the course of that mighty effort they threw some unneeded junk overboard—junk with names like astronomy and astrophyics and cosmology.

And their descendants, the soft, pretty Nrinas and Fortas and Frits, had never seen any reason to revive them.

Except for little Balit. Balit wanted to hear everything Viktor had to say—about the universe itself (especially about the way it had been, in the old days, when there really was a whole universe outside their own little group), about Old Earth, about Newmanhome in the days of its burgeoning glory. It was Balit who came to Viktor with the news that Pelly had landed on Newmanhome. "Maybe he can help you access the old files, Viktor," Balit said helpfully, glancing at his fathers—who, for some reason, were politely saying nothing at all.

"Could he really do that?"

"We can call him to ask," Balit said, now not looking at his fathers at all. "I know how much you want to get that data."

Forta cleared his throat. "Yes, we all know that," he observed.

"But it would be interesting to me, too," Balit protested. "I like it when Viktor talks about those old things."

Forta said, loving but firm, "It's your bedtime, Balit."

"Then Viktor could tell me a *bedtime* story," Balit pleaded. Viktor surrendered. He followed the boy to his bath and sat with him as, damply clean, Balit rolled himself into the soft, gauzy bedclothes and looked up at him expectantly.

Viktor found himself moved by the situation, so familiar, so different. It made him think of telling stories to his own children long ago on Newmanhome, and before that hearing his father tell them to him ages past on the ship. He reached out to stroke Balit's warm, fuzzy head.

"Shall I tell you about the beginning of the universe?" he asked.

"Oh, yes, Viktor! Please!"

Obediently Viktor began. "Once upon a time there was nothing, not anything anywhere, except for one little point of matter and energy and space. There weren't any stars. There weren't any galaxies. There wasn't even any space yet, really, because space hadn't been invented."

"What did that point look like, Viktor?" the boy asked drowsily.

"I don't know. Nobody knows, Balit. It was just a—an *egg*, sort of, that held inside itself the possibility of everything that now exists, or ever did exist, or ever will exist. And then that egg hatched. It exploded. Do you know what that explosion was called, Balit?"

The boy searched his memory. "What you called the Big Bang?" he guessed.

"That's right. The Big Bang. It started out terribly hot and terribly dense, but as it expanded it cooled off. It didn't grow *into* space. It *made* the space, as it grew, and it filled it with things—and finally we came along."

Balit blinked up at Viktor. "Were we the only ones who came along, Viktor?" he asked.

"I don't know the answer to that, either, Balit. I haven't heard of any others. There could have been. There might have been millions of different kinds of people. They could have evolved and developed and then died away, just as human beings did—except for us few."

"It must have been beautiful, when there were all those stars and galaxies."

"It was. But stars die, too. All things die, even the universe, even—" To Viktor's surprise, he found his throat tightening. He had to turn his head away for a moment.

"What's wrong, Viktor?" Balit said in sudden alarm.

"Nothing, Balit. I think you'd better go to sleep now."

"No," the boy insisted. "You looked very sad just then. Was it about something bad? Was it—" He hesitated, then said in a rush, "Was it about the love partner you told me about?"

"It was about my wife," Viktor corrected him.

Balit nodded soberly. "I know how Frit or Forta would feel if one of them lost the other," he told Viktor. He looked at him for a moment, then said, sounding very tentative, "Viktor? Didn't Nrina say she could make you a mate? Don't you think you might let her?"

Viktor glared at him with a sudden near-anger. Then he relaxed, took a deep breath, and tousled the boy's hair. "You're officially grown-up," he said, "but I think you've got a little way to go in some ways. That isn't how it works, Balit."

"Then how does it work, Viktor?" Balit persisted.

Viktor shook his head. "For me, now," he said, "I don't think it's ever going to work again at all."

The mechanics of calling someone on Newmanhome were not that difficult, especially after Balit showed Viktor how to use the desk to do it. Actually making the call, however, was a lot harder.

Once again, it was a matter of that unbreakable speed limit of light's velocity. (The human race had never managed to use tachyons or the Einstein-Rosen-Podolsky effect for any practical purpose. With only their own tiny little cluster of astronomical objects to work on, they hadn't really needed to.) At their current orbital positions, Moon Mary was a good five hundred million miles from Newmanhome—nearly three-quarters of an hour each way for a message to arrive. You couldn't converse. It was more like sending a telegram and waiting for a response, though of the course the "telegram" was a television message.

So Viktor, with Balit beside him to help, put through a call to

Pelly, all those hundreds of millions of miles away. "Hello, Pelly," he said, as though reading from a script. "This is Viktor. I was hoping—" He came to a stop there, and looked to Balit for help. "Tell him what you want," the boy prompted.

"Everything I want?"

"Yes, exactly, everything," the boy ordered, sounding exasperated. "How will he know if you don't tell him? Tell him you would like all the old records—about Nebo, about astronomical observations, everything you wish."

So, gathering speed as he went along, Viktor did. It made a formidable list. When he was through, Balit leaned past him and turned off the desk. Viktor looked at him inquiringly. "What do we do now?"

"We do nothing now," Balit told him. "It will be hours at least before Pelly can reply, and perhaps he is busy doing something else, and perhaps what you ask takes time."

"I imagine it will," Viktor said gloomily. Balit laughed.

"Oh, Viktor," he said with affection, "it is only hours, perhaps, not forever. Come and walk with me. Perhaps when we get back there will be a response."

When they had taken that belly-twisting elevator drop down to the parklike grounds around the building, Balit said curiously, "Would you really go to Nebo if you could?"

"In a hot minute," Viktor said emphatically.

"Even though it's dangerous?"

Viktor thought. "I'm not sure it's dangerous anymore," he said. "They did let that party land—"

"But then some of them were *killed*!"

"Yes, because they tried to force their way in," Viktor agreed. "That might not be necessary. There are other ways of investigating what's in those structures. Not X rays, probably; but ultrasound ranging, perhaps, or something like a neutrino source that can look right through them—"

"No one has any 'neutrinos,' Viktor," Balit said in reproof.

Viktor laughed. "All right then. Maybe all we'd really need is a really big can opener. And some dumb volunteer to run it— like me."

Balit shuddered deliciously at the thought. Then he asked, "Viktor? What's a 'can opener'?"

There wasn't any answer to Viktor's call when they got back, or the next day, or the day after that.

By the end of his third week on Moon Mary Viktor had begun to wonder just how long a guest was supposed to stay. When he touched on the subject with his hosts they were invariably hospitable, and invariably hard to pin down. "Oh, but Balit loves having you here, Viktor, and Forta's been dying to have you show him some more of those quaint old dances."

"And it's so good for your leg to heal here," Forta put in helpfully.

"But Nrina—" he began.

"Oh, Nrina," Frit said, affably dismissing Nrina. "She'll be in touch before long, Viktor, you'll see. That reminds me, I've been meaning to ask you something. Do you think those Nebo colors— the ones you showed us the other day—do you think they would make a good costume for Forta?" And then that inevitably led to a few hours with Forta in his studio, demonstrating the waltz and the Peabody, to be worked into a dance Forta was planning on the heroic subject of the disastrous landing on Nebo.

It was not merely Viktor's desire to be a good guest—that was to say, one who left before his hosts began to despair he would ever go—that made him begin to be uncomfortable. He also had another problem that was growing larger. Moon Mary was a big place. It was full of people, all kinds of people, and Viktor could not help noticing that some of the ones he passed in the parks and streets were female—were so conspicuously female, to all of his senses, that sometimes he almost thought they were scent marking the shrubbery. It distracted him in ways he had almost forgotten.

To put it more concretely, he was getting pretty horny.

When Pelly's answer came at last it wasn't very help-
ful. The broad pumpkin face looked a little annoyed. "I'll ask around
about what you want to know, Viktor, but I don't know much
about that sort of thing myself. Markety might know; he spends a
lot of time digging up old stuff, and so does his wife, Grimler.
Unfortunately they're not here now, and I'm leaving myself pretty
soon. Listen. While I think of it, if you see Nrina ask her how she's
coming with my gillies. They need some more here. And say hello
to Balit for me."

That was it. Viktor looked helplessly at Balit. "Who are Markety and Grimler?"

"I guess they're people who live on Newmanhome—I mean real
people. Well, you know what I mean, Viktor," he finished, half
apologizing. Then he thought for a moment and added, "I think
Markety studied with Forta for a while, when I was little."

"Do you mean he's a dancer? What would a dancer be doing
on Newmanhome?"

Balit grinned. "Dancing, I guess. Don't you think you should
give Nrina her message?"

"Oh, well," Viktor said, stalling, "yes, maybe . . ."

But in the long run he did—hesitantly; he had always thought
that Nrina should be the one to call him. But when he saw her lean,
wide-eyed face looking up at him out of the desk panel he was
unexpectedly happy. Conscious of the boy beside him, Viktor said
stiffly, "How are you, Nrina? I've missed you."

It was a downer that she didn't respond right away. She was
gazing up at him without speaking for several seconds, but just as
Viktor was beginning to feel insecure she spoke up. "That is good
to hear," she said, smiling. (Oh, of course. Distance again. Only a
matter of seconds, this time, because Nrina's habitat was less than
a million miles from Moon Mary—but that was something like
five seconds travel time each way. Quite long enough to be disconcerting.)

She did, Viktor thought, still seem affectionate. He gave her
Pelly's message, and Nrina thought for a moment. "The gillies are
young," she said doubtfully. "I wasn't going to send them for another couple of seasons. Still, it might be better for them to finish
growing up where they're going to live. These are special gillies,

you know. They're almost as strong as the original 'gorillas' you talk about, I think, but a lot more tractable. Like you," she finished, with an affectionate grin. "Oh, and I'm not too happy with the DNA from the stiffs I've still got. If you talk to Pelly tell him to bring me some more—no," she corrected herself, "I might as well call him myself. Well. It's been nice talking to you. Balit, is that you? How are you doing with your genetic studies?"

"All right, I guess, Aunt Nrina," the boy piped up. "Of course, I haven't had much time, helping Viktor and all."

"I believe that," she agreed ruefully. "He does take a lot of time, doesn't he? But he's worth it." And she blew them both a kiss and was gone, and she hadn't said a word about his coming back to her.

Nor did she in the days that followed. Nor did Pelly call back. When Viktor grumbled to Balit the boy said, "He's probably on his way home now, Viktor. But I'm sure he got your message to those other people."

"Then why don't they answer?" Viktor demanded. The boy shrugged, and Viktor's temper rose. "I could understand it if it was all lost! It's wonderful that it *hasn't* been lost, but you tell me they've had power all along, the geothermal generators have kept right on working, so the data's *there*, only nobody ever wants to *look* at it!"

"Please don't get excited, Viktor," Balit pleaded.

"I can't help it. Doesn't anybody care?"

"I care, Viktor. Really, though, you should be more calm." Balit hesitated, then said with determination, "Do you know what I think, Viktor? I think you are building up too many tensions."

Viktor gave him a hostile look. "What tensions are you talking about?"

Balit's expression seemed to show he was sorry he'd brought the subject up, but he took the plunge. "Why don't you have a sexual partner, Viktor?" he asked with determination.

Viktor flushed. He was taken aback. "I—" he said. "I, uh—" He was having trouble responding; the last thing he had expected was to have to discuss his sex life with this child. He managed to get out, "Well, if I did, it wouldn't be, uh, safe for the woman—"

"Because you are potent, yes, of course," Balit agreed earnestly.

"That can be fixed, just as it was for me. In a few days the rest of my residual sperm will be resorbed and my brand removed, and then I can have sexual intercourse freely again, just as you could."

"Wait a minute," Viktor said, staring at the boy. "Again?"

Balit looked puzzled. Then he said, in a self-deprecating way, "Of course, before I was mature it was only with young girls. For practice, as we say—though I did enjoy it very much. Soon it will be with real women. It can be for you, too, Viktor, if you want it. It doesn't hurt a bit," he added encouragingly, "well, except for a little bit, right at first. You know, you don't have to have a *wife*. You don't have to agree to a pairing right at first; hardly anybody does that."

"So it seems," Viktor growled, thinking of Nrina.

The boy's puzzled look returned, but he just asked curiously, "Have you ever done that, Viktor? Paired, I mean?"

"Sure I have," Viktor replied. Then, more slowly, he said, "I was married for a long time. Her name was Reesa—Theresa Mc-Gann—but she's dead' now."

Fascinated, Balit went on, "And did you and this Reesa Theresa McGann have actual children together? I mean, born out of her body?"

"Yes, we did," Viktor said shortly. His discomfort was growing. It was not often that he thought of those long-dust members of his family, and it felt as though thinking of them now was likely to begin to hurt.

"And did you love her?" Balit demanded.

Viktor looked at the boy. "Yes!" he shouted. And realized again, quite a lot too late, that it was very true.

Time passed slowly for Viktor. He spent a lot of time in his room, waiting for the message from Newmanhome that might answer all his questions, but it never came.

There was no point in calling Pelly again, because the space captain was well on his way back to Nergal. Viktor hesitated about trying Markety or Grimler, whoever they were, but finally impatience won over hesitation and he placed a call to each of them.

There were no answers to those, either. Balit counseled patience. Balit himself was always patient with Viktor, when Viktor was gloomy or stormy; but Viktor's patience was running out. He spent more and more time with the desk, searching out every scrap of information he could find that bore at all on anything astronomical.

None of it was any help.

There was plenty of data, to be sure, on the universe as it was— nothing on how it came to be that way. For a while Viktor interested himself in the atlas of the skies. There wasn't much of it: their own planets, just as he had known them in his first years on Newmanhome, the habitats, Nergal itself.

Their paltry group of surrounding stars had been studied, after a fashion—long enough to give them names, not much more. There was one group of four stars usually called "the Quadrangle"—their names were Sapphire, Gold, Steel, and Blood, taken, Viktor supposed, from the way they looked in the sky. There was Solitary— all off by itself in its part of the sky; a natural enough name. There were the binary pair, now called Mother and Father, with a period of about eight hundred years. There was Neighbor, the nearest star at less than three light-years distance, but an uninspiring little K-8.

Then there was Milk. Viktor studied the pale glow of Milk carefully, because it was the corpse of one of the stars that had flared in his own long-ago skies. The desk could tell him little, for no one lately had seemed to care why stars were different in color, and certainly no one had thought much about stellar evolution. But Viktor was nearly sure that what they saw wasn't the star itself anymore, but the shell of expanding gases it had thrust out of itself, now lit from within.

Then he discovered that someone, sometime in the past, had taken the trouble to look a little more closely at all those stars and had found out that Gold had six detectable planets.

Planets! And yellow Gold was a G-4—close enough to their own stellar type, indeed to the type of Earth's own sun.

Was it possible that someone had lived on one of Gold's planets?

By the time he could talk to Balit again he was bubbling with excitement. "It all fits together, Balit!" he cried. "There's a planetary system, not very distant at all. Suppose there's life on one of those planets, Balit!"

"You mean people like us?" Balit asked, wide-eyed.

"I don't know about that, Balit. Probably not very much 'like' us, if you mean two arms, two legs, two eyes—I don't have any idea what they might look like. But like us in that they've developed intelligence. And technology! Why not? They might even be a little farther along in science and technology than the human race ever was—it wouldn't have to be very far to make a big difference!"

"With spaceships, you mean?"

"Exactly! With *interstellar* spaceships. Suppose these Golden aliens, for purposes of their own—and how could we ever guess what their purposes might be? Suppose they decided to move a little furniture around. A dozen stars or so, for instance. Suppose they sent a crew to Nebo to build the machines that would take the energies of our sun, and use them to propel these few stars at high speed across the universe. Don't you see, Balit? It explains everything!"

"And if we studied the things on Nebo very carefully we might know how to do things like that ourselves? Or at least know *why*?"

"Exactly!" Viktor cried in triumph.

But the triumph didn't last, for a guess was only a guess, and there was no way to test his hypothesis. He spent more and more time in his room, fruitlessly going over the data, wishing for word from Newmanhome. He was gazing at the pale point of light that was the star Gold, when Frit tapped on the door. He was carrying the kitten, and he had an apologetic look. "Balit forgot to feed her, and now he's in bed," Frit said. "Can you help?"

"Sure," Viktor said, not very graciously. The kitten was big enough to eat regular food now. "I'll come out. You don't have to carry her," he added. "Put her down; if she's hungry she'll follow us."

Frit politely set the cat on the floor and led the way. To Viktor's surprise, Forta was in the "kitchen"—that was the only way Viktor

could think of the room—sipping a glass of wine and looking ex-
pectant. Viktor found the little container of scraps of food, opened
it, and set it on the floor. The kitten strolled over, sniffed at it, and
then looked up at him. He smiled. "She's just being polite," he said.
"That's what she wanted. See, she's eating now."

As he turned to leave, Forta said, "Why don't you have a glass
of wine with us, Viktor?"

Viktor perceived that it wasn't just a casual invitation. He sat
down and let Forta fill a glass for him before he said, "You didn't
really need me to feed the cat, did you?"

Forta dimpled. "Not really. We wanted to talk to you, after
Balit was asleep."

Faint alarm bells sounded in Viktor's head. "Is something
wrong?" he asked.

"Not really wrong, no, Viktor," Frit said honestly. "It's just
that we're a little bit concerned about Balit."

"About Balit's *future*," Forta amplified.

Frit nodded. "We've always hoped he would want to become
an artist of some sort—a dancer, perhaps, like Forta."

"He wouldn't have to be a dancer, as long as it was something
that used his creative ability. Nrina thinks he has real talent as a
gene worker," Forta added. "That's a kind of art, too, of course."

"But lately he's been so—well, so excited about these stars and
things of yours, Viktor," Frit finished.

Viktor took a sip of his wine, feeling the strain between the
obligations of a good guest and that burning need to *know*. "Balit's
a very intelligent boy. He's really interested in science, too," Viktor
said. "I think he could be good at it."

"Yes, we're sure he could, Viktor," Forta said reasonably. "But
what kind of a life would Balit have if he confined his talents to
'science'? Nobody's a 'scientist.' People will think he's odd."

"In my time it was a highly honored profession," Viktor said
defensively—and, he thought, not entirely truthfully; for it depended on which "time" he was talking about. Certainly the icy
Newmanhome of the four warring sects had offered few honors to
scientists.

"In your time," Forta repeated. His tone wasn't exactly disdain-
ful, but the best you could say was that it was forgiving. "Anyway,

Viktor, it's not *creative*, is it? There's nothing *new* for him to do—you said yourself, all this sort of 'science' thing was well known thousands and thousands of years ago."

"Not all of it, no. No one really understood what happened to our stars! Even the parts that were understood then—the basic astrophysics and cosmology—nobody seems to know anything about them now. They need to be rediscovered."

Frit said earnestly, "But don't you see the difference? Rediscovery, Viktor dear, is not the same as *creation*, is it? You can't blame us for wanting something grander for our boy."

"Oh, Frit," Viktor said, despairing, "how can I make you understand? What could be grander than answering the question of what happened to the entire universe? Maybe Balit can discover that! He's interested. He's smart. He simply doesn't have the education. First he needs a grasp of cosmology and nuclear decay and—"

"No one knows those things anymore, Viktor. Truly. They simply aren't interesting to us."

"But they must be on record somewhere," Viktor said, clutching at straws. "I know the data banks in *Ark* and *Mayflower* had all that material—"

"They don't exist anymore, Viktor. What was left of them must have been salvaged for structural materials thousands of years ago."

"But they were copied onto the files on Newmanhome."

Frit gave Forta a meaningful look. "Yes, Newmanhome," he said.

Forta sighed. For some reason the thought of the files on Newmanhome seemed to make him uncomfortable. "Well," he said, "we'll see what we can do."

"I hope I can repay you," Viktor said.

Forta gave him a strange look. "That's all right," he said, sounding insincere. Then, "Do you know a lot of stories like the Big Bang one you were telling Balit?"

"Oh, dozens," Viktor told him, aware for the first time that the parents had been listening in. In fact he did. In fact he had all the stories his father had told him still well in mind—the story of the carbon-nitrogen-oxygen cycle that fueled the stars, the story of the death of massive stars in supernovae and the birth of pulsars and black holes, the stories of Kepler's Laws of Motion and of Newton's, and of Einstein's superseding laws, and of the rules of quantum mechanics that went beyond even Einstein.

"Yes, of course," Forta said, yawning. "Those are very interesting. I know Balit loves to hear about them—"

"But not all the time, please, Viktor," Frit finished. "If you don't mind."

Then the long-awaited transmission came in from Newmanhome, and it was not at all what Viktor had expected.

To begin with, of course it wasn't Pelly calling—the space captain had to be halfway back to Nergal by now. The face on the screen was a man wearing a sort of floppy beret, pulled down almost to his eyebrows; he was a habitat person, all right, but he was actually wearing clothes. "Viktor," he began without preamble, "I'm Markety. I'm just here for a short time, but I've managed to collect some of the material for you. Give my respects to Forta, please—he is one of my heroes, as I am sure he knows. Here's the material."

Eagerly Viktor watched the screen on the desk as new pictures began to appear. Puzzledly he stared at them. After months he knew what sort of thing the desk produced when interrogated; these were quite different. They were simply a series of—well, photographs! The first batch was pictures of bits and pieces of machinery, some of it the same shiny lavender metal as the keepsake Balit proudly kept by his bedside, some of unidentifiable materials that could have been steel or glass or ceramic. It dawned on Viktor that they were the odds and ends that had been salvaged from the surface of the planet Nebo—but there was no explanation for any of them, no hint of what they might be for, or what studies might have been made of them.

The next batch was more puzzling still.

It had to do with astrophysics, all right, but it was not data displayed from a computer file. It was pictures—pictures of pages of manuscript, or log books, or even a few pages from a book here and there. They seemed to have been taken from the freezers.

They were all fragmentary—a couple of pages of something, without beginning or end; the pages themselves as like as not torn or frayed or spotted into illegibility. Some of them made Viktor blink. Some of it went so far back that his father's own observations were there.

For a while at least, someone had been faithful at keeping records. (Billy Stockbridge, perhaps, loyal to Pal Sorricaine to the last?) There were spectrograms of the sun as it cooled; of the star burst as it grew; of the dozen stars that still remained in their sky—dimmer than before, but not swallowed into the star burst.

None of them were anything like the spectrograms Pal Sorricaine had so doggedly gleaned of the stars that had flared and died all about them. The Sorricaine-Mtiga objects were still unique.

None of the spectrograms made any sense to Viktor, either. The dead observers had left their own speculations, but none of them was convincing. None of them explained what it was that had stolen most of the stars out of the sky. And they were all so very old that there was nothing at all about the fireball that had dominated the sky for so long.

When Balit came back from school Viktor was still puzzling over the transmission. He displayed it all over again for Balit, but repetition didn't make it clearer. Balit didn't do any homework that night. He and Viktor ate quickly and returned to the desk. It was the objects from Nebo that seemed most fascinating to the boy. "But what can they be?" he asked, not for the first time, and, not for the first time, Viktor shook his head.

"The only way to find out is to investigate them. Somebody made them, after all—somebody from Gold, or somewhere else, but still some *person*. They can be opened up."

Balit shivered. "People did try, Viktor. More than twenty of them were *killed*."

"People die for a lot less important reasons," Viktor said roughly. "Naturally it would have to be done with a lot of precautions. Systematically. The way people used to defuse bombs in wars."

"What are 'wars,' Viktor?"

But Viktor refused to be sidetracked. They pored over the material until it was late and Balit, yawning, said, "I don't know if I understand, Viktor. Are our stars the only ones still alive, anywhere?"

"That's the way it looks, Balit."

"But stars live *forever*, Viktor," the boy said drowsily.

"Not forever. For a long time—" Viktor stopped, remembering a joke. He laughed as he got ready to tell it. "There used to be a story about that, Balit. A student is asking his astronomy teacher a question: 'Pardon me, professor, but when did you say the sun would turn into a red giant and burn us all up?'

"The professor says, 'In about five billion years.'

"So the student says, 'Oh, thank God! I thought you said five *million*.' "

But Balit didn't laugh. He was sleeping. And as Viktor carried the boy to his bed, he wasn't laughing, either.

Viktor sought out the one of Balit's parents at home. He found Frit painting something on a large screen. "I'm sorry I kept him so late. We got to talking about why all these things had happened—"

"Where you go wrong, Viktor," Frit told him serenely, "is in always asking why. There doesn't have to be a why. You don't have to understand things; it's enough to *feel*."

Viktor looked uncomprehendingly at the designs Frit was painting on the screen. The screen, he saw, was flimsy, it would be transferred to the wall of the room that would some day be Ginga's. It was a wall poem. He laughed. "So I shouldn't try to understand why you're doing that? When Ginga isn't even born, and won't be able to read for years yet?"

"No, Viktor, that is very easy to understand," Frit said indulgently. "When Ginga learns to read I want her first words to come from her father. No," he went on, brushing in another character in a chartreuse flourish and looking critically at the result, "it is this obsession of yours for understanding the sky that worries me. It upsets Balit, I'm afraid. What's the use of it? The sky is the sky, Viktor. It has nothing to do with our lives."

"But you've written poems about the sky!"

"Ah, but that is *art*. I write poems about what people *feel* about the sky. No one can experience the sky, Viktor; one can only look at it and see it as an object of art." He shook his wooly head in reproof. "All these things you tell to Balit—hydrogen atoms fusing into helium, suns exploding and dying—there's no *feeling* there. They're just horrid mechanical things."

In spite of himself, Viktor was amused. "Aren't you even curious?"

"About stars? Not at all! About the human heart, of course."

"But science—" Viktor stopped, shaking his head. "I don't see how you can talk that way, Frit. Don't you want to know things? Don't you want to have Balit understand science?" He waved an arm around the future nursery. "If it weren't for science, how could you and Forta have had a child?"

"Ah, but that's *useful* science, Viktor! That's worth knowing about—not like your worrying about whose lines are where in which spectra. It's good because it makes our lives better. But I'm not at all curious about why stars shine and what makes them hot—and least of all about where they've all gone—because there's nothing anyone can do about it anyway. Is there?"

By the time word came that Pelly was back in the habitats Viktor was beginning to feel as though he had seriously outstayed his welcome on Moon Mary. Balit was still loyal. Frit was unfailingly polite. Forta, at least, had a use for their guest; he borrowed Viktor for an hour or so almost every day to dance with him. Forta appreciated it, and for Viktor it seemed good exercise for his nearly healed leg, though Frit did not seem to approve. Viktor heard them talking, not quite out of earshot, and Frit was being reasonable. "Folk dancing? Oh, yes, Forta dear, but what is folk dancing, after all? It's simply what primitive people used to do when they didn't have professionals to watch. But you are an artist!"

"And you," Forta told him good-humoredly, "are a little jealous, aren't you?"

"Of course not! On the other hand, dear . . ."

And the rest of the conversation Viktor could not hear, which was probably just as well.

Viktor was leading Forta through the familiar, sweet Misirlou when the package arrived from Pelly. Viktor opened it with excitement—something from Nebo for him to study, something more informative than the broken bits and pieces like Balit's keepsake?

It was not from Nebo. It was human-made and very old. Pelly's message said, "This appears to have come from one of your old ships, Viktor. I thought you'd like to listen to it."

The last time Viktor had seen that object was on old *Ark*, just before the fatal attempt at landing a team of investigators. It was, in fact, *Ark*'s own black-box recording log.

It even still worked—more or less; someone had been repairing it, somewhere along the line, and much of the material was erased, much more so deteriorated in sound quality that Viktor could hardly make it out. But there was one tiny section that was loud and clear—and the voice that was speaking on the log was one Viktor knew well.

Jake Lundy. It was the voice of Viktor's rival speaking from the grave.

When Balit came in, an hour later, he found Viktor sitting over the log, listening once again to the voice of his long-dead rival. ". . . have now been in this ship for fifty-seven days," it was saying, the voice weak and cracking. "I can't hold out much longer. The others are dead, and I guess—"

That was all that was still intelligible.

Balit put his arm around Viktor in compassion. He listened to the tape with Viktor, then listened again. "I know how you feel, Viktor," he declared. "It must be awful, hearing your friend's voice when he's been dead for thousands of years."

Viktor looked at him without expression.

"Jake Lundy wasn't a friend," he said.

"Then why—"

But Viktor could not answer, because he couldn't find words to tell the boy how the voice of Reesa's long-dead lover had suddenly started a hopeless longing for the long-dead Reesa herself.

That night, dancing Misirlou again with Forta, Viktor found himself near to weeping.

"Is something wrong?" Forta asked worriedly.

Viktor just shook his head and went on with the dance. When Frit came in, looking faintly jealous at the sight of Viktor holding Forta, he said, "Listen, something's come up. I've been talking to

Nrina. She thinks we should come to visit her—look at the sketches and talk to her about Ginga."

The principal thought in Viktor's mind was that he was not, just then, ready to resume his affair with the woman who had brought him back to life.

When they reached Nrina's habitat she was there to greet them, proudly exclaiming over Balit's now blemishless forehead. "No brand! Oh, and you'll be making love first chance you get now, won't you?"

"Of course," Balit said sedately. Then Nrina whisked them off to her laboratory—all but Viktor. Viktor was not involved in the planning of the new baby. He was given the freedom of her quarters to wait for her pleasure instead.

It was a long wait. Then, when she did arrive, her words were not of love. For the first time in Viktor's experience of her, Nrina looked angry. "Do you know how much it *cost* Frit and Forta to dig up all those old records for you?"

He was taken aback. "They didn't say anything about the cost," he protested.

"Of course not. You were their guest."

Viktor said doggedly, "I'm really sorry, Nrina, but how was I to know it cost so much money? Nobody ever said anything to me."

"*Said* what it *cost*? Oh, Viktor! Did you really think that two sensitive, artistic, decent people like Frit and Forta would say anything so *vulgar*?"

"I'm sorry," he grumbled. And then, defensively, he said, "What does it matter? You people are closing your eyes to what's really important—what's happening to the universe."

He stopped, surrendering because he could see that she was looking at him with resigned incomprehension. She said, obviously trying to be reasonable, "But Viktor, you said yourself all these things were zillions of miles away and they took millions of years to happen. How can you call them 'important'?"

He ground his teeth. "Knowledge is important!" he barked. It was an article of faith.

Unfortunately, Nrina was not of his religion. She took a turn or two around the room, looking at him in bafflement.

Viktor did not like the feeling that he had committed a terrible social blunder. "I could get a job and pay them back," he offered.

"The kind of job you could get, Viktor," she said with a sigh, "would not pay them back in twenty years. What can you do?" She hesitated, then plunged in. "Viktor? Who are Marie, Claude, Reesa, and Mom?"

"*What?*"

"They are names you used to say. When you were feverish from freezer burn," she explained. "Sometimes you called me Marie and Claude, sometimes Reesa. And just at the beginning I think you said 'Mom.' Were these women you loved?"

He was flushing. "One was my mother," he said gruffly. "Marie-Claude and Reesa—yes."

"I believed it was that." She sighed, twirling a lock of his hair in her slim fingers. Then she looked at him seriously. "Viktor," she said, "I could design a woman like you if you wished. I could make one from your own genes, as I did with Balit for Forta and Frit. Or, if you can describe this Reesa and this Marie-Claude, I could make one like them. Or with the best qualities of both, if you wish. She would be physically of your kind, not as tall and slim as we are. Of course," she added compassionately, "it would take time. The embryo must gestate, the child grow—twenty years, perhaps, before she would be of mating age . . ."

He looked at her with a sudden shock. "What are you telling me?" he demanded. "Do you want to stop our, uh, our—"

She let him flounder without an ending to the sentence. When it was clear he couldn't find one, she shook her head affectionately. "Come to bed," she ordered. "It's late."

He obeyed, of course. And when they had made love, and Viktor rolled over to get some sleep, it seemed that it was only minutes before Nrina was poking at him.

It must have been later than he thought, because she was fully dressed, gauzy work robe over her cache-sex, hair pinned up out of the way. "Get up, Viktor," she ordered.

He craned his neck to blink at her. "What? Why?" It wasn't

uncommon for Nrina to have to get up early to work, but she didn't usually insist on his own rising.

She looked serious. "I want you to go to Newmanhome with Pelly," she told him.

He gaped at her. "Newmanhome?"

"He is leaving tomorrow," she said.

Viktor rubbed his eyes. He was having trouble taking in what she had said. "Are you angry because of the money?" he asked plaintively.

"No. Yes, but that isn't why. It is simply time for it to be over, that's all."

"But—but—"

"Oh, Viktor," she sighed. "Why are you being so difficult? You didn't think I would pair with you *permanently*, did you?"

Pelly's ship was as impressive inside as out—only a chemical rocket, to be sure, but a huge one. Viktor was impressed all over again at the richness of a society that could afford to build such vast, sophisticated machines for so little purpose.

To Viktor's surprise, Frit, Forta, and Balit turned up at the launching, Forta and Frit almost weeping as they kissed their son. It looked exactly like a farewell. "Balit!" Viktor cried. "What is this?"

"I'm coming with you," the boy said simply. Incredulous, Viktor turned toward the parents—and recoiled from the anger in their eyes.

"Yes, he is going to join you, Viktor," Frit said bitterly. "We have discussed it all night, but Balit insists. He is freed now; how can we stop him? But I cannot forgive you, Viktor, for putting these ideas in his head."

CHAPTER 27

In the middle of that feebly expiring universe, Wan-To suddenly felt almost young again. There was still nuclear fusion going on somewhere!

Then the last of the ancient memories fell into place, and his next thought was to curse himself.

He had been such a *fool*. Why hadn't he thought ahead? Why hadn't he planned for this? It would have been so *easy* for him to do this same trick on any scale he liked, to send whole galaxies of stars off in the long-term storage of fast-as-light travel, so that he would have billions upon billions of them ready for his use in this time of his need!

For that matter, why hadn't he built some sort of homing impulse into the matter-doppel's instructions, so that they could have returned to normal space nearby?

The list of charges Wan-To could make against himself had suddenly become almost endless, but he gave up on them as common sense reasserted itself. Self-recrimination wasn't really Wan-To's style. Anyway he had more exciting things to think about.

Yes, yes, the memories were clear. There were twelve stars, and they were still alive! Still even *young*! And all *his*!

True, they had been somewhat depleted by the drain of energies that had been needed to send them hurtling across the universe, and certainly they were now a terribly long way away—but they were *his.* He searched eagerly through his specific memories of that off-hand action. There was not much there, but he was certain that some of them had billions of years yet to go even on the main sequence—then they would be long-lived dwarfs for much longer than that.

Cheerful for the first time in many eons, Wan-To began the task of planning how to make use of this wholly unexpected new gift.

CHAPTER 28

Landing on Newmanhome again was a thrill for Viktor Sorricaine. For one thing, it was real spaceflight! The vessel was a real spaceship landing shuttle, and Pelly let him sit in the copilot seat as they brought it in. Just *being* on Newmanhome was an even greater thrill; it was home again. His real home. The place where he belonged—even though, shockingly, the place was no longer anything like the green and promising land he had grown up in. (Nothing green had lived through Newmanhome's ages of ice. Nothing was alive anywhere at all on Newmanhome, except what the habitat people had put there.) Yet Viktor even had friends there! Jeren was waiting eagerly for him, shy and dumb and devoted; and Korelto. Even surly Manett managed to grumble a greeting as he clasped Viktor's shoulder. His eyes, though, were fixed on little Balit as the boy was helped out of the lander and onto a carrying chair. "He's really Frit and Forta's kid?" Manett whispered. "He actually came with you? Fred! Then maybe something's really going to happen around here after all!"

"Sure things are going to happen!" Jeren rumbled loyally. "Viktor's here now!" Then he wheedled, "But leave him alone, you guys, all right? He needs time to get settled in, doesn't he? Now, look, Viktor, I fixed up a place for you. I can take you there any time. Are you hungry? I could make some rabbit stew—real rabbits, Viktor; we've got a whole flock of them breeding now ..."

Viktor hardly heard any of that. He was gazing around at the
planet he had left. It wasn't all depressing. Although the hills were
brown and bare, the bay was clear blue. So was the sky, with cotton-
ball clouds dotted out over the ocean. And there was definitely a
certain amount of life on Newmanhome again. Human life, anyway.
Practically the planet's whole population—nearly sixty people!—had
come to greet the new arrivals, like the citizens of any frontier town
gathered at the railroad station to see the train come in.

"I'd better help Balit," Viktor said—to no one in particular, to
all of them. He hurried over to where the boy was painfully levering
himself into the sedan chair, with a pair of squat, husky gillies standing ready to take up the carrying rods. Balit looked up at him,
trembling—partly with the effort of holding his head straight in
Newmanhome's gravity, to be sure, but also with sheer excitement.

"This is *wonderful*, Viktor," he breathed. And then he fumbled
a metal case from his pouch. "Hold still, please."

Viktor allowed his picture to be taken, then ordered parentally,
"Put your hat on. You don't know what sunburn can be like; you're
not used to it." As the boy obeyed, Viktor looked up. Pelly was
escorting a lean habitat man over to join them. The man was hob-
bling on two canes, and he had a blue beret pulled down almost to
his eyes. A woman, as tall and thin as himself but almost as pretty
as Nrina, limped after them.

"Viktor," said Pelly, "this is Grimler, and her husband, Markety. They're the ones who sent you the data you asked for."

"Tried to anyway," the woman said, giving Viktor a hug of
greeting. "I hope it was some use for you—I admire you so much,
you know."

While Viktor was still blinking in surprise at that, the man was
going on. "It's harder from the actual stores," Markety apologized.
"You'll see. We can take you there any time you like."

"Any time," the woman echoed hospitably. "Do you want to
go up there now?"

"Oh, *yes*," Viktor said.

It was a good thing they had built the datastore and the freezers adjacent to the power plant up in the hills instead of in Homeport itself. There wasn't any Homeport anymore. At least, there was nothing left of it that was visible. The place where the city of Homeport had once been was now at the bottom of the bay.

The bad thing, however, was that a hill was still a hill. To go up it took *work*.

Balit, Grimler, and Markety didn't even try to climb it themselves; that was what the gillie litter bearers were for. Their squat bodies were solid muscle; Nrina's arts had seen to that. Viktor envied them. His own muscles, softened by so many months in the soft gravity of habitat and Moon Mary, complained of the task of lifting a human body so far. Halfway up, Viktor had to pause to catch his breath.

When he looked around for familiar landmarks there weren't any. "I don't see the power plant buildings," he protested.

From beside him, Korelto said reasonably, "Of course you don't *see* them, Viktor. They got buried." He wasn't out of breath at all— of course, Viktor reflected, he'd had more time to get in shape on Newmanhome.

"But the plant's still running," Jeren assured him. "You can hear it if you listen, and the buildings are still there. And lots of the things in them are still okay. Come on, it's just another twenty minutes or so."

"Just give me a minute," Viktor said. He turned as the gillies brought Balit up next to him and set the chair down. The boy looked up at him, weary but grinning and game.

"Are we there yet, Viktor?" he asked. And then, without waiting for an answer, he pulled his camera out again in excitement. "Look up there! Aren't those things *clouds?*"

Viktor nodded, without answering. He was listening. Apart from the occasional sounds of the climbing party, the silence was almost absolute. A faint sigh of wind. Some distant machine noises from the little cluster of buildings at the foot of the hill, where Pelly's ship was being unloaded.

And—yes—a high-pitched, almost inaudible whisper from farther up on the hillside. The sound was familiar to Viktor, even after all the time that had passed. "Is that the power plant turbines I hear?" he asked.

From his own sedan chair, now coming up even with them, the man named Markety said, "Yes, of course it's the turbines. Are we going to stand here and talk or go on? I thought you people were used to this kind of drag. You two," he ordered Balit's gillies. "Pick the chair up and let's move."

"Do you want me to give you a hand, Viktor?" Jeren asked anxiously. "I know how I felt when I got back here, the first few days. Weak! I never felt like that before. But it'll pass, honest it will, Viktor."

"Of course it will," Viktor growled, panting hard, waving off the offer to help. The other thing about Newmanhome he had almost forgotten was that it could be *hot*. He was not only fatigued but sweating profusely when the trail turned. A shaft entrance lay ahead—something new; something dug recently to get down to something else long buried beneath the surface. Pairs of gillies were coming out of it, carrying freezer capsules.

"Let them pass," Markety called from behind. "They've got cargo to take down to the ship."

Viktor was glad to oblige. He gazed around, wondering. There was a time—oh, a long time ago, a *terribly* long time ago—when all this hillside had been green and sweet, and people had gathered around to picnic and dance and listen to old Captain Bu's speeches. This had to be the same place. But how sadly it had changed. He remembered that he had been there with Reesa and Tanya and the baby, before they married . . .

He had to look away, for his eyes were stinging. He saw Jeren looking at him worriedly and pulled himself together as the gillies lumbered past on their way downhill.

The turbine scream was louder now, unmistakable. There was another throbbing sound that was harder to identify, until Viktor saw a stream of muddy water gushing down alongside the trail.

Jeren saw what he was looking at. "That's from the pumps," he explained. "They have to keep pumping the water out, of course."

"Pumping?" Viktor repeated, and his heart sank.

For it had never occurred to him that freezing meant ice, and melting meant flooding.

Viktor turned to Markety, whose chair was just coming up behind him. "Is that why you had so much trouble retrieving the
data?" he demanded. "Because the datastores were all under water?"

Markety looked astonished, then, as understanding dawned, the
expression turned to compassion. "Oh," he said. "I thought you
knew that."

Viktor had not forgotten what homesteading a new
world was like, not entirely, anyway. What he had forgotten was
how much *work* it was.

Annoyingly, everyone he saw seemed to think that he had come
there for no other reason than to take part in the work—if not in
fact to oversee it. They did need overseeing. When Viktor explained
what a well was, and a septic tank, and why the former always had
to be dug uphill from the latter, Markety was almost pathetically
grateful. "How did you get along without me?" Viktor asked, half-
amused, half-aghast at these inept pioneers.

"Very badly, I'm afraid," Markety said at once. "We need you.
After all, you're the only person who's ever seen Newmanhome the
way it ought to be."

So, willy-nilly, Viktor was drafted into every project. The good
thing about hard, demanding work was that it kept one too busy
to dwell on defeats. Well, it almost did; but nothing could quite
wipe out of Viktor's mind the thoughts of those ruined stacks of
magnetic fiches that had once held the sum of human knowledge.
Meltwater had done what time alone could not. All the chambers
that had held the datastores had been under water. And even the
parts that had now been pumped dry were a soggy ruin; steel was
rust, silicon was cracked and crazed; everything was caked in mud.
To restore any of the lost information would be something like
burning a book in a crucible and trying to read its contents in the
smoke.

Meanwhile, there was the work.

The most important job on the reborn planet was providing
enough food to keep the people alive. Naturally, Pelly's ship brought
tons of food on every trip, and the first habitat visitors had installed
gillie-manned hothouses to grow the kinds of things they were used

to eating. It wasn't enough. The revived corpsicles, who were by far the greater part of Newmanhome's tiny population, had to find ways to feed themselves.

It was Manett who led Viktor to the scratched-out plot of hillside ground that was their first attempt at a farm. It was fortunate that Jeren's promise had been kept: Viktor's muscles had accustomed themselves to carry his full weight around again—there were aches, but they did their job. Even Balit was getting used to the demands on his artificial muscles, though on the trip to the farm plots Jeren carried the boy on his back.

As soon as they had reached the plot Jeren set the boy down and turned to Viktor, his face grinning with pride. "What do you think?" he asked modestly, waving at the irregular rows of green. "I didn't do all of it. Markety let us use the gillies for some of the work. And Manett helped, and some of the others."

Viktor studied the spindly shoots. The mere sight of growing things was a lift to the spirits, among so much bare desolation, but there was nothing there that grew higher than his knee, and nothing resembling fruit on any of it. He asked apologetically, "What are they?"

Jeren looked surprised. "Potatoes," he said, pointing. "All those right there. And there's carrots, and cabbage—you had some of that last night, remember? And we tried tomatoes and peppers, but they didn't come out real well."

"They came out *terrible*," Manett growled. "The carrots get all squashed and funny-looking, too."

"The rabbits like the green stuff, even if we can't eat it. Besides, the carrots taste all right," Jeren said defensively.

"They taste like carrots, sure," Manett agreed, "but even in the caves we used to grow carrots that were four times as long as those. What's the matter with them, Viktor?"

Viktor was conscious of Balit's eyes on him. "I wasn't ever a farmer, really," he apologized. No one said anything. They were waiting for him to go on. He said uncomfortably, "Has anybody tested the soil?" Blank looks gave him the answer. "They might need some kind of fertilizer," he explained. "Minerals or something. I wish we could get at the datastores. I'm sure they'd have all kinds of agricultural information."

"You know we can't do that, Viktor," Manett snapped.

Jeren pointed out, pacifically, "See, Viktor, none of us ever tried to grow anything out in the open, like this."

Viktor nodded in silence. He knew they were waiting for him to speak. He knew, too, that the most honest thing he could tell these people would be that he didn't know how to help them. He even opened his mouth to say as much, but Balit was speaking ahead of him. The boy said confidently, "Viktor will take care of it. Back on Moon Mary he told me lots of stories about when people were growing things on farms. Didn't you, Viktor? I remember you talked about irrigating the fields. And what was the other thing, something about seeding the ground with earthworms?"

"Well, yes," Viktor said unwillingly, "I saw all that kind of stuff done. But I never—"

He stopped there, looking around at the way they were hanging on his words. Even surly Manett was gazing at him with hope.

"But," Viktor corrected himself, "I, uh, I—" He looked around the field for inspiration, then finished, "I don't see any way of watering these crops. Some of the plants look pretty dry."

"It *rains* on them, doesn't it?" Manett growled.

"It only rained once in the last three weeks," Jeren corrected him. "Maybe Viktor's right. Look, there's plenty of water down there in the bay. We could take some of the pumps from the freezer—"

"No!" Viktor yelled, shocked. "That's *salt* water! That'll kill them."

"Oh, sure," Jeren said remorsefully. "All right, then there's a creek that goes down by the landing strip, how about that?"

But by then Viktor had an idea. "Why pump it uphill?" he asked. "There's all that water that's being pumped out of the power plant area. I saw it running down by the trail. We could get the gillies to dig a ditch, divert it to here. Or, even better in the long run, we could start a new farm, wherever the water comes down."

He stopped, because they were all grinning at him. Balit's face was shining with particular pride. "I told you Viktor would know," the boy informed the others. "Now what do we do about this fertilizer stuff, Viktor?"

Viktor thought for a moment. "I suppose if we sent some soil samples back to Nergal somebody could test them and tell us what to do," he said slowly. "Then, I remember we seeded earthworms. I don't imagine any of those survived the ice, but there might be some left in the freezers. We could look. If there aren't any there, maybe Nrina or somebody could make some for us. You have to have something like earthworms to get a good crop, because they lighten the soil and help things grow."

He stopped, because Balit was looking doubtful. "What is it?" he asked.

"Well, there's one thing I don't understand about that, Viktor," Balit said diffidently. "In school we learned about growing things, and nobody ever said anything about earthworms."

Viktor frowned, trying to remember what the farms in the habitats had been like. "Maybe they prepare the soil a different way on the habitats," he hazarded. "Probably they do—I'm sure the crops on the habitats don't grow in plain dirt. It's bound to be something artificial—really special—probably with all the minerals and so on that the plants need measured out exactly. But here we're talking about trying to restore vegetation to a whole planet, Balit. The earthworms would do it all for us, you see. And—yes, now that I think of it, you might need other kinds of bugs, too. Bees, for instance. Some kinds of plants have to have bees, to carry the pollen around so the seeds will develop."

He stopped, startled by the expressions of relief on every face.

"I told you," Balit repeated happily.

And Jeren said with pride, "I knew things would be all right as soon as I saw you get off the ship, Viktor."

By the time Pelly's ship took off again for the return flight to Nergal, Viktor had come to terms with his worst defeat . . . almost.

It wasn't easy to do that. The destruction of the data files meant the end of a lot of hopes for him, but the thought of bringing Newmanhome back to life provided a different kind of hope. Almost as good. Not quite.

But everyone around him seemed almost cocky with expectations for the future, even Pelly. In the last moments before takeoff,

Pelly took time out from shouting at the gillies as they finished loading the lander to clasp Viktor's shoulder awkwardly and say, "I'm sorry about your files, Viktor. Listen, if there's anything I can do—"

"Thanks anyway," Viktor said.

Pelly paused to study him thoughtfully. "You know," he said, "sometimes when things are at their rottenest something nice happens. Maybe something that you don't even expect. You could turn out to have a pretty happy life here, Viktor, with a little luck."

"I know that," Viktor said, summoning up a smile. It wasn't a smile of amusement or pleasure, but the kind of graveside smile a widow gives to the friends offering condolence. "Jeren's been telling me the same thing. You're both right, of course."

But it didn't feel as though they were right, and he was glad enough when Pelly had to break off his efforts at consolation to give orders to the gillies. And then, very quickly, Markety finished the last of his weepy farewells to his wife, who was going back to Nergal for a visit; and the last of the capsules containing corpsicles for Nrina's lab were stowed, and the gillies were herded away out of range of the rocket's exhaust, and Pelly waved a final good-bye from the port . . . and then the port was closed. Everyone retreated to safety, Jeren carrying Balit and anxiously urging Viktor on with them. The lander motors spilled out a little wisp of flame, then roared. The ship picked up speed as the noise became deafening— rolled away—began to lift—and was suddenly only a dot in the sky, disappearing over Great Ocean. Everyone was watching. No one spoke. Viktor caught a glimpse of Balit, staring wistfully at the vapor trails the lander had left behind, and behind him Markety, looking very tired and staring sadly after the disappearing ship that was carrying his wife away.

Then the ship was out of sight. The last fading thunder of its engines died away, and the silence of lonely, empty Newmanhome came in around them.

It was Manett who broke it. "Well," he said, his tone angry as he challenged them all, "now we can get back to digging those irrigation ditches."

Two weeks later the ditches were dug and a trickle of muddy water seeped into the soil of the farm plot whenever somebody, usually Jeren, lifted the flat panel that served as a gate. It hadn't rained, but the plants were already looking a little healthier. Korelto and half a dozen others were spending their days in the cryonics chambers, looking for the earthworms and bees that Viktor had prescribed, or for anything else that might be useful to their task—without much luck so far, but still hoping.

Viktor did not go with them for that. Viktor did not like being in the place where he had lain as a corpsicle for all those centuries; it was too much like visiting his own grave.

In any case, there were plenty of other things to keep Viktor busy, and some of them were even pleasant. One morning he sought Balit out and offered him a treat. "Markety's got an inflatable boat, and there's something I want to look at. How would you like to go out on the bay?"

Naturally the boy had only one answer to that. "Oh, Viktor," he sighed when they were afloat. "I didn't know people could go floating out onto all that *water*—without even getting *wet*! No one I know has ever done such a thing!" And he dabbled his bare feet into the water, squealing in pleasure at the unexpected cold.

Viktor pulled them a few hundred yards away from shore and then rested on his oars, looking about. Balit had his camera out again, taking pictures in sheer joy of everything he could find. But when Viktor looked at the same things—the barren hills, the empty skyline—it all seemed bare and hopeless. The idea of a living Newmanhome seemed like a mirage. Apart from the handful of revived corpsicles, no one seemed to care. Even Markety. If these were the most enterprising people alive, Viktor thought sourly—and people like Markety and Pelly had to be that, since they were the only ones who bothered to come here—then the human race was in bad trouble . . .

But the sun was warm, and the water gentle. The only breeze was mild and on-shore; there were no waves to speak of, and no risk of being blown out to sea. "What was it you wanted to see, Viktor?" Balit inquired.

"Look down into the water," Viktor ordered. "See if you can find anything that doesn't look natural." And then, as the boy leaned precariously over the side, Viktor pulled him back, laughing. "Don't fall in. You don't know how to swim yet."

"But there are some funny-looking things down there, Viktor. Are they what you mean?"

Viktor leaned over to look. It took a moment to be sure of what he was looking at, for they were nearly buried in mud, but then he nodded in satisfaction. "I thought they'd be there. They're Von Neumanns."

"What are Von Neumanns, Viktor?"

"Do you know the things that bring metals in from the asteroids? The things your grandparents use to manufacture things with? Those are Von Neumanns, too. These are the same kind of thing, only these don't travel in space—they feed on metals in hot springs under the sea. And it looks like they went right on doing it for a long time! There are thousands of them here, Balit." And he tried to explain how the Von Neumann nautiloids had gone out for untold centuries, even under the ice when Newmanhome was frozen, eating and reproducing, and then returning as their chemical sniffers sorted out the flavors of Homeport, as salmon did on Earth, and their tiny brains told them to return for harvesting.

"But there wasn't anyone here to harvest them," Viktor said somberly.

"So they're no good anymore?" the boy asked.

"Not at all! I'm glad to see they're really there. They could be pretty valuable, if we had any way to use them. Pure metals, already refined, all sorts of raw materials ..." He grinned wryly. "If we had factories we could do a lot of manufacturing. If we had food to feed the people to run the factories. If we had the people to grow the food to feed the people. If—"

He broke off as he realized Balit was holding the camera on him. "Come on, Balit, what are you going to do with all these pictures? Why don't you turn that thing off?"

"No, it's really interesting, Viktor," the boy protested. "What do you mean, if you had people?"

Viktor resigned himself. "All right, let's start from the beginning. The whole planet's bare, right? Which means there's no ground cover to hold the soil in place. So it's been washing down into the sea for a couple of centuries now, which means that if it isn't stopped fairly soon Newmanhome will *stay* dead." He paused for a moment, trying to remember the bright, promising early days of the first colony on Newmanhome. "So what has to be done, as soon as possible, is get some kind of vegetation going, all over the world. That means planting seeds—a whole planet's worth of seeds, Balit; millions of tons of them. I suppose they'd have to be sown from airplanes—if we had airplanes. If we had the seeds to sow. Then— are you sure you want to hear all this?"

"Please, Viktor!" the boy begged.

Viktor shrugged. "But we need people to do the work. Not only to sow the seeds planetwide, but to grow food to feed everybody doing it. And to build the planes, maybe; and before that to build the factories to build the planes. Balit," he said earnestly, "I've been through this before, and it's *hard*. When the first Earth ships landed here they had a few thousand people, and all kinds of machinery designed for every purpose you can imagine—and still everybody was working night and day for years. How many people are on Newmanhome now?"

"Sixteen," the boy said promptly. "I mean, sixteen from the habitats, plus forty-two like you, and all the gillies."

"Sixteen," Viktor said, nodding. "Plus forty-two like me. Of course there are a few thousand more—like me—in the freezers, but we can't do much about it. Manett says they tried to revive some on their own, but most of them died. Freezer burn, over all that time, the only chance is to take them back to the habitats where somebody like Nrina has all the equipment and can do the job right. No," he said, staring emptily at the brown hills, "I don't see how it's possible. We just don't have the resources to stay alive here, much less try to figure out—"

He stopped himself, then grinned at the boy. "I was all set to go on about Nebo and what happened to the universe again, wasn't I? And you've already heard enough about that."

"Never enough, Viktor," Balit said seriously, but he turned off his camera. Then he said, "There are plenty of people on the habitats, you know."

"Sure there are. They stay there, too. They don't come to crude places like this."

"I'm here, Viktor."

Apologetic, Viktor reached out to stroke the boy's shoulder. "I know you are, Balit. I appreciate it. But—let's be serious, Balit. How many people are willing to leave the habitats and come here? And the ones who do come, how long can they stay? You can't tell me you're *comfortable* here."

"It's not so bad, Viktor," the boy said, trying to sound as though he meant it. They were silent for a moment, then Viktor pointed down through the water.

"See those lumps down there? Not the Von Neumanns, the square-edged ones? I think those were the docks of Homeport. Of course, they're buried in mud now, but I'm pretty sure that's what they were."

"Wouldn't the docks be at the water's edge, Viktor?"

"They were. But that was before the ice pushed the land down; that happens, sometimes." Viktor looked around. "I'd bet," he said, "that we're floating right now just about over where Homeport was!"

He stopped paddling and gazed at the water, trying to reconstruct the plan of the old town. It could have been so. This could have been the waterfront—that patch back there where his home had been—up higher, near where the present shoreline lay, perhaps the old site of the schoolhouse where he had first met brash, red-headed, teen-aged Theresa McGann . . .

"Is something the matter, Viktor?" Balit asked anxiously.

Viktor blinked. After a moment he managed a grin. "It's all right," he said. "I was just remembering."

Balit nodded, studying Viktor's face. Then he said hesitantly, "Viktor? Has—ah—has Nrina called you?"

Viktor looked at the boy. "It wasn't Nrina I was thinking about," he said.

"I know," the boy said. "I just wondered." And then he said, "When we give Markety's boat back to him, do you think we should ask him to show us the Nebo things?"

"Oh, my God," Viktor said, shaking his head in astonishment. Because, incredible as it was, with all the other things that had been going on since he arrived back on Newmanhome, he had almost forgotten "the Nebo things."

The things weren't in a museum, or anything like one. They were in a shed on the outskirts of the little colony, and most of the space was full of junk that no one wanted but no one was willing to throw away. Since that exactly described the artifacts from Nebo, they were there—half-concealed behind a litter of broken dune-buggy wheels, stacks of cracked crockery dug out of the ice-age warrens, and other unnameable debris.

When, with Markety's help, Viktor and Balit got to the Nebo things they were not much better. The largest of them Viktor had already seen, on Nrina's desk machine, a lavender metal object as big as a man, more or less cubical in shape. Viktor poked it cautiously. It was very solid. "Why weren't these things taken to the habitats?" he asked.

Markety looked astonished. "They might be *dangerous*, Viktor. You know what happened on Nebo when people tried to poke into that sort of thing. They're better here, so that in case anyone does anything risky there would be less damage—I mean, to anything *important*," he explained.

"You mean if anybody tries to see what's inside them," Viktor said, nodding. "Maybe you're right, but it has to be done."

Markety's astonishment turned to worry. "I don't know if that's a good idea, Viktor."

"It doesn't have to be done here. Maybe they could be taken to some other part of Newmanhome—maybe we could work out some kind of remote-controlled machinery to try to open them up—I don't know, maybe the best place to do it is on Nebo itself. But in the long run we have to take the chance, because we do have to know!" As the words came out of his mouth Viktor heard, surprisingly, that he sounded as though he were actually growing excited again.

"Pelly says maybe it could be done in space," Balit offered eagerly.

"Just so it's done, I don't care how," Viktor said. "Those Nebo machines did things human beings couldn't even imagine—ever—even when they could travel from star to star."

Markety coughed. "We know they were pretty good at killing people, anyway," he conceded.

"I don't think those deaths were on purpose," Viktor argued. "Not all of them, anyway. At least we know that they actually helped some people—the ones I saw land on Nebo; we have the tapes to prove it. Yes, they died after a while, but they weren't simply murdered . . . God knows why," he finished. Then he went on. "I haven't said all of this even to you, Balit, but I have a kind of an idea. I think there's another civilization around—not human. At least, I think there was, and that they sent somebody to Nebo long ago—very long ago, even before the first *New Ark* landed here from Earth."

"Nobody's ever said anything like that, Viktor," Balit said worriedly. "Where would those people come from?"

"I don't know. The star Gold has planets, according to Pelly. Maybe the people who landed on Nebo came from one of those planets. Anyway, I think that for some reason—I can't even guess what it might have been—they constructed those machines on Nebo to tap the energies of our sun, and use them to accelerate this whole little group of stars."

"Why would they do that?" Markety asked good-naturedly.

"I have no idea. I said so. But we'll never have any hope of knowing 'why' unless we can figure out 'how'—and that means taking some of those machines apart to see what made them run!"

There was a moment's silence. Then Markety said diffidently, "Viktor? You don't mean you're going to, well, just try to break one of them open by yourself, do you?"

"If there was no other way, I would," Viktor said uncompromisingly.

"My," Markety said, pursing his lips. He studied Viktor's face uncomprehendingly, then sighed. "Well, let's talk about something more cheerful. Are you getting hungry?" he asked. "I was hoping you two would join me for lunch—I have some good things Pelly brought from home. What about it, Balit?"

But Balit wasn't listening. His eyes were on the door. "Viktor? Why is it getting so dark outside?" he asked.

Viktor turned to look. It was true; the bright day had turned gloomy. The sun was gone, and the clouds were thick and black. "Well," he said, "if we're going anywhere maybe we'd better hurry. I think it's going to rain."

Rain it did—the first big warm drops splashing on them even before they reached Markety's home, then crashing torrents when they were safely inside. Balit was delighted. He kept jumping up to the doorway, to take more and more pictures. It was coming down most imposingly, with thunder that made Balit hold his ears and lightning strokes that made him squeal—not in fear, or not all in fear, but mostly in a thrill of excitement at this unprecedented, unimaginable spectacle of the elements at work.

The lunch was all Markety had promised, and he was a cheerful host. "I do apologize for not knowing more about those Nebo things, Viktor," he said, steadying his hand to pour wine. It took both his hands to hold the decanter against Newmanhome's pull, one to support the other. "It was my wife, really, who was interested in them—Grimler, you remember? You met her when she arrived."

"Oh," Viktor said, trying to recapture the memory of a slim, pretty woman. "I think I did."

"And she went back with Pelly, unfortunately. I really miss her . . . But I can't say she knew very much about them, you know, it was just that she thought they were interesting."

"I'd like to talk to her anyway," Viktor said.

"And so you shall, as soon as she gets back." Markety sipped the wine, made a critical face, then beamed. "Yes, I think it's all right. Balit? If you can sit still for a moment I'd like to offer a toast to your wonderful parents."

"Just a minute," the boy called from the doorway, fascinated as he took his pictures of the bright violence in the sky and the muddy rivulets that were running down the walkway outside. "Oh, Viktor," he breathed, "I just can't wait till I send these pictures to my class—they'll be so *jealous*." Then he recollected himself. "You wanted to drink a toast, Markety?"

"To our great artists, Frit and Forta," Markety said, lifting his glass with ceremony. Then, when they had drunk, he added, "They're part of the reason Grimler sent the data to you, you know. Of course, she was interested anyway, but she would have done anything if Frit or Forta asked her to—any of us would! Did you see his new dance-poem about the kitten? No? Perhaps it was while you were in flight, but we saw the transmission here. *Marvelous!*"

"Did you know that Viktor has danced with Forta?" Balit put in.

Markety blinked at him in astonishment. "This Viktor? He dances? He's danced with *Forta*? Why, that's wonderful, Viktor," he said enthusiastically. "I had no idea. I really envy you, Viktor. Actually—" He permitted himself a rueful little smile. "At one time, you know, I wanted to be a dancer myself. I even hoped to study with Forta for a time. It didn't work out. He's kind enough to say he remembers me, but I think he's just being polite. I didn't really have the talent, I'm afraid, except in a very amateur way. And in this gravity of course I can't dance at all."

"Viktor can," Balit pointed out. "He grew up here."

Markety stared at the boy, then, with sudden respect, at Viktor. *"Really,"* he marveled. "Could you some time, Viktor? Perhaps after Grimler comes back? I know she'd be thrilled."

"Certainly Viktor will dance for you," Balit said graciously. "We'll need music, but I'll ask Forta to transmit some."

"Wonderful," Markety breathed, and if he had been a hospitable host before, now he was almost overwhelming. The scariness of Viktor's ideas about Nebo were forgotten. Markety selected the finest fruits for Viktor and Balit, and would not eat himself until convinced they were satisfied. But he was beaming. "Isn't this fine? The rain, and such good company, and all these things going on around us? I can't tell you how glad we are that we're here—Grimler and me—I mean, when she's here."

Maybe it was the wine. Certainly there had been a lot of it, but for whatever reason, Viktor couldn't help asking, "How come? I mean, I didn't think you habitat people liked planets all that much."

Markety looked both proud and embarrassed. "Grimler and I aren't like all the habitat people," he stated confidently. "I admit some of our friends think we're crazy, but—actually, we like it here. Grimler's said many times things are just too easy in the habitats. There's no *challenge.* And here's a whole planet that we can make live again—we just want to do our little part in bringing that about. So our lives will be worth something, do you understand? And she'd be here now, except for—"

Markety hesitated for a moment, then, grinning, pulled the blue beret off his head.

It was the first time Viktor had seen him bareheaded. Beside him, Balit made a startled little sound as they both saw that Markety's forehead was emblazoned with the fertility emblem.

"That's right," he said, with that same mixture of pride and embarrassment. "Grimler and I decided we even wanted to have our *own* baby! Not that there's anything wrong with what Nrina does," he added swiftly. "That's all very well for those who prefer it. But we wanted one who was our *natural* child, not programmed ahead of time, and so . . . well, we just went ahead and did it, the old-fashioned way. We made Grimler what you call 'pregnant.' "

"I'm amazed," Viktor declared truthfully.

"Oh, everybody is," Markety said modestly. "But that's what we want—someone who can grow up here on Newmanhome, and not have to take all those pills and injections, and—well, to be more or less just like you, Viktor!"

And that was when there was a scrambling at the door and Jeren turned up, soaked and glistening with rain, his face white with misery.

"Viktor!" he croaked. "The farm! We were just up there checking on everything, and it's gone! All of it! All the seedlings! They're just washed away!"

And behind him Manett came raging in. "Curse you, Viktor! You made us dig that ditch, and now it's just ruined *everything!*"

And when the worst of the storm was over, and bits of blue were beginning to appear in the east, and Viktor trudged up to look, every word had been true. A healthy stream poured through the new aqueduct, and right on through the little planted area. Not everything was gone, quite. But only a few rows highest up, farthest from the irrigation ditch, survived; everything else was furrowed and glistening mud.

"We should have directed the ditch into some kind of holding pond," Viktor said remorsefully. "And we shouldn't have planted on a hillside like this in the first place—I didn't think about erosion. Especially with all that bare ground up the hill." He shook his head in self-reproach. "I should have known," he said.

"Damn right you should," Manett snarled.

———

The next day it was as though the storm had never been, the sky cobalt, the sun warm, hardly a cloud in the sky.

But the storm's traces had not gone away. It wasn't just the farm. The street of the little community was ankle deep in brown, gluey mud. Nothing with wheels could move in it. Even the gillie litter bearers could make little headway, their furred feet turning into balls of clinging, sticky stuff; the habitat people painfully picked their way along, one slow step at a time, when they had to go out. Most of them chose to spend the day indoors.

Yet Balit was entering the communications shed at the end of the street. Viktor saw the boy and felt a moment's surprise, but he was talking to Jeren. "We'll have to find a new place for the farm," he said. "On a level. Preferably with some sort of a ridge between it and the hills, so if there's a flood it'll be diverted away from the plants. And near enough to a stream so we can irrigate."

"I don't think we can go looking for a place today," Jeren said doubtfully.

"No, not until the ground dries out a little," Viktor agreed. "And we'll have to do something here, too. I don't suppose we can pave the street, but maybe we could plant grasses all around the village to hold the soil when it rains."

"We can do that," Jeren agreed, looking over Viktor's shoulder. "Viktor? I think Balit's waving to you."

When Viktor turned, he saw it was true. When he trudged his way to the communications shack, the mud sucking at his feet at every step, the boy was bubbling with pleasure. "Viktor, come inside, please. Right away! I've just had a message from Moon Mary that I want you to see!"

There was no denying Balit's excitement. Viktor supposed it would be another loving communication from Frit or Forta, or both of them; for those came almost every day.

It was neither Frit nor Forta. When the picture came on it was a cluster of Balit's schoolmates, laughing and excited. They weren't in their classroom. They were gathered around a plot of ground with bright-green, healthy-looking seedlings poking out of it. "See, Viktor? They did what you said," Balit said proudly.

"What I said?"

"That we should have the soil analyzed. Pelly had some clods on the cryonics capsules he was bringing back, so I asked my school to take it on as part of their project."

"*What* project?" Viktor demanded.

"They've taken on Newmanhome as a project," Balit explained. "Not just the soil—that's only part of it. But they had it tested to see what it needed, and then they added things. Look at the difference now!"

Viktor stared at him, incredulous. "One little class of kids did that?"

"They're not just kids, Viktor—they're as old as I am. Besides, Grimler helped."

"Grimler? Markety's wife?"

"Yes, of course. She's there, too; you'll see her in a minute. And it wasn't just my class, anyway," Balit declared. "All over the habitats there are schools that have Newmanhome projects. You wanted to know what I was doing with all the pictures I took? Half the schools in the orbits have been watching them. All the kids are getting into it, Viktor—and, look, there's Grimler now!"

Indeed, there she was, slim as ever, looking radiant. "Pelly's going to bring two tons of the 'fertilizer' stuff on his next trip, Balit. And, oh, has Markety told you the good news? He's a boy," she said, glowing with pleasure. "Perfectly healthy, and he is going to have Markety's hair and eyes. Isn't it *wonderful?*"

"Well, I'll have to congratulate Markety," Viktor said with warmth. "I'm delighted, only—" He was staring at the woman on the screen. "Had she had the baby already?" he asked, gazing at Grimler's flat midsection. "I didn't think there was time—"

"Oh," Balit said, looking faintly repelled, "it isn't *born* yet. I mean, honestly, Markety and Grimler certainly wanted to go back to the old ways, up to a point, but not for Grimler to have to *bear* it. No, the reason Grimler went back was so dear Nrina could remove it and check it for defects and so on, and then let it come to term properly; it'll be a season or two yet before they have it."

The boy turned off the picture. "Aren't you pleased about all this, Viktor?" he asked anxiously.

Viktor thought about it. "Of course I am," he said, when he was sure he meant it. "Only—"

"Only what, Viktor? Is something wrong?" And when Viktor didn't answer Balit sighed. "Never mind. But, honestly, I think things are going to go a lot better now."

As a matter of fact, they did. Not well enough to lift Viktor out of the shadowy depression that hung over him; well enough so that there was, actually, progress in the things that mattered to the community.

As soon as the ground was dry enough Viktor and Jeren found a spot that was level enough to suit Viktor's strictures. It was protected by a rise just above it, which, he thought, would divert any future floods; and the gillies began grading it for planting at once.

Viktor was on the scene every day, prowling around worriedly when he wasn't manning a shovel himself, trying to remember what things had been like. It was Viktor who decided they needed to heap up a berm of earth around the farm plot, to retain rainfall when it came, but needed also to gate it, so that if the rains were too heavy they could drain standing water off the plots. It was Viktor who demanded a catalogue of every decipherable label of stored genetic materials in the freezer, poring over them to see if he could figure out which might be plants they could use and which would turn out to be merely some peculiar subspecies of cactus or jungle creeper or moss that someone once had thought might sometime be useful, or at least desirable, somewhere—under some conditions—but could do nothing to feed them now.

Viktor kept himself busy. Harshly he told himself that the absence of hope was no reason at all to stop *trying*. Funnily, it seemed to work.

Whenever there was some good development, whenever Viktor found himself tempted to optimism again, he tried his best to quell the feeling. He didn't want hope. He didn't want the disappointment that hope would bring. He was often the only dour face in an assembly of smiles. Jeren, Balit, Korelto—even Manett and Markety, in their own very different ways—they were all charged up with the excitement of bringing a whole planet to a new birth. Viktor tried not to be. After all, he knew exactly what that was like, for he had lived through it once already, in those first frontier days, thousands of Newmanhome years before.

"But don't you see, Viktor?" Balit said reasonably, in a break between work sessions. "That just means that you, of all people, ought to know that everything we're hoping for can really happen!"

Viktor didn't answer. There was no point in telling the boy the other things he knew—for example, how great the differences were. When the ships from Earth had landed on Newmanhome the colonists they carried had been chosen people. They had been trained and equipped for the job. They had all of Earth's technological knowledge base transported with them to fall back on. More than that, they were all *young*, and full of the juices of hope—and, most important of all, the planet they conquered wasn't a corpse. It was already a fully living world with an existing biota of its own.

And none of that was true now.

So Viktor refused to hope. When Manett, glowing, told him that Dekkaduk was going to bring them a whole revivification system for the remaining corpsicles in the deep freeze, Viktor's congratulations were perfunctory. When Markety bashfully begged permission to name his forthcoming son after him, Viktor refused to be touched. When Balit announced with delight that a dozen schools had clubbed together to launch a new space telescope— maybe even to settle the question of whether Gold's planets had any possible inhabitants—Viktor's heart trembled for a moment, but he quelled it.

But when Balit came shouting his name—

When Balit came shouting for Viktor, what he was saying was, "Come quickly! She's called! It's Nrina!" And when Viktor came stumbling out of his workroom, rubbing his eyes, it wasn't just Balit. Markety was there, face transfigured with excitement, calling, "Go to the communications shack right away, Viktor!" And Jeren was there, blinking back tears, babbling, "I wasn't *sure*, Viktor! I thought it was her, but I didn't want to say." And Balit was saying, "And there was freezer damage, so Nrina wouldn't let us tell you until she was sure it would be all right—"

But then, when Viktor got to the communications shack, finally daring to hope, his heart in his throat, the face that looked out at him from the screen was the well-remembered one, and what she was saying was, "Hello, dear Viktor. They didn't like me any better than they liked you, you see, so they popped me in the freezer, too . . . and, oh, Viktor, I'm all right now, and I'm coming *home.*"

CHAPTER 29

The eons of stagnation were over for Wan-To. He was not merely busy—busier than he had been for at least some sextillions of sextillions of years—he was in an absolute fury of action.

It might not have seemed that way to a normal Earth human being—if there had been such a person to observe him, if observation of Wan-To had been possible in the first place. Wan-To had no way to move *fast* anymore. A single thought took him weeks. To make a plan required centuries. If the imaginary Earth human could have known what Wan-To was up against, the spectacle might have reminded him of a some Earthly watchmaker, feverishly trying to assemble the most delicate of clockwork in a desperate rush to save his life—and trying to do it, moreover, while he was submerged neck-deep in quicksand. For that was how it was for Wan-To. At every step he was impeded by the thick, suffocating medium of the dead star he inhabited. Actually Wan-To was worse off than even the drowning watchmaker, because at least the watchmaker retained his memories, while the particular skills Wan-To needed now were no longer part of his active consciousness. They had been "put away" long before. That was one part of the price Wan-To had had to pay for continued existence in the feeble energies left to him in the dying star, for to save energy he had long ago had to download immense portions of himself and his memories into a kind of standby storage. So first of all he had to find and reawaken those parts; it was as though the watchmaker had to find his instruction manual before he could fit the first gear to its bearing.

It was not enough for Wan-To to make the decision to cut himself loose from the decay of his dying star and go off to revel in the hot energies of those distant, invisible suns. Making the decisions was quick enough. The hunt for the "how" of doing it was much longer.

Wan-To knew the starting point, of course. He would have to reconstitute himself as a pattern of tachyons. *Fast* tachyons, which fortunately were low-energy ones. It was a pity, he reflected, that he couldn't use the extreme minimum-energy tachyons that were the fastest of all. Unfortunately, that was impossible; the minimum-energy tachyons couldn't carry enough information to encompass all of Wan-To. No matter. The ones that were available would do the job. He would copy himself onto a tachyon stream and make his way to this unexpected oasis of life among the desolation.

There wouldn't be much difficulty in finding his way to the little cluster of surviving stars. The sensors had not only transcribed the message; they had very accurately recorded the direction it came from. All he had to do was backtrack. Once he got anywhere near that little cluster of living stars they would be easy enough to find, for they would be bright beacons of light, the only light in a dark and entropied-out universe—beacons of hope for Wan-To.

Unfortunately, even low-energy tachyons took energy to make. That meant some pretty drastic economies for Wan-To. For quite a long time—some tens of thousands of years, he calculated—he would have to shut most of himself down. He would have to eliminate every possible activity except those barely necessary to keep him alive in a sort of standby state, so that he could hoard that pitiful trickle of energies from dying protons, storing it up to use in one prodigal burst that would send him to his resurrection.

Then even the trip itself would take measurable time. Even with the highest velocity tachyons that could do the job, say those moving at some large exponent of the speed of light, it would surely be a matter of some thousands of years. How many thousands he could not say until he got there; the location he had was only a direction. It gave no hint of distance, but there was no doubt that in this sprawled-out emptiness the distance would be considerable.

But, oh!, at the end of that immense journey . . . Wan-To had never felt such anticipatory joy. It was almost enough—no, he told himself, of course it was far *more* than enough—to make up for the great pain of what he had to do to prepare himself for it. For that was no less than the amputation of large parts of his memory, of his knowledge—of huge sections of everything that made up what was left of Wan-To himself. They were excess baggage. However treasured, they could not be taken along. Like any desperate refugee, Wan-To had to sacrifice everything that was merely dear to him for what was wholly essential.

CHAPTER 30

When Pelly's ship brought Reesa to her waiting husband on Newmanhome she did not come alone.

Of course, the only person Viktor saw in those first moments was Reesa herself—familiar Reesa, dear Reesa, loved and lost and restored Reesa. When she came out of the lander she was as warm and solid in his arms as she had ever been, in spite of everything. But the ship was heavy laden. Dekkaduk was on the same lander, with all his equipment to revive corpsicles on the spot and heal whatever had happened to them in their icy millennia—those who could be healed at all, anyway. So were Balit's grandparents, come to visit from their manufacturing habitat, grotesque in their temporary muscles but excited as teenagers at what they were doing.

Pelly's lander had to make three trips to bring down all the cargo that time. There wasn't room in his spaceship's hold for everything. Some of their larger, ruder, sturdier things had made the voyage from Nergal strapped to the outside of Pelly's ship. It was a slow trip, and cranky piloting for Pelly, with all that added mass. It wasn't just Dekkaduk's defrosting clinic. The grandparents had not come empty-handed, but with thirty tons of equipment from their factory habitat, seeds of a machine shop to begin working the treasures the Von Neumanns had patiently brought back to Homeport. Nor did Markety's wife, Grimler, want their son growing up in a world without conveniences. So she had provided, among other things, three additional wheeled vehicles and small aircraft—now at last the people on Newmanhome could explore more of their re-born world!

For Viktor, falling peacefully asleep that night with Reesa breathing gently on his shoulder as she slept by his side, it was not just another day, it was the start of a new calendar, the beginning of another new life—and maybe, he thought, the best of them all.

In the second year of that private new calendar the human population of Newmanhome passed a thousand—nearly a hundred of the newcomers being people just arrived from the habitats, young ones mostly—and Grimler's baby was born out of its test tubes and brought to join them, and Jeren found a wife. In the third year Jeren's son added to the population—now nearly doubled again—and the machines that Balit's grandparents had brought had built the machines that built the machines that were now building vehicles and pumps, earthmovers and cranes, engines and appliances made on Newmanhome itself. The new farm plots withstood the worst of the drenching spring rains and flourished, and Newmanhome was feeding itself. And in the third year . . .

In the third year Balit went back to his home on Moon Mary—"Only for a short visit, Viktor," he said earnestly. "Believe me, I'll be back—" and almost as soon as he had arrived he was sending messages to Viktor. "Come to see us here, please. With Reesa, of course. Everyone's excited about the idea of seeing you!"

And, of course, on Pelly's next trip back to Nergal Viktor and Reesa went with him.

        For Reesa, of course, it was all a wonderful new thrill. She had never seen the spindly, graceful homes of Moon Mary—had hardly seen even the habitat where Nrina had coaxed her back to life, for as soon as she had been well enough she had been on her way to Newmanhome and Viktor.

It was more than a tour. It was very close to a Grand Procession. They were met on Moon Mary by more than a thousand people. Frit and Forta were in the very foreground, of course, taking turns to hug Viktor and Reesa when Balit left either long enough to give them a chance. Nrina was there, too—as she pressed herself fondly

against Viktor he glanced worriedly at Reesa's face; but Reesa only
put her own arms around the slim woman, and if there was any
jealousy there, or resentment, it never came to the surface. Some of
the others Viktor recognized, or almost recognized—Balit's old
schoolmates, some of the friends and family members from Balit's
coming-of-age party—but there were hundreds, *many* hundreds,
more he did not know at all. "I have some surprises for you, Viktor," Balit said proudly, pulling a slim young woman out of the
throng. "This is Kiffena. Do you remember her? She was in my
class when you visited, and we're going to be married."

She came willingly enough to Viktor, who naturally put his
arms around her. He did not remember her out of the gaggle he
had met at Balit's school, but she was certainly a pretty little thing.
As he hugged her in greeting he was surprised to feel the corded
muscles in her lean body—preparing for Newmanhome? Yes, of
course, that would be it, he thought; Balit had promised he would
be back, and certainly it would not be alone. Grinning, Viktor
slapped the boy—no, the *man* now, certainly—on the back. To the
girl he said, "You'll be a wonderful couple."

"We know you'll be very happy," Reesa said.

Then the girl moved her lips for a moment and said, "We know
we will be happy, too."

Viktor blinked at her in astonishment, for she hadn't spoken in
the tongue of the habitats, but in old English. She grinned. "I had
to learn it for my work," she said, half-apologetically.

"Well, she really is a surprise, Balit," Viktor said. "And a very
nice one, too. Congratulations."

Balit looked astonished. "Oh, no, Viktor. Kiffena isn't the surprise. Kiffena is the one who's going to *tell* you the surprise—one
of the surprises, anyway. But let's go home now, please? After dinner we can talk in peace."

Frit and Forta had prepared a handsome meal. "Nothing elaborate," Frit said modestly, handing around grapes the size
of a baby's fist, "for it's just family, you know."

"I'm really honored to be a member of this family," Reesa said,
and took Frit's hand to kiss it before she let him go on with the

grapes. "Balit's been a really good friend to us on Newmanhome, and—" Suddenly she was startled, almost panicked, as the room swayed under her. "Dear God! What's *that*?"

Viktor, after a moment's shock of his own, laughed at her. "I forgot to tell you about earthquakes. Moon Mary does this kind of thing every once in a while."

"But we're perfectly safe here," Forta said reassuringly. When he was sure that Reesa was over her startlement, and everyone had had everything they wanted from the meal, he stood up again. "I've got to practice," he sighed. "I'm going to perform a new dance—I hope you'll enjoy it, Viktor and Reesa, because it's partly for you. But I won't dance it properly if I don't rehearse it again, so, Frit, will you come and count for me while I work at the bar? You'll forgive us, won't you, Reesa?"

"Of course," Reesa said politely. But her eyes were amused, and when Balit's parents were gone she turned to him. "They're leaving us alone on purpose, aren't they?" she asked. "Does this have anything to do with those surprises you were talking about?"

Balit leaned back, his eyes twinkling. "You are very clever," he said. "You are also correct. Let me begin by telling you about Kiffena. She is a specialist in datamachine architecture."

"I didn't know," Viktor said, smiling across the table at the pretty young woman. "In fact, I didn't know there were any people like that at all."

"I began the study when Balit was sending all those exciting stories back to us," the girl said, smiling back. "It seemed such a pity for all that information to be lost."

"She's been studying the datastore, Viktor," Balit said with excitement. "It may be that not everything was lost."

That stopped Viktor. "What are you talking about?" he demanded.

Kiffena said with pride, "Balit sent me some of the data fiches from the store. I've managed to reclaim most of one fiche and part of three others, Viktor. They were magnetically stored, you see. Most of the magnetism was lost because of flooding, but there is a little residual—sometimes too little to make out, but sometimes not."

"It's not about astrophysics, though," Balit apologized.

"No," the girl said, shaking her head. "I'm not sure what the

main fiche is about, Viktor. We tried to have it translated, but some
of the words just don't make sense. Look."

And she keyed Balit's desk and displayed some sections of what
looked like a printed book.

"Oh, I know what that is," Reesa said suddenly. "It's case law.
I mean, it's what judges decided in some lawsuit or criminal trial,
long and long ago. People used to worry about those things a
lot, back on Earth."

"But that's wonderful, Kiffena!" Viktor said. "If you can get
anything at all out of that mess, maybe we can get some of the good
stuff. You said you unscrambled parts of three others?"

"I don't know if they're much better," she admitted ruefully.
"One was something about history. Have you ever heard of a man
named Artvasdes? He was what they called the 'king' of something
called 'Armenia' on Earth, long ago, and he had a war with someone
named 'Cleopatra.' "

"I've heard of Cleopatra," Viktor said. "Not the other
fellow, no."

"And then there's a story about some people that, really,
Viktor, seemed to spend an awful lot of time worrying about
things that didn't really matter—it's called *Remembering Bygone
Times*—"

"*Remembrance of Things Past*. Marcel Proust," Reesa said, laughing. "I read that once."

"You said there was more?" Viktor asked.

"Yes," said Balit ruefully. "That really looked good for a while,
Viktor. It had a lot of data about Jupiter, Venus, the Sun, the
Moon—the Old Earth Solar system—and about a number of
asterisms—"

"The fiche called them 'constellations,' " Kiffena corrected him.

"Constellations, then. Groups of stars as seen from Earth. They
were called things like Libra and Sagittarius and Aries. We thought
it might be something like a child's primer on astronomy."

"But what it was," Kiffena said ruefully, "was some sort of
magical system for forecasting events."

"I think it's called 'astrology,' " Viktor said.

"I would have liked to try it out," Kiffena said, "but of course
we don't have any of those planets or constellations any more."

"But that's *wonderful*," Viktor cried, suddenly realizing what all this meant. "Do you think you can restore much of the store?"

Balit looked downcast. "Not much, Viktor," he said regretfully. "I picked out some of the best-preserved fiches to send Kiffena. Most of it is just—well, pulverized."

"But a lot of it, yes, Viktor," Kiffena said encouragingly. "The thing is, it's not organized anymore, so we can't pick out one section—say, astronomy—and work on that part. There's no way to know what any particular fiche holds until we start to restore it."

Viktor shook his head wonderingly. "I had no idea," he said. "How did all this happen?"

"Balit," Kiffena said, hugging the young man proudly. "Balit made it happen. Didn't you know he was sending back reports every day?"

"I knew he was taking a lot of pictures, yes."

"Pictures of everything that happened, Viktor! It was so exciting for us in the school to see—well—*thunderstorms*! And rainbows, and swimming in the ocean, and clouds, and—everything. And then, of course," she said happily, "we all got interested. That's when I began studying datastore architecture, Viktor. We all began things like that, and in the other schools—"

Viktor blinked at her. "What other schools? I only went to yours."

"But of course we didn't keep Balit's reports to ourselves, Viktor," she said patiently. "No, not at all. Half the schools in the world were getting them—all over the habitat system and on all four moons. Different groups took on different projects, and even some of the grown-ups got interested."

"Newmanhome," Balit said sincerely, "was the most interesting thing that ever happened to us, Viktor. And, of course, with all those people taking it up, a lot got done."

Viktor looked at the boy. "I see that," he said. "Well, do you have any more surprises?"

Balit grinned at him. "A few," he said. He keyed the desk again, and a big torpedo-shaped object appeared. "This," Balit said, "is sort of like what you call our Von Neumann machines, only bigger. It's going to go to Gold."

Reesa blinked at him. "The star?"

"That's right, Reesa, the star—the one that we think has planets. Viktor thinks maybe the machines on Nebo came from Gold, so we're sending this automatic spaceship out to survey it and come back to report. Of course," Balit added ruefully, "it will take a while. Gold's nearly eleven light-years away, and this ship can't even get up to the speed of light."

"But really, Viktor," Kiffena said, "those planets don't seem inhabited anyway."

"So this ship is just to make *sure*. And then there are a couple smaller ones—" He keyed the desk again, and three smaller torpedos appeared. "—which will orbit Nebo, keeping a watch on it before someone lands again."

"Lands again!"

"Oh, yes, Viktor," Kiffena said comfortably. "I think I will, if nobody else does. After all, those machines seemed to operate automatically, didn't they? So they had to have some sort of data storage and control systems. And decoding their architecture shouldn't be that much harder than trying to restore your Newmanhome store."

Viktor stared at her, then at Balit. He was almost in a daze. "I had no idea," he said. "I can hardly believe it."

"Believe it, Viktor," Reesa advised him. "When a few million bright young people get excited about something, a lot can happen."

Balit grinned at them, his arm around Kiffena. "And most of it," he said, "is still *going* to happen."

They didn't stay for Forta's new dance. They couldn't. The messages from Newmanhome were too urgent and too imploring—for, although there were a couple of thousand people now alive on the planet and busy about the work of bringing it back to life, Viktor and Reesa were the only two who knew what it should be.

They didn't return empty-handed, either. In the cargo hold of Pelly's ship were forty new artificial wombs for Dekkaduk's laboratory, to speed up new births; and genetically improved strains of kelp to seed the empty seas; and a dozen species of tailor-made fish to feed on the kelp when it had had a chance to grow. One of the school groups had taken on the problem of seeding the bare South

Continent, and so in the cargo hold of Pelly's ship were two new little airplanes specially designed for dropping pelleted seeds of specially designed ground-cover grasses. Kiffena's group had given her a ton and a half of instruments to go on with the work of trying to recapture lost data from the files. Balit had persuaded a dozen youngsters, from his school and others, to come to study the fascinating and unprecedented subject of Newmanhome's weather, and naturally they had a ton or two of meteorological instruments of their own. Once again Pelly's ship was grotesquely deformed, with odds and ends of gear stuck to it all through the flight from Nergal, and it took four trips in the landing shuttle to get it all to the surface. And then, somehow, time had to be found to get all those things started . . . and to plow new farmland to feed the growing population . . . and to find new geothermal sources away from Homeport so that more power plants could be built so that other little communities could be launched elsewhere on the barren world . . . and to do—to do *everything*, really, and to do it all at once.

Everyone else was almost as busy, of course—with the work of resuscitating the planet, and with their own affairs, too. Every week a dozen or so newly awakened people came wonderingly out of Dekkaduk's thawing pens to join in the great task, and of course the pressure was intense to ensure that many of them were female. Families began to happen again on Newmanhome. Jeren's tall wife was bulging at the belly—neither Jeren nor she had been willing to wait for a turn at the artificial wombs. Markety's baby was walking sturdily where his parents still sometimes tottered. The freezers were still nowhere near emptied; each trip of Pelly's ship brought more people from the habitats, then went back; and yet the principal element in the population growth was already beginning to be newborns.

And then Reesa sprang her bombshell.

As they lay spooned together in bed, at the end of one long, wearying day, she whispered to the back of his neck, "Viktor? Are you asleep?" And then she went on quickly. "There's something on my mind."

"Oh?" he said—not wanting to say yes, sure, he'd noticed her frequent abstraction, supposing it to be the shock of coming to this new, unexpected and highly confusing new life.

But then she said, "I talked to Nrina while we were on Moon Mary."

"Oh," he said, in quite a different tone. He was at once wide awake. "Reesa, darling," he said, guilty, placating, "I hope you understand—I mean, I thought you were *dead*."

But her finger was over his lips, and she was laughing at him. "You're always talking when you should be listening, Viktor dear," she told him. "I'm not interested in what you did while I was dead. Only I'm not dead anymore, you see, and Nrina—Nrina took me aside to tell me something. She said she had cell samples from both of us. She said it didn't matter, of course, if I couldn't bear a child myself anymore, because I wouldn't have to. Not as long as she had the samples from both of us. She wondered if you and I wanted—"

She stopped there. Viktor squirmed around on the bed to face her in the gloom. Then, looking him in the eye, she finished, "A baby."

"Oh, my God," Viktor whispered softly. He was silent for a long moment. A baby! A baby would not replace lost Shan and Yan and Tanya and little Quinn, but still . . . "What did you tell Nrina?" he asked.

He was not surprised to see her cheeks were damp. "I told her we'd think about it, Vik. And I'm thinking about it very hard right now."

When Forta performed his new dance the whole community took time off to watch.

It wasn't Forta in the flesh, of course. Forta in the flesh was still millions of miles away, on the moon of ruddy Nergal. But Forta in the live broadcast from his own stage on Moon Mary was still wonderful, brilliant Forta, and he danced beautifully. Viktor saw with pleasure that there were traces in Forta's dance of the Yemeni step and the dip and curtsy Viktor had taught him. But there was more to it—so much more!—that was all Forta's own genius: grace and passion, yes, and courage and hope, too.

When it was over Forta returned to the cameras to say, breathless and happy, "I've dedicated this new dance, 'The Greening of Newmanhome,' to my son, Balit, and his bride, Kiffena, and most of all to our dear friends Viktor and Reesa and all those who join them in the real greening that is going on on Newmanhome now. All of us wish them well!"

Of course, there was a party to follow the performance, a happy one that lasted a long time. When it was over Viktor could not sleep. He got up from the bed where Reesa was peacefully smiling in her slumber and walked out into the dark streets, gazing up at the five lonely stars in the black sky.

Lonely . . .

What had *happened* to everything? Viktor scowled at the unanswering sky. He walked past the communications shack, one of the few lighted structures in the little settlement, down toward the water. Behind him he heard a door close, but he didn't turn. He stopped a few yards from the edge of the bay. There was nothing to be seen out over Great Ocean, not even a line of horizon, only darkness. Near his feet the little waves peacefully ran up the gravel and retreated, with a sighing sound.

Behind him Balit's voice said, "Viktor? I thought that was you. I called Forta to congratulate him on his performance, and I've just got his answer. He's been so busy, Viktor! He said he's been getting calls from all over the habitats—not just fan calls, calls from people wanting to know how they could help us here!"

Viktor turned and peered at the gangling young man. "That's nice," he growled.

Balit blinked at him but went on enthusiastically. "Yes, and do you know what they've done? Three of the other schools got together, and they've launched a new observatory! A really big one this time. Big mirrors and radio webs—it'll be looking for infrared and radio and gamma radiation and all those things you've been talking about. And Forta says they're even talking about moving one of the habitats, or building a new one, in orbit around Newmanhome!"

He broke off, aware that Viktor was not matching his pleasure. "Is something the matter, Viktor?" he asked worriedly.

Viktor flung his arm up toward the black sky. "Look," he said. "It's all gone! The whole universe, it's simply grown old and died on me!"

Balit was silent for a moment. "That might be," he admitted.

"But really, Viktor—don't you remember all the things you've told me? That's *there*. This is *here*. Our own sun isn't old. It's got billions of years left—much longer than all the time life's existed in this system."

"I know that," Viktor said wearily.

"But, Viktor—what does it matter what happened to the rest of the universe?"

"It matters that I don't *know* what happened," Viktor said tightly. "And I never will! Oh, it's wonderful that Kiffena's trying to patch up some of the old records, and people are starting to look for new answers again, and—it's all wonderful, I admit it! But it's all taking so *long*. And even if sometime people do find out what was going on on Nebo, and what caused our stars to do what they did—I won't live long enough to find it out!"

"But Viktor," Balit said lovingly, "I will."

CHAPTER 31

$\mathbf{W}$hat Wan-To was doing was pruning himself—as surgically as any horticulturist trying to save a winter-struck shrub.

Wan-To didn't call it that, of course. He had no experience of horticulture. He had never seen a flower garden in the dying fall of a year, when the plants prepare themselves for the death of winter; roots are allowed to die, stalks wither, flowers turn brown and fall to the ground—everything is sacrificed to the growth of the healthy seeds that will bring the new plant to life again when the soil warms.

But what he was doing in that moribund universe was the same thing. Everything had to be allowed to die except that one little kernel of self that was the essence of Wan-To. Eyes were allowed to go blind. Thought processes were rigorously pruned. Memories were abandoned—oh, so many memories! Memories of the eternity of Wan-To's life, the eons of joyous frolicking in his thousand giant young stars, the pride of creating his own stars, his own galaxies, his own copies. Everything had to go. All the memories of Wan-Wan-Wan and Kind and all his other copies—gone. The taste of a G-class star turning red giant, forgotten. The delights and terrors of warring against his competitors, abandoned. There was simply no room for any of these things in the little tachyon seed that would be Wan-To, speeding across the dead emptiness toward his rebirth. Even the tiny trickle of energy that was spent in hoarding them could be squandered that way no longer but had to go toward creating the tachyon pattern itself.

There were some memories that he couldn't bring himself to throw away. He could not force himself to discard the memory of that tiny group of stars itself—could a dying man make himself forget the promise of Heaven?

So when almost everything else was gone . . . when the task of turning himself into a seed was almost complete . . . Wan-To allowed himself the luxury of retrieving all that he knew about that wonderfully preserved cluster.

Yes, yes, it contained three medium-sized stars, just the size he liked! (A fourth, unfortunately, in some disrepair because it had been zapped in that long-ago war—but no doubt more or less healed again, in all this time.) Several other stars, not as pleasing as habitats, but still so very welcome. And even solid-matter planets, yes. Even those were precious to Wan-To now, in his final poverty.

And on those planets—

A thrill of memory shook Wan-To. He had not remembered the strange thing Matter Copy Number Five had told him, but there was the datum, long neglected, now recalled at last. Yes. It was so. The planets were known to possess that strange and unhealthy phenomenon, living matter.

Some parts of them were *inhabited.*

Wan-To stopped what he was doing for a moment to think that over. Could that forgotten fact be in any way important?

Then common sense took over. Of course not, he chided himself. How could it? They were so tiny and helpless. Why, it was even possible that they might be quite amusing—even a kind of company for him, more or less as Kind and Sweet had been long, long ago. In any case, they could not possibly be a *threat.* With a healthy star behind him, he could easily enough annihilate them, if that proved necessary—as he had with creatures like them, so many times before.

It had never occurred to Wan-To to think about what those silly, short-lived little creatures might become . . . in some tens of thousands of years.

ABOUT THE AUTHOR

Frederik Pohl has been everything one man can be in the world of science fiction: fan (a founder of the fabled Futurians), book and magazine editor, agent, and, above all, writer. As editor of *Galaxy* in the 1950s, he helped set the tone for a decade of sf—including his own memorable stories such as *The Space Merchants* (in collaboration with Cyril Kornbluth). He has also written *The Way the Future Was*, a memoir of his first forty-five years in science fiction. Frederik Pohl was born in Brooklyn, New York, in 1919, and now lives in Palatine, Illinois.

DATE DUE
